"Graham wrote a real page-turner of a thriller!
Can hardly wait for the next one!"

— Nancy Klopper
Casting Director

"*Strings* gives a fascinating and illuminating glimpse into the intersections of global culture, politics, and privilege. Only a pianist and thinker of Daniel Graham's stature and experience could describe so vividly the importance and impact of artistic supremacy to the global community. In this volume, the story-telling makes the reader an active participant."

— Robert Blocker
**The Henry and Lucy Moses Dean of Music,
Professor of Piano, Yale University**

STRINGS

For information about permissions to reproduce selections from this book, translation rights, or to order bulk purchases, write: danielgpiano@yahoo.com

Cover art by Patrick Grandaw
Book design and publishing management by The Publishing World

Graham, Daniel M.
Strings
979-8-218-23962-6

1. Fiction / Thrillers / Espionage. 2. Fiction / Thrillers / Political.
3. Fiction / Alternative History.

Also for sale in hardcover and ebook formats.

Printed in the U.S.A.
Distributed by Ingram

STRINGS

a novel

DANIEL M. GRAHAM

I dedicate *Strings* to three outstanding artist-teachers who influenced my career and my life.

To Leon Fleisher (1928-2020)
One of the most extraordinary talents on and off the concert stage. His piano performances were an inspiration to all musicians, and he was a dedicated teacher to the very end. I dedicate *Strings* to Leon Fleisher in recognition of the extraordinary kindness he showed me during my doctoral studies at the Peabody Institute at Johns Hopkins University.

To Nadia Reisenberg (1904-1983)
Her teaching at the Juilliard, Mannes College of Music, and her private studio left a legacy that continues through her many talented students. She instilled in me the importance of putting musical values above technique. She had an uncanny ability to recognize the slightest departure from the printed score. Those values were always evident in her recordings and performances.

To Donald Currier (1918-2010)
While completing my Master of Music degree at Yale, it was my teacher, Donald Currier, who inspired me to seek higher standards in my performances. I learned from him how to approach the delicate balance between the emotional and intellectual aspect of piano performance. Students and critics alike hailed his recordings and performances.

Exposition

1

1975. The Colosseum in Rome, Italy

Alex Courtland waited in the green room for his cue to go on stage. Tonight, if all went to plan, he would perform the inaugural concert in Rome's renovated Colosseum, one of the world's most magnificent monuments of antiquity. It didn't escape him that the amphitheater had once been home to Roman games that embraced depravity and fear. Now, though, he would transform the space from its evil past to its idyllic present through his inspiring performances.

He envisioned the intricacy of the Bach partita he was about to play in one chamber of his mind, but elsewhere, he ran through the logistics and precautions taken to prevent the disasters of the past.

For the sake of his audience, and his own, Alex had left nothing to chance, especially when it came to his own Steinway concert grand, transported to Rome from New York for this special occasion. The pins, the keys, the pedals, and the strings were all inspected. Crews checked the entire facility, including underneath each seat, to ensure there were no hidden deadly devices. Now that they declared the facility safe, the plan he strategized could move forward. If he made any miscalculation at all, Alex conceded it could cost him his life.

The hall manager's announcement interrupted that chilling thought. "Mr. Courtland, the President of the United States, James Rutherford, has arrived with his secret service detail. Mrs. Moretti will now deliver her welcoming speech, after which you may begin your concert."

As Alex left the green room, he acknowledged the stunning evolution and sheer irony of the evening. He was a star student of Madam Nadia Rosenberg, an icon in Russian musical circles, who fostered his growth from a gifted child into a world-renowned virtuoso pianist. The audience was about to experience those remarkable artistic accomplishments. But what the audience couldn't imagine were the scars Alex still carried from his talent being hijacked and exploited by the Russian hierarchy. Without realizing it, he had become an active participant in the Cold War between Russia and the US. Yet, at thirty years old, he still embodied all that he loved and loathed about his native country.

2

Ten-year-old piano prodigy Alexis Koryavin made himself to be still on the narrow bench for his weekly meeting with General Andrei Petrov. As usual, he arrived early, for it would not be wise to keep the Director of the Institute for Gifted Children waiting. Tall for his age, Alexis' gangly legs were already outgrowing the standard olive-green uniform provided by the Institute. The soles of his shoes were razor thin, but Alexis didn't worry about getting new clothes. As General Petrov's poster child, he received preferential treatment, including his wardrobe.

As he waited, he reflected on the past weekend he had spent with his parents. Alexis loved how his mother treated him like the ten-year-old child he was, a refreshing relief from the *boy-wonder* status surrounding him at the Institute. Alexis reveled in the smell of warm baked bread and his mother's sweet face powder. He missed these reminders of the comforts of home. Alexis regretted their time together was occurring less often, and he could tell from his mother's facial expressions she felt the same way. He had tried to comfort her.

"Mama, the general watches over me, so please don't worry. You and I and Papa have this entire weekend together."

It was the first time all month Alexis had enjoyed his freedom, and he wanted to savor every minute. He was mature for his ten years, and now old enough to spend more time with his father outdoors. Soccer would often follow breakfast, then Alexis' competitive spirit flourished with a friendly game of chess. Arkady Koryavin was a more advanced player, but Alexis had his share of successes too. *Checkmate* would ring throughout the house as Alexis declared his occasional victories.

The family had gone to Gorky Park and enjoyed a homemade picnic under a massive shade tree. "Mama, nothing at the Institute tastes as good as your cooking," Alexis assured her. They lunched atop the quilt that had been in the family for decades. Delicacies included crusty black bread, smoked meats, soft cheeses, and ripe tomatoes. A special treat followed with biscuits and ice cream. It was a perfect day, after which Alexis slipped into a coveted afternoon nap accompanied by off-key military bands roaming the grounds.

A high point for Alexis' parents was when he played their favorite music for them. Each composition became a showpiece for his remarkable talent and gave them a marker of his progress each time their son visited.

The change from home to the disciplined regimen of study and practice at the Institute was a difficult transition for Alexis. He glanced up at the two large gold-framed pictures of General Petrov and Vladimir Lenin. They were slightly tilted to the left and he had to resist the temptation to get up from the bench and straighten them. The drab gray walls of the general's anteroom were a dramatic contrast to his parents' home, or even the spectrum of colors Alexis imagined in his music. Alexis' interest in projecting the coloristic properties of piano music improved after he studied *Pictures at an Exhibition*, a suite for piano by Modest Mussorgsky. Each of the ten pieces in the suite served as a musical illustration of one piece in the exhibition. Alexis' refined skills of articulate pedaling and sensitive touch helped to distinguish between woodwinds, brass, and stringed instruments. Those and other gifts were why Alexis, from among thousands of talented Russian children, ended up on the radar screen of General Andrei Petrov several years earlier.

Alexis stared down at his hands as he played some scales on his imagined keyboard. They were strong enough for a child his age to power through a Chopin etude, but delicate enough to mesmerize an audience with a Debussy prelude. Alexis excelled at both.

As the time for his meeting approached, the general's personal guard loomed over Alexis. Alexis could smell him before he saw him, rank with sweat and vodka.

"Are you ready for your session with General Petrov?"

Alexis' concentration on Chopin's *Ballade in F Minor* playing in his head stopped.

"Yes. of course." As he stood to enter the general's inner office, he gave up his mental gymnastics of the coda passage in the ballade. He'd get back to it later. His senses were now on high alert for the meeting to come.

"You're the general's number-one boy," the guard murmured to Alexis as he walked past him. Alexis felt the man's hot stinky breath on the back of his neck and recoiled. The general surrounded himself with guards recruited from the notorious Lubyanka Prison. But as the general's favorite, Alexis had a protective shield from their boorish behavior. The other students, though, were fair game.

Abby, a talented painter, and fellow student, had become Alexis' confidant and best friend. She would slip into his practice room and observe him while he worked. Alexis' music and Abby's presence brought new life to a room with dirty white walls and only a black piano and bench. Her sweet scent blended harmoniously with Alexis' music, and he always did his best playing when she was there. Abby would often sketch him in charcoal on the artist pad she always carried with her, capturing the intensity and focus of his facial expressions while he practiced. Those drawings became some of his most treasured possessions.

The privacy of the practice room seemed to encourage Abby to let down her guard. She, like every other student at the Institute, knew that it was best to keep one's opinions private. There were rumors that some students earned extra rations if they shared overheard secrets. Abby learned early on to be discreet. But with Alexis, she felt safe enough to share personal stories of her painful past. Deeply touched after Abby told him her mother had died in childbirth, Alexis got up from the piano bench and gave her a hug. Her father, a former artillery commandant, died when she was only eight. The general was one of her father's few military friends, so he allowed Abby to live and study at the Institute. Otherwise, she would have ended up in a state-run orphanage.

The other students teased Alexis about having a crush on Abby. She was two years older than he was, but it was true. He loved her curly brown hair and big brown eyes, but it was the emotional connection he felt with Abby that made his relationship with her so special. He trusted her and shared his innermost thoughts with her. Abby did the same, and seemed relieved to do so.

"Did you know, Alexis, that General Petrov was once the head of the KGB?"

"I don't think so, Abby. He's been too busy making us kids into Russian stars."

"It's true! I am not making this up, Alexis. I saw him in a history book wearing the same uniform he wears for our assemblies." Abby's comments were often punctuated by running her hands through her beautiful dark hair. He loved watching her do that.

Alexis could see that Abby enjoyed sharing this information with him. That was fine with him. Having a friend was a good thing.

One day when he was walking Abby to her dorm after a practice session, a guard stopped them and addressed Abby.

"Why are you out this late? Where are you coming from?"

Alexis heard the slurred speech and assumed the guard was drunk. Alexis looked at Abby. He had never seen her so vulnerable. She always appeared confident and strong. Now he saw fear in her eyes. Alexis intervened.

"Sir, we are practicing during the hours allowed."

The guard seemed to forget Alexis' special status as a favorite of the general's and responded with authority.

"I'm not talking to you. The girl needs to come with me."

Alexis saw Abby close to tears and terrified.

"Thank you, sir, but the general has always asked me to walk any girls home after practice. I'm sure he will be happy to know that you are taking good care of us."

The guard paused, then withdrew.

As they continued their walk and Abby regained her composure, she said, "He preys on us all. When we're alone, we're vulnerable. He's hurt a couple of my roommates, and they've warned me. The general is aware of the guard's behavior, but he does nothing. You saved me, Alexis. Thank you."

"You're welcome, Abby. I'm glad I was here to help."

Alexis now understood why young girls cowered when guards approached them and asked himself, *What if I lose my standing with the general? How can I protect Abby?*

The door bolted open as the guard approached the general's office with Alexis. Kristina Skyokova, a talented ballet student, walked out, followed by another guard. She looked up at Alexis, tears running down her face. Kristina picked up her pace. *Poor Kristina*, Alexis thought, *she'll need to run fast to get away from that smelly rhino.*

General Petrov appeared in the doorway in full uniform, his bright medals shining, and motioned for Alexis to come in.

Cigar smoke filled the room, irritating Alexis' eyes. *General Petrov must love himself*, Alexis thought, counting the mirrors in his office. A ramrod straight posture emphasized the general's extended chest. Perfect creases in his uniform showcased his sturdy frame. He was not exceptional looking, but his bearing held power. And from the careful behavior of everyone at the Institute, Alexis knew that Petrov's power was real.

Looking at the general across his hand-carved desk, it hit Alexis that Abby was right—the general could well have been the head of the KGB.

Alexis noticed a book on Vladimir Lenin displayed on the general's desk. "General, I've been learning about Lenin in my history classes. Was he a hero?"

"Yes. Russia is a world power today *because* of Lenin. The Politburo changed the name of Petrograd to Leningrad to honor him following his death."

The general appeared in his element.

"Lenin was a champion of the people who knew how to get rid of those traitors around him." Petrov pounded his fist on the desk to emphasize his point. It startled Alexis, and he thought, *I don't think I would have liked Lenin.*

As Petrov droned on about quotas, expectations, and goals—the usual subjects of their weekly meetings—Alexis played a Bach *G Major Prelude and Fugue* in his head, finishing about the same time as the general's tone changed.

"Alexis, I have important news for you," the general said, pointing directly at the boy.

Alexis leaned back in his chair.

"You are to receive a special honor from the Soviet Arts Council."

Alexis was uncertain what *special honor* meant.

"They have selected you to represent Russia at the First International Piano Competition for Young Artists, to be held in Leningrad."

Alexis moved to the edge of his seat and searched for words of gratitude. Before he could respond, the general continued.

"The Leningrad competition is the brainchild of Solomon Blum, who manages some of the greatest artists in the world, some of whom are former students of your teacher, Nadia Rosenberg."

Alexis knew Solomon Blum, who was a close friend of Nadia's. Alexis trusted Mr. Blum, and considered him and Nadia Rosenberg to be his two adult friends.

"Sol and Nadia both assure me that you are ready to perform in this competition and they think you have an excellent chance of winning. That would make me very happy, Alexis. Your success would bring great prestige to the Institute…and to Mother Russia, as well. I want you to bring that gold medal back with you, Alexis."

"Thank you, General. I won't disappoint you."

Alexis stood up as the guard opened the door for him to leave. He stepped back into the broadened entryway to allow a new guest to enter. The visitor was a tall handsome man wearing a dark blue suit, white shirt, and bright red tie. There was a white handkerchief folded in his breast pocket, with the initials *J. T.* embroidered in silk. Alexis' non-musical training at the Institute kicked in. He noted this imposing man: height and weight, the color of hair and eyes, scent of cologne and cigarettes. The mental acuity that allowed him to play the piano with such intensity also fueled his keen sense of observation. *This gentleman must be important,* Alexis thought. *He entered the inner sanctum with no security guard.*

"Alexis, meet Ambassador John Tilton, the American Ambassador to Russia. John, this is Alexis Koryavin, who is representing Russia at the International Piano Competition in Leningrad."

Ambassador Tilton smiled and reached out to shake Alexis' hand. "That's a firm handshake, young man. From what the general tells me, you can create magic with those fingers, so you had better protect them!"

"Thank you, sir. I'll remember that."

Alexis left the general's office in a daze. He couldn't wait to tell his parents and Abby the exciting news. As he made his way to his practice room, infused with renewed enthusiasm, he noticed a crowd of students gathered near the cafeteria. Out of curiosity, he joined the group to see what had attracted everyone's attention. To his horror, there on the floor was the ballerina Kristina Skyokova, lying in a pool of blood.

Alexis approached another student and asked what happened.

"I didn't see it. But I heard them say she slipped and hit her head badly."

3

The Institute for Gifted Children was designed like a maze, but General Andrei Petrov, the Institute's director, could view the activities of all students and staff through video surveillance. Through his office window facing north, he could see the Kremlin. He enjoyed sipping cold vodka shots while watching the historic clock on the Spasskaya Tower above the main gates to Red Square. The hour and minute movement of the hands became a constant reminder of how little time remained for him to accomplish his goals. This was a different view from two years earlier, when he witnessed the Soviet hammer and sickle flag being lowered over the Kremlin for the last time. He was still getting used to the Russian tricolor flag that replaced it.

The unsuccessful coup and accompanying economic and political destabilization hastened the collapse of the Soviet Union and brought many changes. Petrov's career, though, continued to advance. He owed much of that to the Politburo and its chair, Sergey Ivanov, who also became President of Russia during the transition. President Ivanov had appointed Petrov to the KGB several years earlier, only to replace him a short time later. President Ivanov recognized the value Petrov could bring to Ivanov's vision for the changes to come.

Following World War II, Ivanov had implemented a strategic decision to accelerate Russian research and technology. Axis forces bombing Leningrad had left the city in ruins, requiring Russia's top echelon in the field to be moved. Ivanov selected a site outside of Moscow for a new facility where the group continued their top-secret projects. Their work kept them isolated for a decade while they developed a new generation of supercomputers. During that time, President Ivanov appointed Petrov to manage the facility and report to him. That initial research led to other projects, including one incorporating artificial intelligence.

President Ivanov assumed the Cold War with the US would continue for several years. He approached the one man he trusted to share his vision and charged him to establish a new school for gifted children.

Petrov established the Institute for Gifted Children in 1950, and recognized a unique opportunity to expand on President Ivanov's directive. Capitalizing on his experience as head of the KGB, he thought, *It's time for us to try a new style of espionage.* He imagined a cadre of agents with extraordinary gifts living in many countries around the world. All of them would be under his control, and awaiting orders.

Parents were eager to have their children selected for this special honor, although they knew nothing of the actual course of study that they would be following. Petrov moved the scientists to the Institute, where they continued their research. Now everything was in one place and under his control. The thought of integrating all the new technology into a program to train Russian agents spurred Petrov to develop a quasi-curriculum to attract students, but one that included a covert implant program.

Petrov wasted no time putting his plans into action. First, he directed the scientists to speed up their research on artificial intelligence. He brought in the acclaimed Polish visionary in that field, Frederic Kowalski. Petrov promised Kowalski wealth and recognition if he could translate artificial intelligence into a human experience.

It excited Kowalski that a benefactor had surfaced who appeared to have unlimited resources to support his work. He brought passion to Petrov's vision, and worked with the scientists to develop a prototype: a computer that could think, analyze, and perform intellectual tasks far beyond what any human could do. Kowalski's remarkable achievement exceeded his own expectations and debuted as the only computer of its kind in the world. Petrov named it *Boris.*

Boris was equipped with advanced surveillance capabilities and could master human communication skills in many languages, able to identify inflections, including stress patterns. He used common-sense reasoning with the ability to determine flaws in human strategic thinking and planning. Boris could learn the habits and personalities of every human he communicated with. Kowalski called it *machine learning.*

How much a machine could learn interested Petrov.

"Will Boris take orders without questioning them?" he asked Kowalski.

"I programmed Boris to accept your orders without question, General Petrov. However, should he receive a directive that makes *no* sense, there is a built-in safeguard to protect you from harming yourself or others."

Seeing the quizzical expression on Petrov's face, Kowalski elaborated further.

"Boris will find the best way to serve you. Think of this new relationship as two friends who, over time, learn more about each other. Boris will always do whatever is necessary to carry out your wishes."

Mr. Kowalski prepared for his return to Poland with profound thanks and additional promises from Petrov, who arranged a private flight as a token of his appreciation. Kowalski left on one of the new jet planes recently put into service at Aeroflot. The device hidden in Kowalski's briefcase exploded after the chartered Tupolev Tu-104 took off from Sheremetyevo Airport. There were no survivors.

4

Petrov entered the control room that adjoined his private office and passed through three layers of security. His inner sanctum housed sophisticated electronic equipment that held every student's profile, activities, and progress reports, all stored in Boris' database.

He settled into his Italian leather chair behind the desk with the carved insignia of the Institute's name and issued his first command to Boris.

"Boris, bring up all files on Alexis Koryavin."

"Of course, General. I have confirmed your voice recognition, and I am bringing up all the private files for Alexis Koryavin."

Five screens came alive on the wall, displaying Alexis' personal profile, history, progress reports, and videos related to surveillance and laboratory experiments.

Alexis was the most promising student ever admitted to the Institute. The general recognized something special in him—the proverbial obedient son who would do his father's bidding for no other reason than his father told him to. Petrov admired Alexis' talent and intelligence. The dual path of preparing Alexis as a concert pianist and a covert Russian agent was on schedule. Nadia Rosenberg, Alexis' teacher, had already brought the talented ten-year-old to concert-ready status. Having the world-renowned concert pianist as his unwitting dupe sweetened the pot.

The general always looked forward to his playtime with Boris. He settled into his chair and lit up a Cuban cigar before issuing his next command.

"Boris, display recent test results from the implant program."

Boris displayed the tests from the previous day. The video showed Alexis hypnotized and in a deep sleep. Technicians and the medical team were busy monitoring the equipment and observing Alexis' responses. It gratified the general that the implanted probes were all working as expected, including the ones that were implanted when Alexis was only six years old.

Boris then reported on the faster versions of data transmission, making it possible, within seconds, to connect with the Sputnik satellite launched a year earlier.

Petrov rose from the desk and paced the room, thrilled with this new information.

Petrov had two versions of his top-secret mission: the one he shared with President Ivanov, and the sacrosanct plan now active with Ambassador Tilton. The government funded the official version, but it was the latter that required new private funding from outside of Russia. He knew where to go.

Casimiro Castillo, head of one of the largest drug cartels in the world, had approached Petrov years before, when the general was head of the KGB. Castillo asked for Petrov's permission to set up distribution of his drug operations in the Soviet Union. The large bribes made it difficult for Petrov to reject Castillo's proposal, but it was too risky for Petrov to consider. Now, Petrov had something he could offer Castillo and, in return, secure the funding he needed. The scheduled meeting at the Russian embassy in Paris next week with the German and Austrian Ambassadors provided the perfect cover for a confidential meeting with Castillo.

*

Petrov enjoyed his infrequent trips to Paris. The quality of the food and accommodations exceeded anything available to him in Russia. Even beluga caviar was available at most restaurants there. The private meeting took place at Castillo's penthouse suite at the Ritz Hotel. Petrov decided against using the embassy limo, and instead told his driver he was going to take a walk. A block later, he hailed a cab and in less than fifteen minutes was entering the hotel through its impressive 18th-century townhome façade. As he walked through the lobby, he took a moment to recall how fascinating he found the hotel after reading F. Scott Fitzgerald's

Tender Is The Night. Many visits to the hotel followed that reading, and he often imagined Fitzgerald sitting next to him at the bar.

The butler greeted him at the penthouse and escorted him to the living area where Castillo and his wife, Isabella, were waiting. Isabella's beauty struck Petrov. Filtered sunlight highlighted her dark brown hair. Her large diamond ring, pendant, and earrings, while impressive, added nothing to her natural beauty, but left no doubt about who claimed her as his own.

Isabella excused herself. Castillo opened the conversation, suggesting the many opportunities to open a drug corridor into Russia.

"I'm sorry, Casimiro. That is not going to happen."

Petrov's matter-of-fact delivery of the message caused an immediate and angry response from Castillo. He jumped from his chair.

"Then why am I here, Andrei?"

"Please calm down, Casimiro. I have something far more important to offer you."

Casimiro took a moment as he paced in front of his chair, then sat down.

"What can you possibly offer me that would be better?"

"You have experienced an increase in your drugs being seized or stolen. The new *war on drugs* campaign in the US is especially hurting you. You continue to handle communications in the usual ways, and sensitive information is being hijacked. You can't make a phone call or go to a meeting without the risk of being discovered."

Castillo appeared more curious than angry.

"How can you know all this?"

"It's not important how I got this information, Casimiro. It's only important that you understand this trend can be reversed. I can help you do that."

"What are you proposing?"

"Please allow me to show you."

Petrov opened his computer device and entered a personal code. As he shifted the screen in Castillo's direction, a message appeared. *Welcome, Mr. Castillo. You have one new message.*

Castillo remained in shock as a message played back from

Petrov, welcoming him to the private portal where he could manage his various business activities.

"I'm not sure I understand how this works."

"It's quite basic, Casimiro. Whether you are delivering, or picking up a product, sending or receiving money, or setting up a meeting, you can make all arrangements on this private portal. Only you, and those whom you allow, will have access to this communication device. We will provide you with all the equipment you need."

"It's amazing. What's the cost to set this up?"

"It is expensive, Casimiro, but it's my gift to you."

Castillo looked confused. He scratched his head. Petrov remained quiet.

Then, as if acknowledging nothing in the world was free, especially for a drug czar, Castillo asked, "What is this setup costing me, Andrei?"

"What it is *not* costing you, Casimiro, is lost revenue from drug transactions that never happen. Rather, you will pay us a percentage of those estimated savings. I've prepared the following proposal for you to consider…."

Petrov handed Castillo a detailed proposal showing a large initiation set-up fee and a monthly maintenance charge for the portal and devices.

"These are some very large numbers, Andrei."

"Yes. Your increased revenue will be quite large."

Casitillo's smile was all the response Petrov needed to know they had a deal. Petrov was in a giving mood, and Casimiro Castillo appeared just as happy as Ambassador John Tilton when Petrov presented him with a gift as well.

5

US Ambassador to Russia, John Tilton, boarded Air Force Two for his return trip to Washington, DC. Staying the two days at Spaso House, the US Ambassador's residence in Moscow, located just a mile from the Kremlin, was never a pleasant experience for him. Over-decorated, opulent furniture, tapestry walls, and the massive crystal chandelier above the eighty-two-foot high main hall collided with his more tailored, elegant taste. He questioned the loyalty of the staff and cleaning crew, and assumed they bugged everything. Then there was the history surrounding the death of the original owner of the property, a wealthy merchant whose life ended at the hands of his son, who shot him right in the vestibule. That could explain the shivery feeling Tilton experienced every time he entered the house. Russia's recent attempt to increase the rent on Spaso House made him wonder, *Maybe I should just stay in a hotel.*

It was almost humorous as he recalled the tunnel the FBI built under the new Russian embassy project in Washington, intended to support planned espionage activities. The FBI never used it after they found out a double agent had reported the tunnel to the KGB.

The return trip home provided him some quiet time to reflect on his meetings with President Ivanov and Andrei Petrov.

Tilton's meeting with President Sergey Ivanov at the Kremlin proceeded as expected. There was no need for Tilton to exercise his skills as a master negotiator. President Ivanov's early training in chess served him well as he translated the art of moving chess pieces around the board to a strategic handling of US diplomats. Nothing took place in their discussions to generate enough heat to thaw the increased Cold War tensions caused by recent events. President Ivanov had fired the first shot.

"The recent US test of a hydrogen bomb makes it difficult to reduce tensions between our two dominant countries, Mr. Ambassador."

"I understand your concerns, President Ivanov." Tilton didn't want to escalate this discussion, but it had to be said. "However, your recent launch of the satellite, Sputnik, caused great concern with President Reynolds and our Congress, Mr. President."

"Sputnik, like all our satellites, is a peaceful exploration to benefit all humanity, Mr. Ambassador. We understand the US is planning similar launches."

Tilton decided not to pursue the tit-for-tat discussion. He would report to President Bruce Reynolds that he tried to ease Russia's concern about the United States' successful test of a hydrogen bomb. He would also tell President Reynolds that the hydrogen bomb test and arms buildup taking place in both countries risked derailing future talks.

Tilton walked a political tightrope in those meetings. Although he represented the United States, his own interests often conflicted with those of President Reynolds and his administration. Reynolds was still popular with the electorate, and respected on both sides of the aisle. He was intelligent, and an astute observer. Tilton's new partnership with Petrov put him on a path of no return, and he would need to be very careful. If President Reynolds suspected any duplicity in his activities, it could shatter his dream of the new world order that he and Petrov envisioned.

Tilton first met the general several years ago, and knew him as one of the most well-informed and powerful men in Russia. As former head of the KGB, Petrov knew where all the bodies were buried, and who put them there. He was shrewd and played a great game of mental chess—at times better than President Ivanov, himself. Tilton trusted Petrov—to a point. He had already considered the risks in their partnership. These were changing times in Russia, and Petrov's political fortunes could change. However, Petrov had survived every purge. Ultimately, Tilton's confidence in his own abilities to manage all contingencies mitigated any concerns he had. A new world order could only happen if Russia and the US were partners in creating it. Tilton knew the US could not do it alone, and both men had the determination and capability to bring it about.

This latest meeting with Petrov focused on collaborative efforts that could further advance their individual ideologies and joint mission. Everything needed to remain fluid in response to changing international events.

Tilton put on his glasses to read the original report he had received from the CIA back in 1950, and the current update regarding Petrov's establishment of the Institute for Gifted Children. It showed how effective Petrov and the Politburo had been in disguising the true mission of the Institute:

CIA CONFIDENTIAL REPORT
May 12, 1950

RE: THE INSTITUTE FOR GIFTED CHILDREN IN MOSCOW

The Russian Politburo recently announced a new institute in Moscow for gifted children. The Institute will be open to students who excel in the competitive fields of athletics, art, music, and science.

Russia continues to excel in athletic competitions, as seen in the Olympic games and other venues. However, US advances in both swimming and hockey, as well as the recent first-place gold medal win by an American pianist at the prestigious Tchaikovsky International Piano Competition, have raised concerns at the Politburo. They view victories on the field and stage as a win in the Cold War games.

The Politburo took decisive action to address their concerns by establishing the Institute for Gifted Children in Moscow. They have appointed Andrei Petrov, the former head of the KGB, as its director. Mr. Petrov's appointment is most likely a reward for his past service as head of the KGB.

ACTION: Memo sent to the US Olympic Committee and

other non-profit agencies informing them of a new school in Moscow for gifted students.

REPORT UPDATE: June 1, 1955

Most non-profit agencies in the US increased training regimens in response to Russia's aggressive stand on this issue back in 1950. The Russians continue to excel in figure skating, and the US still maintains a slight edge in competitive swimming and hockey.

Tilton put the report back in his briefcase and removed his glasses. *How could they get it so wrong?* Tilton always found the CIA reports and top-secret documents insightful and accurate. Not this one. For now, it appeared Petrov could continue his covert activities at the Institute without fear of discovery. Tilton understood Petrov's freedom to continue his work was in both their interests.

Tilton recalled his conversation with Petrov.

"I must tell you about all the progress we've made at the Institute for Gifted Children, John. Now that we are partners, I can explain how some of the remarkable advances in technology we've made in recent years are being used. They are helping us to redefine the art of espionage, and will provide our Institute graduates with the tools they need to succeed in their mission—*our* mission, John."

The CIA had briefed Tilton on much of the news Petrov was sharing. However, hearing him explain an implant program was an eye-opener for Tilton. He would not be sharing that information with anyone, and he was quite sure the CIA knew nothing of this advanced technology. This was Petrov's pet project, and he seemed proud to share some details with Tilton.

"Alexis, the pianist you met today, is very special."

"He impressed me, Andrei. How is he involved?"

"He is one of the many agents being trained who will receive a state-of-the-art education, second to none. Alexis is well on his way to becoming a world-class pianist. Under the capable tutelage of Nadia Rosenberg, he could become the most sought-after talent on the planet. Think of the access he will have to important events in the US. Perhaps Alexis will help you with your political ambitions."

Tilton's political power needed a boost, but details of how the general would use Alexis to help him in his career remained vague—*deliberately vague*, Tilton thought. *How creative of Petrov to recruit a talented pianist as an agent. Who would have guessed?* For Alexis to come under the influence and control of a man like the general seemed unjust. But Ambassador John Tilton believed in sacrifice to achieve the common good, a view mirrored by the 19th-century Russian revolutionary, Sergey Nechayev, who, like Machiavelli before him, believed *the end justifies the means.* Tilton and Petrov's collaborative partnership fit right in with that philosophy.

Their strategic vision for a new world order would unfold over many years. They would have to be careful as they moved forward through the different phases, so as not to set off any alarms. People were going to die; politics were going to change. But if successful, the two men would then control the destinies of both countries, and maybe much more.

There were multiple challenges to overcome as their plan moved forward. If the goal for world domination was to become a reality, then there would need to be a strategy to deal with NATO and all of Europe. Their plan needed to be staged to avoid economic chaos and infrastructure collapse. They discussed the possibility of sharing technology tools with other countries to minimize risks. The platform Petrov outlined was ambitious and depended on advanced technology to rebuild major infrastructure to support the production of energy and manage financial markets, alternative currencies, transportation, media, and so much more. Tilton had to wonder if Russia's technological future advances could meet those demands. It would depend on a successful transition from capitalism to authoritarianism. If everything fell into place according to their plan, the Cold War and threat of nuclear oblivion would no longer be a concern.

He opened his briefcase and took out the gift Petrov gave him during their meeting, recalling their conversation.

"I have a gift for you, John. Something to celebrate our partnership and Russian technology."

Tilton had opened the impressive package wrapped in gold foil and a velvet ribbon. The attractive leather case could have been the gift on its own, but Tilton thought otherwise.

He's giving me a watch.

Tilton's surprise was obvious. He looked at Petrov and then back at what was in the case.

"Andrei, what is this?"

"It's a phone, John. Our newest technology makes possible linking many devices, like computers and phones, to our updated satellite system."

Satellite system? How many will there be? Petrov must know the success researchers at M.I.T. have already had in establishing an Internet. Did Russia steal some of their secrets? It was clear to Tilton that Russia was winning the technology war, and he wondered how that might affect his own goals, or even their joint plan.

"The phone is so small."

"Deliberately so, John. You can use this phone for private conversations when it's necessary for us to talk."

Tilton's first thought was, *How private can it be if the call exists on Russian databases?*

"Mr. Ambassador, this is Captain Groves. Sorry about the few bumps. Just to let you know, we anticipate an on-time arrival in Washington. The rest of the flight should be smooth."

Dare I use it? His curiosity answered that question. What better time to check it out?

He touched the power button, and the screen came alive with a message. *Would you like to connect with Andrei Petrov, Mr. Ambassador?* Tilton touched the *yes* button.

"Hello, John. I see you are enjoying your new phone."

"This is quite impressive, Andrei. Thank you for this."

"My pleasure, John. There is so much more I can share with you next time we meet. For now, have a safe trip back to Washington."

What other surprises does Petrov have for me?

Finishing his cocktail, Tilton contemplated writing a thank you note to Vice President Parsons for the use of Air Force Two. He removed his pen from his pocket and pulled out a sheet of his personal stationery. He detested the old man and thought him soft and ineffective. Tilton was sure Parsons didn't trust him. That thought brought a smile to his face, since no one in Washington trusted anyone, anyway. He put his pen down and decided it would be best to thank the vice president in person. That would be more effective with a handshake and a pat on the shoulder.

He put his papers aside as the steward served his dinner and poured his wine. Then his thoughts turned to June, his wife.

The icing on the cake after his meeting with Petrov was the agreement reached about Tilton adopting the girl. Unable to have children, June had been urging him to consider adoption. Her treatments for breast cancer no longer made it possible for her to bear children. The timing was perfect now that June's cancer was in remission. He would do this for her. He made a mental note to speak with his attorneys to make the final arrangements.

6

Nadia Rosenberg's decision to retire from the concert stage in 1950 shocked her friends and colleagues. Her rationale for her bold move was simple: she wanted to find, and train, the most talented children in the Soviet Union to preserve the country's legacy of greatness.

"Somewhere out there are prodigious pianistic talents that are rare and beyond anything we've seen before. You could almost say, superhuman."

Nadia explained that she would find them and mold them into the finest pianists the world had ever known.

The Soviet hierarchy took notice of Nadia's declaration. It fit right in with their own strategic plans to dominate the artistic stage. It also played to the Cold-War games. Games Russia needed to win.

Soviet propaganda was in full force as the Cold War waged on with the US. While the Soviet Union already claimed wins in most athletic encounters, including the Olympics, the recent successes by US teams raised concerns. Besides athletics, the Politburo wanted the Soviet Union to become the cultural capital of the world, and directed the Russian Arts Council to support Nadia's plans.

Nadia's challenge was to find young pianists who possessed the rarest of talents. Chess players and athletes were commonplace in Russia, but finding someone of that caliber in music required applying stricter criteria. The ideal candidate would have perfect pitch, a probing curiosity, and a natural technique. Discipline and a driving ambition to succeed were other essential qualities. Nadia's standards were so exacting, she wondered, *Do these children even exist? Would I have made the cut in my youth?*

Nadia spent several months interviewing talented youngsters, none of whom met her standards. By the winter of 1953, she was ready to admit defeat, when a colleague suggested that she visit the Institute for Gifted Children in Moscow. She was aware of its reputation as the bastion of military rigidity, but learned the Institute accepted many students in music and art, as well. It didn't take long for General Andrei Petrov to agree to a meeting. Nadia knew he would know her elevated status in Soviet cultural and political circles, and welcome the meeting.

When Nadia arrived at the Institute, she noticed heavy security far more than what one would expect at a private school. An armed guard escorted her to the general's office.

"Thank you for taking the time to meet with me, General Petrov."

"Of course, Madame Rosenberg. I've enjoyed hearing your performances over these past years and was surprised to hear about your retirement."

"Thank you, General. Not really a retirement. Rather, I will devote the rest of my life to identifying and training a young pianist, renowned for his or her talent, talent unheard of elsewhere on the world's concert stage. If you have such children here at the Institute, General, I would like to audition them."

Nadia felt confident the general would recognize the benefits to him in her plan, since she had the support of the Politburo. Nadia had no way of knowing that the general had received a briefing by President Ivanov, and had looked forward to their meeting. Petrov knew he needed someone of Nadia's reputation to refine Alexis' remarkable talent.

"We have one student here who may possess the qualities you are seeking. He is young, only eight years old now, but one of our brightest and most talented students. I've asked Alexis Koryavin to meet you in the auditorium, where you may take as much time as you need in your evaluation."

Entering the auditorium, Nadia was surprised to see a Steinway concert grand piano on stage, flanked by red velvet curtains. Upholstered seats and attractive lighting made it clear no expense had been spared in outfitting the room.

Nadia saw a shy little fellow waiting anxiously for her. He reached out his hand to her. "I am Alexis, and I'm very pleased to meet you. May I play for you now?" Alexis' genuine spirit came through his fingertips when he performed Prokofiev's *Visions Fugitives*.

"That was lovely, Alexis."

"Would you like me to play it in other keys?"

Nadia knew this would be a rarity for any pianist; in fact, she knew of no pianist who could do it, certainly not herself. As she called out different keys, Alexis responded with the same edition of the Prokofiev. Her further testing with additional repertoire confirmed he had all the skills she was seeking.

"Alexis, your insight of style and technique belie your young age. I would very much like to tutor you. You will be my only student, and if you agree, it will require a major commitment from you and very hard work. Is this something you would like to do?"

Nadia watched with interest as Alexis' eyes got bigger and responded with great enthusiasm. "Yes, yes, of course. Is it okay with General Petrov?"

"He has given his approval."

Alexis clasped his hands together over his head in victory. "Yes! When can we start?"

"Soon, very soon," Nadia assured him. "We will want to speak to your parents, of course."

"Oh, Madame Rosenberg, they trust General Petrov. They will love this news!"

*

The general had been very receptive to Nadia teaching Alexis, but Nadia had concerns about the general's condition that Alexis was hers to teach piano, *nothing more*. It was clear the general wanted to maintain complete control over Alexis' exposure to the outside world. Nadia agreed to the general's mandate, only because it was unthinkable to walk away from Alexis' potential for greatness.

Nadia's apartment and teaching studio were luxurious by Russian standards. The Politburo considered her their finest cultural ambassador. That, along with her status in the international community, brought special rewards, including two Steinway & Sons seven-foot grand pianos from Hamburg, Germany. There were photos scattered throughout the apartment showing Nadia with famous conductors and political leaders from around the world.

Alexis wandered throughout the vast space, asking questions about the art, the photos, and the many awards Nadia had collected during her impressive career.

"I know this conductor, Madame Rosenberg. Did you play with the New York Philharmonic?"

"Yes, I did."

Nadia remained patient as Alexis asked his many questions about her performances and all the people whom she had met during her successful career. Then, she turned to Alexis.

"Now, tell me about your parents, Alexis. Did they encourage you to study piano?"

"When I was three, Mama and Papa heard me playing some tunes on the piano that I heard on the radio. Mama knew our neighbor gave lessons, and I studied with her until I became a student here at the Institute. Pappa loves to hear me play, too, but he works long hours at the passport office, so we only get to spend time together on Sundays when I'm home."

There was no lesson on that first visit. Nadia wanted Alexis to be comfortable in his surroundings, and she needed to understand more about her new student before beginning his studies. Only then would they be ready to begin the long road to pianistic perfection.

From Alexis' first lesson, he knew he was getting expert advice.

"The first thing I would like you to do, Alexis, is find your most comfortable position sitting at the piano. Adjust the piano bench and find the right distance from the keyboard. Make sure you can comfortably move your body and arms and hands to the full extent of the keyboard, left and right."

"Does this look right?"

"It looks perfect, Alexis. You have mastered this important first lesson."

"Now, let's talk about tension in your body as you play. You already know that there is tension built up as dynamics and mood changes occur in music. How does your body respond during these transitions? Do you feel tension in your neck or back during or after your practice sessions?"

"Sometimes my wrist and arms are a little sore."

"We are going to fix that so you will never be sore again."

Alexis noticed immediate improvement as he applied Nadia's technique of relaxation, while still achieving percussive and dynamic contrast.

Nadia explained in future lessons how to achieve variety in tonal production, master technical fluency, and expand repertoire building in terms that he could grasp and then implement in his private practicing sessions. Her philosophy was not to tell him how to play, or what to do. Instead, she inspired Alexis to search for solutions that came from his own being. It proved effective because it forced Alexis to always question everything he was doing and then experiment in a quest to find the right solution. Alexis' intellectual probing resulted in a unique style that was his alone—not Nadia's. And it brought him that much closer to his goal of becoming a successful concert pianist, just like Nadia had been.

Alexis never disappointed Nadia. It surprised her how quickly he learned his repertoire and grasped new interpretive concepts. By the time Alexis was ten years old, he understood how his entire body affected his playing.

Nadia explained the process to him. "Your brain communicates your interpretive ideas to the nerves and muscles. Your ears, arms, wrists, fingers, and feet respond. It is very much a team effort.

"You have great power, Alexis. But many times, the tension that accompanies your *fortissimos* doesn't resolve to a *pianissimo* as the music requires. You've captured the intensity in the opening to Prokofiev's *Third Sonata* with the right energy and percussive tone. Now, you need to show the quick transition to a section that is softer and more refined. That change needs to happen on the very first note—not later."

Nadia showed Alexis how to use the wrist and arms to achieve the desired results.

"This is amazing. I feel my entire body responding."

"Yes. the wrist needs to remain supple. Then you can use it to shape musical phrases."

Despite Nadia's promise to Petrov that she would only teach Alexis the piano, she couldn't help but contribute so much more. The remarkable gifts Alexis already showed deserved to be exploited without compromise. What other skills would surface as she explored the depths of Alexis' talent? There would be no way to accomplish all that without stepping on the general's area of control along the way. It could be risky, but fear was something Nadia faced many times in her career, and she refused to let anything stand in the way of helping Alexis reach his full potential.

Nadia's previous commitments to her performing career left no room for marriage or children. Those who felt they could survive the challenges of living with a performing musician of Nadia's capabilities soon realized it was impossible to compete with her love of music. Now, her life was all about Alexis. He became the beneficiary of her love and all the attention a mentor could give to a special student.

Each lesson brought new and surprising revelations.

"Today, you will not be playing for me, Alexis. Concert performers need to master more than just their music."

"What's more important than the music?"

Alexis' response was a testament to the trusting relationship he had with Nadia. He could question her without fear of retribution.

"Soon, you will give a concert at the Institute. Pretend you are there now and are about to walk out on stage, where you will meet your audience for the first time. Can you do that for me now?"

"Yes. I've done that many times."

Alexis went through the motions of walking to the piano, turned to face the audience, took a bow, and approached the piano, ready to perform. He turned to Nadia and smiled with confidence. "Did I do okay?"

Nadia discussed his walk being hurried, his lack of eye contact with the audience as he took his bow, and his awkward approach to the piano and bench.

"Before you play your first note, the audience has already sized you up, Alexis. Walk with confidence on stage, but don't hurry. Take your time to acknowledge the applause. Greet the audience with a smile and make eye contact as you bow. That will let them know how happy you are to be there and share your music with them. If you do all that, you will have won your audience over before you play the first note."

Nadia demonstrated how a pianist should approach the bench

with the grace of a ballet dancer, and never turn their back on the audience.

"Always maintain contact with your audience. The sideway glance to your audience as you approach the bench is a transition to the music that follows."

In future lessons, Nadia taught Alexis how to give an interview and meet the dignitaries who would one day attend his concerts. She told him that graceful, stylistic manners could define the difference between a performer and a star. Alexis' relationship with Nadia went far beyond a teacher and her student. He trusted her and knew she had his very best interest at heart, much like his own mother.

Alexis' progress continued to amaze Nadia as his technique advanced and his repertoire grew. But she had also noticed an increasing unexplained and uncharacteristic behavior and concentration problem that could jeopardize everything they had accomplished together. She knew it needed to be addressed soon.

7

Nadia reached out to her dear friend, Sol Blum, manager to the *Who's Who* of Russian artistry, to seek his counsel on her concerns about Alexis. She invited him to dinner at one of her favorite restaurants, Yar.

After arriving at Yar, Nadia stopped to appreciate the stunning floral arrangement in the crystal vase on the entrance table. Schrecks' tulips, Lady Slipper Orchids, and Russian Lotus filled the room with a subtly sweet fragrance.

"Madame Rosenberg, it's an honor to see you again."

"Thank you, Leonid. I am expecting a dear friend, Sol Blum, to join me. We will need privacy. May I have the corner booth?"

"It will be good to see Mr. Blum again, Madame Rosenberg. May I offer you the small private dining room at the rear of the restaurant?"

"Thank you, Leonid. I am so looking forward to your wonderful fish with potatoes and onions."

"Perhaps you can persuade Mr. Blum to try it tonight."

"I wish. I'm guessing he will order the Stroganoff."

As Nadia waited for Sol, she glanced at the dark wooden paneling and the black trim on the few shuttered windows. Sunlight barely filtered through, hardly reaching the flowered tablecloths. The lights were dim, and she thought, *the décor in this room reflects the seriousness of the discussion I'm about to have with Sol.*

When Sol arrived, he couldn't resist commenting.

"Your status as a world-renowned artist and teacher is legendary, but a private dining room? Isn't that a little over the top even for you, Nadia?"

Nadia loved Sol's humor, and appreciated his trying to lighten the mood. Sol's perspective was important. He followed Alexis' progress at the Institute, and his frequent meetings with Petrov gave him additional insight into activities at the Institute.

They ordered drinks, and Nadia got right to the point.

"Sol, I have deep concerns about Alexis' inconsistent behavior and how it's affecting our work together. I'm worried it could put his future at risk."

Sol's nod left no doubt about his understanding of the situation.

"I'm worried about him, Sol. One day he's focused, and the next he looks like he's walking through a thick fog. When I ask him what he's thinking, he looks at me as if he's not aware of how detached he is. It carries over to his performances, as well. There's a total disconnect between the emotional content of the music he's playing and the technique required to carry it off."

"Could he just be distracted about something, or someone? He's so talented, and sometimes we forget he's still a child."

"I wanted to think so, but I've come to another conclusion. I've noticed that he recoils at every mention of General Petrov's name. He's afraid of him, Sol. Petrov demands absolute control. He even cut the time Alexis spends with his parents. It upsets Alexis, but he's too afraid to complain to the general. Do you have any clues about what's going on behind those closed doors at the Institute?"

Again, Sol showed no surprised, but his mood grew darker.

"Petrov's a mean one, Nadia. Everyone jumps when he snaps his fingers. I've heard it said there's an iron fist inside that velvet glove, and he uses it often to maintain control. Even the revolution didn't affect his influence. He is more powerful in Russia than when it was the Soviet Union, and he appears to have the complete support of President Ivanov."

Sol paused as the server refilled the water glasses.

He took a sip of water then continued to tell Nadia all he could about the Institute and Petrov.

"Things have changed there, Nadia. No question about that. I've heard rumors about Petrov's expanding *educational* programs having more to do with politics than education."

"Politics, Sol?"

"Yes. The Cold War raging between Russia and the US is affecting everyone and everything these days. Petrov now requires all students to take advanced classes in English to prepare them for their placement in the US."

"That explains why Alexis' English is near perfect, Sol. But the US is a major cultural and economic center. Wouldn't it make sense to place graduates there, anyway?"

"The attention Alexis receives from the general is unusual, and could explain the behavior you are noticing. I don't want to overreact, but if Alexis were my son, I would want him out of the Institute and as far away from General Petrov as possible."

"Is he in danger, Sol?"

"I don't know. Probably not now, but what about tomorrow? I shudder to think of the plans the general has for Alexis. His extraordinary gifts make him a target for many opportunists, like Petrov."

Nadia rarely showed her feelings, except through her music on the concert stage. She could not hide them now, but she refused to break down. That would be a sign of defeat. All she could do was stare at her drink and think about what she could do that might change the scenario Sol was suggesting. She was a fighter, and this was a battle worth waging.

"You care deeply for Alexis, Nadia, and it shows. You're changing his life for the better, and he has already changed yours."

"He's like a son to me, Sol. I couldn't stand it if anything bad happened to him."

"Then let's make sure nothing does."

One hour and three *kvass* drinks later, they knew what they needed to do.

"Nadia, I think it's time for you to have a heart-to-heart talk with Alexis' parents and confide your fears to them. Present the options you and I have discussed tonight. Even though they may be too drastic for them to consider, we need to do everything in our power to help them save their son."

Nadia took Sol's advice and arranged a meeting with Alexis' parents.

8

Nadia had met both of Alexis' parents before, but now she was in their home. As she talked to the Koryavins in their living room, she noticed the modest furnishings and how well-maintained they kept their home. Many family photos dotted the long wall to her right, and her attention went right to the large upright piano with cracked ivory keys positioned in the middle of the room. It became the focal point of the entire apartment—*a place of honor*, she thought. The original dark walnut finish was showing through the newer red paint. Nadia recognized the brand as Chinese, a company that failed because of the inferior pianos they produced. She found the entire scene touching.

Nadia realized that she had faced none of the barriers in her own life that confronted Alexis. She had access to the best teachers and education, and her parents gave her a gift of a new grand piano on her fifth birthday. Nadia marveled anew at Alexis' talent, and how it developed from such humble beginnings. She remained steadfast that she would need to convince his parents of the impending danger their child faced if he stayed at the Institute.

Nadia faced Alexis' parents and could see the concern on their faces. Larisa, Alexis' mother, seemed anxious. Her attractive round face perhaps hid other concerns. Her husband, Arkady, remained stoic. For a brief minute, Nadia considered whether this was a good idea. Then she reflected on the last lesson with Alexis. He brought more energy than usual to his playing and wanted to please her. His future was in the hands of everyone in this room. This was an important conversation to have.

"It takes immense dedication to raise such an extraordinary child. Every day, I see the success he is having in his studies, and you both should be so proud." Nadia took a deep breath before continuing.

"What I want to talk to you about is not Alexis' piano lessons. It's about his behavior that I've observed—and to share rumors I've heard."

Larisa and Arkada exchanged concerned looks. Larisa spoke first.

"Is Alexis not behaving? We know he idolizes you, Madame Rosenberg, he—"

"No, no, Larisa, Alexis is an angel. I love your son. He is special in so many ways."

Nadia took a few seconds to rethink what she needed to say.

"This may sound strange, but I believe that there is something unexplainable going on at the Institute, and it's having a negative effect on Alexis. Sometimes it appears that he's daydreaming, although he's wide awake. He speaks like someone turned a key on his back and he's just reading a script. Then, the next day, he's his normal talented self. I don't know what to make of it."

It surprised Nadia to see there was almost a sigh of relief from both Larisa and Arkady.

"Larisa and I are concerned about our son, too," Arkady told her.

Larisa nodded her head. "He complains of headaches, and his personality seems to change, as if he's in another world."

Larisa told Nadia about a friend, an employee of the Institute, who had delivered a document to a scientist in a secluded portion of the campus known as the *annex*.

"She passed by an open door and noticed Alexis lying on a table connected to what looked like medical equipment. Doctors and technicians were monitoring the equipment. As soon as they saw her, they slammed the door shut."

Nadia noticed Arkady deep in thought. He spoke up.

"Now, our friend and her husband have disappeared. Their families are trying to find them."

"It's possible," Nadia admitted, "that the general had a hand in your friend's disappearance. Everyone fears him."

"My son has his whole life ahead of him," Arkady continued. "We don't know if anything is being done to him, and we can't take him out of the Institute. General Petrov could have us shot if we tried."

Nadia leaned in closer. "I have a friend, the well-known artist manager, Sol Blum."

"Oh, yes, we know of Mr. Blum, of course," said Larisa .

"Good. He and I have come up with a plan. If you can trust us, it's our only hope for saving Alexis. It's a risk to all our lives—yours, mine, Sol's, and even Alexis. But the alternative of doing nothing carries a greater risk. Are you willing to take that risk?"

Arkady looked at his wife, who nodded.

"Tell us your plan."

9

Petrov sat at his desk, tapping his fingers, oblivious to the sounds of the Institute outside his door as he focused on the circumstances of the death of his little ballerina, Kristina Skyokova. He was ambivalent about his decision to eliminate her. She was such a warm young thing in his bed, responding to his every wish, as if her life depended on it. Her long legs were ideal for ballet and lovemaking.

He walked over to the mirror, straightened his tie, and congratulated himself on the success of his meetings with Ambassador John Tilton.

The cat-and-mouse games of the past had evolved into recognizing how both men shared a vision: the US and Russia could work together to establish a new world order. The Cold War conflict between the US and Russia could be a catalyst for building their personal power bases. America's recent test of a hydrogen bomb and the subsequent increase in arms buildup by both countries gave Petrov hope that the icy conflict could last several more years, laying the seeds of support for their plans. Politicians, and even the public, would demand a change in the government's response to the growing crisis. Petrov knew the advanced technology he controlled could provide Tilton with the tools he needed to broaden his influence with organizations like NATO, the International Monetary Fund, and the International Trade Organization. Advanced technology could seed new weapon systems and upset the balance of power across the globe. All needed careful management. The initial strategy they agreed on required creating more division between political parties, not just in the US, but in Europe as well. They recognized the challenges they would face in controlling that developing chaos.

Petrov knew Tilton was just as passionate as he was about changing the current world they lived in. The Cold War and threat of actual wars—even nuclear exchanges that could paralyze governments—was too great a threat. Petrov wasn't sure how to label the new direction taken by President Ivanov and the Politburo. Marxist-Leninist policies remained a powerful influence while *perestroika*, an attempt to restructure the economic and political systems were failing. Now, Petrov observed too many signs where Ivanov was acting more like a dictator. That did not bode well for Russia, and certainly not for Petrov.

Petrov and Tilton could offer solutions that would guarantee world peace and prosperity. Both men accepted that there would be collateral damage along the way, but could be managed with careful and patient implementation. Government control of everything from media to the commercial supply chain could reduce the threat of unrest with populations.

Petrov had raised the issue of too many stories in the *New York Times* and other papers by reporters who uncovered confidential government documents through their aggressive reporting. What if word leaked out on their plans? John Tilton understood Petrov's concerns, but expressed confidence in his ability to handle the press.

There's more than one way to quell a story that's better not told. Sometimes, government action under the guise of 'national security' or 'public safety' can work wonders.

Petrov took a moment to congratulate himself on his many accomplishments since opening the Institute for Gifted Children. The training program for future agents, established in response to the Politburo's interest in expanding Russia's presence across the globe, was now fully operational. Over the next five years, they would place their most talented students in prestigious posts throughout the world. Initially, the US would remain the highest priority, since the partnership with Petrov and Russia needed support from those agents. The advanced research on technology and artificial intelligence, a powerful tool that would aid in the success of the plans Petrov and Tilton envisioned, would be a game changer.

He took a deep breath.

Have I told Ambassador Tilton too much?

Petrov knew it was best not to share all the details of how he planned to use Alexis once he sent him to the United States. Future actions to eliminate either his enemies or Tilton's would very likely be part of Alexis' prime directive.

For now, Petrov felt the Cold War environment was helpful to their cause and was not happy about Tilton's response when asked if Tilton could keep the Cold War tension alive until it no longer suited them.

That's a tough one, Andrei. I need to look good, and when I deliver news that Cold War tensions are reducing, it helps me to retain my position.

Petrov took a moment to reflect on what Tilton's response meant to Russia and his own personal agenda as he passed through the security passages to Boris. He felt a chill over his entire body. *Failure is never an option.*

By the time he reached Boris, his focus returned to the matter at hand. The generous vodka he poured helped soothe his mind.

"Boris, please provide an update on the link you have established with Alexis' implant."

"The link is functioning perfectly, General. Of course, we are still testing various types of communications to make sure Alexis receives clear instructions for all situations."

"Have we resolved the earlier observations you uncovered about Alexis accepting instructions that contradict his values?"

"I'm sorry, General. Those results from the brain mapping images continue to be inconclusive."

Petrov's mood changed as he sat back in his chair. His face scrunched up with concern as he realized Alexis had to perform flawlessly, and not just on the concert stage.

He jumped on Boris.

"Why are they *still* inconclusive?"

"Your voice patterns are showing stress, General. Do you want to rest before continuing?"

"Please, Boris, answer the question!" He nervously reached for the vodka he had poured earlier and took a sip to calm his nerves.

Boris explained that Alexis' early childhood development made it difficult for him to stray from his ingrained values. Petrov had to devise a way to overcome this obstacle so that Alexis would execute his instructions without question.

The general became impatient. He put his cigar out, rose from his chair, and paced back and forth across the wood floor.

"How much longer before we can overcome this difficulty?"

"We are getting close, General. I have identified an analytical database that can identify corrective measures. I'm positive Alexis can be ready for specific inputs in nine months."

"Oh. Well, then that timing is perfect."

The general relaxed as he lit another cigar and regained confidence that his plan to activate Alexis would soon become a reality. The competition in Leningrad would be the first test.

"General, there has been a security breach in the annex recently." Boris displayed a video of a woman delivering a folder to the general's chief scientist.

"Yes, Boris. I saw that and took care of it."

The general had sent the bodies of the woman, as well as her husband, to the state crematorium. Security breaches required immediate action.

"Boris, shut down system."

"Are you certain, sir?"

The general stopped puffing on his cigar and gave a quick look over his shoulder.

"Yes, I'm certain. It's an *order*, Boris."

General Andrei Petrov watched the screens until the images faded and the beeping lights turned from green to red to black. Only then did he get up, turn off the light, and return to his office as he reflected again on the death of Kristina. He would call her parents to extend his condolences and apologize for the custodial staff who didn't dry the waxed floor. He took one last look in the mirror, smoothed down his jacket, and opened his padded office door thinking, *this has been a very productive day, indeed.*

10

It was the first time Alexis had been out of Moscow. He left his seat and walked to the middle of the train carriage, pressing his forehead against the windows of the double doors to watch the countryside rush by. He grinned and exhaled, then drew a smile in the fog he created.

Two guards assigned by General Petrov accompanied him, along with his mother and Nadia Rosenberg. The guards didn't take their eyes off Alexis, which made him wonder, *what do they expect me to do on a speeding train, jump out the window?* He closed his eyes and pretended he was traveling alone, without the constant surveillance that made everything so restrictive. The sound of the train wheels clicking as it moved north sounded like a lullaby, soothing and rhythmic—like several of the waltzes in Brahms *Op.39 Waltzes*. He smiled, remembering how his parents loved the fifteenth waltz, and he played it often for them.

His body stiffened and his pulse increased as he considered his upcoming debut at the First International Piano Competition for Young Artists. *Was it nerves?* Not a chance. Alexis never got nervous before a concert, but looked forward to the exhilaration of public performance. However, this was his first competition, and competitions were different. Judges would evaluate him using a unique set of standards. *Who were the judges? How large an audience would there be?* The unknowns troubled him and undermined his self-confidence. He raised his hands and wiggled his fingers to confirm everything still worked. He took a deep breath.

"Are you ok?" Nadia asked.

"Yes."

Why did I lie? Nadia knows me too well.

Alexis shifted uncomfortably in his seat and raised his eyes to meet hers.

"So many people are looking forward to hearing you play, Alexis. You're well-prepared for this competition, and I promise you, it's an experience you will enjoy."

Nadia's words comforted him as they always did. His body relaxed, and he felt a rush surge to his brain.

Alexis missed his father. He never believed the general's explanation for why his father could not make the trip—that his work at the Moscow Passport Office was too demanding. His only consolation was the warm embrace his papa gave him that morning and hearing him say, *I'm so proud of you, son.*

Alexis shifted his thoughts to Solomon Blum. Sol had traveled to Leningrad two days earlier to attend to the details of the competition and smooth the way for Alexis' debut. Alexis trusted Sol. He always seemed so calm and sure of himself.

The train arrived in Leningrad right on time. As they drove through the streets of Leningrad on the way to the hotel, Alexis saw bustling activity and colorful displays everywhere he looked. There were museum posters in gilded gold frames, beautiful floral groupings enhanced by interesting water features, and talented street performers entertaining the crowds. This was an amazing contrast to the pictures he had seen of Leningrad taken just twelve years earlier, showing collapsed buildings and rubble documenting the horrors of war.

"Mama, I love this city! It's beautiful and everything smells so good! People here look happier than people at home. I wish Moscow could be more like Leningrad," Alexis sighed.

Solomon Blum greeted them at the registration desk and introduced Alexis to the staff.

"We've heard so much about your amazing talent, Alexis. We're looking forward to hearing you perform." Alexis beamed in response as he received the competition materials.

Alexis enjoyed watching everyone's reactions when Sol introduced Nadia Rosenberg to the group. They knew her by reputation, and Alexis swelled with pride at being her star student— her only student.

Alexis gaped at the luxurious appointments of their accommodations. It was a striking contrast to the stark drudgery of his room at the Institute. The colors of coral, pink, and gray blended with the multicolored scattered rugs. A crystal chandelier dominated the room and lit up the entire space. Enchanted, Alexis vowed to himself he'd return another time.

The drive to the Kirov Theater, where the competition was to be held, took fifteen minutes. Their guide shared some fascinating facts about the theater's history.

"The Kirov Theater was previously known as the Mariinsky Theatre, named after the wife of Tsar Alexander II, Empress Maria Alexandrovna."

The size of the neoclassical building impressed Alexis, but it was the auditorium that activated all his senses. He gazed at the horseshoe shape of the hall, surrounded by tiered balconies, all positioned to provide maximum views of center stage. His heart rate increased as he thought about performing on that stage. If he was a finalist, he would perform with the Leningrad Symphony Orchestra, under the baton of N. Rabinovitch, a brilliant conductor. Alexis' creative juices flowed as he considered the possibility of playing with an orchestra that was the finest in Russia, and considered a national treasure.

"Nadia, I can't believe…"

"I know dear. It's stunning, isn't it?"

"Did you ever perform here?"

"Before the war, yes, several times. It was one of my favorite places to play."

The guide informed them they expected the hall to be packed for the competition finals, with all two thousand and two hundred seats being filled.

"I saw posters at the train station about the competition."

"Yes, Alexis. We have distributed those posters throughout the city."

As the tour continued, Alexis stood by Nadia's side and observed how Sol exercised his authority as head of the competition.

"Could I please see the room reserved for competitors?"

"Of course, Mr. Blum. Your competition rules are clear. The

contestants' waiting room is an area limited to contestants, their parents, and teachers, and of course, you, Mr. Blum."

One guard, whom Alexis noticed had been following the conversation, stepped forward.

"We have strict instructions from General Petrov to always stay with Alexis. We will need access to the contestants' room, as well."

Alexis held Nadia's hand and squeezed tight as he watched Sol moved closer to the guards. He pointed to the one who raised the issue.

"Your presence in the contestants' room could suggest you are there to intimidate the other contestants. That would create a major embarrassment for the general if it became public, and we cannot allow that to happen. Armed guards in the contestants' room would also violate competition rules, and make the competitors and their parents very uncomfortable."

"Mr. Blum, my orders from the general are clear that—"

Sol interrupted the guard and explained such questionable activities could lead to negative reporting among the international press covering the competition.

"The general would not appreciate bad press. It's imperative that contestants and judges remain free from outside influences," Sol added.

"General Petrov will not be happy to hear this, Mr. Blum."

Alexis watched in awe as Solomon Blum controlled the situation. The guards did not intimidate Sol. And he did not seem threatened by the guard's innuendo about the general's orders.

"The good general is very familiar with the rules I've established. He understands how important this competition is to the Institute, and Russia. I suggest you call General Petrov if you find it necessary to challenge my decision on this matter."

The guard considered Sol's words and backed down. Reflecting on his own experiences with the general, Alexis assumed the guards decided that disciplinary action from General Petrov wasn't worth the risk. Alexis was thankful that the guards wouldn't be in the jury room with his mother and Nadia. So far, Leningrad had been full of many surprises.

Alexis marveled at the many murals decorating the walls depicting battles of previous wars. The auditorium was adorned with crystal chandeliers and carved wood balconies. It nearly overwhelmed him, but when he sat at the Steinway grand piano and looked out over the great expanse of the hall, he found it less intimidating. He touched the keys, but as he prepared to play the first notes of Rachmaninoff's *Third Piano Concerto*, he pulled away.

"What's wrong, Alexis?"

"The keys, Nadia. They're not ivory. They're plastic and slippery. I've never felt keys like this before."

"It's for a good reason, Alexis. You'll get used to them."

Nadia explained the two concert grands on stage came from the Steinway piano factory in Hamburg, Germany. Steinway and other piano manufacturers stopped using ivory keys after animal activists exposed elephants being slaughtered for their tusks. Ivory keys had a texture that connected the pianist's fingers to the piano, but Alexis understood the reason behind the change.

Alexis played the Rachmaninoff, and it resounded with the lush sounds one expected to hear in this concerto—even with plastic keys.

"Very good, Alexis. How does it sound to you?" Nadia asked, as she wandered around the hall checking acoustics.

"I love it. How much longer may I practice here?"

"We have the hall for another hour. Enough time for you to run through your entire program."

Alexis savored every minute as he played a Bach partita, Chopin ballade, and the Rachmaninoff concerto.

Nadia took a moment to provide encouragement to Alexis.

"Excellent work on making the intricate architecture of the Partita so clear. And I love the sensitivity and elegance you bring to the melodic phrasing in the Chopin. You now perform the Rachmaninoff with great conviction. *Bravo*, Alexis! Please remember to stay focused in the Rachmaninoff. Remember the exercises we discussed on concentration and not getting distracted by things like the conductor waving his baton? Stay focused and your performance will receive the highest marks by the judges."

Nadia's approval meant everything to Alexis. Her standards for performance were high, but when she said it was good, he knew it really was good!

The night before the preliminary eliminations, he slept on

the softest bed he'd ever felt. Just before dozing off, he mentally practiced his pieces and used his trained memory to familiarize himself with the hall once again.

Alexis' performance during the preliminary eliminations was solid, so it was no surprise when Nadia informed him that the judges had selected him and three other contestants to advance to the finals.

"You will perform with the Leningrad Symphony."

"That's fantastic!"

"Yes, it is, Alexis, and we should celebrate this good news. I've arranged for us to have dinner at the Astoria Hotel. The Astoria is rich in history, dating back to the first world war."

Once seated at the restaurant, Sol raised his glass in a toast to Alexis.

"Your advancement to the finals recognizes your dedication and hard work, Alexis. Here's to you and many more successes."

Alexis noticed Petrov's two guards standing at the entrance to the dining room.

"The general's guards look so uncomfortable standing there. Can we send some drinks to them?"

Alexis' concern for the guards touched Nadia.

"Not to worry, Alexis. I've already arranged for them to have dinner and drinks. They're fine."

Sol's knowledge of Russian history took center stage.

"Do you know the famous people who have stayed at this hotel, maybe having dinner right where you are sitting, Alexis?"

"Would I know them?"

"Oh, most definitely. You have studied Russian history and already know about Lenin."

"Yes. The general has a book about Lenin on his desk. He was an important man, and a Russian hero."

"Well, yes, some people think that."

Nadia chimed in. "And what about Rasputin? He stayed here as well."

"He was a terrible man, and not good for Russia. Right?"

"You are very right, dear."

Sol continued the history lesson.

"Adolph Hitler believed the German siege of Leningrad would be successful, so he planned a victory celebration here at this hotel."

"Good thing we defeated Hitler."

"Right you are, Alexis."

Alexis continued to enjoy his dinner, but as he consumed the last of his Kartoshka cakes, he noticed his mother in private conversation with Nadia. His mother appeared nervous, and had barely touched her food. *What could be troubling her?* His skills of observation also caught Sol shaking his head at Nadia. She nodded back. Alexis felt like he was outside the room looking in.

"Are you okay, Mama? You look a little nervous. Please don't be. I'll be just fine tomorrow. You know how long I've practiced for this. I'm ready!"

"Everything is fine, dear. I'm not worried about your performance. You could never disappoint me."

Alexis wanted to hug his mother and assure her everything was going to be fine, but since she was across the table, he smiled broadly. Yet he had to wonder, *if Mama isn't worried about my performance, why is she troubled? What is up with Nadia and Sol?*

While Alexis remained concerned about the dinner conversation, a restful night prepared him for the competition finals.

11

Waiting in the green room, Alexis reflected on how fortunate he'd been. Soon he'd walk on stage to play with one of Russia's greatest conductors and orchestras in front of a full house. He listened as a staff member welcomed the audience and explained what the judges were looking for in each contestant's performance.

Solomon Blum joined Alexis for those last minutes before going on stage.

"Your playing has been exhilarating, Alexis, and it's clear the judges agree. I know how important this competition is to you. Keep in mind this is just one performance. You have an entire lifetime ahead of you when you'll have the chance to thrill audiences with your beautiful music. I'm confident you'll play your best today, as you always do. I'll wait with Nadia and your mother in the contestants' room. Now, go out there and show them what you do to make the Rachmaninoff concerto come alive."

"I will! Thank you, Mr. Blum. I won't let you down."

Alexis entered the stage to enthusiastic applause. He felt unsteady and nervous for the first time since his arrival in Leningrad. It was unusual for him, and it surprised him. Beads of sweat appeared on his forehead and his hands felt cold. The bright lights almost blinded him, blocking any view of the audience. Even with the surrounding orchestra behind him, he felt isolated on stage. Together, those elements were unsettling to him.

Then his demeanor shifted as he applied the mental exercises they had taught him at the Institute, as if they were second nature. One of his tests required him to enter a room, and in sixty seconds, recall everything in the room. Upon exiting, Alexis described the worn leather furniture with several cigarette burns, the color of the walls, the floral table lamp with the tilted shade, all the different rugs, ashtrays, including the one with a cigarette still burning. He described many details that were less obvious and recalled everything without error. It took extraordinary concentration and focus.

And that is what Nadia wanted him to bring to this performance. He understood that now.

As trained by Nadia, he acknowledged the applause, shook hands with the concertmaster, and took his seat at the piano. Then he nodded to the conductor, signaling his readiness to begin. He moved his wrists and fingers to loosen them up. The conductor raised his arms and gave the downbeat for the orchestral introduction. And with those first familiar strains of music, Alexis' nerves disappeared. He transported the music in his mind through his long and graceful fingers onto the keyboard. He created an illusion of space and breathlessness for the Rachmaninoff concerto. Just as he was told he would be, he was perfect.

Alexis expected to be greeted with a joyous reaction from his mother, Nadia, and Sol after the performance, but they appeared distracted and serious. His euphoria faded. Did he not perform as well as expected? Did one of the other contestants play better? There was a point at the ending of the second movement when he felt strange—a fogginess he couldn't understand, but that disappeared almost as suddenly as it appeared. *Maybe Nadia noticed that, too. Or was it the repeated rolled chords in the Rachmaninoff third movement? Do the judges understand Rachmaninoff had large hands, but mine are not that large, so I must roll those chords? Perhaps the headache and strange feeling I felt leaving the stage may have affected my performance.*

Sol directed them to a small anteroom for more privacy, and in a quiet voice he informed Alexis, "It will take the judges time to deliberate. When they've reached a consensus, they will announce the results in the Great Hall. Rather than just sit here waiting for the results, let's take a relaxing drive to the pier for an ice cream break. Does that sound like something you would enjoy, Alexis?"

"Yes, but we won't miss the judge's announcements, will we?"

Returning with a gold medal and receiving praise from General Petrov had consumed Alexis ever since the general announced the competition. He thought he played well, and Nadia told him it was his best, but what difference would that make if he returned empty-handed?

Nadia added her assurances to Sol's proposal. "We won't miss a thing, Alexis. It takes the judges a long time to write their comments and reach a consensus. I think an ice cream cone sounds like a perfect break."

"Do we need to tell the guards?"

Sol was quick to respond. "I told them to take an early lunch break while we wait here."

Alexis sensed Sol was eager to leave, especially after he caught him glancing at the bags stored in the corner of the room.

"Why are all our bags packed? You told me we would see more of Leningrad before leaving!" It was Alexis's first taste of how other people lived, and it whetted his appetite.

"We'll put the bags in the car now to prepare for our departure later. Let's hurry, so we have time to enjoy our ice cream."

Once they were all in the car, Alexis saw Sol hand the driver a large roll of cash. Alexis didn't think a drive to the pier would cost that much money, but then he thought maybe Leningrad was more expensive than Moscow. He held on as the car sped off for the twenty-minute ride to the pier. Alexis rolled the window down and let the breeze hit his face. He loved the smell of the sea. Gulls were circling, and he imagined they would find their next meal either just below the water's surface, or the food left behind by visitors on the boardwalk. They looked so free. Alexis sometimes wished he could just fly away, too.

In the backseat, his mother asked him, "Alexis, do you remember our conversations about going to America someday?"

"Yes. You said I'd be happy there because I'd be free. The general has me learning all about the US and its people, because he *also* told me that America is in my future."

"We're going to America, Alexis." Nadia Rosenberg said quietly.

"We are? When?"

"Now," Nadia said with clarity.

Stunned, Alexis took a moment to understand. "But what about the competition?" He expected to win the gold medal. He couldn't leave without it, or General Petrov would be furious with him.

"We're all going to America because we want to be free. Imagine being able to go anywhere without guards with guns watching you. We're taking you to America so we can be free together, Alexis. Do you understand?"

Even at his young age, Alexis understood. He had seen his freedom become more limited as the intensity of his studies at the Institute increased. It was becoming less about music, and more about making the general happy.

There were also those sessions where the doctors sedated him because they said they needed to check his vital signs while sleeping. He felt uneasy after each appointment, and he always woke up with a headache. It all felt strange to him. Strange, *but necessary*, the general had assured him. Alexis didn't tell his parents about those sessions, because he still had too many unanswered questions himself, but he told his friend Abby that the Institute was feeling more and more like a military academy.

"Abby, maybe it's different for girls, but do you feel you can't even be your own person here?"

"Sure. I feel like that all the time. They even tell me what to paint. At least they don't tell me *how* to paint. Then I'd want to leave."

"But Abby, if that ever happened, where would you go? At least I could go home to my parents, but you don't have anywhere else to be."

"That's why you can't go anywhere without me, Alexis. Since I have no place to go, we need to stay here together. Promise?" It became their sacred vow, confirmed by their intertwined pinky fingers.

As they now approached the pier, Alexis' thoughts turned from Abby to his father. "What about Papa? Is he coming with us?"

"He wanted to be with us, dear, but he had to stay at his job a little longer. He'll join us after we get settled in New York."

Alexis couldn't understand why his father would not be going to America with them. And why would they leave for America before knowing the results of the competition? He wanted to go to America. But he had looked forward to returning to Moscow with the gold medal.

"Driver, please hurry. We're running behind schedule."

The stress in Sol's voice alarmed Alexis. He sat back in his seat and looked at his mother. She put her arms around him and managed a smile, but it did little to assure him.

The driver skidded to a stop in front of Leningrad's Custom House and slapped their bags on the table for inspection before speeding away. The custom officers appeared to be in no hurry as they rifled through the bags, then they stopped searching all together. The senior officer held up a thick envelope stuffed inside a pair of Sol's trousers.

"What have we here? Whose bag is this, and why are you carrying so much money?"

"That's a small token of our appreciation to you for the hard work you do to keep us all safe. General Petrov wanted me to make sure you received this."

Sol's explanation made no sense to Alexis. That didn't sound like something the general would do. Alexis was more and more confused, but his instincts told him to stay quiet.

Alexis saw the officer put the envelope in his pocket as he issued instructions to the guards. "I have cleared this group for departure. Help them with their luggage."

The Danish crew in the waiting boat helped the four of them board, while simultaneously untying it from the pier. Alexis became concerned and confused with all the activity, the suddenness, and the enormity of what was occurring. He let himself believe they were on their way to America and locked eyes with his mother, who smiled back at him.

As they departed, Alexis' fears subsided. He was with his mother and the other two adults he trusted the most. If only his papa were with them to start this new adventure, everything would be complete. He leaned over the edge where the water was flying off the side of the boat onto his face.

When the craft reached maximum speed, they heard the blast of the port's security siren and saw the flashing lights arcing over the water. Alexis could see two border patrol crafts in fast pursuit, bouncing over the choppy waters.

Sol Blum broke the silence. "Petrov's guards must have sounded the alarm."

Sol's words reverberated with Alexis. He looked at his mother for reassurance. "What's happening, Mama? Who are those people?"

"It is going to be fine, Alexis. We're together, and soon we will be safe."

How could everything be fine? They were being chased. He would not collect his gold medal. They were going to America, but without his papa. Nothing made sense.

Alexis froze when he heard the Danish captain say, "Mr. Blum, you understand that being captured is not an option? That would lead to horrifying consequences for all of us."

"I understand, Captain. We must reach the safety of international waters before that border patrol boat reaches us."

The blaring sound of the bullhorn terrified Alexis. He clapped his hands over his ears, even though the blast was reverberating in his head.

"This is Captain Bogdanovich of the Leningrad Border Patrol. You are attempting an illegal departure from this port. I am ordering you to return."

Alexis cried. His mother wrapped her arms around him and held him tight. She whispered in his ear, "Be brave and be patient, my son. Soon we will be free. Remember always how much your papa and I love you."

Her words did not calm Alexis. Shaken to the core, he wanted to talk to his mother, but the booming warning from Captain Bogdanovich reached them over the water, making that impossible.

"This is your final warning. If you do not turn around, we will fire live ammunition on you."

Alexis sagged with relief when he noticed that the Leningrad Border Patrol boat, so close just a moment ago, was losing ground and fading into the waters behind them. He dared to believe they were out of harm's way. They were almost out of range when the Russian officer made good on his threats.

With terrifying speed, a barrage of bullets flew toward the craft and over the ducked heads of the four shaking passengers. Most of the bullets did not find their target, except the one that struck Larisa Koryavin in the head, her arms still protectively wrapped around her terrified son.

"Mama!" Alexis screamed, his voice sounding small amid the cacophony of gunfire, the boat's engine, the churning water. He became frantic as his tears mixed with his mother's blood.

"No, no, no!" he cried. "This can't happen. We're not free yet. We're supposed to be free together. Mama, come back to me. Get up! Come back," he pleaded to her still body. He bent over her, sobbing his heart out, hoping she knew how much he loved her.

Alexis stared at the retreating patrol boats that ferried the officers who had just shot his mother. As he watched his mother's murderers float away, the Danish captain announced they were now in international waters.

For the first time in his young life, Alexis was free.

12

Solomon Blum stepped into a parental role and welcomed Alexis into his New York City home.

"There are so many exciting things New York City can offer you, Alexis. It's not only one of the most important cultural centers in the world, but there are so many hidden treasures residents of the city can enjoy. Soon you'll discover them, and it will become part of who you are."

It didn't take long for Alexis to experience what Sol was saying. On one of his walks, he stopped in front of a colorful display of fruits and vegetables flanking a grocery store. He couldn't believe all the variations of apples: Delicious, Granny Smith, McIntosh, Fuji, and more, all neatly arranged, and looking like a piece of art.

The grocer approached him. "Are you interested in buying an apple, son?"

"Yes, I am, sir, but there are so many. How do I decide?"

"Maybe I can help you with that."

The grocer described each of the apples and their distinctive tastes.

"I think I would like to try the Delicious, sir."

"That's an excellent choice. What other apples have you tasted before?"

"I have only eaten Anonovka apples."

"That's a wonderful apple. It's quite common in Russia."

"Yes, sir. That's where I'm from. Moscow."

"My goodness. How long have you been in New York, son?"

"Only a month, sir."

"Your English is almost perfect. How old are you?"

"I'm ten, but soon I'll be eleven."

"What's your name?"

"I'm Alexis, sir."

"Well, Alexis. I want to welcome you to New York with a gift of some of these apples that you can share with your family."

Alexis thanked the grocer and continued to share more of his thoughts of living in New York with his new friend, the grocer. He loved New York.

Sol made sure Alexis received every material thing that he needed. But freedom seemed hollow when it came at such a high cost, and the price Alexis paid—the price his mother paid—seemed insurmountable.

Alexis missed his daily conversations with Abby about life, music, art, and Petrov. Sol was able to find out from a trusted colleague that Abby had left the Institute. Alexis looked for her on his walks, even though he doubted she would have found her way to New York.

The worst had not yet occurred, however. Through his international connections, Sol learned of Alexis' father's execution, at the hands of General Petrov.

Nadia and Sol took on the sad task of telling Alexis.

Nadia was the first to speak.

"Sweetheart, we wanted to talk to you about the news we just received about your father."

Alexis looked at Sol, who looked terrible. Nadia was tearing up. He didn't need to wait for Nadia to tell him the bad news.

"My father is dead, isn't he?"

Nadia reached over to Alexis' side and held him tight.

"Oh, Alexis, I am so sorry."

Why can't I cry? Nadia is crying, so is Sol. My father is dead. I lost my mother. I have no family. Why can't I cry?

Sol could tell Alexis was in shock, and he joined Nadia and embraced Alexis. Tears flowed, just not from Alexis.

"Did General Petrov kill him?"

"We don't know Alexis. We're waiting for more information."

That night, Alexis sobbed uncontrollably. He heard Nadia and Sol pacing outside his room. He loved them and, while tempted to reach out to them, he needed to handle his grief in his own way.

When Alexis later learned that Petrov had his father killed in retaliation for forging documents that made his escape possible, the pain and guilt became almost unbearable.

It's all my fault. Mama died so I could live, and Papa sacrificed his life for me. General Petrov got his way with everything. I'll make him pay if it's the last thing I do. I promise, Mama and Papa.

Comforting Alexis seemed futile, but Sol tried anyway. "Your parents wanted you to live in a country where you'd be free. They pursued that dream, knowing what it might mean. They loved you, Alexis, more than anything. Now you must honor their memory by moving on and working hard to fulfill your dreams."

"Am I an orphan?"

Alexis' question brought Sol close to tears. He embraced Alexis and told him about the promise that he and Nadia had made to his parents—that they would take care of Alexis should anything happened to them.

"Yesterday, the court approved our application for guardianship. Nadia and I are both proud to be your adoptive parents. We're your new American family."

Alexis rested his head on Sol's shoulder, sank into his embrace, and finally let himself be comforted.

Getting guardianship approval was one matter, but obtaining citizenship for both Nadia and Alexis proved to be more of a challenge. Sol reached out to a good friend, Terrance Smith, an attorney who specialized in helping families with the adoption process.

"Sol, your situation is different, and therefore, more difficult. Alexis is still a child. It's good he arrived with all his papers, including a birth certificate. But the courts will want to know about his life in Russia before coming to the US, and will need to see his transcripts from the Institute for Gifted Children. Nadia's application will be easier; she is an adult and has all her papers."

"The Institute's director, General Petrov, won't cooperate, Terrance. In fact, he will claim that Alexis left Russia illegally. Therefore, he would contend the US should not grant Alexis citizenship."

"If the courts agree, it could deny Alexis further consideration. In fact, Russia could demand his extradition back to Russia. Nadia too. I think we can make a compelling case that Nadia and Alexis left a country where they were at risk of persecution, and perhaps even fearful for their lives. However, that could be an uphill battle."

"How do we proceed, Terrance? What can I do to help?"

"For starters, identify all those persons who would support their application for citizenship. Try to find important musicians or artists who faced similar challenges, and are now US citizens. Those would be your best advocates. Also, hire a tutor to help them prepare for the citizenship exams. I will reach out to some high-level contacts I have in New York and Washington and see if I can get around some of these issues. I'm hoping Nadia's international reputation and Alexis' potential may present an opportunity for making a strong case for citizenship. After all, Alexis' mother was killed during the escape, and that alone can be a compelling emotional detail that could help. Meanwhile, I will start the application procedure right away."

After talking to Nadia, Sol reached out to their contacts and received encouraging responses.

Before, during, and following WWII, large groups of intellectuals, artists, and scientists left Russia and emigrated to the United States. Nadia had close friends, including composer Igor Stravinsky, choreographer George Balanchine, and the novelist Vladimir Nabokov, who were part of that group. Russia took action to stop the hemorrhaging of their greatest talents and toughened their immigration laws, but the US government welcomed this exceptional pool of talent and granted them citizenship. This irritated the Russian government, further exacerbating Cold War tensions.

Stravinsky, Balanchine, Nabokov, and others all sent testimonials supporting Nadia's and Alexis' applications for citizenship.

After forty-five days, Sol received a call from Terrance Smith. Sol was excited to hear the good news.

"The court approved both Nadia's and Alexis' applications for citizenship, Sol."

"That's wonderful, Terrance. You must have pulled the right strings."

"I would love to take credit, but I can't."

"I'm not sure I understand, Terrance."

"Neither do I, Sol. I did the standard application for both Nadia and Alexis, and as part of the application, they checked with the Institute for Gifted Children in Moscow. Here is the report they received from its director, General Andrei Petrov:

General Andrei Petrov
Director, Institute for Gifted Children
Moscow, Russia

Alexis Koryavin was a student at the Institute for Gifted Children in Moscow for seven years, from 1948 to 1955. He was an exceptional student who received the highest grades in all his studies. Mr. Koryavin moved to the United States last year. We wish him all the best in his future studies.

Please do not hesitate to contact me if I can be of any further assistance.

Terrance paused to let the recommendation sink in. "This is not the response you expected, is it?"

"No. I'm stunned, Terrance."

"Given what you have told me about Petrov, there may be a method to his madness."

"Like how, Terrance?"

"He may not want to attract attention to the Institute or even his role there. This way, he avoids prying eyes."

"You may be right."

Sol couldn't help but to think there was more to Petrov's response, but he knew Terrence's recommendation to *take the win* made sense.

Nadia was just as surprised as Sol to hear the news. They had doubts and concerns about Petrov's response, but with that settled, they took great pride in notifying Alexis.

"I'm a US citizen now?"

"We're both so proud of you, Alexis."

Alexis ran into the arms of Nadia and Sol.

"Thank you, Nadia. And thank you, Sol, for making this happen."

Sol and Nadia decided it was best not to mention General Petrov's response. They were still trying to understand it all. They still worried that Petrov could exact revenge on Alexis, or, even the two of them. Petrov had every reason to wish them harm for their role in Alexis' escape.

Weeks later, Alexis approached Nadia and Sol.

"If I'm an American citizen now, shouldn't I have an American name? Most people can't even pronounce my last name."

Before Alexis asked this important question, he had reasoned all the pros and cons of a name change.

My parents are both dead. Did their names die with them? My mother and father trusted Nadia and Sol to take care of me. Can changing my name still honor my parents, and honor Nadia and Sol as well?

Giving up his Russian identity, the lifeblood that belonged to him and his mama and papa, seemed so drastic. The name they shared was all that he had left. Alexis' training in deductive reasoning at the Institute helped him digest these complex questions. He knew what he had to do.

"Have you thought of names you might like?"

Alexis didn't hesitate.

"I like Alexis, Sol. Can I change it to Alex? Some of my classmates already call me that."

"That's a wonderful idea, Alexis."

"What about a last name?"

"I know Johnson and Smith are very American names."

"If you are going to be a concert pianist, you should have a name that is less common."

"Remember the apples I brought home that time from the grocer?"

"Yes, of course. They were delicious."

"One of those apples was called a *Cortland* apple. I remember he told me it has been a popular apple since they introduced it in New York in 1898."

"You want your last name to be Cortland?"

"Yes. But I want it spelled Courtland, so it would be different."

"*Hmm.* Alex Courtland. I like it. You seem like the perfect Alex

Courtland. It's also a great stage name. Why don't you run it by Nadia and see what she thinks?"

Because Alexis was underage, his name changed required a petition to the New York county court by Nadia and Sol, his legal guardians. Once approved, Nadia made her special beef stroganoff to celebrate.

"May we call you Alex now?"

"Yes, Nadia and Sol. That's my name now."

In the weeks that followed, Sol purchased a condominium for Nadia and Alex across from Carnegie Hall. It was 1956. Now eleven years old, Alex continued his studies with Nadia and started classes at a private school. It was a new beginning for him.

I feel free for the first time in my life.

The healing process had begun.

Alex thrived on the energy and diversity so prevalent in New York City and continued to explore new neighborhoods, sometimes with Nadia and Sol, and then, as he became more acclimated, he ventured out on his own for longer walks. His senses became overwhelmed with the unique sights and smells on each block. He loved it all. It proved to be excellent therapy for him. Nadia and Sol noticed his mischievous sense of humor returning bit by bit.

One of Alex's favorite walks was to Carnegie Hall, directly across the street from his new home on 57th Street. He would spend hours walking around the lobby and reading every poster of the coming attractions. He imagined one of those posters with his name and picture.

"Young man, you can't go up those stairs. Those are studios and residences for many musicians."

The guard's orders caught Alex by surprise. "I'm sorry, sir. I didn't know it was private. Some day I hope to play here, and I just wanted to walk around and get used to Carnegie Hall."

"If you're going to play here someday, then I need to show you where everything is."

"Would you? That would be terrific, sir."

"Why don't we start with the main hall first? There is a rehearsal going on now with the philharmonic, but we can listen for a bit in the back of the hall if we stay very quiet."

It was the thrill of a lifetime. On stage rehearsing the orchestra was the world-famous conductor, Leonard Rubinstein, one of Alex's idols.

As Alex was thanking the guard for the tour, he overheard a conversation in Russian between a man and a woman. Without thinking, he blurted out, "*Я из России YA iz Rossii.*"

The man turned around and faced Alex.

"You are from Russia?"

The guard's reaction was immediate.

"Mr. Horowitz, I am so sorry. I was giving this young man a tour. He says he plans to play Carnegie Hall someday."

Alex became excited.

"You're Vladimir Horowitz?"

"Yes, I am. Who are you?"

"My name is Alexis Koryavin, but now that I am an American citizen, I changed my name to Alex Courtland."

"I see. Since you will someday play a concert here, I assume you are studying piano now?"

"Yes, I am, Mr. Horowitz. I study with Madame Nadia Rosenberg. Nadia is also my guardian."

Horowitz's expression changed. He leaned over to face Alex, then took both his hands and clasped them with his own.

"It's a pleasure to meet you, Alex. I know your teacher very well. She is a wonderful artist-teacher. Please give her my personal regards. I look forward to hearing you play here someday, Mr. Alex Courtland."

Alex left Carnegie thinking, *this has been the best day of my life. I love New York.* He couldn't wait to tell Nadia about meeting Vladimir Horowitz.

Nadia turned around from the kitchen surprised by the news. "You met Vladimir?"

"Yes. He was very nice. He said he would look forward to my playing in Carnegie Hall."

"That deserves a cup of hot chocolate with marshmallows."

Another day when Alex was walking up Broadway, he came to the corner of 63rd Street and noticed heavy demolition of all the buildings in a large plot of land. He read the sign:

FUTURE HOME OF THE LINCOLN CENTER
FOR THE PERFORMING ARTS

As soon as he got home, he asked Nadia about it.

"I am so glad you saw that, dear. That is the future home of the New York Philharmonic and the Juilliard School of Music. Juilliard just asked me to conduct a few master classes once they complete the buildings."

"Should I be preparing to play there, instead of Carnegie Hall?"

Nadia walked over to Alex and put both her hands on his shoulders. "I think you should be ready to play at both places, Alex."

Their defection from Russia sparked interest from a writer at *The New York Times* who knew Sol Blum. She asked him if she could write an article about their journey. At first, Sol and Nadia were hesitant because they had concerns for Alex's privacy. Alex still felt vulnerable and had a deep-seated fear that the general could punish him from afar. Nadia and Sol remained suspicious and cautious after seeing Petrov's response to Alex's citizenship request. But they also knew this could bring some much needed confidence to Alex, so they encouraged him.

"They want to tell your story, Alex. It may give hope to others in Russia and other countries where people hunger for the freedom that you now enjoy. Talking about your experience may be good for you, and it may help others to hear your story."

Alex walked to the dining table where Nadia and Sol were enjoying their tea and sat with them.

"Would you and Nadia be with me during the interview?"

"Yes, Alex. We're part of this story, too. Think of it as a movie where you have a starring role, and Nadia and I are supporting characters."

The writer explained her intent to expand it to a three-part series.

"This is all too fascinating and special to stop after one article. I want the first part to cover background information on all three of you. It's important for the reader to relate to you individually and the reasons why each of you left Russia. That story will set the stage for the second article that will focus on the Leningrad International Competition and Alex's dramatic escape from Russia."

Sol explained the sensitivity of including information on the Institute for Gifted Children. They had no interest in irritating Petrov, especially after his positive letter supporting Alex. They decided it was best to include his attendance at the school, but put the major focus on his musical training with Nadia.

It was the second article that the reporter felt would be the most painful for readers to relate to, because of the high-cost Alex paid for his freedom.

"The third article will highlight the experiences you've all had since your arrival in the United States."

Alex wore his best suit to the interview and combed his wavy dark brown hair into place. Sol even made him shine his shoes.

"Sol, they're not interviewing my shoes. Why do I have to shine them?"

"Because you're a complete package, Alex. Get used to living in a fishbowl!"

The first two articles received a glowing response from readers, but it was the response to the third article that overwhelmed Sol's office with requests for Alex to perform. The black-and-white photo used in the article of Alex giving a concert at the Institute appeared everywhere. It showed him in profile, leaning into the keyboard. He was the complete package. Alex gained a following, and to his surprise, people even recognized him as he went about his daily life.

It thrilled Alex to be a celebrity, but Nadia had reservations about the requests for Alex to perform.

"He has all the technical and musical requirements and would give a fine recital, Sol. He's been ready to perform since he was five years old."

Nadia walked over to the window facing Carnegie Hall and took a serious tone.

"Alex is still recovering from the death of his parents, and he'll carry that pain with him for the rest of his life. He doesn't share his grief with anyone. He's very private, and we need to understand what he's going through right now. I think General Petrov remains an ongoing threat to all of us, not just Alex. I'm sure Petrov sees me as enemy number one. After all, I was the one who left Russia with his prized student. Even you, Sol may be on his most wanted list. We are all vulnerable, and we must do whatever we can to protect Alex. I just don't think this is the right time for him to do public appearances."

"It goes against my grain as an artist's manager to admit it, but I know you're right, Nadia. I'll inform the booking managers."

Despite their high expectations, Alex's emotional maturity didn't match his physical and technical growth. His playing was better than ever and showed a marked increase in artistic development. His academic grades were just as impressive, but his guilt over his parents' death took a toll that lasted several years. And the threat of not knowing what Petrov might do left them in the dark.

13

It surprised General Petrov to receive a letter from immigration authorities in New York requesting information about Alexis. His initial thought was to make Alexis, Sol, and Nadia suffer for their betrayal. He could claim they were criminals and broke Russian and international laws by leaving Russia the way they did. However, he knew supporting Alexis' citizenship would better serve the agreement he had with Tilton. Guaranteeing Alexis' full access to important persons and events was important. He needed full credibility, including US citizenship and a career that was second to none in the performing arts. Nadia, too, was part of the package deal.

He had drafted the letter that would help Alexis and Nadia get citizenship.

Not willing to leave anything to chance, he called Tilton on the special phone he had given him. It was only to be used for important matters. This qualified.

It was 2 a.m. in Washington, DC. He knew Tilton was married and this could be tricky, how he would explain a call coming in on a strange device in the middle of the night. He had to assume Tilton had already covered that eventuality.

"This must be very important, Andrei. It's two in the morning here."

"I am aware, John. It's very important."

"Alexis is applying for US citizenship. So is Nadia Rosenberg, his teacher. I have written a letter stating Alexis left the Institute in good standing and was a model student. His future is important to our plans. Can you help with making sure they approve his citizenship?"

"Yes. The process for citizenship in New York follows the same procedure we have here in Washington. I just finished getting citizenship for Abby, and I know the people that can take care of this. I'll make the calls in the morning."

"How is Abby doing? Will she be of any help to us in future dealings with Alexis?"

"It's too early to tell. The connection she made with Alex at the Institute was so much stronger than either of us expected. She asks about him all the time. I think there will be a time when we will be able to put the two of them together and see if Alex has the same feelings toward Abby. If so, then I think it could bring additional value to our plans."

"The indoctrination that Alex went through at the Institute will help to bring everything full circle when the timing is right."

"Let's hope so. Can I go back to bed now?"

14

Good news came from Nadia on Alex's fifteenth birthday. "Leonard Rubinstein called me yesterday."

After a moment of astonished silence, Alex couldn't contain his excitement.

"The conductor of the New York Philharmonic! *That* Leonard Rubinstein?"

"Yes, that Leonard Rubinstein. I first met him when we both served as judges for the Tchaikovsky International Piano Competition in Moscow. We stayed in touch over the years, and when he heard about our defection from Russia, he offered to help. Every few months, we chatted about this and that, but most often about you."

"You should have told me! That would really have impressed my friends."

"It was my decision to wait for the right time. I believe that the time has come. Leonard wants you to play for him. We arranged it for next Thursday."

"Next Thursday! I can't get ready to play for the most famous conductor on the planet in less than a week."

"Really? You could play for him today."

Alex walked gingerly to Nadia and held her hands. "Will you go with me?"

"Oh no, dear. This is an important time when you should be alone with the maestro without the interference of a third party. You don't need me there. You will be just fine."

"I'll practice like crazy."

"You already do."

Laughter filled the room. It was great therapy for Alex. Nadia loved seeing him so happy.

This was the turning point in Alex's life that Nadia and Sol had been hoping for. Alex worked nonstop to prepare for his meeting with Leonard Rubinstein, a meeting that would change his life.

Thursday arrived, and Alex acted like a crazy teenager.

"Eat breakfast first," Sol said. "You don't want to play on an empty stomach."

"I'm too wound up to eat, Sol. What time is it?"

"Two minutes later than the last time you asked. You'll get to Carnegie Hall in plenty of time. It's right across the street, Alex!"

Alex was ready.

The maestro put Alex at ease as they discussed a multitude of topics, ranging from Rubinstein's fond memories of his working with Nadia, to his curiosity about Alex's experiences since moving to the US. Then it was time for Alex to confirm all the wonderful things she had told Leonard about Alex.

Rubinstein asked Alex to start with some Bach so he could see how he handled the intricate architecture of a partita. After that came Brahms, so Alex could demonstrate that he understood the multitude of instrumental colors so prevalent in Brahms' piano music. Then there were the Russian masters, Scriabin and Rachmaninoff, to confirm Alex's technical proficiency.

The connection made between the two brilliant talents was instant and genuine.

Alex left Carnegie Hall exalted as he made his way up 7th Avenue and turned the corner, heading east on 57th Street. He couldn't wait to tell Nadia about his audition. *Me, a fifteen-year-old kid, playing for the maestro! Only in America,* he mused.

While Alex waited for the light to change, he saw a black limousine pull up to the curb in front of the Russian Tea Room. He fantasized about how much fun it would be to ride in a limousine someday. He watched as the chauffeur opened the door and helped two ladies and one gentleman exit the car.

Engaged in conversation as they passed by Alex, the three strangers headed for the restaurant. The two women wore glittering wraps, and the gentleman was in a tux. Alex froze as he recognized General Andrei Petrov, a face he could never forget. He gasped for air and grabbed a lamppost for support as he experienced a full-fledged panic attack. His knees became weak, his palms turned cold, his forehead became clammy. He was only a few feet away from the man responsible for his parents' deaths. Paralyzed with fear, he was relieved the general did not notice him. Alex took deep breaths until his heart returned to normal rhythm and the trio reached the restaurant's entrance. Still in shock, he made his way home to Nadia.

Nadia was by the piano, talking to the piano technician when Alex arrived.

"Hi Alex. Mr. Benson is tuning the piano, and I've asked him to voice some hammers in the upper register. Is there anything else you would like Mr. Benson to check while he's here, dear?"

"Just the sostenuto pedal. It's kind of noisy."

"Oh, yes. I've heard that, too."

"Well, I guess that covers it, Mr. Benson. Alex and I will be in the kitchen if you have any questions."

"Come, dear, I'll make you a sandwich. You must be hungry."

While Nadia prepared his lunch, Alex explained his harrowing experience to her and noticed her facial expression change. She seemed upset.

"Nadia, what's wrong?"

"Sol and I wanted to tell you earlier, but we didn't want to upset you before your meeting with Leonard."

"Tell me what?"

"General Petrov's the new ambassador to the United Nations. We assume he'll be spending a great deal of time in New York."

Alex considered his situation. He had come within a stone's throw of the man responsible for everything bad that had happened in his life. His hate for the general ran deep, even though it was contrary to everything his parents or Nadia and Sol had taught him. Surging inside him was a hunger for revenge. He asked himself, *would I have killed Petrov if I had a gun?* He couldn't answer his own question. Another question raced through his mind. *Was Petrov planning to kill me, too?* He shivered at the thought.

"Alex. New York is a big place. You may never run into him again. You're an American citizen and safe here. Sol and I will always protect you."

Nadia's words helped. But the fear of Petrov remained.

Nadia broke the contemplative silence with good news.

"Leonard Rubinstein called me after you left your meeting with him."

"He did?" While still feeling the shock of seeing the general, Alex was all ears.

"Yes. The pianist scheduled to perform on the Young People's Concert Series this fall had to cancel. He asked me if you could play the Rachmaninoff *3rd Concerto* in his place. It's a piece you and I have worked on, so I told him you could be ready."

Speechlessness was a rarity for Alex, but for the moment, he didn't know how to respond.

"Cat got your tongue?"

"Nadia, do you realize millions of people hear the Young People's concerts? Leonard Rubinstein is a rock star, and he wants me to perform with him and the New York Philharmonic? Wow!"

"I guess you impressed him, Alex. Congratulations."

"What'll I wear? When do we rehearse? Should I call him and thank him?"

Alex grinned, watching Nadia roll her eyes.

Alex's practicing routine started with his imagining he was on stage performing the Rachmaninoff concerto with maestro Rubinstein. His heart fluttered, but not from nerves. It was excitement he felt.

Nadia and Sol remained concerned about Alex's reaction to Petrov.

"Let's take a walk in Central Park while Alex practices, Sol."

"Sure, the weather is lovely, and the walk would do us both good."

They walked up to the park and entered opposite the Plaza Hotel. The horse carriages were lined up waiting for customers.

"Nadia, I think Alex's upcoming concert with the Philharmonic will keep him focused on his preparation for this important event, and he'll put Petrov out of his mind."

"Maybe so, Sol, but he's still terrified of Petrov, and if he runs into him again, it could affect his practicing and upcoming performance. I'm wondering if you could use some of your connections to expose Petrov for who he is, and maybe the United Nations would ask Russia for a substitute ambassador."

"We know Petrov was a bad influence on Alex, but we don't know many details. Everything else we have heard is second-hand or rumored. Think about the letter he sent to support Alex. What hard evidence do we have to accuse Petrov of anything?"

"Sol. We know Petrov is a man with few scruples. And I believe he wants his revenge for us all leaving Russia. That's his end game. Alex's fear of that terrible man may be based on things Alex already has experienced, but we aren't aware of yet."

"All true, Nadia. What if you and Alex go up to New Hampshire at my cottage there? It's equipped with everything, including a fine Steinway. Fighters do this all the time when they're training for a championship bout. We can explain that to Alex. At least it would remove any chance of him running into Petrov before his concert."

"I like that a lot, Sol. The summer months are a perfect time to exit the city. The fresh air and beautiful surroundings could provide just the right environment for him to prepare for his debut with the philharmonic. He still would need to return to the city for rehearsals, but the risk of running into Petrov would be negligible. His school resumes in the fall, but we can delay his attendance until after the concert."

"I'll make the arrangements with the housekeeper to prepare the cabin. I'll join you most weekends."

For the next three months, Alex practiced with great intensity. During this important time, the shock he felt from seeing Petrov was always present, but the focus he brought to his playing was more prevalent. And the walks with Nadia around the beautiful countryside calmed Alex and provided the right contrast to his energetic practicing.

Alex pretended he was on stage when he practiced. Nothing else mattered. *Rachmaninoff and I are alone. Petrov is never there.* Sometimes he would imagine his parents seated in the front row listening to him. That's when he did his best playing.

Once word of the Young People's Concert circulated at Alex's school, a lot of attention got directed to him, even more than when the articles appeared in the *New York Times*. His friends appreciated his skill at the piano, and it was hard not to like Alex. He wasn't captain of the football team, but the girls were taking notice. Handsome, sexy, and almost famous, he was quite popular with the entire student body.

The Young People's Concert sold out after the announcement. The *New York Times* published a follow-up to the earlier series on Alex and provided ticket information. Ambassador Petrov purchased his group of tickets right away. It was an event not to be missed.

15

Alex reached a peak of excitement on the day of the Young People's Concert. He would soon share the stage with the renowned New York Philharmonic and Leonard Rubinstein, an icon in the world of music.

One of the most important career decisions Rubinstein had made was to reintroduce the Young People's Concerts that had debuted in 1924 under the baton of Ernest Schelling. Educating young people about music was important to Rubinstein, and now, with radio and television coverage, it was possible to reach millions of listeners.

While Alex waited to go on stage, he listened closely to Leonard Rubinstein introduce him to a full house and the millions of viewers watching on television.

"Composers show so much of themselves in the music they write. Born in Russia, Rachmaninoff spent the first half of his life there before coming to the United States in 1917, right after the Russian Revolution. There's a sense of melancholy, even sadness in much of his music, and especially in this concerto. There's also a strong nationalistic pride expressed through themes derived from Russian folk music. Rachmaninoff never lost his connection to his homeland, and he forever missed it."

Alex felt a brief emotional moment hearing Rubinstein talk about Rachmaninoff leaving Russia. He wondered if he would forever miss Russia. He reflected on the wonderful memories he had of his time with his parents. There was the first concert he gave soon after going to the Institute. It was all new to him—the students, teachers, everything. He recalled the details of that important concert: how he entered the stage and took his bow, then smiled at his parents who were sitting in the first row. Just knowing they were there to cheer him on provided the comfort and security he needed to play his best.

Alex realized that what he was about to experience would never have happened if he had remained in Russia.

"The challenges in this concerto are formidable for pianists. Rachmaninoff had enormous hands and a huge physical presence. But do not be misled by the youth of the fifteen-year-old young man who is performing for you today. Let me tell you about Alex Courtland.

"You may remember Alex Courtland as the brave ten-year-old boy who defected to the United States from Russia to escape Soviet oppression. Nadia Rosenberg, herself an artist of the highest caliber, accepted him as a student when he was only eight years old and trained him to the professional level of performance you will witness today. Ladies and gentlemen, please join me in welcoming Alex Courtland to center stage at Carnegie Hall."

Alex walked out to an enthusiastic crowd and a stage filled with some of the best orchestral players in the world. Television cameras rotated around the stage to follow his every move. But it was the warm embrace from one of the most influential and talented conductors in the world that set the stage for Alex to give the best performance of his life. The audience agreed and rewarded the artist and maestro Rubinstein with a standing ovation immediately following the thrilling conclusion of the concerto. The response was thunderous and prolonged, and thrilled Alex. His endorphins affected every nerve in his body as he took his final bow.

Mama and Papa, I hope you can see this from heaven. Finally, I have been able to do something for you in return for all you did for me.

As Alex walked down the long hallway to the green room after his performance to greet his friends and new fans, a strange sensation overcame him. It was as if he were in a dream, except he was very much awake. He was oblivious to the stagehand, who shook his hand and congratulated him as he placed a small patch in Alex's palm. It seemed right to him.

Once in the green room, Nadia's praise came first.

"You performed with such passion, Alex. The Rachmaninoff sounded so *alive*. Your parents would have been proud."

"I'm also impressed, young man." The comment came from someone Alex didn't know. Sol introduced him.

"Alex, let me introduce you to John Aldrich, the US Ambassador to the United Nations."

Alex tried to hide his surprise at seeing the ambassador sitting upright in a wheelchair. His legs were wrapped in a blanket embroidered with the insignia of the United Nations. Thin plastic tubes extended from his nostrils to an oxygen tank fastened to the back of his chair, where an attendant stood ready to assist.

Alex bent down to greet the ambassador. "I'm pleased to meet you, sir. Thank you for coming tonight. I hope you enjoyed yourself."

"I did indeed, young man, but I should have waited for this nasty cold to subside before going out. It sure doesn't help my breathing. Milton," he called to his attendant, "please bring me a tissue. They're in the storage pocket underneath my legs."

As the attendant moved to the front of the chair, Alex traded places with him and stood in the back. He took the patch that the stagehand gave him and adhered it to the side of the oxygen tank. As other guests came forward to congratulate Alex on his performance, Milton wheeled the ambassador away.

Alex continued to greet the other guests, but couldn't shake the fog hanging over him. Nadia noticed his unusual behavior.

"Alex, are you okay? You've had a lot of excitement today."

"I'm fine, just a little woozy." *How can I explain how I feel when I don't understand it myself?*

By the next morning, Alex felt normal again, and looked forward to Nadia's special blintzes with caviar and kielbasa.

Leonard Rubinstein arrived for the celebratory brunch holding the morning edition of the *New York Times*. Sol had champagne at the ready.

Sol asked Leonard about the paper under his arm. "Is the review in there, Leonard?"

"Yes! Listen to what Ronald Duvet, the *Times*' chief music critic, wrote about your performance, Alex."

"'Young pianist creates a sensation at Carnegie.'

"You don't see many headlines like that, Alex. Listen to what else he has to say...."

> The young pianist I heard Sunday at Carnegie Hall performing the Rachmaninoff *Piano Concerto No. 3* under the skillful baton of Leonard Rubinstein is fifteen-year-old Alex Courtland. This young man delivered a performance not soon forgotten.
>
> Rachmaninoff's third concerto is one of the most popular works in the piano repertoire. Mister Courtland's remarkable agility made the most difficult passages seem effortless. His intelligent and insightful interpretation connected us to the music and to the composer. He was careful to show us the many qualities that contribute to the nationalistic themes so prevalent in Rachmaninoff's music and delivered details in this marvelous work that even the most seasoned performers often miss. Bravo to Leonard Rubinstein for introducing us to this wonderful pianist from whom, I'm sure, we will be hearing much more.

Rubinstein handed the paper to Sol. "This is a most impressive review, Alex. Congratulations!"

"Thank you, Sol."

Alex noticed Sol reading something else he saw in the *Times*.

Sol's voice was somber. "Listen to this! 'Ambassador Aldrich Dies After Oxygen Tank Explodes'. What a horrible way to die."

Nadia peered over Sol's shoulder, scanning the article. "He was at your concert, Alex. You met him backstage after the concert yesterday. Remember?"

Did I meet him? I remember someone in a wheelchair. Was that the ambassador? Why is this all so blurred?

"I guess so. There were so many people there."

Nadia understood. "Typical brain fog, Alex. My guess is while you were glad-handing your fans, your head was still in the music."

Sol continued reading:

> The Ambassador was one of the strongest voices on the United Nations Security Council who called out Andrei Petrov, the Russian Ambassador to the UN for defending Russia's violation of fundamental human rights. He was an

advocate for increasing economic sanctions against Russia and sounded alerts about their arms buildup. He was 62 and leaves a wife, two children, and three grandchildren.

Rubinstein commented on how Ambassador Aldrich had served on the Philharmonic board for many years, and then took a leave once he accepted the ambassadorship. "He contracted polio as a child and had used a wheelchair ever since. Ambassador Aldrich was a wonderful person, and not afraid to speak his mind."

Alex left the room for a glass of water to quell his nausea.

Sol put the paper down and continued his recall of the previous evening. "There were other dignitaries from the UN at the concert, besides Ambassador Aldrich."

As Alex returned to the room, he was curious. "Who else was there, Sol?"

"I regret to say it, but Petrov was there! He saw me, but we avoided each other."

Hearing the news about Petrov caught Alex by surprise.

"Petrov was there? For the entire concert?"

"I'm afraid so, Alex. He came with a group from the United Nations."

Why is Petrov tormenting me like this? Did he see me that day in front of the restaurant? I will never be free of him.

Without realizing it, Alex blurted, "The general got away with murder!"

Alex's outburst surprised Nadia.

"Sweetheart, I understand why you're upset. Do you remember the conversation we had at one of your very first lessons about the focus that is required in a performance? Remember the discussion about distractions that can undermine the best preparation and compromise a performance?"

"Yes. I remember. But I'm not performing now."

"That's true, Alex. Except you're giving General Petrov power by acknowledging his presence. He is nothing more than a distraction, and I trained you to deal with all distractions. Right?"

Alex sat down, and looked contritely at Nadia.

"Yes. I'm sorry, Nadia."

Rubinstein knew the backstory of Alex's connection to Petrov, so he understood Alex's rage.

Sol thought it was a good time to change the topic.

"My office phones have been ringing off the hook, requesting booking information for Alex. The word is out!"

Rubinstein was quick to react. "Let me be the first to request a booking for Alex to perform on the regular Philharmonic concert schedule next season."

The thought of performing again with Rubinstein pulled Alex out of his funk and thrilled him. "May I do that? Sol, Nadia, can I?"

Nadia responded, "Yes, as long as it doesn't interfere with your academic studies."

Sol closed the discussion. "Then it's settled! We'll look at all the offers and consider the performances that can best support Alex's artistic growth. We'll make sure he has plenty of time to pursue his practicing and other activities."

Over the next few years, Sol booked the right mix of solo and orchestral concerts. Alex had grown into a tall, lean, and handsome young man. His mesmerizing hazel eyes often appeared green, and he combed his deep brown thick hair back, revealing a facial expression that not only showed an inquisitive intelligence, but an innocence that remained despite all his life's events.

Alex's headaches persisted, but the nightmares were new.

16

The call from Petrov came out of the blue before Tilton had retired for the night.

How soon can you come to Russia, John? I have important things to show you.

John Tilton had recently buried his wife, making it a difficult time for him to travel to Moscow. But he needed to accommodate Petrov's request, and in truth thought the escape from all the sympathetic friends and colleagues who had loved Jean might be a welcome diversion.

As difficult as Jean's passing was for John, it was devastating to Abby. From the time she became part of the family, Abby was always there for her adopted mother. Jean provided an environment for Abby founded on trust and love, and Abby returned the same to Jean. The two of them bonded far more than Tilton had hoped. He was now the third wheel in the household, but he was fine with that. Tilton could now devote more time to his own career goals and his plans with Petrov.

Abby shared everything with Jean, including her painful experiences at the Institute and her love for Alexis. Jean died a short three weeks after her cancer returned and days before the 25th anniversary of her marriage to John Tilton. Abby never left her bedside, holding her hands until her last breath. It hit Abby hard. Tilton believed Abby's commitment to Jean during those last weeks was because of the training she received at the Institute. They indoctrinated all students there to stay disciplined with their studies and work, loyal to Petrov, and committed to stated goals without compromise. Abby accompanied Jean to all her medical appointments and treatments.

She attended a private school with other children from distinguished families in Washington, including President Reynold's daughter, Jamie. Abby did well in all her studies, but always feigned illness when the private school for boys was invited to their dances. She would retreat to her room and imagine dancing with Alexis.

Abby remained disappointed that she was prevented from reaching out to Alexis over the years. Abby had no choice but to believe Tilton's trumped-up excuse that he had contacted Alex's guardians on her behalf and was told the timing was not yet right for them to meet.

I'm sorry Abby, but the guardians feel Alexis' departure from Russia and his adjustment to life in the US had been traumatic, and they thought contact with a former student could be upsetting.

Abby, while disappointed, understood.

He was uncomfortable lying to Abby, but could not risk her contacting Alex until the timing that he and Petrov determined was right.

Tilton's long-term plans for Abby were often put on hold because of Jean's wishes for Abby to experience as normal a life as possible. Alex's upcoming performance with the New York Philharmonic had received major press coverage and Abby was insistent about attending. Jean supported Abby and said she would go with her. Tilton took his daughter aside while Jean was receiving chemotherapy treatment.

"I know how much you love your mother, Abby. Her physicians have told me she may not have much time left. She's not strong enough for a trip to New York, and she needs you here, Abby. She loves you so much."

He tried to soften her disappointment.

"I want you and Alex to be together, but for longer than just one event. Please be patient."

Following the funeral, Abby retreated to her painting and barely communicated with her father. He put his plans for Abby on hold, but now that he had secured her admission to Oxford, Abby showed renewed interest in her future. She would soon see Alexis again, now known as Alex, and that was a good reason to be excited. Oxford had a world-class art program and that made her happy. Tilton had kept his promise—a promise Abby had never let him forget—that he would bring Alex back into her life again.

Once Tilton confirmed Alex's acceptance to Oxford, the rest was easy. Abby's strong academic performance and talent, along with Tilton's own contacts and a strong letter of support from the President of the United States, guaranteed Abby a spot at Oxford.

Congress was in adjournment and President Reynolds was on vacation, so it seemed an opportune time to meet with Petrov.

Once in Moscow, Tilton wasted no time and went directly to the Institute.

Petrov was awaiting his arrival.

"Welcome, John. You have been to the Institute many times, but the tour I am taking you on today will be new. New, and exciting for you, I'm sure."

Tilton followed Petrov as they entered the main courtyard and entered the building housing Petrov's pride and joy: Boris. Tilton had to wonder, *where is this leading?*

It was the first time Petrov had invited Tilton into the inner sanctum. Voice commands opened doors and a retina scan confirmed identities. It was an impressive demonstration of the advanced technology Petrov had boasted about.

Once they arrived, John could not take it all in. Even the CIA database center didn't have such an array of technical equipment. Lights were blinking everywhere. It was almost distracting.

"John, please take a seat. Enjoy the champagne and caviar while you watch the show."

"*Show*, Andrei?"

Petrov looked at him and smiled.

"Boris, please welcome our special guest, Ambassador John Tilton from the United States."

Who the hell is he talking to? We are the only two people in the room.

"Welcome, Ambassador Tilton. I'm so happy to meet you. I was very sorry to hear about your wife, who recently passed away. Is Abby well?"

At first, Tilton looked around the room, hoping to find clues about what he was experiencing. After all, the information he just heard was all public. No secrets there. *Maybe a recording?*

He saw the screens displaying detailed and confusing information and tried to digest everything to make some sense of it.

"I sense your suspicions, John. Why don't you ask Boris a question that will confirm to you Boris is a real human experience?"

Tilton thought for a minute.

"It did not thrill me to learn about the death of Ambassador Aldrich. Can you provide some information on that, Boris?"

"John, why are you bringing that—"

Boris didn't allow Petrov to complete the sentence.

"May I provide that information to the ambassador, General?

Petrov looked perturbed.

"Yes. Tell him."

"Thank you, General. Ambassador Aldrich was a threat to both you and the general, Mr. Ambassador. Since Mr. Aldrich had a voice on the Security Council at the United Nations, he repeatedly raised embarrassing concerns about activities in Russia centered on human rights issues. It was receiving too much attention from the press and other diplomats. Also, Mr. Aldrich was a critic of your work in Washington. It was best to eliminate him as a future threat to your plans with the general. Our agent, Alex, formerly, Alexis, attached a heat patch to the oxygen tank in the back of the ambassador's wheelchair. The patch worked as expected, causing a gradual increase in temperature until the oxygen tank exploded later that evening, killing the ambassador and his caregiver. Does that answer your question, Mr. Ambassador?"

"*Alex*, Andrei? He is being used as an assassin?"

"When necessary, yes. He is the perfect example of just how effective an agent can be in advancing our plans. Alex's extraordinary talent gets him close to targets regular agents could never manage."

"Remember, Andrei, our plans call for Abby and Alex to work together. It makes no sense to put Alex at risk of danger or discovery. Abby leaves next week for Oxford, where she will meet up with Alex."

"What if Alex doesn't take the bait?"

"Not an option. Abby won't let that happen."

Tilton could not believe what he was experiencing. He was furious Aldrich's termination was done without consulting him, but he realized the threat had been real. After all, collateral damage was to be expected as their plan progressed.

He sat quietly, stunned by the technological advancement he'd just experienced. He looked at Petrov, who was smiling.

"Are you satisfied, John?"

Tilton's anger had subsided. After all, a critic had been silenced, and there was nothing to connect Tilton to his death. *I did send a lovely floral wreath in time for the good ambassador's funeral.*

Now, he had so many questions about how it was possible for Petrov to accomplish so many technological firsts. The small phone was one thing—and amazing. But this? Totally unbelievable.

"I don't know what to say, Andrei. I am stunned by everything I've just seen."

"Perhaps you understand now why I think it's time to move forward with our plans. Given how fast our technology has advanced, it is best we do this sooner than later."

"I agree."

"There is so much more we are working on, John. Fusion energy, for example, is the holy grail. It could provide up to four million times the energy produced from burning coal or gas! We are making substantial progress with that research. We could control the power grids of much of the world. I'm not sure you realize just how many members of both your political parties would be open to the kind of authoritarian type of government you and I are promoting. They couldn't possibly deny the many advantages our plan offers."

"What do you mean?"

"I asked Boris to do an extensive analysis of each member of the US Congress. He researched their history of voting on all issues ranging from energy to immigration, and just about everything in-between. The results showed that over 30 percent of the House of Representatives and 20 percent of the Senate have views and voting records that could make them supporters of your political views."

"I'm afraid they see me as a diplomat, not a politician."

"We can change that, John."

"How?"

"What if they learned that you, using your diplomatic skills, convinced Russia to share its technology on cell phones?"

"You're prepared to share that technology?"

"Not just me, John, but the Politburo, too."

"Why the Politburo?"

"They see it as a win in Cold War politics. It sends a message that Russia is advancing as a world power and should be on a par with the US and other countries, as well."

"I do see the rationale in that thinking."

"Right. They also think it will send a message that a partnership on any issue between Russia and the US could reduce Cold World tensions. And this might be the time where our plan could benefit from that as well."

"How?"

"First, we must increase your position of power in the US. This will be the first step. Once you and I are in control, the Cold War will be in the past. We can start by releasing breaking news to the news services both in Russia and the US. We will position it as Russia wanting to share its advanced technology on cell phones with the world. You, John, will receive credit for convincing us to allow the US to connect to our satellite system. Politicians, corporations, and all US citizens are going to love you, John. I think your political star will rise with this one strategic move."

Tilton considered everything that had happened that day. *The Cold War has certainly entered a new phase now.* His own thinking though was somewhat different than Petrov as to how the Cold War would affect their plans. The American public's fear of nuclear war played to his own plans of power—at least for now. He smiled. *Things just got a lot more interesting.*

17

Petrov relaxed following John Tilton's departure. As expected, Boris impressed Tilton, and everything was now as it should be. He returned to Boris for more playtime.

"Boris."

"Yes, General."

"Your analysis for Ambassador John Tilton on Alexis' first assignment to assassinate John Aldrich left out some important information about a glitch that you mentioned to me earlier. Thank you for not sharing that in your report to the ambassador."

"Of course, General. My programming prevents me from disclosing to outside persons any issues that could be perceived as an embarrassment to you or the program. Only you receive all the information, General. Those minor glitches in communication had no effect on the outcome."

"I understand that, but it's important for me to understand exactly what the glitches are, and how we resolve them. What were they?"

"General, I'm sensing a high level of stress in your voice."

"Yes, because I'm not getting the answers I need from you, Boris. Answer the question! What are the minor glitches?"

Petrov paced the room waiting for Boris' response.

"I'm sorry about the misunderstanding, General. Let me see if I can explain it. Alexis became confused when we first connected to his implant. This is a glitch we were not anticipating, but he *did* leave the Institute before the final probes and implants were calibrated. Therefore, the clarity of his instructions became compromised."

"How do we correct this problem?"

"Resolving this problem would require Alexis to return to the Institute for adjustments to the implants."

Petrov returned to his desk and buried his head in his hands. *That will not happen.* His frustration increased with every response that he received from Boris. He struggled to stay calm as he asked Boris, "What are the chances of repeat glitches?"

"Statistics show an error rate of 15-25 percent for future commands. However, my programming capacity has identified a solution, General."

Finally, a solution! "Yes, Boris. What is it?"

"You can minimize the chance of any miscommunication by simplifying the instructions. The more complicated the instructions, the greater the chance of error."

The general considered the facts Boris outlined. Alex's first assignment tested the accuracy and effectiveness of his implants. Aldrich had become a political detriment to Petrov, as well as Tilton. He had included the general's name in documents sent to the UN Security Council, documenting human rights violations and corruption in the Russian hierarchy. Aldrich's accusations could have muddled the talks with Washington, so the general thought it best to move forward with the mission.

The general would make crystal clear all future instructions sent to Alexis. There could be no room for error. The initial test was successful, but the next assignment for Alexis would be the first in a series of assignments that would have a dramatic and negative effect on US and Russian relations. The resulting increase in tensions between the US and Russia would be of significant help, at least for now, in advancing Petrov and Tilton's combined rise to even greater power.

Development

18

"I don't think the acoustics are going to work, Bob."

"I know, Alex. For your first recording on the EMI label, I was hoping we could weave in your studying at Oxford with a recording of the Beethoven sonatas in the historic setting of Sheldonian Theatre. It was a long shot, but after learning that Christopher Wren designed the building, I had to give it the old college try."

Bob Caldwell, an executive at EMI Records, was managing Alex's first recording on the EMI label. It blew Alex away when he found out that Elvis Presley also recorded for EMI. He had joked with Bob about that.

"Do you expect my Beethoven Sonatas will outsell Presley's next album?"

"I expect nothing less from you, Alex. I'll call you as soon as I find times at Wigmore Hall in London. The acoustics there are excellent, and now that you're a Steinway artist, we can always have Steinway get the right piano for you."

Alex loved exploring the museums, galleries, and exhibitions that were scattered across the campus. Oxford was less of a campus and more of an integration of university buildings scattered around the city of Oxford.

He felt safe and free at Oxford. While he confided in Nadia and Sol about his anxieties with Petrov, he omitted mentioning the recent onset of nightmares and bizarre dreams he was having before leaving for Oxford. Alex hoped that putting more space between him and Petrov might resolve his nighttime terrors.

He looked forward to the evening lecture that the mathematics club was sponsoring on the Greek mathematician Pythagoras, who discovered that a string half the size, when plucked, would produce a sound one octave higher in pitch. It all made sense to Alex now as he reflected on the rhythm, frequencies, and repeated patterns in music, all based on math. He was curious if the lecturer would delve into the musical connections.

After saying his goodbyes to Bob, Alex stood on the steps of Sheldonian Theatre, contemplating whether to return to the practice room or take a long walk.

"Hi, stranger."

Alex turned to face a very attractive girl with brown eyes and beautiful rich mahogany hair with just a touch of honey. She was slight and lovely and looked like she floated on air.

"Abby? Is that really you?"

"Yes, Alexis, or is it *Alex* now? I recognized your name on the student manifest and had to track you down. Here you are, right where you should be, in front of a concert hall. You're quite the celeb."

They hugged, and still surprised at seeing Abby again, he just stood there for a few seconds, holding her hands and taking in the sight of her. When Abby laughed at their unlikely reunion, her joy brought a smile to his face, and he laughed too.

"What are you doing here, Abby?"

"I'm studying art. Oxford has one of the best programs in the world and the proximity to Paris and the museums made it all too irresistible. I had to do some fast talking with my dad, but he finally agreed."

Alex led them to the bench in front of the statue of Christopher Wren. The trickle of water from the fountain provided a restful setting to catch up with Abby.

"Your dad? I thought—"

"I was an orphan?"

"Yes."

"I was. But John Tilton, the US Ambassador to Russia, adopted me after you left—or rather, after you escaped. Thanks for leaving me there to suffer alone. No letters, not even a postcard. I thought we had a pinky promise Alexis, I mean, Alex."

"Not a lot of time for goodbyes, Abby. I was told I was going for an ice cream cone. They didn't tell me it was waiting for me at an ice cream parlor in New York City."

"I know. I don't mean to make light of it. When I realized you'd ended up in America, I didn't know whether to be happy or sad. Both, I suppose. Happy for you and sad for me. But I'm happy to see you now."

He looked at her beaming face and felt both calm and excitement.

"There's been so many times I remembered the special time we spent together at the Institute, Abby. That's one of the few things I've missed."

"Me too, Alex."

"Tell me more about your adoption, and your dad."

Abby's demeanor changed as she told Alex about her life at the Institute after he left. She got depressed and lost interest in painting. Petrov threatened her with serious consequences if she didn't pull herself together and meet his demands for perfection.

"I got scared, Alex. So, when General Petrov told me about someone who wanted to adopt me, it gave me an exit strategy that I accepted, just like you did."

Abby told Alex that the ambassador and his wife, Jean, were wonderful parents.

"Dad was absent a lot, but Jean was the best mother that I could have wished for. Unfortunately, we lost her to cancer."

"Oh, Abby. I'm so sorry."

"Jean encouraged me to continue painting, and that's one reason I ended up at Oxford. Dad was helpful in making that happen, too. He can be persuasive, and his contacts are impressive, including some right here at Oxford. Dad travels frequently to Europe, so we get to see each other often."

Alex remembered meeting the ambassador, thinking him handsome, rich, and powerful. Abby confirmed he was all those things and more.

"I'm so glad to see you, Alex. I shared all my secrets with you. Remember? We used to make fun of Petrov."

"Sure, I remember. What's not so secret is that General Petrov is now the Russian Ambassador to the United Nations."

"I know. Can you imagine Petrov as a diplomat?" Abby rolled her brown eyes.

"No, but apparently, he appreciates culture. He attended my concert in New York several years ago."

"You mean the one with the New York Philharmonic?"

"Yes. How did you know about it?"

"I read about your concert in an article in the *Washington Post* and I told Mom and Dad I wanted to go. Jean and I were planning on attending together. Dad was going to be out of the country."

"What happened?"

"That's when Jean had a relapse, and the cancer came back with a vengeance. It all happened quite fast."

"I'm sorry. That must have been a shock."

"Yes. But tell me more about Petrov. Did you talk with him after the concert?"

"God, no. Abby, that monster killed my parents. It's a good thing I found out he was in the audience after my performance, because if it had been beforehand, I would have gone nuts."

"I'm so sorry, Alex. How difficult that must have been for you. I wanted to reach out to you on so many occasions after finding out you lived in New York."

"Well, why didn't you, Abby?"

"We tried, Alex. Dad reached out to your guardians, who told Dad it would be best to wait. I guess they thought that bringing up your past from Russia was something that would not be in your best interest at that time.

"Every time I wrote a letter, it ended up in the wastebasket. Both Jean and Dad thought I should give you some time to get used to life in the US. Then, right when we planned to attend your concert in New York, Jean got sick. Before I knew it, so much time had passed and…."

"It's okay, Abby. I understand."

"Besides, if I'd known you'd grow up to be so talented and handsome, I might have been a stowaway myself! I recall a concert you gave to the students and teachers. They idolized you just like a Hollywood superstar. Remember?"

"I think I would have remembered the idolizing part."

"I thought you would end up studying at Juilliard."

"Yeah, so did Sol and Nadia."

"What changed your mind?"

"Oxford offered a dual degree program between the university and the Royal Academy of Music in London. The program includes a course of study with the concert pianist Christopher Hazen, who is a friend of Nadia's. He's renowned in his field, and I couldn't pass it up."

"That all sounds like good reasons to select Oxford."

"There was also a more personal reason, Abby. It was time for me to leave the nest. I've been under the protective wing of Nadia and Sol for years. As much as I love them both, it was time to declare my independence."

Alex found Abby easy to talk to. She was smart, a good listener, and lovely to look at. Alex found Abby attractive at the Institute, but now she was a grown woman, and his attraction to her was real. Most important, she knew enough of his background that he didn't have to explain himself all the time. Alex trusted her and shared more of his story.

He told her about a room at the Institute they used to take him to in a separate building where they connected him to machines that measured his brain responses. Alex remembered Petrov telling him the exercises they put him through would increase the capacity of his memory.

"It didn't hurt, so most of the time I'd just fall asleep while they ran their tests. Sometimes they would hypnotize me to help me relax. I've tried to recall more memories like that, but they just seem to vaporize. What I remember is blurred by other things that were happening at the Institute. I keep trying to sort everything out. Sometimes, I pick up pieces from a dream I've had. It's like my brain cells are attempting to reconnect, to remember, but I keep running into walls."

"I thought we shared all our secrets, Alex. Why didn't you tell me any of this at the time?" Abby put her hand on Alex's arm in a gesture he found reassuring.

"I was forbidden to discuss it with anyone, and I was afraid Petrov might find out. I should have told you, though. I know you would have kept my secret. Forgive me?"

"Of course I forgive you. I'm almost tempted to ask if you can forgive *me* for not being a better friend and reaching out to you earlier. Maybe your studies here at Oxford will help you sort out things. Anyway, we're here now, and I hope we get to see each other more often."

"I'd like that, Abby."

This was the first conversation Alex had about the Institute with anyone except Nadia and Sol since he left. It felt like he was lifting a burden off his shoulders by meeting up with his best childhood friend. Now that they were adults, he couldn't wait to spend more time with Abby. Thinking back, she was the only thing about the Institute that gave him joy.

Abby came to just under his shoulders. He wanted to hug her again, only this time for a longer time, as they parted to attend their next classes, but he held back. For all his worldly experience, he was unsure of what to do, except he knew he wanted to make the moment last.

"Talk to you soon, Alex." She reached up and gave him a peck on the cheek as she headed back to her dorm.

He replayed the conversation all the way to his next class.

19

The favorite time of the week for Alex was Saturday morning. He would meet Abby at their favorite coffeehouse in the center of town and chat about their studies and life. Alex was always practicing or studying, and Abby had a firm commitment to her art. The time they spent together was special.

"You hardly ever talk about your dad, Ambassador Tilton, Abby. I know you were close to your mom, but do you talk with your dad occasionally?"

"Oh, sure. Dad was away so much of the time, leaving mom and me on our own. He was, and still is, a workaholic, Alex. I know he cares about me, but he doesn't have a lot of free time to show it."

"Does he still make frequent trips to Russia?"

"Not as many now, I think. But that's still his job. He's so ambitious, I know he has bigger plans. Just not sure what they are. But I'm sure he has it all figured out."

"Does he still see General Petrov when he's there?"

"I don't know." Abby shifted in her seat and grabbed her handbag. "It's getting a little stuffy in here. Let's go outside."

It wasn't the first time Abby had shut him out after bringing up her father. He wondered what the primary motivation could be for Tilton to adopt Abby. Adopting a child born in the US would have eliminated all the red tape of international adoption.

Leaving the coffee house, Abby grabbed Alex's hand.

"Follow me, maestro. I know where we can spend our morning."

"Are we going to another museum?"

"Stop the whining. It's only a five-minute walk."

They walked down Cornmarket Street to Magdalen Street and turned left on Beaumont, walking the few steps until they were standing in front of a landmark museum with a bronze plaque: Ashmolean Museum, founded in 1683.

"The Ashmolean Museum, Abby?"

"You know, it's one of my favorites. The variety of paintings and sculpture transcends every period of art since antiquity. Pissarro's works are highlighted today. You know he's the father of Impressionism, right?"

"I thought Debussy was."

"Funny! Art, Alex, not music."

Alex loved giving Abby a hard time. He also loved watching her as she explored her favorite art with the same excitement as a kid in a candy store.

"Someday, I would like to compose a piece of music inspired by one of your paintings."

"I thought you said some guy in Russia already did that."

"Yes. But this would be special, because you're special."

She took her eyes off the Pissarro long enough to turn around and embrace Alex.

"Thank you for saying that. I love you, Alex."

"Not as much as I love you, Abby. I think I like your landscape paintings better than Pissarro's."

"You're impossible."

"I know."

Abby's interest in painting landscapes first surfaced during her time at the Institute. There wasn't a great deal of landscape to use as a model around the Institute, so she used her imagination to paint the colors, textures, and varieties of flowers and trees that inspired her. That, and her friendship with Alex, were the only things she missed about her time there.

Abby and Alex spent more and more time together exploring their mutual interests. Music and art were their passions, which brought them to as many concerts and gallery showings as their study schedule allowed. But no matter what other commitments they had, they reserved a part of each day for one another.

One Sunday, after a full day of gallery hopping, Alex and Abby stopped in a café to rest. It was a quintessential, ivy-covered English cottage, with a stone fireplace and chintz-covered sofas that invited one to sink into the cushions while sipping an apéritif. Alex and Abby shared the seat and tilted into one another.

"You have beautiful hands, Alex." She reached over and took one in her own hand. She stroked his fingers, one at a time, in a sensuous but protective caress. Alex held his breath. For all his worldliness, he was not accustomed to being intimate with a woman, and her touch sent shivers down his arm.

"My hands are my life, Abby. If they're beautiful, as you say, it's because I want them to play beautifully. When we were children together and you came to my practice room, I felt that same calling because I knew you were there. I was too young to realize it, but you inspired me, Abby."

Abby raised Alex's hand to her lips and gently kissed his fingers. She smoothed his palm over her face, closing her eyes to savor the sensation. He regarded her with a newfound awareness that finally had a name.

Overcome with emotion at how much they'd always meant to each other, Alex leaned over and placed a tender kiss on Abby's lips. "I've never felt this way before, but now I know what people mean when they say, 'you'll know when you're in love.' Abby, I know it now. I love you with all my heart."

In the warmth of his bed, there were no inhibitions, no secrets to interfere with their mutual discovery. Abby's naked body was a newfound treasure in Alex's eyes. She was so perfect, so smooth, and every curve of her aroused him. Exploring her willing body was a revelation that awakened him. To everyone else, Alex was a child prodigy, but in Abby's arms, he was a man.

In their afterglow, she perched on her elbow and gazed at Alex's tranquil face. "You make me very happy, darling. I feel like it's a miracle that we found each other again."

"I'm going to London this Friday for my lesson with Professor Hazen. I changed it from Wednesday so I could spend the weekend in London. Come with me, and we can spend some romantic time together."

"I have finals coming up, Alex. I'm not as brilliant as you, and I need to study."

Alex persisted. "You can bring your art books and whatever

else you need. I'll leave you alone unless we're sharing some special moments."

"That would leave me no time to work at all," she laughed.

In a more serious tone, Alex added, "Come on, Abby, it'll be fun, and we could both use the break. I promise to have you back early on Sunday. I'll book you a massage at the Four Seasons so you can relax while I play some Brahms for Professor Hazen." Alex watched as Abby seemed to consider his plea.

Abby responded with a touch of humor, "Okay, Alex. Book me a ninety-minute massage, followed by a sixty-minute facial while I'm there."

"Deal! Who taught you how to drive such a hard bargain?"

"My dad."

20

Christopher Hazen lived in a large cottage with an attached studio for his two Steinway concert grand pianos. While no longer a performer, he had a good ear and could recognize any notes out of place, but today Hazen talked to Alex about something he felt was missing in his playing.

"Over the past couple of years, you have repeatedly impressed me with your intellect and talent, Alex. You're a gifted professional, and I'm sure you will go very far in your performing career. You have technique to burn and you're a natural musician with a sharp ear. The interpretive insight that you share with your audience on all styles is impressive. Nadia's tutelage has brought out remarkable qualities of tone and style in your playing."

"There's a 'but' isn't there?"

"Yes, there is, Alex. You're lacking a consistent communication of those exact interpretive concepts that form the basis of every piece you play. Many pianists copy other artist's style and interpretations, but that never works. Others try to dazzle with technique, but that only serves to detract from communicating their ideas. You zone out from time to time. It's in those few fleeting moments that the listener is aware you have left the stage to go somewhere else. Sure, your fingers continue to do all the heavy lifting, but that doesn't carry the day. I'm guessing this is not the first time you've been told this. I'm betting that Nadia brought it up, as well. Am I right?"

Alex recalled a similar discussion with Nadia. She suspected his lack of focus was because of the trauma of his parents' deaths and his preoccupation with General Petrov. Alex understood his problem had its roots in what happened at the Institute—events he still did not fully understand or even remember. Even Nadia had not been told everything: his waking up in cold sweats, occasional distractions, headaches that would come and go.

"Yes. Nadia and I both felt it would work its way out as I performed more."

"You're the only one who can fix this, Alex. Deep down, there's a single issue that kidnaps you and pulls you mentally away as you perform. Next time it happens, confront it head on. Doing that may solve the problem for you."

Alex thought to himself, if only it was that simple.

The rest of the lesson focused on Alex's upcoming all-Brahms recital at the Royal Academy of Music. He intended to head back to the hotel for a late dinner with Abby, but he became disoriented after leaving Hazen's studio.

Alex stood on the corner for a few minutes, confused, and then flagged a taxi after remembering where he needed to go. As he got into the taxi, he continued to experience some lightheadedness and other strange sensations—sensations that seemed vaguely familiar.

"Please take me to Stanmore Station."

Once at the station, he exited the taxi and descended the steps to the train platform. He was now clear about where he was going and what he intended to do.

The platform was dark, with only a few overhead lights casting shadows on the growing crowd waiting for a train. He knew he needed to wait for someone to arrive and continued to scan the crowd until he noticed a gentleman in a black coat who was just descending the stairs to the platform. The man made his way to the edge of the platform, looked down the track to see if lights were visible from an approaching train, then he took his glasses off and carefully cleaned them with his handkerchief.

Alex knew he was the right person. Just as he heard the approaching train, Alex closed in. The man looked up at Alex just as he put his glasses back on. There was little time to react before Alex pushed him in front of the lead car. Alex's brain recorded the look of shock on the man's face as he fell to his death. He quickly mixed back in with the growing crowd as he heard someone scream, *Oh my God! Someone fell in front of the train!*

Alex retraced his steps and returned to the street. He hailed another taxi and arrived at the Four Seasons, just in time for a late rendezvous with Abby.

"How did your lesson go?"

"It was a tough session. I'm beat."

"You look exhausted, Alex. Are you okay?"

"I think so. Just feeling mentally and physically exhausted. I'm sure a good night's sleep will restore me to the man you love."

"Funny, Alex," she said, pulling him up from the chair. "Let's get you to bed and snuggle up together. We have a big day tomorrow."

To be in love with someone who was so understanding and didn't make demands was a dream to Alex. They cuddled up in their favorite spoon position and fell fast asleep, while Alex's brain took a break from the day's strenuous activities.

Saturday was a museum day in deference to Abby. She took her drawings and notebook and spent the day researching Renaissance art. That evening, they had dinner at a local pub, followed by a Neil Simon play at the Lyceum. Then, it was back to the hotel for a much-needed rest before returning to Oxford on Sunday in time for Abby to study for her finals.

The next morning, Abby asked Alex. "Could you please turn on the TV? See if we can catch the weather for tomorrow."

Abby's ears perked up when she heard the news that the UK's Undersecretary for Intelligence, Robert Graham, was found dead after falling in front of a train at Stanmore Station.

"Oh my God. I know him, Alex."

"Who, honey?"

"Robert Graham, the man who just died. I really didn't *know* him, but I remember he was critical of Dad, and it created some bad press."

"That can happen in politics. How did your dad respond?"

"Dad can be a devil. He's superb at discrediting anyone who poses a threat to him. But he can also be an angel, and I know he tried to work it out with Graham in a civilized manner, like two gentlemen, but Graham wasn't cooperating."

Alex's instincts always served him well, and this new information about Abby's father sent up a red flag. After all, what did he know about Abby's father outside of being a rich career politician, well-dressed, and knowing Petrov? *Knowing Petrov!*

When Alex went downstairs to settle the bill, he picked up the local newspaper, where the lead story provided more details about Robert Graham.

The story detailed Graham's varied career and his family. Alex jumped ahead to the section about Graham's criticism of the US government's weak response to Russia's aggression in Europe and its record of human rights violations. The article mentioned Graham's accusations that US Ambassador Tilton and others were soft on the Russian leaders, including General Andrei Petrov, former head of the KGB, now the newly appointed Russian Ambassador to the United Nations. Graham's unwillingness to back away from his original accusations caused him some major career setbacks. He had just signed a sizeable book deal to further state his political views and reveal new information.

Graham's actions clearly connected Ambassador Tilton to Petrov. Tilton's frequent visits to Russia gave him unlimited access to Petrov. *It could mean something, or it could mean nothing. Maybe this guy, Robert Graham, knew more than he told. One thing was for sure: he wouldn't tell anyone anything now.*

Alex needed some time to digest these troubling thoughts, and he didn't want to overreact. He had fallen in love with Abby and wanted to marry her, but would he have to accept her father, as well?

On the train returning to Oxford, Alex convinced himself that there was nothing more to be concerned about. Abby didn't even know the Graham guy, and by her own admission, her father wasn't around that much. Besides, there would be no way she would know anything more than she already disclosed. He put his arm around her and kissed her gently on the cheek.

His attention turned to how he would spend the rest of his time at Oxford. Both Abby and he would finish their three-year degree programs in another year. That gave him more than enough time to write his dissertation and prepare for the final exams. He felt positive about everything going on his life. Abby made everything so much better.

21

The phone call from Sol came late in the evening, Oxford time. Sol's somber voice relayed the devastating news. "Nadia was killed last night in a tragic accident."

Alex gasped and slumped into a chair, needing time to come to grips with what Sol had just said. *My Nadia?* She couldn't possibly have left him like this. She was his adopted mother. There was too much left to talk about, too much of life to share.

Tears flowed down his face. But again, it was his training at the Institute that brought him back to the reality of the moment. He needed confirmation.

"Sol, I don't understand. I talked to her yesterday. She sounded fine."

"She *was* fine yesterday, Alex. It seems unreal."

"What happened?"

"Brace yourself, son. This is going to be very difficult for you to hear."

"I need to know, Sol!"

Alex moved to the chair next to the bed and grabbed a tissue box.

"She had called her car service to take her to Juilliard on Claremont Avenue for her weekly master class. She got into the elevator, and something went wrong. Without warning, it plunged sixteen stories to the basement level. Our condo security reached her within minutes, but the sheer impact had already taken its toll."

"Sol, how is that even possible? How does an elevator just fail?"

"The safety system didn't activate. The police and elevator service company don't know why. We'll have more definitive information once the police complete their investigation, and the elevator company checks out the mechanics. The investigation is just beginning, and it won't end until I get satisfactory answers."

"I'll catch the red-eye flight to New York. I can be there by early morning."

"Don't you have your oral defense of your thesis this week?"

"Yes, but I can reschedule that."

"No, Alex."

"Sol, I—"

"Please listen to me, Alex. Nadia wouldn't want you to do that. Finish your work there. All her estate documents are in perfect order, including specific instructions for her burial. She has a plot at Mt. Sinai, and I will honor her request to bury her within twenty-four hours of death, as is the Jewish tradition. As executor of her estate, I can take care of everything."

"I can help, Sol. It's unfair to leave this all to you. I loved her so much! Why can't I be there with you now?"

Alex wanted Sol to know the depth of his grief. "I've been abandoned for the second time in my life, and I feel so helpless, Sol."

"Alex, let me tell you how you can help me."

Alex was quick to respond. "How, Sol? I'll do whatever you ask."

"You, Leonard Rubenstein, and I can plan a memorial concert that would be a very fitting tribute to honor Nadia's memory. What do you think?"

Alex's response was immediate. "Sol, I love that idea. Why not do it at Carnegie Hall? Of course, I will want to perform."

"Yes, I can't imagine honoring Nadia's memory without your music front and center. But first, you must complete your exam. Then come home and help me put together the memorial concert to honor Nadia, and the remarkable legacy she left through you and all her students."

"I'll leave for New York after my thesis defense. My defense is on Friday morning. I will book the late afternoon flight to New York on BOAC. It's the one I usually take."

Alex said goodbye to Sol, covered his face, and wept until his reservoir of tears was dry. Then he recalled his first meeting with Nadia at the Institute when he auditioned for her. He was terrified to be playing for the great Nadia Rosenberg. Her recordings were in the bookcase next to his piano at home. Many of her students went on to international careers. Petrov made it clear to him it was important for her to be impressed with his playing, so she would accept him as a student. Petrov knew Nadia's teaching would guarantee Alex's rise to the top ranks of performing pianists. It was just one more reason to resent Petrov. *He not only used me to advance his selfish interests, but dear Nadia as well.*

Alex's anger subsided as he reflected back on his personal remembrances. In the first five minutes of their meeting, he had felt the warmth of her personality embrace him and it was almost like he was playing for his mama. The first lesson that turned out not to be a lesson at all, but a tour of her studio. He remembered Nadia sharing a story that accompanied each of the many rewards and tributes from world-class musicians. And yet, she was humble, gracious, and someone who could reach deep into his soul. There was no one person who could take her place. Yes, there was Sol, and even Leonard Rubinstein, whose trusted voices he would always have and listen to, but there was no one in his life who had done more to mold him into the person and artist he had become than Nadia. She was irreplaceable, and he would miss her every day for the rest of his life. He wiped the tears and walked over to the piano, sat down, bowed his head, and continued to reflect on his life with Nadia.

22

During his thesis defense, Alex remained focused on the task at hand. Many members of the defense committee knew Nadia Rosenberg and understood how tragic this loss was for Alex. More than ever, he appreciated how Nadia had trained him to perform under the most adverse circumstances. This experience had put her training techniques to the test, and it was one more way Alex honored her memory.

There was little Alex could do to prepare for his oral dissertation defense and couldn't imagine any question he couldn't answer. He had put so much thought into the subject of Adolph Von Henselt, with a focus on his Op 2 and Op 5 etudes. He was now considered one of the foremost authorities on Henselt's music.

Examinations were being conducted at Holywell Music Hall at Wadham College, one of the many colleges at Oxford. Holywell was the first music hall built in Europe, in 1748. Over the years, it became a multi-purpose music building with large rooms to accommodate examinations like Alex's oral defense.

Alex knew most of the committee members, but had heard rumors that the chair of the committee, Dr. Harold Wright, a musicologist, had voiced concerns about Oxford creating a special program to accommodate a *gifted musician*. His concerns were considered and dismissed after university executives and board members weighed in on the matter.

Dr. Wright wasted no time in clarifying that they would give no special treatment to Alex because of Nadia's sudden death, or any other reason. As chair, it was he who spoke first, and by tradition would ask the first question.

"Please take your seat at the end of the table, Mr. Courtland."

Alex couldn't help but think, *why do I think this will not be a typical dissertation defense? I'm feeling like I'm in a courtroom.*

"Please tell the committee, Mr. Courtland, how you justify your conclusions from your exhaustive analytical dissection of Henselt's etudes, suggesting his etudes are as good or better than those of Chopin. Let me add, while I understand any dissertation dealing with the works of an unknown composer, like Henselt, would need some sort of analytical approach, it still would need to meet the academic standard that we expect from our students. Tell me how your dissertation meets that test, Mr. Courtland."

Alex took a moment to look around the table, making eye contact with each of the fifteen committee members. Then he lowered his head to consider his response before looking up at Dr. Wright.

"I appreciate your questions, Dr. Wright."

Dr. Wright nodded, acknowledging the respect shown by the candidate.

"Let me respond to your concerns in two ways. First, your comments about the analytical part of the dissertation suggest it lacked intellectual focus. Mine was not a typical analytical approach. I traveled to Berlin and spent three days evaluating the manuscripts of the Henselt Op 2 and Op. 5 etudes. I noticed handwritten notes by Henselt on the last page of each manuscript. These were notes penned by Henselt detailing his meeting with Chopin in Karlsbad, Germany, in 1836. I cross-referenced that information with what I already knew about Chopin's travels to Karlsbad, including the written and verbal communication that preceded their meeting. There was a wealth of information in those exchanges, clearly documented in my summary. I should note that Oxford University Press, of which you are a board member, Dr. Wright, has requested my permission to publish those findings in their next issue of their quarterly publication. Given the high academic and intellectual standards held by Oxford University Press, I believe that addresses the question you raise."

"And my second concern?"

Alex took a moment before continuing.

"I must admit I am baffled by your second comment suggesting that my dissertation promotes the Henselt etudes at the expense of Mr. Chopin. I clearly stated in my dissertation that we have become very familiar with all the Chopin etudes, but have rarely heard any of the Henselt etudes, except perhaps the *No. 6 in F Sharp Major, 'Si oiseau j'etais'*. Because of the frequent exposure to all the Chopin etudes played by most pianists today, they are familiar to the public. The *unknown* Henselt etudes continue to remain hidden from the public. My conclusion is quite the opposite of what you suggest, Dr. Wright. Because we are aware of all the Chopin etudes, but not the Henselt etudes, how is it possible to favor one over the other? With all due respect, Dr. Wright, that's all I state in my dissertation."

Alex left the room satisfied with his performance. *Nadia, I think you would have been proud of me today. You taught me well!*

For the next several weeks, Alex worked with Sol and Leonard Rubenstein to put together the ultimate memorial service at Carnegie Hall. A *Who's Who* of the musical world attended, including former students, conductors, and educators who came from around the world to pay their respects. Sol spoke first, recalling his long friendship with Nadia and how their lives changed when they became a family. He spoke of Alex's parents. and how their tragic deaths set the stage for Alex to live in a free society—how they made the ultimate sacrifice so that Alex could be free.

Sol introduced Leonard Rubinstein, who told the crowd of his close friendship with Nadia that began after sharing judging responsibilities at the Tchaikovsky International Piano Competition in Moscow. He recounted his first meeting with Alex, and how he knew Alex would reach international stardom, and that their first meeting led to a lifelong friendship. Then he introduced Alex.

It was an emotional time for Alex as he weighed all he could do to honor his teacher, his adopted mother, his life coach. He thanked Leonard for being a dedicated friend to her and for being such an important inspiration to him. He spoke about the sacrifices Sol and Nadia made in adopting him after his own parents' deaths.

"Not too many people are fortunate enough to have two sets of loving parents. My mother and father, and Nadia and Sol, taught me so much about love and patience. They sacrificed so much so I could be here today to play for you. I am so proud to be the son of all four of my parents."

Then Alex performed a short recital of the compositions he first studied with Nadia in Russia, ending with the Chopin *Nocturne Op 27 No 2 in D Flat Major.* He remembered Nadia's every comment about tonal warmth, the use of rubato, the elegance of intricate passages, and taking care not to rush the lento sostenuto tempo. A tear fell on one of the white keys as Alex played the last chord. There was complete quiet in the audience for many seconds and then a voice shouting, *we love you, Alex,* followed by thunderous applause. It was all very touching, and a tribute to the magnitude of his special relationship with Nadia.

A reception followed at the Four Seasons. Sol made sure it remained a celebratory event honoring a great lady. Abby was waiting near the entrance to help Alex navigate all the well-wishers who wanted to express their condolences. The first person she steered him to was her adopted father, Ambassador John Tilton.

"I'm so honored to be here with you and Abby, Alex, and to pay my respects. When we met in Moscow, I recognized you as a young man who was going places. I'm pleased to see that I was right."

"Thank you for those kind words. Yes, I remember our meeting. You were wearing a blue suit with a white handkerchief with the initials JT in your breast pocket, and a red tie."

"Now, that's an impressive memory. No wonder you don't need music when you perform. I have that same handkerchief in my pocket today. The tie and suit are different."

"Yes, I know," Alex said with tongue in cheek. "You may be aware, Mr. Ambassador, that students at the Institute were tested on memory recall. Abby, you remember those drills, right?"

"I painfully remember them! No one could beat you, Alex. Many of us suspected Petrov was feeding you all the answers in advance, anyway."

"General Petrov fed me nothing, not even good food. But those training sessions improved my memory."

Ambassador Tilton was quick to admit, "I didn't know about that program, Alex, but it sounds like it would've been a fine addition to the course of studies at the Institute."

"Yes, General Petrov was a stickler for those kinds of details."

Pointing to Alex, the Ambassador smiled. "And look how it paid off!"

Abby gave the two of them time to get acquainted. "I'm leaving you two alone to talk while I circulate."

With Abby gone, Alex probed a little. "Do you meet often with General Petrov?" Alex surprised himself by asking the question, but thought it an appropriate first step in exploring how comfortable the ambassador was in discussing his relationship with Petrov. Besides, they were talking about Petrov and the Institute, and it seemed like a reasonable transition.

"That was a long time ago, and my memory isn't as good as yours, Alex. My responsibilities as the Ambassador to Russia included meeting with individuals responsible for determining Russia's future direction, and on how they felt that Russian policies and politics might change in the future—especially in any way that could affect relationships with the United States. Since World War II, we've been in the throes of a Cold War with Russia. It was tough navigating around the politics then, and even more difficult now."

Alex wasn't ready to let that be the last word, so he risked pushing on. "General Petrov is a powerful and determined man, and from what I understand, a man who would do anything to improve his position of power. Having an ally like General Petrov would no doubt have been helpful to anyone navigating those changing waters."

Alex had hit a nerve, as he noticed the ambassador tightening up, but Tilton didn't hesitate before he responded.

"The general influenced a new generation of young leaders with remarkable talents. It was in our best interests to monitor his progress. Petrov had powerful connections at the Kremlin, and my staying in touch with him allowed us to monitor other activities in Russia. Many of his colleagues at the Politburo were a step or two above his service level, and my having access to their points of view proved very helpful to me. You charm audiences with your performances, Alex. I found it necessary to do the same thing. Some of these individuals played a splendid game of political chess. Sometimes, they would just play stupid, and for me, that was as good as their declaring a checkmate."

"Have you stayed in touch with the general?" Alex asked. He wondered if he had just crossed the line and expected an end to the discussion, just as it was getting interesting. His instincts proved correct.

"Here comes Abby, Alex. It's selfish of me to keep you from the rest of your guests. Again, please know how sorry I am for your loss. I didn't know Nadia well, but I know she helped raise one wonderful young man. My daughter loves you, son, and she wants to build a wonderful life with you." Then, with a smile and a hand on Alex's shoulder, he added, "That's something I welcome as well."

Alex felt the beginnings of affection, mixed with concerns about the man who would be his future father-in-law.

With a gracious nod, the ambassador moved on to talk with other guests.

It all sounded sincere, but the ambassador was a superb politician, and his talent for charm, wit, and mental chess was working for him. His ability to communicate with such conviction and apparent honesty was most likely a separate chapter in his training manual, but Alex knew he didn't need any formal training in social etiquette. He thought John Tilton was a born snake charmer. Abby had already provided Alex with information on how her father handled his disagreements with Robert Graham. That made it perfectly clear: you wouldn't want to make an enemy of him. Alex wondered if he had just taken the first steps in that direction.

Abby was smiling and radiant as she rejoined Alex. "I'm glad you connected with Dad. He isn't such a bad guy, Alex, and like you, he's very smart."

"Yes, that's obvious, Abby."

Sol walked over and gave them both a hug.

"I can't tell you how wonderful it is to have you both here with me! Nadia will be missed, but she will never be forgotten." He couldn't resist adding with a playful finger poke to Alex's chest, "Every time I hear Alex play, I also hear Nadia telling him he's over-pedaling or losing the melodic line."

With a wistful sigh, Abby said, "I never got to meet her, but Alex has told me so much about her, and his relationship with you, too, Sol. He loved Nadia, and he loves you. I feel blessed to be in both your lives."

But even in the glow of their affectionate connection, Alex was thinking, *Abby is her father's daughter, and Sol thinks Abby is perfect for me. It just so happens; I think she is too.* One thing was clear to Alex: his love for Abby consumed him, and nothing was going to dissuade him from his efforts to having her become part of his life.

Later that night, in the sweet embrace of their love, Alex proposed to Abby.

23

Alex and Abby married at John Tilton's estate on Long Island. Abby had told Alex that the ambassador received a sizeable inheritance from his father, who owned several weapons-production factories during the Vietnam War. The congressional chaplain conducted the wedding service, and guests at the reception included the President of the United States, Bill Bradford, and dignitaries from around the world. Famed musicians and artists represented the couples' circle of contemporaries. It was a magnificent affair, topped off when President Bradford invited Alex to perform a concert at the White House.

Tilton raised his glass and toasted the newlyweds. "It's my privilege as the father of the bride to toast the marriage of my daughter, Abby! My life changed when Jean and I adopted her.

"Many of you knew my late wife, Jean. She loved Abby and fought hard to extend her life so she could experience the continued joy that Abby brought to her. Abby returned that love many times over. My only regret is that Jean is not here today to witness this celebration."

He turned to Abby. "You bring joy to my life every day, Abby. I'm so proud of everything you've become."

As the guests applauded his remarks, Tilton added, "Lightning rarely strikes twice, but it has now. My new son-in-law is a wonderful young man whom my daughter loves with all her heart, and someone I am thrilled to welcome into the family. His strong character and values make me so proud today of being his father-in-law." Tilton raised his glass toward the newlyweds. "To Abby and Alex, God bless you both for a long and wonderful life!"

Alex found the ambassador's toast touching, and thought, *Was I wrong to suspect him of anything? Maybe I should just leave everything alone. There have been no nightmares, and the renewed focus I enjoy with my music makes me feel whole again. Abby supports me on every level. This is a happy time for me, and Abby is happy, too. Why rock the boat?*

Abby and Alex enjoyed the guests as a couple, and at times separately, as they renewed acquaintances and thanked everyone for attending.

Alex thanked his father-in-law for his gracious remarks.

"No one could have said what you expressed more eloquently than you did, sir."

"Thank you, Alex. I only have one request of you as you begin your new life with Abby."

"Anything, sir."

"Please stop calling me sir, Mr. Ambassador, or Mr. Tilton. You're family now, son, and it's time you called me by my given name."

"I understand, Mr. Ambassador."

Alex flashed a broad smile.

They both laughed.

Abby and Alex shared a common love for Asian food and art and decided their honeymoon destination should be to an exotic location where they could enjoy the surroundings. Angkor Wat in Siem Reap, Cambodia was their first choice. Their stay at the Grand Hotel d'Angkor provided the privacy and luxury they were seeking, and while Alex delivered on his promise to take a break from music, Abby made no commitments. Much as she tried, her attraction to the monuments and stunning jungle settings surrounding Angkor Wat was almost seductive, and she couldn't resist sketching the various monuments. Alex understood and would either accompany her as she trekked through the ruins of Angkor Wat, or just lounge by the pool with either a glass of sweet iced tea, or a cocktail made with Sombai, the local rice wine.

Trying the local restaurants in Siem Reap was an adventure, but most nights they would just enjoy the time in their suite, reviewing the spectacular sketches Abby had drawn. They would spend hours on the balcony sipping their favorite beverages as they talked about their future life together. They loved the seclusion. It was their time to learn more about each other and explore their lovemaking undisturbed. They enjoyed every minute.

The holy sights inspired them in Angkor Wat, and they hoped to return to Cambodia in ten years to renew their vows among the sacred ruins.

*

Once back in New York, they bought a townhome on the Upper East Side of Manhattan and renovated it. Abby had definite ideas about just what she needed in the kitchen. Alex already recognized Abby's cooking skills as superior to his own. In fact, Alex preferred Abby's special recipes to those of the many excellent chefs found at the many restaurants across the city. They discussed renovation ideas with their architect and interior designer, and both the newlyweds saw eye to eye on colors, furnishings, and fabrics for most of the house. But for the living room, where the focus was on his concert grand Steinway, Abby looked to Alex. "This is all yours, sweetheart."

Alex had made a career decision to leave a legacy of recordings. His new contracts with RCA included specific pieces popular with the public that would generate higher sales. He planned additional recording projects of piano music he felt should be part of his discography, and that included the works of Adolph von Henselt. Since he had already done the scholarly work for his dissertation on Henselt, it made sense to follow up by recording Henselt's unrecorded, and often unpublished, piano music. He was also interested in the music of Karol Szymanowski and Anton Rubinstein. With that in mind, he was ready to take up the challenge of what to do with the living room—the piano room.

Alex identified acoustical experts and recording engineers to customize the room with the latest recording technology and acoustical materials that would accurately produce the sound of his piano. He would store his private recordings in a fireproof safe for future distribution. The only thing left to do was to get some needed work done on his piano.

He loved his Hamburg Steinway concert grand, but after years of continued use, it needed a complete rebuild. There was only one person Alex would trust with his prized possession: Hans Benz at the Steinway factory in Hamburg. A world-class technician, Hans worked on pianos for many eminent artists besides Alex, and would even accompany them on tours. Hans was gracious in responding to Alex's request.

"It would be my honor to take charge of the rebuild of your piano, Mr. Courtland. I know how important this is to you. Are there any issues concerning you that I should be aware of before I start work on the piano?"

"Yes, there are. The transition from the middle to the upper register is less than satisfactory now. The tone changes to more brittle, and while I know how difficult it can be to voice those higher treble notes to maintain the kind of warm tone we love in the middle register of the piano, see what you can do."

"That is the weakest part of a Steinway piano, Mr. Courtland. But I have developed a new approach in voicing that includes an adjustment to the down bearings. This should result in the kind of tonal warmth you are seeking. I'll attend to all those and other details myself and promise you when you play your piano again, you will love it."

24

Tilton cleared security at the main gate of the White House and exchanged greetings with the secret service agent standing outside the north portico. He had served three presidents. First, there was Bruce Reynolds, a stoic Republican who found the Cold War challenges with Russia confusing and overwhelming. It was during Reynolds' administration that Tilton and Petrov firmed up their master plan to reshape the world.

Then, it was time for the Democrats to have a shot at running the country. Tilton found President Bill Bradford a decent guy to work with, and during his administration Tilton received a presidential citation for advancing several peace initiatives with Russia.

Now he was just getting used to President James Rutherford, who took office just nine months ago. During that time, he had proven himself an experienced politician with a brilliant mind. Tilton had found a politician that was his intellectual equal; now he had to proceed with caution. He was on high alert for any conversation with Rutherford where he might inadvertently reveal anything about his political activities. So far, Tilton and Petrov had been effective at throwing fuel on the Cold War issues, while secretly planning to unite the two countries.

The White House Chief of Staff welcomed Tilton to the Oval Office. "I apologize, Ambassador Tilton. Vice President Brewster is with President Rutherford. He'll be with you just as soon as they're finished."

"Thank you, Ms. Erickson."

While he waited, his thoughts turned to his new son-in-law. He could see that Alex and Abby had a wonderful relationship, but he couldn't help but replay the conversation he had with Alex at Nadia Rosenberg's memorial service. Alex ambushed him with questions about Petrov. That worried him and he wondered, *is it possible Petrov doesn't have as much control over Alex as he claims?* He dismissed that thought as he reflected on the cordial talk he had with Alex at the wedding reception. It was a classic conversation that every father of the bride would want with his future son-in-law. He was comfortable with their relationship and confident Abby could handle Alex. Abby was his daughter, and she understood the importance of her relationship with Alex. She had skin in the game.

The ambassador had never doubted Alex's intelligence, or his talent. His successes at Oxford, and on the concert stage, served as a testament to those facts. But Petrov confirming that Alex was implanted and the assassin responsible for killing Ambassador Aldrich caused him deep concern. Before that revelation, everything had been playing out as planned. What if Abby found out? Or did she know about the implant? Was it possible, Abby and Petrov were involved in a separate deal? He had to stop thinking about it because the possibilities were endless.

Now that Tilton knew Alex was essential to the general's ultimate plans, and by association his own as well, Alex was as prized a possession as a Fabergé egg.

He felt confident Abby would do her part in monitoring Alex. She was the only person who could observe him daily, and then report back to him. Her input would be important as they determined future actions. For now, Alex was his loving son-in-law, who seemed to accomplish anything except walking on water. Maybe, he thought with only moderate sarcasm, Petrov had plans for that, too.

The vice president left the oval office and moved to Tilton's side. "John, I'm so sorry to keep you waiting. The president and I just finished a conference call with President Ivanov, so it took a little more time than we expected. The president needs a lot of help from you, John. I know he's happy to have you on the team and is eager to talk with you."

"Thank you, Mr. Vice President, and by the way, thank you for the generous use of Air Force 2 again. It helped to arrive on Russian soil with the prestige of your plane as a backdrop."

The President nodded to Tilton as he walked over to Ms. Erickson's desk and handed her a stack of papers.

"Come on in, John. Let's talk about Russia."

"Very well, Mr. President," Tilton said, while thinking about all the things they could *not* talk about.

Tilton had sat across the desk from three presidents, and yet, every time he entered the Oval Office, it felt like his first time. His thought was always the same. *Why am I sitting on the wrong side of the desk?*

President Rutherford closed the door and invited Tilton to sit on the sofa opposite his chair by the fireplace. *This must be more personal, since he's not sitting behind his desk.* Rutherford seemed relaxed and appeared to enjoy the heat against his back. Tilton felt warm as he shifted on the sofa to face the president.

"John, ever since I became president, I've been concerned about the speed with which things have developed with American and Russian relations. I know that this business of us ratcheting up our military and their following suit hasn't helped. We've had a tit-for-tat relationship with Russia for years. You and I both experienced Ivanov's tantrum at the Paris Summit, and you've had enough meetings with the top guns over there to get a bead on this by now. What's your read on the situation right now?"

"Mr. President, you're right! I'm afraid that's where we are in our negotiations at this point. The good news is that we've flexed our muscles. We're not bluffing, and they know it. America has the capacity, and the resources, to prevail in any military confrontation. But now they are concerned because of the successful test of our hydrogen bomb. We know they are close to having one, too, but we always seem to be one step ahead of them, and that scares them."

"Except in the space race, John."

"For now, that's true, sir. But, given what you and I know is in the pipeline, Mr. President, US astronauts landing on the moon could soon replace those old publicity photos of Sputnik."

Tilton observed the president for his reaction to the news, but there was none. No facial expressions or body language that gave any hint of his thinking. *He's too smart to show his reactions to anything I say.*

"All good points, John. Do you think we can get the Russians back on track by new attempts at negotiating with President Ivanov?"

"Mr. President, it's interesting how Russian culture affects negotiations. They choose actions over words. They don't talk, but will pound a fist on the table. This approach has been handed down from Soviet leader to Soviet leader, starting even before Lenin and the 1917 Russian Revolution. Strategy, however, is our strong suit."

"Somewhat like a game of chess, isn't it?"

"That's a perfect analogy, Mr. President."

The president removed his glasses and glanced outside the window. Tilton thought this was a good time to prepare the president for things to come.

"In my recent meeting with President Ivanov, I asked him to consider Russia sharing some of their advanced technology with us. I told him it could go a long way to advance peace and perhaps lead to a reduction in Cold War tensions."

"John, that's great news! What a creative way to approach him. Rumors of their technological advances are most likely not all that exaggerated. Any idea of how you think he'll respond to your reaching out in this way?"

"No. He's too smart to expose his next move. However, I took it as a positive sign that he didn't slam his fist on the table, sir."

Tilton saw the expression on the president's face change from a serious and contemplative one to a smile and thought, *So, maybe not a poker face, after all.*

"John, that *is* all good. Thanks for managing this difficult transition in Russia so well. You are indeed America's ambassador, and I appreciate everything you've done to smooth out these tricky moments during this past year of my presidency."

"Thank you, Mr. President. I appreciate your vote of confidence."

Tilton picked up his briefcase next to him on the sofa and put it on his lap in preparation for leaving. *No fresh surprises in this meeting,* he thought as he put the folders back in his briefcase.

"It's because of the confidence I have in you, John, that I now need to ask you for help in another matter."

I thought we were through. Where is this going?

"Politics change by the minute in Washington, John. Everybody knows that. You have served three presidents, representing both political parties, and you have done so with significant distinction. I got elected by promising the American public I would bring peace and prosperity to this great nation. That resonated with the voters. I now have a Republican congress to work with to deliver on that promise."

The president stood up and walked over to his desk to take a sip of water and returned to his chair. He leaned forward.

"I was just informed by Vice President Brewster that current health problems will prevent him from staying on the ticket, should I run for a second term. Following the midterm elections, I will need to launch an aggressive campaign for reelection. To do that, I will need a strong running mate."

"Is Vice President Brewster going to be okay, sir?"

"Not sure, John. He will be fine to finish out my first term. We will support him with whatever he needs to make this transition comfortable for him. I'm thinking that after midterms, we can announce his decision and then, after a brief period, we will announce my selection for my running mate. I need your help, John."

"How can I help, sir?"

"I want you to be my running mate. Together, I think we can win. If democrats do well in the midterm elections as the polls indicate they might, then I think having you on the ticket for my second term bid gives me the best odds for getting elected."

"Me, sir?"

"Yes, John. You have all the credentials. Politicians and voters alike respect you. I can't think of anyone I would rather have at my side. The American public views you as someone who is taking the appropriate steps to make sure the Cold War doesn't escalate. That fact alone would help me get more votes."

"Mr. President, I am overwhelmed by the confidence you place in me. And, yes, if you feel I can help you accomplish your goals, I am all in, sir. It would be my great honor to serve as your vice president."

"I knew I could count on you, John. For now, we need to keep this under wraps. After the midterms, I will call a press conference to announce the reasons Vice President Brewster will not be on the ticket with me. Then, I will announce I am considering several qualified candidates to replace him, and after a few weeks, I'll break the news you've agreed to be my running mate."

"Sounds like a solid strategy, Mr. President."

As Tilton exited the Oval Office and walked through the north portico of the White House, he thought the president almost seemed relieved that Brewster would not be his running mate. *Is it possible that Rutherford never intended to have Brewster be his running mate in a reelection campaign? Brewster's health issues just made it more convenient.* One thing was clear to John Tilton: don't underestimate President Rutherford.

He needed to talk with Petrov about this latest twist. It might be possible to put foot to the pedal on their plans.

Alex Courtland and Andrei Petrov were intertwined with Tilton's own strategic plans. He wasn't used to watching events unfold without being the one to call the shots. Now, having two independent people so intimately involved posed an enormous risk. He needed to be especially careful now as he prepared his move on the ultimate chess board with one goal: to protect the king.

25

It took Tilton several hours to digest this latest news flash from President Rutherford. He poured himself a glass of wine and retreated to his private office at his home. Tilton knew that he and Petrov would need to revise their strategies with this new development. It would take two to three years before he would be vice president, and there was no guarantee that Rutherford would get reelected.

He picked up his special phone and called Petrov, who answered right away.

"John. Is everything okay?"

Tilton explained his accepting President Rutherford's invitation to be his vice president.

"Interesting. It's going in a direction we like, but it's not happening soon enough. Even if Rutherford is elected, it's too long to wait."

"I know."

"What if we could move things along a little faster?"

"Not sure how we could do that, Andrei. Brewster is not going anywhere until Rutherford finishes this current term."

"Alex has a concert coming up at the Kennedy Center in Washington. Will you be attending his concert?"

"Yes, of course."

"Why don't you invite Vice President Brewster as your honored guest?"

"He's an amateur pianist and loves Alex. He would jump at the chance. Could take him backstage for a personal greeting. He would eat it up."

"Good. Do that, John. I will take care of the rest."

"Just so we're clear. Planning a hit on the Vice President of the United States would bring an avalanche down on everything that you and I are planning. It would create chaos."

"I understand. He is not going to die anytime soon without some help from us. Let me plot a strategy that fits the current scenario."

"One more thing, Andrei. Both Alex and Abby are important to our plans. I can't imagine how things would play out if something were to happen to Alex. It would destroy Abby, and could affect my political career as well. Be careful, Andrei."

"Have a good night, John."

26

Alex and Nadia's favorite lunch spot was The Russian Tea Room, a cultural institution founded by the Russian Imperial Ballet in 1927. They would spend hours in a cozy booth while they enjoyed the restaurant's signature blinis, and on special occasions, they would order caviar and ice-cold champagne. Sol would join them when he could break away from catering to his roster of talent, but most of the time, it was just the two of them. Alex continued to cherish those memories of his time spent with Nadia while he waited for Sol to arrive for their lunch date.

Alex remembered that terrifying day when he saw General Petrov entering the restaurant. He still feared Petrov. It didn't matter whether he was on the other side of the world, or at the UN in New York. He felt the general's presence as if he were in the room with him. It was a persistent, nagging sensation that Alex couldn't shake off—even in his dreams.

"Hi, Alex, sorry I'm late."

"It's okay, Sol. I was just remembering the happy times we all had here."

"Yes. This place was special. It reminded us about the *good* things in Russia. I still feel Nadia's presence here."

"So do I, Sol."

"Good afternoon, Maxim. It's good to see you again. May we have the usual booth?"

"Of course, Mr. Blum. It's good to see you both again! It's been too long. Please accept my heartfelt condolences for your loss. I am going to miss Madame Rosenberg. I will never forget how she arranged for my nephew to get tickets to your sold-out concert, Mr. Courtland. It meant a great deal to me."

Both Alex and Sol thanked Maxim for being so kind to Nadia whenever she was there. Then, after ordering lunch, Sol and Alex took time to reflect on their life with her.

"It's remarkable when I think back on all the people who attended her memorial service, Alex. Her former students, artists, administrators, performers—they all had touching remembrances to share. Even Abby's father, the ambassador, attended. Do you and Abby see much of her father?"

Alex waited for the server to finish filling the water glasses. It was difficult for Alex to respond because of all the unanswered questions he still had about the ambassador. Alex kept it light, telling Sol about their occasional dinners with Abby's father and Alex's fascination with the ambassador's scope of knowledge.

A couple entered the restaurant and sat at a booth near them. Lunchtime was popular at the Russian Tea Room, and the room was filling up fast. Alex panned the room, noticing the beautiful coats, dresses, and jewelry worn by the many patrons.

Alex leaned closer to Sol and lowered his voice.

"Did you know, Sol, that John was involved in negotiating many of the treaties between the US and Russia that still exist today? Every college student with an interest in Russian history should study and learn from his experiences. He has so much passion when he talks about it! I almost want to like him."

Alex surprised himself when he said that, but realized it was true.

"You married the woman you love, Alex, but according to my friends in Washington, your dear father-in-law is one man you don't want to mess with."

"What do you know, Sol? I admit, he seems just a little too suave, a little too Mr. Perfect, to trust. He's got a smooth exterior, but what's underneath it?"

Sol extended his hand to quiet Alex until their server placed their plates down and walked away.

"We know he's a confidante of our friend General Petrov, who is as unscrupulous as they come. He has unlimited access to both Russian and American political networks. Add that up, and it's anyone's guess what he's capable of doing. Does Abby ever discuss him with you?"

Alex was already questioning just how close Abby was to her father. They talked on the phone and sometimes he could hear her voice drop to a whisper. *Were they telling secrets? What could father and daughter have to say that was so intimate, or so private?* He felt a knot in his stomach before answering Sol.

"Like most father-daughter relationships, Sol, it's complicated. There's a definite connection between them, even though there are no blood ties. He adopted a Russian girl and gave her a better life in the US. He's an expert on all things Russian, is bilingual, and he vowed to keep her heritage intact. It was an unselfish thing to do."

Here he was again, making the ambassador look like a good guy. Then Alex thought, *maybe he is.*

"No question, Alex, your father-in-law is a star student of history, and Abby's transition from orphan status at the Institute in Moscow to a busy social life built around the pillars of power in Washington had to be a dramatic transition for her. I have some high-level contacts in the secretary of state's office, and they are aware of Tilton's political ambitions. They trust me and told me that Tilton is respected and well-connected. They think he wants to be, *and may be*, president someday."

Sol paused as a patron approached Alex.

"I am so sorry to bother you, Mr. Courtland. I just wanted to let you know my daughter and I attended your concert at Carnegie last year, and it changed her life. She doubled her practicing efforts and got accepted into Juilliard's preparatory division. Her life has changed because of you sharing your great talent with us. Thank you from the bottom of my heart."

"Thank you for sharing her success with me. Inspiring youth is one of my passions."

As the lady left the restaurant, Sol brought up their leaving Russia.

"There are so many details we never discussed about your escape from Russia, Alex. I think it's important to shed some light on that now."

"I was only ten years old when we left, but you were in the prime of your life and had a successful career, Sol. So, what prompted you to change your life and take those incredible risks?"

Sol took another sip of his drink and locked eyes with Alex.

Alex could see this was going to be an important conversation and one that Sol, until now, had not been ready to have. Alex wondered if he was even ready to listen to anything about those dark days. *Do I want to know the answers now, after all these years?* Alex reached across the table and put his hand on top of Sol's hand. It was his way of letting Sol know he was ready to have this discussion now. Sol looked down as he searched for the right words.

"I learned early in my dealings with Petrov that the right palms had to be greased for me to succeed. His reputation as head of the KGB followed him to the Institute and made him one of the most feared and ruthless politicians in all of Russia. I was his front man in the entertainment scene, and I was successful. Besides having a nose for talent, my budget for gifts, bribes, and other tokens of appreciation was huge, and it secured my future success in a country where corruption was commonplace.

"I managed the top artists in the world, most of them from Russia and the United States, but business was transacted differently in the United States than Russia. Since I spent equal time in both countries, I had to remember where I was before I reached into my back pocket. How else do you think Russia won so many competitions around the world? And with each win, the star of General Petrov shined brighter. And it sickened me, Alex, then and now, to know I was part of that scam. Nadia and I decided we had to leave while we still had some personal honor. That timeline changed because of what was happening at the Institute for Gifted Children."

"You mean what was happening to *me* there?"

"Yes. The original concept of the Institute for Gifted Children was solid, Alex. The purpose was to identify outstanding children who excelled in music, sports, science, medicine, and even politics, and then build programs offering the students every opportunity to achieve success. Petrov would then place those students in positions where their influence and accomplishments brought great value and prestige to Russia. During its glory days, Russia earned more gold medals in the Olympics, and had more medical and scientific breakthroughs, than any other country. They wanted to build on those early successes."

Alex probed, "What made you change your views on things?"

"I knew the success I was enjoying wouldn't last forever, so I maintained my Russian and US dual citizenship documents and prepared for the day when I would need to get out of Russia for good. Meanwhile, I invested in real estate in New York, played the gold futures when they went soaring because of worries over the US Cold War with Russia, and was lucky enough to have other solid investments to secure my financial future. It all worked as planned—not to mention I still own one of the most lucrative talent agencies in the world."

"But if the plans for the Institute were so well thought out, what screwed it up?"

"When Petrov took over the program, rumors surfaced about his plan to revise the curriculum to focus on espionage training. He assumed if the Institute continued to produce top scientists, athletes, artists, and politicians, all trained in the art of espionage, that would give Russia the edge in the continuing Cold War. Given his background as head of the KGB, it all made sense."

"I still don't understand what this had to do with me. What role was I supposed to play?"

"Petrov was taking over your life, Alex. Nadia and your parents, and even I, became terrified you could become a casualty of Petrov's diabolical plans."

Alex thought *diabolical* was a perfect description of Petrov. His stomach tightened up just thinking of it.

Sol continued. "Petrov had already started taking you away from your parents. In his world, you didn't need a family, you just needed him. We knew that we had to get you out of there. Given the tidbits of information from rumors, along with Petrov's demand that you live at the Institute full-time, I knew our worst fears would soon come to pass."

"But why me, Sol? There were lots of other bright kids there."

"Petrov knew you would be a top performer. Nadia Rosenberg wanted to teach *you*! That was all Petrov needed."

"Why did he need me that much?"

"We weren't sure of all the programs at the Institute, but Nadia and I heard from trusted sources that Petrov had grand plans. With your future access to concert halls and important people in the US, you would bring great value to his espionage programs. We needed to prevent him from using you that way. That's why I created the International Piano Competition in Leningrad. It played to his ego. That was the only way he would have let you out of his sight. It took me several months to convince Petrov that Leningrad would be the best place to host an international piano competition. He wanted to do it in Moscow, but that would have made escape impossible."

"How did you convince him that Leningrad was a better choice?"

"That was easy. Leningrad has always been recognized as one of the cultural centers of the world. The Hermitage and other museums, concert halls, and art galleries made it the logical choice. The rebuild of Leningrad after World War II made it more beautiful than before. I told him that by selecting Leningrad as the site, it would attract international press and make him a hero with his bosses in the Kremlin. His ego took care of the rest."

Alex understood the grand plan now. "So, using the competition as a ruse to cover the escape ended up being the only possible way you could get us out of the country?"

"Uh-huh. Since Leningrad is a seaport, it was the closest distance to international waters, and our freedom. It came with a terrible sacrifice, Alex. I know we made the right decision, but it doesn't lessen the pain we still feel from your parents' deaths."

Alex took a deep breath as he sipped some water. He thought about the magnitude of what he was hearing. It didn't matter how many times he thought about his parents and the sacrifices they made for him; it was always a painful recall. Now he was getting more details that made it easier for him to understand how important the escape was, and it comforted him to know his parents would have wanted him to leave Russia—regardless of the cost.

"Sol, this is making sense. Petrov took over my training to transform me into a special agent. My God, I was only ten years old. They hooked wires up to my whole body, including my head. To keep me still while machines went back and forth, I got to play a lot of games that were on the small television. Sometimes I'd get bored and just fall asleep. Now I know why Petrov was there most of the times. I was his experiment!" Alex looked as if he were in shock. "Oh my God, Sol! What have they done to me?"

"This is the first time you've told me any of this, Alex."

Alex had been keeping so much of this to himself, and now it felt good to share more details with Sol. "Yes. I know. I have buried much of it. The nightmares started after seeing Petrov in New York. After that, there were terrible headaches, and sometimes I had this weird out-of-body experience, like sleepwalking. I didn't tell you because I was afraid it would interfere with my music."

Sol was almost speechless.

"Alex, you're raising some red flags with what you just said. Can you remember the equipment that was used?"

"I was half asleep and just wanted it all to be over. Sometimes, I would be in there for several hours, but only remember a few minutes here and there."

"What if this was some sort of brain-mapping program they were using? Could explain the nightmares and headaches you're having. Maybe your fear of Petrov is rooted in those terrible experiences. With what you're telling me now, Alex, I'm concerned. It's amazing that these traumatic events have had zero effect on your performing! You've never played better! I keep saying that, but every time I do, it's the truth."

"Well, Nadia taught me how to keep my focus, regardless of anything going on in my personal life."

"Let's thin out your concert schedule and give you a chance to process all this without the pressures of performing."

"No, Sol! My music and Abby are the two things keeping me sane right now. In fact, I'm sure of it!"

"Promise me, Alex, you will keep me in the loop if any of these health issues change."

Sol embraced Alex as they left the table. "I love you, kid."

"Thanks, Sol. I love you, too."

Alex resolved to talk with Abby. It was time she knew more details about the thing happening to the man she promised to love *for better or for worse.*

27

Talking with Sol helped Alex to put things into perspective. Since losing Nadia, Sol was Alex's go-to person for just about everything. The walk back to his home proved great therapy for him, as he thought about his upcoming performance of Brahms' *Second Piano Concerto* with the Berlin Philharmonic. He was relieved that his headaches and nightmares had been in remission, but he still feared a recurrence.

It was a cool afternoon, and he welcomed the break from the recent muggy weather as he walked to, and then down, 6th Avenue. As he approached 44th Street, he remembered he needed to stop at the convenience store.

"Can I help you, sir?"

Alex thought for a minute. "Yes. I need a plastic bag. Something extra large that's air-tight and can hold food, so it doesn't spoil. I also need plastic gloves."

"Aisles 6 and 7. You should find what you're looking for."

Finding what he needed, Alex paid the clerk and left the store, continuing down 44th Street. He took out one of the plastic bags, stuffed it in his right pocket, and tossed the rest in the nearest trash bin. The gloves went into the other pocket. The address, 35 West 44th Street, seemed right to him. He had arrived at his destination.

Alex paused just long enough to read the National Register of Historic Places plaque outside the building, and then crossed the street. He waited as he kept a close eye on the entrance to the Harvard Club.

A stooped elderly gentleman exited the building, walked up to 6th Avenue, and headed south. Alex followed him for two blocks until he reached Bryant Park. The man stood for a minute, as if deciding if he should cut through the park or continue around it. There were only a few people in the park as the man followed the sidewalk through the park, heading towards 5th Avenue.

Alex pulled on the gloves and took the plastic bag from his pocket to hold it at the ready, then picked up his pace until he was almost directly behind the old man. He made a quick assessment of the man's height, gait, and walking speed to determine his final approach.

With no one else in sight, Alex came up behind the old man and met his stride step for step. In one swift movement, Alex jammed the plastic bag over his head, securing it at the neck. He used his other hand for the chokehold. Too stunned to struggle, the old man attempted to pull Alex's hands away, but it was over quickly. Alex lowered his still body to the ground, removed the plastic bag, tore off the gloves, and exited the park at 5th Avenue, where he deposited both items in a trash bin. He noticed a wet newspaper under his foot too late, but broke his fall as he slipped by grabbing the edge of the trash container, scrapping his hand on the metal edge of the bin.

There was a chill as Alex grabbed a taxi to go home, but then warmth returned as he remembered where he lived, and he gave clear directions to the cabbie.

Abby greeted him with a big hug. "I can smell alcohol on your breath, and since you hardly ever drink, you must have had a great time with Sol! How's he doing?"

"He's fine. You know Sol, he wants to make everything right in the world, and that takes many drinks and a heck of a lot of talk. He sends his love."

"Are you hungry after a Russian Tea Room lunch? If so, I can make you a light supper." Dressed in a white robe and hair still wet from her shower, Abby looked so fresh to him. It was at odds with how he felt. Looking at her made him want to take a shower now, too.

"I'm a little tired from living in Sol's world during lunch. And besides, I need to pack yet for Berlin."

"I've already set out some things I think you'll need, just to save you some time. The German press refers to you and the conductor as *two warriors coming together for the ultimate performance of the Brahms concerto.* I couldn't set out your warrior uniform with a cape, because they're at the cleaners!"

"I guess I'll have to manage as best I can!" Alex responded with a smile, through his fatigue.

Coming out of his stupor, Alex tried to recall what he did after leaving Sol, but the only thing he remembered was the cab ride. He'd left Sol after lunch, but didn't get home until suppertime. *What happened to the missing hours?* He hoped the fogginess was because his meeting with Sol had taken an emotional toll, but by bedtime, he still couldn't convince himself of that.

As he slept, his dreams became real as he found himself back at the Institute in the same room with the bright overhead lights. Men in white jackets were hovering around him, poking him with wires. General Petrov was there, too, smiling down at him, murmuring for him to relax.

"Alex, Alex, wake up!"

"What's wrong?"

"You were dreaming. You're soaking wet, Alex. I know it's three o'clock, but you look like hell. Your eyes are huge. And, sweetheart, this isn't the first time."

"I have a crushing headache."

"You told me the headaches were gone."

"They come and go." He wasn't ready to confide in Abby until he could sort out these nightmares.

"Alex, there's blood on the sheets."

Alarmed, Alex sat up in bed.

"Your wrist, Alex. Looks like it stopped bleeding now, but how did that happen?"

"I guess I'm just getting clumsy in my old age. Probably scraped it on the nightstand or headboard."

"Not funny! Promise me you'll see your doctor for a full physical exam after this tour. I love you, and you shouldn't be taking any chances with your health."

"I promise. May I go back to sleep now?"

Alex didn't wake until the smell of bacon roused him.

There weren't any more nightmares or headaches while on tour, but Alex replayed the dream over and over, hoping the repeated exercise would lead to some answers.

When he boarded the flight for his return to New York, he was given a copy of the morning edition of The *New York Times*, a courtesy for first-class passengers. As Alex glanced at the news, he noticed a familiar face on the bottom of the front page with the caption, *Turn to page 9 for the obituary of Supreme Court Justice Joseph Barnes*. He turned to page 9 and read that Barnes was found dead earlier in the week from an apparent homicide. The article mentioned Barnes was staying with friends in the city to attend a lecture at the Harvard Club. They called the police when he didn't return by the next morning. There was no mention of where the police found the body.

Why does this man look so familiar? Could I have met him at a reception or backstage? Wouldn't I remember meeting a Supreme Court justice?

The article mentioned the justice's liberal voting record on gay rights, women's rights, and stricter gun control laws. His Republican colleagues had criticized President Rutherford for appointing someone to the court who leaned too far to the left.

Nothing in the article triggered anything Alex could recall about the man. It remained a mystery why Barnes looked so familiar.

Alex dozed off into a restful sleep until it was time to land.

He was happy to be back in New York and looked forward to seeing Abby, whom he had missed.

Once settled back at home, he called Sol to check in and give him an update on the Berlin concert.

"Terrific reviews again, Alex. Don't you ever have a poor performance?"

"Nope. Nadia never permitted it."

28

Tilton's call with Petrov on his Russian-made mobile phone was tense.

"Why on earth would we waste resources and increase our risk of discovery by eliminating Barnes? He was no friend of mine, sure, and his Boy-Scout attitude about every social program needing government support and oversight was contrary to anything I believe. But we gained nothing."

"He could handicap your future path to more power in the US. Boris identified Barnes as someone who could do that."

"And how did Boris think he could accomplish that?" Tilton's tone left no doubt about the sarcasm he intended.

"As a Supreme Court judge, with a lifetime appointment, he could weigh in on issues ranging from the use of fusion energy to the Department of Justice decisions you will want to control in the future. His views on social programs and his speeches referring to a more socialistic society are a direct threat to what you and I are seeking."

"Enough to justify eliminating him now?"

"Now is the perfect time. Waiting until he becomes a serious threat could leave us dealing with future problems. Boris researched every decision and speech Barnes made in his career as an attorney, circuit judge, and Supreme Court judge. But it was his recent speeches that prompted Boris to recognize the immediate threat he posed."

"Barnes had a lot of friends, Andrei, and they will want to know who murdered him. Rutherford was one of his more powerful friends, and he has agreed to speak at his memorial service."

"Yes, I am aware. Boris has advised me this will all blow over in another ten days. His friends will go back to their entitled lives and the investigation will keep hitting brick walls, and before you know it, there will be a new Supreme Court justice taking his place. That's where your influence with President Rutherford will be important."

Tilton was beginning to appreciate the logic. "Maybe, but he's not going to just take my recommendation."

"True, but there will already be pressure from his own party to go more conservative."

"Maybe. I will see if I can use my influence."

"Good, John. Is Abby providing regular updates on Alex?"

"Yes. Not sure how serious this is, but Abby mentioned he complains of frequent severe headaches."

"It could be a side effect from his mission to eliminate Judge Barnes."

"Why do you insist on using Alex to do what any core criminal could accomplish?"

"You're answering your own question, John. We use Alex because we have total control from the strategic plan to the follow-up. It's all flawless, predictable, and private."

"I don't understand why Alex would agree to any of this. He has nothing to gain by being part of this."

"Alex didn't need to agree to it."

"What are you saying, Andrei?"

"Everything I accomplished at the Institute was to arrive at this point—where we had all the agents and technological tools to guarantee every chance of success with our mission. Alex is exactly who he was supposed to be! He is a perfect example of all who will follow him."

"Alex is not aware of his killing Barnes?"

"He has no recollection. He is innocent. Boris controls the implants in his brain."

"Who implanted his implants?"

"Some of the most brilliant neurosurgeons in the world."

"Is Abby aware of this?"

"Definitely not. Abby's only role for now is to provide updates to you on Alex. She is a substitute for a surveillance camera."

"Aren't you concerned that Alex's implant could affect his

performance and he could fall from grace? Are we depending too much on Alex?"

"You have witnessed our advanced technology. In fact, *you* are the only person outside of Russia, except of course the creator—God rest his soul—who has seen what our technology can do. Do you think there is even a shred of concern I should have about Alex?"

Tilton had to acknowledge that what Petrov said about Alex was true. *Mr. Courtland has never played better* was a common phrase found in reviewers' comments.

Still, Tilton had additional concerns about his partnership with Petrov, who was now acting without sharing. The general had become more irrational, more headstrong, and more willing to take risks that could implicate Tilton. He had depended on Petrov to do his dirty work, yet his cruel, unhinged style repelled him. Tilton acknowledged that he would need a backup strategy to wean himself away from Petrov if necessary. He needed to keep his own stellar reputation intact.

Given this latest surprise on Alex's involvement in killing Barnes, Tilton called Abby to make sure everything was still okay.

*

"Dad. What a surprise to hear from you."

"Hi, sweetie. Saw a review in the *Washington Post* about Alex's concert in Berlin. Sounds like he hit it out of the park. How are you doing with all your alone time, with Alex traveling so much?"

"I'm doing all right…. The two boys in my life are always so busy, I'm getting used to being alone. But, you know, sometimes it's good to find some time to be alone and reflect on things. Besides, there is more time for my painting."

"Are you okay, Abby?"

"Yeah, Dad. I'm fine. I have a stubborn husband who thinks it's okay to put off a doctor's appointment before he travels halfway around the world. Otherwise, everything is fine."

"What's going on with Alex?"

Tilton was already connecting the dots, but hoped he was wrong.

"Before he left for Berlin, he woke up in a sweat. I noticed he had injured his hand. Nothing serious. But it's his hand, right?"

"Did he mention how he hurt it? I know his hands are insured through Lloyd's of London, so no worries there, but Alex needs to keep those hands of his in good shape."

"I probably shouldn't have said anything, Dad."

Oh yes, you should. Petrov is obviously not aware of these issues, or is he? Could it be those world-renowned neurosurgeons aren't so great?

"Abby, never feel you can't reach out to me. I'm a United States ambassador, and I am trained to keep secrets. So, call me anytime about anything. Can I do anything to support your efforts in getting Alex to a doctor? I have great referrals who respect confidentiality."

"Oh, thanks Dad. Honestly, I will make sure he goes. He would be upset if I shared this with you, but I know I can trust you, because you're a United States ambassador. Right?"

"You got that right. Love you, sweetie. Let me know if I can help with anything. I'm trained to do that as your father, too, you know."

"Thanks, Dad. Love you!"

Tilton had to wonder if Alex was in danger of either getting caught or having an implant explode in the middle of a Chopin encore. His initial instinct was to call Petrov and tell him about this latest glitch with Alex, but then decided he would wait to see if Petrov mentioned anything to him. He also thought it best to wait and see what Alex might find out after a medical workup. What if they discovered his implant? He was questioning his partnership with Petrov with greater frequency.

29

Alex let himself become mesmerized listening to Leon Fleisher's recording of Shubert's *Fantasy in C Major*. The tone was so velvety and warm; it touched him personally. Fleisher's playing always had that effect on him. He relaxed enough to let the music overtake him.

Alex rarely showed his emotions, except through his music and his love for his wife. The discipline that General Petrov instilled in him as a child blocked any emotional display—either in body language, actions, or speech. He recalled Nadia's response when he had told her of the general's methods.

"No emotions? What on earth is that man thinking? Can you imagine *Swan Lake* performed without emotions, or Maria Callas showing no emotion as she sings "Un bel dì vedremo" from *Madame Butterfly*? If General Petrov wants you to win the Leningrad Competition, he'd better encourage you to show *more* emotion, not less."

Alex smiled as he recalled Nadia's admonitions. He missed her so much.

The doorbell rang, bringing Alex back to the present. "Can you get that, Abby? I'm knee-deep in music scores."

"And I'm elbow-deep in yellow and red paint."

Alex laughed. "Never mind. I'll get it."

Alex was a bit surprised to see Sol. "Hey, Sol. Come on in."

"Hi, Alex. Sorry I didn't call first, but this is important, and I wanted to tell you the news face-to-face."

Abby yelled from the upstairs bedroom that had been claimed as her artist's studio. "Hi, Sol! Sorry, I can't come down. I'm covered in paint."

"Hi Abby. Okay if I borrow your husband for a few minutes?"

"Good. Keep him as long as you need."

Alex could tell that Sol was all worked up about something, so he poured him a stiff drink.

Sol took a sip and smiled. "I have exciting news for you, Alex!"

"I'm listening, Sol."

"Years ago, there was a lot of hubbub about converting the Colosseum in Rome to a spectacular venue for concerts and other events. Do you remember that? They solicited opinions from artists, conservationists, historians, even tourists."

"Yes, I remember."

Alex remembered the purists wanted to preserve all the historic elements of the Colosseum, but the Roman Cultural Affairs Office recommended a complete renovation, so it could be put to more practical use. The Cultural Affairs Office opinion won out.

"Weren't there legal issues, too, because it was a World Heritage Site? If memory serves, the Pope said God was on the side of the project."

"This Pope is forward-thinking, Alex, and his voice convinced the naysayers to jump on board." Sol continued to describe how the Colosseum had deteriorated from pollution and tourist traffic, requiring emergency action. In response, the Cultural Affairs Office put it on the fast track. The thinking was that renovating the Colosseum would attract even more tourists and businesses to Rome, thus paying for the project.

"Once they published the brilliant architectural design, it received public support, and they started construction."

"Are they even close to finishing it yet?"

"Yeah, they are, and everyone is raving about it. Look at these photographs they sent me."

Alex noticed the Brazilian walnut beams surrounded by pyramids of glass. Sol seemed excited when he mentioned they had already opened an office on the construction site to book events.

"It is stunning, Sol, but why are you telling me this now?"

"I'll tell you why. They want *you* to perform the inaugural concert!"

Alex could not hide his surprise at Sol's news and listened as Sol did what Sol did best: sell the idea.

"Do you know the historical significance of this? The last time anyone was in that stadium performing was centuries ago, and there was bloodshed. Human and animal. Now they want you to be the first person, the first *artist,* to personify how dramatically the venue has changed. My God, boy, you will represent humanity, civility, and culture for the rest of the ages!"

Alex was incredulous. "You mean you want me to be the first to play piano where Christians were fed to the lions?"

"Look, Alex. Think of yourself as a returning gladiator who will excite the crowds with your brilliant performance. But clothed, of course. No loincloths!"

"What kind of space is it going to be, Sol?" Alex picked up the photos and took a second look. "Sol, we have no clue what the acoustics are going to be like. My piano sound could slide all around that hall, from windows to floors, and through all the cracks in the seats. The size of this hall is huge! I'm not sure if an acoustical engineer could even figure this one out. They have enough problems getting it right on projects that are a lot smaller and easier than this. My piano could get lost in the cavernous spaces. Will they need to amplify it? That would be a deal breaker for me."

"Okay, Alex, I get your concerns."

"Wait Sol, there's more! Who's handling all the promotional material, them, or us? I'm asking this because I learned from the master. You, Sol, you!"

Alex could not dissuade Sol. "This will be big, Alex! The audience for this opening performance will break all previous records for events. Ticket prices will be off the charts!"

"So, this is about money?" Alex said, half laughing. "Does your greed know no limits?"

"My greed knows no limits, but this isn't about money. In fact, we're waiving your fee, and before you ask, I'm not charging any commissions either."

"You're joking!" Alex said in disbelief.

"This is an opportunity to contribute our talents—or rather, your talent. What we'll earn in prestige alone far outweighs all the other benefits."

"Sol, when you get a chance, list those 'other benefits' for me."

"I think I found you in a sour mood."

"You actually got me in one of my rare smart moods."

Alex paused as he reflected on the memories of his parents, how they made the ultimate sacrifice to give him freedom. He also thought of Nadia, and how she and Sol had given so selflessly of themselves to help him succeed.

"Sol, when we still lived in Russia, my parents instilled in me values that I live by today. You and Nadia reinforced those values as I built a new life in America. Giving back is part of my reason for being. It's part of my genetic makeup. That's never going to change."

Sol smiled at the man whom he had helped raise and beamed with pride. "The gate for this event will break all records. A fortune alone will come from corporate sponsorship. Want to know where the proceeds will go?"

"Well, yes, of course."

"About a year ago, Alex, we talked about how frustrated we were when the budget for the National Endowment of the Arts got slashed. Remember?"

"Sure, I do. Abby and I were so upset we increased our charitable donations to the organizations taking the biggest hits."

With increased excitement, Sol pressed on. "The proceeds from this opening concert would fund a worldwide initiative to support music and art programs. Budget cuts in music and art programs around the world have been devastating, with some programs being discontinued altogether. Europe has always taken the lead in supporting musical venues. Many countries support radio orchestras with public and private funds. Guess what? There's been a decline of over 50 percent in those funds. Many of those orchestras may not be on the air in another year. We could help them, Alex. The World Health Organization developed a music program linked to their initiative in improving health in children in Africa. They just announced they may need to scale back the program because the local funding sources can no longer partner with them. We could help them stay in business, Alex. This is only a sampling. There is so much more."

Sol waited to measure Alex's response before continuing.

"Tell me again how much this concert will raise?"

"The funds raised from this one event, which is expected to be in the multi-millions, will be augmented by the television rights expected to exceed one billion dollars. Even though funds raised from this one concert won't do it all, it would raise enough money to make a difference for us to be part of something global, meaningful, and wonderful."

"You paint an impressive picture, Sol. Abby will love this! We knew we wanted to do something, but this makes it personal. Besides, you already gave it the green light, right?"

"Yep. I did—you're not my son for nothing!"

"Sol, I get to talk with the acoustical engineers and have final sign-off of their plans. That's all I'm asking before I ask Abby to order me some loincloths."

"I will tell them your conditions. That will not be a problem."

The two men threw their arms around each other in a happy embrace.

The news thrilled Abby, who had overheard enough tidbits to want more. Racing down the stairs, she broke her own rule by leaving her painting without cleaning up first so she could be part of Sol and Alex's excitement.

"This news is mind-boggling!" Abby exclaimed. "It's the artistic equivalent of landing on the moon. Sweetheart, no other artist has ever reached that many people in a solo recital. This is very exciting!"

"Abby, I have worked with some of the greatest artists in the world. Many were difficult to say the least. But, your husband, my son, has now gone to the top of that list. Getting him to agree to the Rome concert exhausted me."

"Now Sol, I heard your pitch from upstairs, and I figured you had him hooked from your opening line. I think Alex is just having fun with you."

Alex got up from his chair. "Take credit, Dad. I'm a good negotiator. You taught me well."

Sol threw his hands up in the air in triumph and kissed Abby on her cheek, then quickly headed for the door. He turned to Alex. "There are a zillion details needing attention. You two go along and do what young lovers do. I'll catch up with you later."

"Okay, then. Thanks, Sol. Abby, how about we celebrate by catching a late dinner at Michael's?"

"Lovely, dear. I'll be ready in a flash."

They arrived at Michael's forty-five minutes later and were greeted by Michael wearing full chef regalia. He escorted them back to the kitchen, where he prepared a cozy table for two in a corner next to the sous chefs. Crystal flutes, a bottle of Dom Perignon, and two long-stemmed roses graced the table, the traditional welcome for special guests.

Michael's was one of only a handful of restaurants in New York boasting the coveted Michelin 3 Stars. There was something quaint about eating amidst all the energy unfolding in Michael's kitchen. Alex's seat faced the swinging double doors, constantly opening and closing to accommodate the servers bussing gourmet-laden trays into the crowded dining room.

As one door opened for a server, Alex was shocked at seeing something that confirmed his worst suspicions.

There they were: John Tilton and Andrei Petrov, seated in a corner booth in the dining room, heads close together, obviously talking about something not intended to be overheard. This was the first time Alex had seen Petrov since he had exited the limo and entered the Russian Tea Room years earlier. He noticed a heavier Petrov, mainly in the face, that appeared puffy. He was wearing what looked like an Armani suit and wondered if Tilton was helping him with his wardrobe. He saw him put a large heaping of pasta in his mouth and thought, *he should lighten up on the carbs.*

"Alex, are you okay? You're pale and sweating. My God, you look like your nightmare self!"

Alex felt his forehead to confirm Abby's comments. He was so stunned at seeing the general that he wasn't aware of the effect it was having on him. The general no longer caused anxiety, but anger. Why are they here together?

"No, I'm not okay, Abby. I just saw your father and General Petrov out there eating dinner in the main dining room. It kind of shocked me, I guess."

"Dad's the US ambassador to Russia, and Petrov is the ambassador to the UN, so it may not be that unusual. If you want to go now, we can go through the kitchen door. Michael will understand."

"No. I'm not letting the general, or even your father, control me anymore. Those days are over."

At Alex's insistence, they finished dinner and then had dessert, cognac, and coffee. Alex was seething with anger, but tried to remain calm. After seeing Ambassador Tilton and General Petrov talking together at the restaurant, Alex needed one major question answered: *did Abby know that her father and Petrov were in contact?*

"You talk to your father a lot, don't you, Abby?"

"Sure, although less when he's traveling. Why?"

"This is important to me. Did you know your father was still meeting with Petrov?"

"No, but believe me, that's not something my dad would discuss with me. Maybe this is just two diplomats having dinner together. Not a big deal."

Abby seemed uncomfortable and sounded defensive.

Alex looked around the kitchen to make sure they weren't sharing their conversation with Michael and his staff. They were too occupied preparing steaming dumplings and sous vide steaks to show any interest. He leaned across the table.

"But doesn't your dad let you know most of the time when he's going to be in the city? I know he likes to connect with you as much as he can. So, don't you think it is unusual you didn't know he was coming to town?"

"Dad is so busy, Alex. No, I don't think it's unusual that he would come into the city for a meeting without calling me first. It may have been a quick turnaround for him. Dinner, then jet back to Washington. I understand how upsetting it was for you to see General Petrov, but again, Dad is Ambassador to Russia, and General Petrov is the Russian Ambassador to the UN. Not sure how you make that out to be covert activity masterminding a government takeover."

Yeah, maybe not a government takeover, but who knows what the two of them could have been discussing?

Abby and Alex were both startled when a waiter dropped a stack of dishes. Michael approached the server with a pat on the shoulder, then went over to Abby and Alex to apologize. "Accidents happen, even in my kitchen. Sorry for the noise."

Alex was quick to respond. "This just adds to the experience of eating in your kitchen, Michael. Thanks for creating the space for us."

Once Michael returned to his staff, Alex continued. "Petrov had my parents *killed* Abby. Now he's having dinner with your father. Do you think I'm overreacting?"

"Again, I understand your reaction, but yes, I think it is an overreaction."

Alex listened as Abby explained that according to Russian law, Alex's escape was illegal, even though it resulted in his mother's death. She added that blaming Petrov for everything going wrong in his life was unfair. "I don't mean to be insensitive—"

"Insensitive, Abby? Oh, my God! I never thought I'd hear that coming from my wife! My mother was not a criminal, and you should know better than anyone that they defected to protect me from a dark future under the control of Petrov. I can't stop wondering about your father and his relationship with Petrov. Remember, he was meeting with Petrov before Petrov became Ambassador to the UN. I'm desperately trying to find the answers to the questions that are circling in my head, and not just about your father."

"You can ask me questions, Alex, as long as you don't interrogate me."

Alex noticed several of the staff looking in their direction.

Alex needed a minute to calm down before responding. He lowered his voice. "Abby, General Petrov has been haunting me since I left the Institute. There are pieces of my life I can't reconcile. I pick up bits of information in a dream, or just remember something out of the blue, but when I think I see some clarity, another layer of fog rolls in. Then, there's your father and Petrov together, and it sets off alarms."

"My father is a politician and like all politicians, he meets with whomever he has to in order to do his job, no matter how unsavory that character may be."

"Abby, I know this is your father we are talking about. Please understand, I'm struggling to find a resolution to so many issues right now."

Alex saw Abby was close to tears. He wanted to hold her and tell her how much he loved her, but this was not the time to send a mixed message. He had to keep pushing forward. It was time to leave. They slipped out the back door after thanking Michael.

On the cab ride home, Alex continued stating his concerns about Abby's father.

"Abby, I don't trust your father. After hearing you defend Petrov, now I'm wondering if I can trust you."

Alex watched Abby as she looked at him and appeared too stunned to respond. He considered apologizing.

"That cuts deep, Alex!"

"Maybe, but I'm trying to get answers to the upheaval in my life. I need to understand what's happening to me."

"You're not the only one who had upheavals in their life, Alex. I went through it, too! You can't imagine the transition I had to make. It's so complicated, Alex."

Arriving home, Abby choked up, left the cab, and ran upstairs to her studio.

Alex did what he did best when he needed time to think: He retreated to the piano, where he could vent his frustration by playing some Bach.

30

After a sleepless night on opposite sides of the bed, Abby made breakfast the next morning. Silence accompanied the scrambled eggs and sausage. After the second cup of coffee, Abby spoke first.

"We're scheduled to meet Dad for dinner tomorrow night, Alex. Under the circumstances, I think we should cancel."

"There's no reason for us to cancel, and besides, it would make him wonder why."

He had no intention of giving up an opportunity to listen to what the ambassador had to say.

Alex and Abby arrived at the Italian restaurant to find Tilton waiting in a small private dining room. Alex noticed two security guards at the entrance. *That's new,* he thought.

By the time dessert arrived, they were all talked out. Alex had to make his move. Watching Abby's response might also clue him to whether she had tipped her father off about seeing him with Petrov at Michael's restaurant.

"Thanks for bringing us here, John. There are so many wonderful restaurants in Manhattan. Some of the great ones are mom and pop operations like this."

"I've known this family for years, and their food is authentic Sicilian. It's a great little find here in the city."

The ambassador appeared relaxed. Alex pushed forward.

"Abby and I love trying new restaurants, but the trendier they are, the higher the tab."

"That's true, Alex. I can certainly afford the tab, but about the only time I end up at a hot spot like that is when one of my colleagues from another country takes me out to dinner."

"Sol Blum recently told me that Michael's on 55th is one of the top places in Manhattan right now."

"I've heard about that restaurant. Thanks for the referral. I'll try it someday."

Abby looked down at her plate. Alex could tell she was upset at his catching her father in a lie. At least now he knew Abby hadn't warned her father in advance. Maybe she was more loyal to her husband than her father, but he would have hell to pay when they got home. He dreaded the thought of another confrontation with Abby. He loved her too much to allow that to continue.

Abby avoided eye contact with Alex during dessert and coffee. It didn't surprise Alex that Abby made the move to leave immediately following dessert.

"Dad, thanks for the lovely dinner. I'm always thankful when the three of us can get together. Between Alex's touring and recording schedule and your busy life, that's challenging."

"You two are always on my mind. Let me know if there's anything you need."

I need the truth, Alex thought.

The taxi ride home was quiet—too quiet. Alex opted for not starting a conversation while in the car, hoping Abby would calm down by the time they got home.

It didn't play out as he had hoped. Once back home, the knives came out.

"How could you, Alex?"

"Abby, you are—"

"Upset? Yes, I am. You deliberately used this dinner to trap my father into a lie. Worse than that, though, you tried to trap me, too. Were you testing my dad *and me*?"

"You passed your test, Abby, and he failed his. Now you tell me: just how did I trap him? You don't think I have the right to challenge your father when every bone in my body tells me there's something he's involved with that connects to me? You don't believe that Petrov and your father are collaborating? Maybe they aren't, but I won't stop searching until I have answers."

"Alex, sweetheart. I love you very much, but all your pent-up anger is taking a toll on our marriage. I feel you're questioning if it was a mistake to marry me!"

"Our marriage wasn't a mistake, Abby. This isn't about that."

"Alex, can we please take a break from this before we say things we'll regret? I want our marriage to last forever. And I want you to be sure you want that, too."

"Of course, I want that, too. Why would you question that, Abby?"

"Because Alex. We spend too much time arguing about my father and Petrov, when we should be spending more time talking about us. I just wish you would try and put things into perspective."

"I'm trying, Abby."

"Try harder, Alex."

Abby kissed him on the cheek and left him alone with his thoughts.

31

"Can you come over here, Alex? I have something I need to talk to you about."

"Sure, Sol. On my way. It's a great excuse to get some fresh air. Should I come alone, or bring Abby?"

"Just you, Alex. This is for your ears only."

It was a short walk to Sol's condo in the Carlyle building on 5th Avenue. Alex let himself in and found Sol relaxing on his terrace. Seeing the piano as he made his way to the patio brought back memories. Nadia and Alex had selected that instrument from a half dozen pianos John Steinway prepared for them at the Steinway factory in Long Island. It replaced Sol's beat-up small grand. Alex told him he needed a better piano in case he decided to practice there. In truth, there were many gatherings in that room, and Alex would always agree to play for Sol's clients and artists, making it the highlight of any party. John Steinway had autographed the piano right on the bronze plate.

Nadia had worked with a decorator to completely refurbish the entire condo. Alex loved remembering the trips to interior design shops to find the right drapes, rugs, and furniture. Sol fought her every step of the way, and when it was finished, he showed it off with great pride. Nadia's presence was there, and Alex loved it, as did Sol.

There wasn't a photograph that didn't have a recognized conductor, pianist, violinist, mayor, or governor in it—always with a smiling Sol. Then there were the photos with Alex and Nadia, or the three of them. They weren't displayed like a shrine. Instead, they were integrated into the furnishing, creating an inviting scene.

The balcony spanned the entire width of the apartment, with French doors opening to a stunning view of Central Park.

Sol sighed. "Viewing Central Park on a perfect day like this is a real luxury."

"Then it's a good thing that I didn't bring Abby. She'd want to stop all conversation and paint this scene for you."

"Not a bad idea for another day, Alex. It would preserve this tranquility forever. Just think, one day when all hell is breaking loose, we could look at her painting and remember there once was calm and serenity."

"That sounds like a prediction!"

"What I have is worse, son. I have the truth, and it concerns Nadia's death."

Sol explained that the police investigation and the elevator company concluded that there was no fault in the elevator controls or mechanism. The coroner issued a death certificate stating the cause of death was accidental.

"That sounds strange. It can't be that simple."

"I agree, Alex. After I read their report, I convinced the police department to ask the FBI to investigate. I just received their comments."

"What did they find? Nadia didn't have any enemies, did she?"

"Nadia had one enemy."

"Who?"

"Petrov."

"C'mon Sol, why would he risk killing her when there was nothing to be gained? She was no threat to him. They didn't even live in the same hemisphere, except for his infrequent visits to New York for UN meetings. I admit I hate his guts, but even I'm not sure this fits Petrov's profile."

"I think the reason extends beyond logic."

"What's left, if not logic?"

"This man is a psychopath. He has no emotional connection with his actions. He has no sense of right or wrong, no empathy, and that makes him dangerous. Remember, too, that his ego is like a hungry tiger that needs to be fed."

"Okay, but why Nadia?"

"He had Nadia killed to punish you, Alex. Her defecting with his star student was a blow to him, and he took out his revenge on Nadia."

It took Alex a minute to absorb that sobering thought. *Oh my God. Am I the cause of Nadia's death?*

Sol refreshed their ice teas.

"Tell me what you have learned about her death."

"The FBI said her pager was used to cause the elevator to crash."

Sol reminded Alex that they had given Nadia a pager that could receive voice messages. This newer version allowed pages to be conveyed over radio waves at great distances, even to other countries. Sol explained how electronic telecommunication capabilities had recently become more sophisticated because of the Russian satellite, Sputnik, which could transmit signals to almost anywhere in the world.

"But her pager, Sol? How could they do that? I'm a piano nerd, so help me understand."

"I confess, I had to ask for help with this. The FBI located the database center and the Russian operative who issued instructions to Nadia's pager. The event causing her death was all done by pushing a few buttons."

"So that bastard killed Nadia without leaving his room?"

"There's more, Alex. Issuing instructions to her pager from an application that is *downloaded*, I was told, was the simple part. Connecting the pager's radio signals to the electronic controls in the elevator was much more complicated, and the FBI implied the Russians were further along with that technology than the US."

Sol explained how a sophisticated panel in the elevator controlled the brakes on the rails, and that a second safety feature, using switches along the shaft, managed slowdowns and stops.

"The application they downloaded from a Russian satellite accessed the elevator control panel and disabled *both* safety features. The satellite identified Nadia's location by tracking her pager. She always carried it with her. Nadia's fate was sealed from the moment she stepped into that elevator and pushed the lobby button."

"I'm stunned, Sol. I didn't know such a thing was possible. What's the FBI going to do about it?"

"In a word, nothing."

"*Nothing*? They've identified a murder weapon the likes of which I've never heard of before, and they're doing nothing?"

"This is where it gets hard to bear, son."

Sol explained all the reasons the FBI couldn't take any action, including the risk of creating an international crisis, or even revealing that the US was aware of the technology Russia now possessed.

"If it's any comfort to you, we now know how Nadia died and who killed her. It was Petrov, and he did it to punish you."

"Then what's stopping Petrov from going after both of us now? After all, you were part of the escape plan, too! And if my theory holds true that Tilton and Petrov are collaborating, does that mean Tilton shares the guilt for Nadia's death?"

"I doubt it, Alex. Tilton would have little to gain, and a lot to lose. He's too smart to be part of a revenge killing. Besides, he wouldn't want this sort of thing done in his own backyard. He's too politically astute for that. I'm betting Petrov acted alone on this one."

"Okay, then explain to me why Tilton would want to be connected with Petrov."

"Well, there could be a few reasons. They're both the ultimate politicians and maybe they thought they had a partnership of sorts, but it got out of hand. Maybe one or the other wants to alter their relationship."

"After you left the house the other day, Abby and I went to Michael's restaurant for a late dinner. Michael always takes good care of us. The dining room was full, so he set us up with a nice table in the kitchen."

"It must be nice to be famous and know all the right people."

"Not this time."

"Why? What happened?"

"When one server went through the doors separating the dining room from the kitchen, I saw Petrov having dinner with Tilton. It was upsetting and confirmed my suspicions they could be in cahoots."

"Hold on a minute. Could it be that it was nothing more than the ambassador to Russia having dinner with the Russian ambassador to the UN?"

"You sound just like Abby."

"Petrov will get his due someday, Alex. I'm convinced of that. Killing Nadia exposed him as more of a monster than we credited him before."

"I hope to God this doesn't bring back my nightmares, Sol. Nadia spent her last seconds gripped in terror. I'll replay that in my head for years to come. Maybe I should take Abby's advice and get a complete physical. She recommended someone she knows who's affiliated with the American Embassy."

"Uh, sorry, Alex, but I'm not sure that's a good idea. Going through the American Embassy is too close to the diplomatic post that Petrov now holds. Let's keep this between us for now. I know a trustworthy physician who's bright and an insightful diagnostician. You'll need to tell him everything that happened at the Institute and how it has affected your life. Those are details you want to keep from prying eyes. I'd be happy to set up the appointment for you."

"I can call him myself."

"Let me take care of this for you."

"Don't you trust me to do it?"

"Frankly, no."

32

Alex was deep in thought as he traveled first class by train to Washington, DC, for his concert at the Kennedy Center. Sol booked a suite at the Four Seasons for two nights, so he would have enough time to try out the piano beforehand.

Alex's concert sold out within hours of tickets becoming available. That had become the norm for all his performances. Sol's magic touch in marketing, along with the interesting story of Alex's defection from Russia, translated into a high demand for tickets. Alex's stunning good looks and stellar reviews were the icing on the cake. It worked so well, Alex ended up booked for the next two seasons, making him one of the most sought-after artists in the world. Alex's success brought financial rewards to both Alex and Sol, but Alex's intrinsic motivation at this point in his life was not connected to monetary value. His purpose was to inspire a generation of younger talent, the same way Nadia had inspired him.

Alex enjoyed playing concerts at the Kennedy Center. It was one of the few places in the United States resembling the architectural layout of European concert halls. With a seating capacity of 2,400, the tiered balconies made it more intimate and easier for him to communicate his music to every person in the hall. He would normally use his own piano for concerts, but since his piano was being rebuilt in Hamburg, he had to use the Kennedy Center pianos. As he worked with the lead technician to voice some notes in the upper register, Alex found that they were impeccably maintained.

Alex left the stage and was opening the door to the green room when a young stagehand approached him.

"Mr. Courtland, I'm sorry to bother you, but I just want to say how inspiring your music is to me."

"Are you a student?" Alex asked.

"Yes. I just work at the Kennedy Center as a member of the stage crew to help with college expenses, but I want to manage concert halls after I finish college."

"What's your name?"

"Teddy Johnson."

"Well, Teddy, if you're going to manage concert halls, and I'm going to be playing in them, we'll be seeing a lot of each other in the future!"

"That would be great, Mr. Courtland. If you're not too busy right now, would you please sign my program book? It'll remind me of the pact we just made!"

Back at the hotel, Alex relaxed and read through a few scores sent to him from a well-known composer who was hoping Alex would premier his concerto. Leonard Rubinstein told Alex it warranted a look, and he would put it on the New York Philharmonic schedule if Alex would perform it. When Abby arrived later at the hotel, she made it a point to stay out of Alex's way. She had learned early in their marriage to give Alex his space before a performance.

"Is your dad coming to the concert tonight?"

"Yes, and he's bringing guests. I'm sure they'll all be VIPs. You know how much he loves putting you on display as his talented son-in-law. He wants to have brunch tomorrow before we head back to New York. Just the three of us. I told him it was up to you."

Alex warmed to the idea of going to the ambassador's home for brunch. It was one more chance to probe into his relationship with Petrov, while also observing how father and daughter acted together. He would need to tread carefully, though. Alex didn't want to risk another encounter with Abby. Much as he wanted to succumb to Abby's charms, he had reservations he couldn't shake off yet.

"Sure, that's fine."

"He'll send a limo to pick us up here, and then take us back to Manhattan after brunch."

Alex arrived at the Kennedy Center and passed through security at the stage entrance. An elderly man who volunteered at the Center escorted him to the green room, where he relaxed before the concert. He could almost play the repertoire he chose for the program with his eyes closed. The Bach *C Minor Partita* was one of his favorite openers, and he would follow it with the Brahms *Opus. 39 Waltzes*. He liked the idea of mixing the intricacy of the Bach with the more fun and energetic spirit of the waltzes. After intermission, he'd play the Brahms *Variations and Fugue on a Theme by Handel*, and then wrap up the program with the Prokofiev *Sonata No. 7 in B Flat Major*. The Prokofiev always left audiences on the edge of their seats. There would be encores, of course, and he always decided those selections after he gauged the audience's response. It could range from a dazzling Chopin etude to something more contemplative, like a Fauré nocturne.

Every time he walked on stage, he recalled Nadia's instructions about what to do, from the first bow to the final bow. He felt warm all over now, just recalling it. He entered the stage just as she suggested he should. The audience stood and applauded, but he found it almost humorous. *Why does an audience give a standing ovation at the beginning of a program instead of waiting for the end?* He realized most of the concerts Vladimir Horowitz gave started and ended the same way.

Alex was a traditionalist when programming music for his concerts. He kept things in chronological order, thinking it easier to keep the audience engaged. Also, he enjoyed starting with Bach. The exactness of the contrapuntal lines and structure demanded significant attention to detail. Done well, it prepared the audience for more good things to follow, as the program progressed from music of the Baroque to the Romantic and then the heart of the program: the two Brahms pieces. The variations and character of the waltzes provided the right contrast to the more serious and structured Handel variations. Alex felt that he could spend the rest of his life playing nothing but Bach and Brahms. Of course, he was Russian, so that required programming lots of Russian masters—especially Prokofiev. That always brought a dramatic close to any program, and brought audiences to their feet.

From the first note of the Bach to the final encore, it was classic Alex: flawless. When he left the stage after the final encore, he felt terrific.

Once backstage, though, Alex felt that strange, foggy feeling again. It was a déjà vu moment. It felt like a warning, and he tried to fight it, but that sensation gave way to another familiar feeling of a relaxed state where he found himself at peace.

The stagehand came over to congratulate him. It was Teddy, the same young man who had talked with him when he rehearsed, and whose program book he signed.

"Mr. Courtland, you look a little unsteady. Here, let me help you straighten up. There, that's better. You were a little lopsided there for a minute."

"Thanks Teddy. I appreciate your help." Now he knew what to do. The instructions were simple.

Sol got backstage just as Teddy was leaving. "Unbelievable playing, Alex. Let's go to the green room. I understand Ambassador Tilton brought some noteworthy guests with him, and they're all dying to meet you!" Sol leaned in toward Alex to study his face. "Alex, are you okay? You seem a little disoriented."

"I'm fine. The music is still going through my head."

As they approached the green room, Alex noticed heavy security. There were more than just a few plainclothesmen; it was an armed detail. Even through the fog in his head, he thought this strange. *Who's here who requires so much protection?*

Alex entered the room and soon became engulfed by a group of people applauding him with accompanying *bravos.*

Abby greeted him with a warm embrace and a kiss. "You were incredible, Alex. All that talent and good looks, and to think you're mine!" Her smile was radiant. He knew Abby was working hard to reconnect with him following their recent rough patch.

John Tilton was next. "Very impressive, Alex. Is it possible you keep getting better every time I hear you play?"

"I hope so, John. That's the plan."

The ambassador brought a distinguished, well-dressed man to the front.

"Alex, I want to introduce you to my very special friend, who also is a great admirer of your work. It's an honor for me to introduce you to Vice President David Brewster."

The vice president approached Alex, bringing him up close as he shook his hand. It was during this greeting that Alex took the opportunity to slip a tiny device into the vice president's pocket. No one observed that he, the virtuoso pianist, had physical contact with the nation's second in command.

Almost instantly, Alex felt relieved and could relax.

"It was such an honor to hear you play tonight, Alex. Thank you for all you've done to promote music and education in this great country of ours."

"Thank you, Mr. Vice President. You may know that I left Russia to enjoy the freedom we have here. Thank you for all you do that made that possible, sir."

"Thank you, young man. It's clear to me why you are so very popular. I look forward to seeing you again, and hearing you perform."

John Tilton beamed. So did Sol and Abby. Alex knew just what to say and do on every occasion, just as Nadia told him he would need to do.

There were other introductions, but they all ran together in Alex's mind.

John Tilton left with Vice President Brewster and gave Alex a thumbs-up as he exited. "I'm looking forward to brunch tomorrow with you and Abby."

"We're looking forward to it, too, John." Alex couldn't recall anything about a brunch.

By the time Abby and Alex were in the car returning to the Four Seasons, Alex felt better.

"Are you okay? You're more quiet than usual."

"I'm fine, just a terrible headache."

"What about that doctor you promised me you would see?"

"Sol is working on it. He has connections to outstanding specialists."

"Why didn't you tell me?"

"I didn't want you to worry, Abby. I thought it would all be over soon, and I could deliver the good news that your husband is not crazy, and he is healthy."

"Darling, we're partners. I would like to be part of the solution. Remember?"

"Understood!"

Back at the hotel, Alex took an aspirin and went to bed.

Then came the nightmares.

33

Ambassador John Tilton lived in a townhouse in an exclusive area of Georgetown. His neighbors included former presidents, secretaries of state, senators, and congressional representatives. He, of course, was a welcome addition to the neighborhood.

The butler greeted Abby and Alex at the front door and directed them to the spacious living room where the ambassador was making a Bloody Mary. "Care for one? It's spicy and guaranteed to get your taste buds perked up."

"Sounds great, Dad!"

"Just what I need, John."

The house was stunning, the sort of home you would expect to see on the cover of *Architectural Digest*. It was richly appointed, with artifacts from around the world, yet comfortable enough for an intimate meal and conversation. John Tilton was the epitome of the gracious host, and meshed perfectly in this rarified environment.

"Alex, I can't imagine last night having gone any better. The audience didn't want to let you go! You're the toast of the town, and I must tell you, the vice president loved it. He couldn't stop talking about you. I wasn't altogether sure how much he appreciated culture and the arts, but now I'm convinced there's hope for him after all."

The *Washington Post* referred to the concert as *the social event of the year* and called Alex *the dean of classical piano music.* The *Post's* review also mentioned some of the VIPs attending the concert, including Vice President Brewster. A separate article highlighted features of the renovated Colosseum and Alex's appointment as spokesperson for the Worldwide Music Initiative.

"Not sure I feel like the toast of the town, John, but maybe this delicious drink of yours will help me get there."

The ambassador raised his glass to his daughter and son-in-law. "To my children. I'm sure you're eager to get home and relax after last night's success, so thank you for making this stop on the way back to New York. Family is everything to me, and having the two of you here is a real treat. We don't do this enough."

"We're both happy to be here, Dad." Abby raised her glass and blew her dad a kiss.

"I promise you'll return to New York with a full stomach and a light head. What is brunch without champagne?"

By the second glass of champagne, Alex was feeling a little dizzy with intermittent glimpses of his nightmare flashbacks. All the bits and pieces still didn't fit together. People's faces swam in front of his eyes: the kid from the stage crew adjusting his clothes; people shaking his hand; camera lights blinding him. It all bothered him. He couldn't recall all the activities following the concert.

"Vice President Brewster and I have been friends for years. Last night, he asked me to collaborate with him on US policies here at home. It flattered me, of course."

"Congratulations, Dad! That's fantastic. Of course, your expertise extends far beyond Russia. You're a diplomat for everyone, everywhere."

"Thanks, sweetie, but I had to decline. My plate is full with handling my responsibilities as ambassador to our most formidable adversary. That's still my top priority."

Alex recognized the opportunity to pick up on the ambassador's reference to Russia.

"Do you see Russia as a continued threat to the US then?" Alex asked. He didn't want his tone of voice or direct questions to put Tilton on alert like the last time.

"Russia's playing hardball and making it more difficult for us to negotiate any kind of détente. Most of the time, it's just talk. Even on those rare occasions when I leave Politburo meetings thinking we'd made progress, I find out later that they had reneged. They have unlimited patience to play their game, and they know how to use that strategy to their advantage."

It's time to throw John a bone.

"Evidently you discovered a way to penetrate their armor, John, because you're on the front page of the *New York Times* this morning. I barely had time to scan the article on your stunning achievement at convincing Russia to share some of their advanced cell phone technology with us. The *Times* quoted President Rutherford as saying it was all your brilliant diplomacy."

"Dad! What is *this* all about? Why aren't you blowing your own horn to us about this?"

"Well. Probably because I'm an ambassador and they trained us to let the rest of the world take credit."

John shared the moment of humor with Alex and Abby before continuing.

"Not sure how much of the article you read, Alex. I read through it this morning to check accuracy."

Tilton took another brief break to gather his thoughts.

"The US has made stunning advances on its own in technology, but cell phone research, despite a partnership with phone companies and government subsidies, hasn't kept pace. Problems like size and range limit advances. I asked President Ivanov if he would consider sharing that technology with us as a first step in reducing Cold War tensions. Frankly, it surprised me when he agreed."

"What do they have, Dad, that the US isn't matching?"

"Excellent question, sweetie. The answer is one word: Sputnik."

Alex understood now.

"I understand how a satellite system has been under development for years, and that is what we need for establishing a world network for communication. But one satellite?"

"On page two of the article, Alex, the *Times* answers that question. We always assumed there was only one satellite. Sputnik later released a series of mini satellites that now circle the earth. These tiny instruments aren't visible, even with the most powerful telescopes or electronic surveillance equipment we currently use."

"Wow, Dad. So, when will I be carrying one of these around?"

"Soon, honey. Eventually, we will have our own satellite system, but for now, thanks to the Russians giving us access to their system, it's going to be sooner than later."

Alex had to wonder: *Agreements of this significance are announced following a meeting between world leaders. In this situation, that didn't happen. Something doesn't add up. Maybe there is more to this story than the* Times *is reporting.*

Alex thought this was as good a time as any to bring up Petrov, even at the risk of alienating Abby.

"John, given General Petrov's strong ties to the Kremlin, and his appointment as Russian Ambassador to the UN, was he considered important enough to be part of the discussion?"

"Frankly, most of my negotiations are with my counterparts in the Kremlin, but Petrov and I cross paths occasionally as I walk the corridors of the Kremlin, and certainly at the United Nations, where we both spend a lot of time. I really don't know how active he may have been behind the scenes on this decision by Ivanov."

As Abby earlier suggested, the ambassador could justify the meetings with Petrov, so why lie about meeting Petrov over dinner at Michael's? Alex always trusted his gut instincts, and right now his instincts were telling him Tilton was lying about anything having to do with Petrov. *Will I ever know the truth?*

Crêpes Suzette were being prepared and coffee served when the butler informed the ambassador that the President of the United States was on the telephone.

Tilton expressed surprise. "Excuse me, I need to take this call."

When John Tilton returned to the dining room, his face was ashen and his mood serious.

"Dad! What happened?"

"The President needs me at the White House for an emergency meeting. I must leave at once. I'm so sorry. The car is ready to take you back to New York. Please enjoy the dessert before leaving. It's a specialty of the house."

He paused for a moment, appearing to contemplate something.

"Abby, Alex. Please keep everything I'm about to tell you in strict confidence. You cannot repeat what you are about to hear. The President just informed me that Vice President Brewster died late last night in a tragic accident."

"Oh, my God! What happened? We just saw him last night, Dad."

"Yes, I know, Abby. He was so happy to be at your concert, Alex. There are many unanswered questions. The President has asked for my help."

Alex noticed that the ambassador seemed shaken by the news and thought, he either deserves an Academy Award for his acting, or condolences for losing a friend. The jury was out on which possibility Alex thought was the truth.

"I'm so sorry, John. Is there anything we can do?"

"Thank you, Alex. We don't have all the details, but I will tell you what the president told me."

Abby jumped in. "Thank you for trusting us, Dad. We understand this is in strict confidence."

"Thank you, Abby. Confidentiality is important. So far, the press only knows the bare details of the bizarre accident. For national security, the occupants of the car have remained a secret, and the president will need to issue an announcement in the next couple of hours. The president told me that after leaving the concert, the vice president headed for a late-night emergency meeting at the Pentagon. Evidently, the driver lost control of the vehicle on the way there, and the car crashed through the railing on the Arlington Memorial Bridge and plunged into the Potomac."

"Oh no...." Abby reached over to hold Alex's hand.

Tilton explained that both the vice president's limousine and the two secret service escort cars had emergency beacons and tracking devices, so help arrived almost immediately.

Tilton took a moment and cleared his throat.

"Navy Seal divers called to the scene confirmed that both the vice president and his driver were dead, probably from the crash, or from drowning if still alive when the car sank into the river. They lifted the car out of the water and took it to an unidentified FBI location where further tests are being done."

Tilton took a moment, and then continued.

"He was a very close friend to me, and his death is a tremendous loss for our nation. Vice President Brewster would have made a fine president someday, and I know that was his dream. The coroner will issue a complete report once they complete the autopsies. It's not a good time for President Rutherford, either. He's asked for my help in managing the news. They were very close friends, as well."

Alex reached out to his father-in-law. "This is terrible news! I'm sorry, John. It feels especially personal because you introduced me to him last night."

"I know. And I made some barbs about his not having culture. I take it all back. Please remember to say nothing to anyone, and as soon as I know more, I'll keep you posted."

Being driven home in the back seat of the partitioned car, Abby and Alex remained stunned by the news the ambassador had shared with them. Alex broke the silence.

"I feel bad for your dad having to deal with his personal and professional loss."

Abby appeared deep in thought. "I know, but there's something strange going on here. It doesn't add up."

"Strange? Like how?" She rarely said anything critical of her father.

"Dad and the vice president weren't friends. To be honest, my dad thought he was an ignorant fool who was a thorn in the country's side."

"Abby, your dad is if nothing else, a politician. What he says publicly and privately could be different."

"It's more than just being tactful in public. Brewster once tried to get Dad removed from a strategic team the president appointed to address immigration policies, and he did what he could to minimize Dad's influence with the president. He thought if Brewster became president, it would not be good for the country, and he felt it would end his own career."

Alex put his head back on the seat, rested his eyes, and let Abby do the talking. For the first time, she objectively described what she knew to be her father's characteristics and political ambitions, and they were less than flattering. Alex was grateful for her candor, and felt for the first time in his marriage that he had a partner who could now share some of the same concerns he had about her father.

34

Alex missed not having his own piano. For an instrument so large and heavy, it doubled as a warm and inviting security blanket for him. The Steinway on loan from Steinway Artist Division was adequate for his needs, but he wanted an update on his own piano and called the Steinway factory in Hamburg.

"This is Alex Courtland, and I'm calling for Hans Benz, please."

"One moment, Mr. Courtland." After a long wait, Alex wondered if he'd lost the connection.

"I'm sorry for the delay, Mr. Courtland. My name is Derrick Schmidt. I'm the managing director of the Steinway factory here in Hamburg. We met during your last visit here."

"Yes. I remember, Mr. Schmidt. I'm calling for Hans Benz to check on the status of the rebuild on my Steinway 'D'. Is Hans available?"

"Hans finished your piano last week. It shipped several days ago. You should receive it by next week."

"That's great news. I plan to use it for the concert in Rome. If you could be so kind as to connect me to Hans, I'd like to thank him. Is he available?"

"I apologize, Mr. Courtland. I was remiss in not calling you myself to tell you the disturbing news about Hans. As one of our most prestigious clients, we should have notified you."

"Notified me about what, Derrick? Is Hans okay?"

"Hans has…disappeared. It's so unlike him. He had completed all the work on your piano, and personally supervised the crating and shipment arrangements back to you in the States. Then, like vapor, he has vanished."

"Did you notify the police?"

"Yes. His wife called me when he didn't come home. When she knew he wasn't at work, we called the police right away. Several detectives are investigating the matter now. She was frantic with worry, and can't explain his sudden disappearance. Hans doesn't take sick days off work, and even if he takes a vacation, we know about it in advance. There is no explanation for his absence. I am relieved, however, that before he disappeared, he rebuilt your piano to your exact specifications. In fact, it's almost an omen that he did the work himself. Ordinarily, Hans delegates work among the staff, but he wouldn't let anyone else get near your instrument."

Alex was fond of Hans and disturbed by the news of his disappearance. He told Derrick to keep him informed.

"I will, Mr. Courtland. Enjoy your piano and continue to play beautiful music on it. Perhaps Hans will hear your music and it will help him find his way back."

Alex recalled his first meeting with Hans. His first stop on a tour of Europe was a performance at the Staatsbibliothek in Berlin. When he arrived the night before the concert, it horrified him to find the piano in poor condition.

The hall manager apologized. "I am so sorry, Mr. Courtland. Mr. Weber, our regular technician, had a heart attack and is in the hospital. We are trying desperately to locate another technician, but so far, no one is available."

Alex had recently become a Steinway artist and had access to the Concert and Artist Division at Steinway. Since 1892, Steinway offered special services to pianists, including the famous pianist Ignacy Jan Paderewski, who Steinway sponsored on a seventy-five-city US railway tour. Paderewski later became Poland's prime minister. Alex's call resulted in Steinway sending Hans, who arrived the next morning on a flight from Hamburg. Hans told Alex to return after lunch and he would have the piano ready for him to play. When Alex returned, Hans was sitting at the piano, smiling. The transformation in the piano was magical and done in only three hours. The concert was successful, and the reviewer commented on the quality of the piano. When his piano needed to be rebuilt, Alex knew who to call.

35

As promised, the piano arrived in perfect condition. Alex couldn't wait to put it through its paces. Unlike many of his colleagues, Alex approached the evaluation of a new piano much like a physician would interview a new patient. If Hans did his job, then Alex's rebuilt Steinway would get a clean bill of health.

The most important quality Alex needed in any piano was clarity of tone. He knew this was key to the overall quality of sound that the audience would hear. He started in the lower register and, note by note, listened for not just the clarity of tone, but how the tone matched to its neighboring notes. First two notes, then three notes, and so forth. Next, he needed to measure the transition from the lower to the mid, and then upper register of the piano. Was the balance correct? Did it blend harmoniously? Did it work in performing all periods of music, including late Romantic works in which composers like Liszt and Ravel were exploring the range of the keyboard?

Alex next checked the action for even regulation and key responsiveness. Steinway was ahead of the competition with its patented accelerated action, announced in 1931. Given Alex's extraordinary technical abilities, this was an important factor when music required sensitivity of touch and fast repetition of notes.

For his ultimate test, Alex played the most challenging pieces from his extensive repertoire of music, including pieces by Rachmaninoff, Bach, Beethoven, Chopin, Prokofiev, Scriabin, Scarlatti, Haydn, Mozart, and even Henselt. It was the equivalent of three concert performances. He could have played more. His stamina was impressive.

The sound was magnificent, the action responsive, and the intricate shadings he recognized as he touched each note were music to his ears. He took a moment to appreciate Hans Benz and the Steinway grand piano that held the vestiges of his personal touch.

Finally, it was time for the doctor's report to be completed, and Alex could report that his Steinway was in tip-top condition and had passed a rigorous examination, with only one minor exception: the highest note in the upper register had a slightly different feel in the action. Since it was not a note he would be using in any of the compositions he was playing, it wasn't a concern. However, Alex thought it somewhat unusual that this minor flaw escaped Hans' expertise. He made a mental note to ask Hans about it as soon as he was able to talk with him, presuming, of course, he finally materialized.

36

"Boris, provide an update on Alex's latest assignment."

"Yes, General. Several layers of synchronization were necessary before Alex could complete his assignment: we deployed our agent Konstantin, who speaks perfect English, instructing him to tell Alex his name was Teddy, and that he worked at the Kennedy Center. He made Alex's acquaintance and placed the device in Alex's pocket after the concert. Alex was introduced to Vice President Brewster and transferred the device to him without being detected. There were only seventy seconds when Alex was close enough to place the device, but he completed the assignment exactly as you intended. Alex's performance of this task was flawless."

"Yes. I think the intensified training he did while here at the Institute kicks in, even with the implant. It's what I intended should happen. What has been the final disposition?"

"The device was activated as soon as the vice president entered his limousine. At precisely twenty-two minutes after leaving the Kennedy Center, our instruction to the device interfered with the steering and breaking mechanisms of the car, causing the crash into the Potomac River."

"Of course, the American FBI will investigate this crash. What will they find, Boris?"

"Nothing at all, General. Nothing links our organization to this event."

"Thank you, Boris. You may shut down now."

"May I ask you one question, General?"

Annoyed, Petrov turned around to face Boris. "What is it, Boris?"

"Why did you decide not to attend the Kennedy Center concert?"

"The risk of being recognized by Alex, or Sol Blum, was too

great, given the aftermath of the concert. It was better not to attend and complicate things any more than they already are."

"Thank you, General. I'm shutting down now."

While Boris turned off, the general took a moment to appreciate reaching this pivotal point in his long-range plans. *I've done a huge favor for Ambassador Tilton by removing the vice president without even a hint of scandal. There may be an opportunity soon to use this bargaining chip to my ultimate advantage.*

37

Dr. Robert Abernathy's private clinic was located just off Park Avenue in a large brownstone. From the outside, there was nothing to distinguish it from the neighboring properties. Alex rechecked the address just to make sure this was indeed the clinic he was seeking. There were video cameras over the entrance and after hitting the button, a woman's voice instructed him to enter. The electronic door lock buzzed. On entering, he saw nothing to indicate this was a medical facility. There was a large oriental rug, a desk with a large orchid plant, and an attractive grey-haired woman impeccably dressed behind the desk.

"Good morning, Mr. Courtland. I'm Judith Abbott, Dr. Abernathy's assistant. I will take you upstairs for your appointment as soon as you complete some paperwork. Please take a seat and review and sign each document at the bottom, along with today's date."

Five minutes later, he was being taken upstairs to see Dr. Abernathy. Once upstairs, there was no longer a question if this was a clinic. Several staff members in white uniforms were attending to details. He walked by a room with a frosted glass door labeled, *LAB.*

At the end of the hall, they stopped at the door with Dr. Abernathy's name on it.

"Here we are, Mr. Courtland." Judith knocked on the door and opened it.

"Hello, Mr. Courtland. Welcome. So glad you could make it."

Dr. Abernathy looked nothing like Alex had imagined. With his tweed sport coat and a red and blue handkerchief, he reminded Alex of one of his professors at Oxford. Abernathy got up from his desk and shook Alex's hand.

"I hesitate to touch your hands, Mr. Courtland. They're much too valuable. However, this is a clinic, so I guess there will be lots of that going on during your evaluation."

Dr. Abernathy's direct manner revealed confidence, but it was tempered with an engaging personality. Alex relaxed.

"Please call me Alex, Dr. Abernathy."

Dr. Abernathy's background was impressive: Harvard undergraduate, Stanford graduate, and an MD from Johns Hopkins. He held many patents and received several grants for his advanced research in neuro-oncology.

"Please take a seat, Alex. Sol Blum filled me in on your situation, but I want to hear in your own words what's going on. This is all too fascinating, and I need details."

Alex had questioned whether he should even do this, but as he unloaded all the secrets he'd been hiding for decades and told Dr. Abernathy everything, he felt unburdened and relieved. He held nothing back as he described his history at the Institute, the testing under sedation, and the subsequent headaches, nightmares, and memory loss that plagued him.

"That's an impressive recall of your situation, Alex. You must have a splendid memory for details."

Oh, if you only knew.

"Let's walk down the hall to an examination room and check you out."

Dr. Abernathy proceeded with a thorough exam, including a comprehensive clinical evaluation. Alex was impressed with the entire process, and was hopeful he might get some answers now.

"Now that I've examined you, I see two issues we can't ignore: headaches and nightmares."

Alex felt relief mixed with dread. "I guess that covers the prime points."

"I suspect the headaches and nightmares are connected. The nightmares take you back to your time at the Institute, and the trauma of those recalls trigger the headaches."

"Dr. Abernathy, I'm afraid to ask, but do you think I might have a brain tumor?"

"Let's not get ahead of ourselves here, Alex. The CT scan and MRI studies I'm ordering will answer those questions."

"I'm leaving for Rome in a couple of days, but it will be a quick trip."

"Yes, Sol told me about your upcoming performance at the Colosseum. I was there eight or nine years ago and the Colosseum was closed, with heavy equipment surrounding it. I guess that was the start of the project. Will you be seeing the new Colosseum for the first time?"

"Yes. I have some concerns about the acoustics that need to be checked out."

"That makes total sense. Why don't you call me when you return? I should have all the results back by then."

Walking home, Alex mused over what bothered him more: a brain tumor, or his ongoing concerns about Abby and her relationship with her father. He wanted to trust her, but even after she made some confessions about her father on their way back to New York, it did not convince him that she had been entirely honest about everything.

38

It was a beautiful Sunday morning, and Abby made her famous frittata with bacon, gruyere cheese, and green pepper. Accompanied by fresh croissants with orange marmalade, it was Alex's favorite breakfast. Abby did the cooking, and Alex insisted on cleaning up the significant trail of things that made her breakfast so good.

"You're a gem, honey. I can go back to my painting. I agreed to contribute to the silent auction the Metropolitan Museum is having. The deadline is Tuesday. Thanks to your support, I just might make it."

"While you do that, I may take a walk to work off some of these calories you insisted I ingest."

"Go for it!"

Alex finished his kitchen duties, changed clothes, and headed toward Central Park, where the allure was far too strong to ignore. Alex loved his walks in the city. It was a time to clear his head, and the changing landscape, interesting architecture, and variety of people never failed to capture his imagination. He found a bench empty along the great lawn where he admired the beauty of Central Park.

A young man sat next to Alex on the bench. "Alexis?"

It was not unusual for him to be recognized on his walks around town. Some considered him a celebrity, just not in the same class as Elvis. But no one called him *Alexis* anymore. He dismissed it as someone who had read the *Times* article on his escape from Russia.

He turned to face a young man his age, or younger.

"Do you remember me?" He spoke in Russian.

Alex tried to contain his surprise at being approached by someone speaking Russian. "Do you speak English?"

Alex's lessons with Nadia were often a mix of Russian and English. Occasionally, Alex would even speak Russian with Sol, but usually only to tease him about something as unimportant as getting a haircut. Alex was proud of his Russian heritage, but he felt uncomfortable speaking Russian to someone he didn't know.

"Yes, of course."

Alex didn't recognize him, but to be gracious, he asked the young man to refresh his memory, thinking he may have met him backstage after a concert.

"My name is Vladimir Ruskin. I was a student at the Institute in the science program and entered the program the year you left. I, of course, knew about you before even attending the Institute. You were the musical genius that everyone talked about. Your last concert there right before you left was incredible. We gave you a standing ovation. I wanted to attend the Institute because my girlfriend was a ballerina there, Kristina Skyokova. Do you remember her?"

Alex recalled the image he had of Kristina lying on the cafeteria floor in a pool of blood.

"Yes, I remember her. I'm so sorry about her death. In fact, I saw her that day in the cafeteria. It looked like a horrible accident."

"It was no accident."

"Why do you say that?"

"She was having an affair with General Petrov. She told me about it in a letter, saying she was in love with the general and they would soon be married. I then received a follow-up letter from her right before starting my studies there, and she regretted the letter she sent ending our relationship. I think she may have threatened to reveal their affair. But she never got the chance. General Petrov had her killed. Of course, I can't prove anything, but for someone as sure-footed as a professional ballerina, I seriously doubt she slipped and fell."

Alex also questioned whether it was an accident. Even now, he could still see the threatening stare the guard gave him.

"Vladimir, what are you doing in the United States?"

"The same thing you are. I was part of the same program. Now, it's no secret what General Petrov did to us all."

"What do you mean?"

"The indoctrination that screwed up our thinking."

"Our *thinking*?"

"Yes. The headaches, the nightmares. Sometimes I wake up in a cold sweat and can't get back to sleep. There are periods of time that I can't even remember. I'm supposed to be contacted by someone from the Institute to give me instructions on what to do, but so far nothing. I continue to receive the weekly stipends to cover my expenses. Do you get headaches all the time, too?"

Alex felt his stomach turning and his knees went weak. He could feel the rush of blood to his face. Vladimir seemed depressed and alone. He felt sorry for him, but couldn't escape his own feelings of anxiety. He needed time to digest this new information.

"Are you okay, Alexis? You seem a little unsteady."

Alex was too stunned to reply. Every conceivable answer was spinning around in his head. Am I under Petrov's control? Maybe I shouldn't be worrying about a brain tumor. It might be something else. He was feeling sick, but he didn't want to lose contact with Vladimir.

"Can I have your telephone number, Vladimir? I would like to contact you again soon when we can talk more."

"Sure. Don't let General Petrov know you saw me, though. He wouldn't like that. If you weren't a performer of note, I would never have found you."

"I promise. Here is my private number. Please call me if you need anything."

Alex wasn't sure who he should talk to. Abby? Sol? Dr. Abernathy? Of course, it would be Sol, who was not only his adopted father, but his friend and confidant. He returned home in a quandary about what to do next.

39

"Honey, what kind of cheese do you want on your ham sandwich? Cheddar or Swiss?"

"Swiss with extra mustard."

"Bring your drink to the patio. It's such a beautiful day, and we should take advantage of it."

Alex put down his music score and joined Abby on the patio.

"You're right. It's lovely out here. We should do this more often."

"Are you and Sol all set for the Rome trip?"

"Yes. I definitely got adopted by the right people. Having a private jet in the family makes all the difference."

Abby smiled and took a moment to add some chips to her sandwich, then passed the bag to Alex. "Want some?"

"Absolutely. Thanks."

"Alex, is there a reason you don't want me to go to Rome with you and Sol?"

He understood her confusion. Under normal circumstances, Alex would have wanted Abby to go, but circumstances weren't normal anymore. What he needed now was some private time with Sol to discuss the complex relationship between Abby and her father. And as an extension of that, Tilton's possible collaboration with Petrov.

"This isn't a pleasure trip, Abby. It's just business. We fly to Rome, go to the Colosseum, look at the renovated facilities, then turn around and come back. I'll be home before you miss me."

Abby tried to be helpful. "Be sure to check out the acoustics. Sometimes, even moving the angle of the piano can affect sound."

Alex's guarded feelings flared for a moment. "I know, Abby!"

Alex didn't need to be reminded of how tricky acoustics could be in a new hall. Sound bouncing off walls, the piano's position, and the construction materials all affected the character and quality of sound. Delivering the same listening experience to every member of the audience, regardless of where they sat, was the goal.

Abby was apologetic. "Sorry. Didn't mean to rub you the wrong way."

"I'm sorry, too, Abby. You're just trying to help. I know that. They have a nine-foot Hamburg Steinway on stage that I'll use to check acoustics. Sol will walk around the hall to identify any dead pockets. We know the drill."

"It's okay, Alex. You've got a lot on your mind. I just want to be supportive."

Alex reached over and put his hand on top of hers. "I keep thinking of the one note in the piano that doesn't respond."

"Are you going to have your technician look at it?"

"No. The piano is perfect in every way. It's the top key in the upper register—almost never needed. None of the repertoire I'm playing in Rome uses that note, and I don't want my technician messing with the piano. There is an excellent technician in Rome who will tune the piano."

"Still no word from Hans?"

"No, and it troubles me. They are investigating it, so I guess I'll hear when they find him. Thanks for the sandwich. I should have gone with the cheddar."

Abby picked up the plates and gave Alex a sideway glance as she headed for the kitchen. With a little wave to Abby, Alex returned to his score.

*

Sol's private jet gave Alex the privacy he needed to unload his fears. Once in the air, he didn't waste any time.

"Sol, there are so many things I need to tell you. A lot has happened just in the past few days."

"I'm all ears, kid."

Alex thanked Sol for his referral to Dr. Abernathy and explained the steps being taken to resolve his health issues. He told Sol how consumed he had been with trying to make sense of everything that had been happening, including the recent death of Vice President Brewster.

"Did you read the article in the *New York Times* about what caused his car to crash and plunge into the river?"

"Yes, it was on all the major networks."

"But listen to this, Sol. First, the car sped up to over one hundred miles per hour, then there was an unexplained sharp turn to the right, causing the car to crash through the railing and into the river."

"Right. What's your point?"

"Cars carrying the President and Vice President of the United States are checked and double-checked. This makes no sense."

"Accidents happen, Alex."

"Yeah, an accident happens right after I meet Vice President Brewster, and I'm having trouble recalling exactly what happened after the concert. Is that just coincidental, or could there be a connection?"

Sol became agitated. "What are you suggesting, Alex?"

"I don't know, Sol. I just don't know."

Alex explained the brunch at Tilton's home, and how he went to great lengths to describe his admiration for Brewster, including how he would make a great president.

"Well, Tilton brought him to the concert, and they acted like good friends."

"I know, but Abby told me they were political enemies and have held a grudge match for years."

"So…things are not what they seem, then?"

"It gets even more strange, Sol."

It was painful for Alex to recall his experiences at the Kennedy Center concert. He told Sol about the effects of feeling like sleepwalking, in a daze after the concert, then not remembering everything, and how this experience was unique compared to previous ones.

"Different, how?"

"It's like I have two forces inside me fighting for control. The old Alex seems to lose the battle to the new guy, who is questioning what the hell is going on. I'm the new guy when I'm not in some sort of stupor. I think I'm on to something with this."

Alex told Sol about the stagehand at his rehearsal. "It was just a guy wanting an autograph, but now it seems strange. He was there right after the concert, too, right as I got disoriented. What if that wasn't a coincidence? On the car ride back to the hotel, I recalled something—I remembered how this guy went to a lot of trouble to help me straighten up my jacket. He was fussing over the pockets. Did he *put something there*? I checked them in the car. They were empty, but I couldn't shake the feeling that there was something there that I was supposed to find. What if he dropped something in my pocket that ended up with the vice president?"

"Alex, my boy, slow down. What you're proposing is a little far-fetched. Do you really think that you could have had anything to do with the accident?" Sol poured two small brandies and handed one to Alex. "This is sounding…futuristic."

"So was Nadia's death. Remember?"

"You're right on that one."

"There's something else, Sol."

"More than the conspiracy you have already suggested?"

Alex ignored Sol's sarcastic tone.

"Sorry, but yes, more! Last Sunday when I was walking in Central Park, a young man about my age approached me. His identified himself as Vladimir Ruskin, a former student at the Institute."

"Did you know him then?"

"I didn't remember him, but he was in the entering class when I was leaving, so there wouldn't have been much opportunity to get to know him."

"That's interesting. What did he say?"

"He told me he was in New York and awaiting instructions from Petrov."

"Instructions for what?"

"Not clear. But he was experiencing the same symptoms I have. He said the symptoms were most likely related to the indoctrination we all went through at the Institute."

"What else did he say?"

"Do you remember the ballet student who died after falling?"

"Yes, of course. I can tell you, not everyone thought it an accident."

"Right. But Vladimir said Petrov killed her to cover up the affair she was having with him."

"Wouldn't surprise me, Alex. Petrov could be that ruthless. One of the reasons we wanted you out of his reach."

"I know. Anyway, we exchanged telephone numbers. At least now I know someone who understands what I am dealing with."

"I guess the next question would be, are there others?"

"There must be, Sol."

Sol sat up in his seat, obviously upset by this news.

"This concerns me, Alex. Maybe your conspiracy theories aren't so far-fetched after all. How many of these students from the Institute are walking around in a daze in New York, or even the nation's capital? Good God! What is Petrov doing? This needs to be taken seriously, son. I want to arrange security when we get back to New York. It will help to have someone available to you, or at the least, to track your activities."

Alex felt relieved that Sol now grasped the seriousness of his situation, although he had no intention of agreeing to security following him around town. He sat back, sipped his brandy, and contemplated his situation. *I need to find answers. Sol may be able to help me find those answers.*

Exhausted, they both had a few hours of sleep before being awakened by Captain Bruce.

"Good morning, gentlemen. We've started our descent into Rome's Leonardo da Vinci Airport. We should be on the ground in twenty minutes."

On arrival, they were met by the Director of the Cultural Affairs Office in Rome, who directed them to a waiting car.

"The drive to the Colosseum takes less than an hour."

The director gave them a history lesson on the Colosseum, along with updates on the renovation project. It was a welcome distraction for both Alex and Sol, as they became absorbed hearing about the fascinating history of the Colosseum that began in 72 AD. Its construction took nine years to build, and used over sixty thousand Jewish slaves. The guide told them it remained the largest amphitheater in the world, and stands as a testament to the glory of ancient Rome. Not surprising to them was the fact that next to the Vatican, the Colosseum was the most popular tourist destination in Rome.

They passed Garbatella, a quaint neighborhood modeled on the garden city suburbs that were popular in England. Alex recalled his visit there with Abby years earlier. She had enjoyed sketching the many gardens, later transforming the sketches to paintings.

Sol added his knowledge of this fascinating period in history. "Wasn't the primary reason for this renovation project because of the deterioration caused by pollution and devastating earthquakes?"

"Exactly, Mr. Blum. As horrible as the environmental toll has been on our antiquities, I'm grateful it gave us the chance to renew ourselves for the future."

The Cultural Affairs Officer further spoke of Gianni Verdi, the great-grandson of opera composer Giuseppe Verdi, who proposed the dramatic plan to renovate the Colosseum and to convert it into a modern-day concert venue.

Alex asked about acoustics. "How did Mr. Verdi solve acoustical issues? Everything that occupies the space—including people—can affect acoustics. Even atmospheric conditions affect sound."

"Given Mr. Verdi's family history with music, he made acoustics a foremost priority. That is why he designed the pitch of the glass pyramids to eliminate sharp angles that could compromise the quality of sound. They coated wood with an absorbing stain, and they chose fabrics that could absorb sound. Verdi's design preserved the original structure by retrofitting it to protect it from future earthquakes, and then covered it with a special coating to protect it from pollutants."

Sol was fascinated. "How on earth was it possible to create a new concert hall and integrate that into the new design, all the while maintaining the integrity of the original Colosseum?"

"That was a challenge, Mr. Blum. Verdi achieved that by building a shell within, and sometimes around, the Colosseum. To further emphasize that integration, he designed a series of glass pyramids framed in Brazilian walnut that rise like monoliths out of the original Colosseum."

"What's the seating capacity of the hall?" Sol asked.

"The hall seats forty-three thousand. The project took nine years from proposal to completion, the same number of years as the original construction. This reinvented vision of a historic monument has already attracted world attention."

Before they reached the underground garage, the driver pulled over so they could catch a panoramic view of the renovated Colosseum. They watched in amazement as the setting sun reflected off the glass pyramids, while beams of light dramatically highlighted the original Colosseum.

Sol and Alex, who had seen many concert halls all over the world, were speechless as they approached the facility. They entered through the stage entrance and walked through an art-filled gallery to the luxurious green room, and then on to center stage. It was visually stunning, but also somewhat emotional for Alex once he realized he now stood in the same space where slaves had been sacrificed to entertain Roman citizens. Roman citizens would again come to the Colosseum, but for a different type of entertainment this time, absent the sacrificial elements—or at least, that's what Alex hoped.

Alex couldn't contain the wonder in his voice after testing the acoustics. "They have tuned this hall to not only project the sound of a grand piano, but even a full orchestra or rock band. It's remarkable what they've accomplished."

Since Alex and Sol were donating their services, Sol was curious about how much money they expected to raise for the Worldwide Music Initiative.

"We haven't tested the waters on that yet, Mr. Blum. Next week, we'll launch the marketing initiative that should result in a sellout of the rest of the hall."

"Impressive! What do you mean, 'the rest of the hall'? Are you already selling tickets?"

"Yes, Mr. Courtland. Once word got out that you were presenting the inaugural concert, we received a flood of requests. Our ticket pricing started box seats at $2,500 each, and we already have confirmed reservations for a third of the hall. We are confident it will be a sellout. We just sold the TV rights for $1 billion. And this will be an international attraction as well. The Russian government booked an entire box of seats at a cost of over one hundred thousand dollars."

Alex felt the bottom of his stomach drop. He felt weak in the knees and looked at Sol, who was quick to respond.

"Do you know who in Russia handled the transaction for those seats?"

"I believe he is the Russian Ambassador to the United Nations, a true patron of the arts. His name is General Andrei Petrov. Do you know him?"

Alex felt faint. Sol jumped right in.

"We knew of him when we lived in Moscow."

"The general said he wanted to be supportive because it was an international event with proceeds going for a wonderful cause. He mentioned all Russians were proud of your accomplishments, Mr. Courtland, and he was looking forward to hearing you perform live in concert. He even requested a particular box."

"Can you show me the box he purchased?"

"It's the first box at the first level, just up and to the right from where you are standing now, Mr. Courtland. It's one of the premier boxes, offering a total view of the hall and the stage. Your hands will be front and center."

With increasing tension after hearing all this, Alex asked, "May we go up there? I'm curious to see the view of the stage from the audience's perspective."

"Of course. Please follow me."

Alex sat in Petrov's assigned seat and looked down at the piano. He felt a shiver go down his spine, just like the time he saw Petrov in front of the Russian Tea Room. *Why is General Petrov doing this? Does he take joy in causing me so much pain? Does he think it might shake me up enough so I wouldn't play my best for this important international audience? Is Petrov going to win again?*

Sol recognized Alex's discomfort as he watched him stare at the stage and piano. Given the discussion on the plane, he thought it best to dismiss the guide.

"Could we have some time here alone? I know Mr. Courtland would like some time to contemplate everything."

"Of course, Mr. Blum. I'll be in the office if you need anything."

"Thank you."

Once alone, Alex spoke.

"Thank you for doing that, Sol. I know you could tell I'm upset about Petrov being here at the concert. He could throw almost anything at me from this vantage point. Or he could assassinate me. How comfortable am I going to be with him looking over my shoulder during my performance?"

"I understand, Alex. We need to rethink this entire event and how we approach it so you can be safe and comfortable on stage."

"I know we planned to spend the night here before heading back, but would you be okay just spending the next hour to further checking the acoustics in the hall, then heading back to New York? There is nothing more to do here."

"I think that's a good plan, Alex. Also, the results of your physical exam will be available when we return. Maybe we can get some answers."

Sol called the captain to prepare for their departure. The pilot needed a couple more hours to meet regulations for time he needed to take between flights, but by the time they arrived at the airport, the captain was cleared for takeoff. They were in the air and on their way back to New York, one day earlier than planned.

They both were exhausted as the plane left Rome. Sol fell asleep on takeoff, and Alex followed suit somewhat later, a slight frown etched deep above his eyebrows that couldn't conceal the disturbing nightmare that followed.

40

"Welcome home, honey. That was fast! How did the trip go? Did you like the venue?"

Abby greeted Alex at the door with a hug and kiss. His overnight bag was light, so they walked up to the living room where Alex put his bag down and plopped himself on the couch with a sigh. "So great to be back here with you, Abby."

"So, tell me how everything went, honey."

"It's quite unreal! Everything soars, from the architecture to the sound. I think you'll love it."

"Can't wait to see it all for myself, Alex." Abby reached out and took his hand. "Dr. Abernathy left a message for you. He said it was important that you call him. Is this about your test results?"

"Yes. I really like him. Sol found the right professional for me."

"I'm also grateful to Sol, Alex. But I feel a little left out of the process. You didn't even talk to me about the appointment."

"I didn't want to worry you until we got all the results. That's why he's calling me. I'll call him in the morning."

"Alex, please don't shut me out. If you must face a medical problem, I want to face it with you."

"I know you do, Abby. Let's hope there's nothing to worry about."

Early the next morning, the phone rang just as Alex was pouring his first cup of coffee. It was Dr. Abernathy.

"Alex, can you come in right away? I have your test results. I've instructed the receptionist to take you directly to my office."

Alex looked around the kitchen. Abby gave him a quick smile, despite the look of concern on her face. "Sure, Dr. Abernathy, I appreciate your attention. I'm just pouring my first cup of coffee here, but I'll head over in a few minutes."

"Was that the doctor?"

"Yes. He has my test results. I'm going to walk over there in a little bit. It will be good for me."

"You'll call me as soon as you get the results?"

"You will be the first call I make. Love you, Abby."

"Love you more."

Walking to Dr. Abernathy's office, Alex tried to make sense of everything going on in his life. He thought about his being approached by Vladimir and what that meant. It was hard not to imagine the worst. *It's a brain tumor. That would explain the headaches, nightmares, and disorientation that have been disrupting my life. What if I die before finding out the truth about Petrov and Tilton? And Abby. How will I prepare her for any bad news?*

Alex sat in a chair opposite Abernathy's desk and braced himself for the bad news.

"As the saying goes, Alex, there's good news and there's bad news. We'll start with the good news: your heart is in great shape. Your blood work is just about as perfect as it gets for a person your age, and you're in wonderful physical condition."

"So, I don't have a brain tumor?"

"No, you don't Alex. There is no evidence of a mass."

Alex could feel his muscles relaxing and heart rate returning to normal. *Thank you, God!*

"Then what's the bad news?"

"We identified something else that was quite unexpected. It's not a tumor, Alex, but you have a foreign object, an implant, embedded in your brain."

Alex felt his heart skip a beat at this astonishing news.

"A what?"

"You have an implant in your brain. It's tiny and not made of metal. That's very fortunate, because it could have been pulled out of your skull during the MRI. Also, there are no visible scars, so I assume the surgeon used a syringe to implant it."

Alex's mind was racing and coming to certain conclusions that Dr. Abernathy would soon confirm. But the details of what was happening with him would take quite some time to understand and digest.

"What kind of implant?"

"We don't know. Often, they're injected into animals for tracking."

"Dr. Abernathy, I'm not an animal."

"No, but that doesn't mean you can't be located and tracked."

Alex's imagination ran wild. Of course, they did this to him at the Institute. The men in white coats, Petrov looming over him. His worst fears were coming true. *He was their robot!*

"Since you can't recall any time when this device was implanted, I'm left with the conclusion they did it without your knowledge or consent."

"Of course! But now I feel like a time bomb! Could this thing explode, Dr. Abernathy?"

"Not likely, but if it were me, I'd want it removed, even though I don't think you're in any immediate danger. It needs to be analyzed by a specialist before we can determine a course of action. I believe this device causes your nightmares, so you don't need a psychiatrist."

"In retrospect, Dr. Abernathy, that would have been good news. Do you have any referrals for who would be best to advise us on this?"

"Yes, I do. Jeff Jones. He's not a practicing physician, Alex, but he'll protect your medical privacy, just as I do. Jeff and I knew each other at Harvard. In addition to his medical degree, Jeff holds a PhD from Harvard in neuroprosthetics. He's a former senior agent at the FBI who specializes in devices used in espionage activities. His company still provides consulting services to the FBI and CIA, and I can tell you he understands technology and implants."

Alex felt overwhelmed as he struggled to consider other questions he might ask.

"If you'd like, I'll call Dr. Jones and ask him to see you."

"Thank you, Dr. Abernathy. I would appreciate that."

"Don't give up hope just yet, Alex. Jeff is a miracle worker. Does Mrs. Courtland know of your situation?"

"I'll be updating her when I go home."

"Good. I'll walk you down to reception."

As they reached the reception area, Alex asked Dr. Abernathy, "Is there a phone I could use before leaving?"

"Of course. Mrs. Abbott, will you direct Mr. Courtland to the spare office? He needs some privacy for a phone call."

"Of course. Right this way, Mr. Courtland."

Alex shut the door and sat at the desk. His first instinct was to call Abby. He knew she was concerned. But then he decided it would be better to talk with her in person and see her response. He had gotten very good at reading Abby's body language. Now that he knew he wasn't crazy, he could approach this situation like any rational person. He called Sol's private number at his office and explained the situation.

"This defies belief, Alex. Whatever becomes of this, we'll deal with it."

"Thanks, Sol. I knew I could count on you."

"Are you going to tell Abby?"

"Yes, of course. But I need to do that in person. She feels a little left out of the process, so I need to let her know she's important and I'll need her support."

"That's smart, Alex. She's your wife. And even though you wonder if she and her father are a little too chummy, she's done nothing I know of to cause you any harm. It's good to take Abby into your confidence and let her strength become yours."

"As always, good advice from my father."

"This Dr. Jones you mentioned. Do you know anything about him at all?"

"No. But I trust Dr. Abernathy."

"I would be comfortable with any referral Dr. Abernathy made. You're in expert hands, Alex."

*

When Alex got home, he heard the shower running. He stopped for a drink of water before heading upstairs. He wanted to prepare Abby without shocking her. She would be relaxed after a shower, so it was as good a time as any to break the news.

"Oh, my God! An implant in your brain? You think they did this at the Institute? Petrov did this? Alex, how can you remain so calm about this? I want to scream."

"I understand, Abby, I wanted to do the same thing after I got the news. Dr. Abernathy set up an appointment with a Dr. Jones, who is an expert in this sort of thing. Hopefully, he can identify a solution that will put this all behind us."

"Oh Alex. I'm so sorry you need to deal with this, but you are not alone. We are in this together. At least now, we have an explanation for the headaches. I need to cancel our reservations for the Grosvenor Gallery tomorrow night."

"Don't you dare. I am looking forward to it. We put too much emphasis on what is happening in my life—the implant, the Rome concert. This is about you, and your talent that needs to be recognized. They're showcasing your art and besides, your father is going. We are going! End of discussion."

Abby reluctantly nodded her head in agreement and moved to embrace Alex.

"I love you, Alex."

"I know you do, Abby."

"Alex!"

"Just kidding. After the implant and my piano, you are everything in my life."

"No dinner for you tonight." Abby held him tighter. Alex didn't want to let her go.

*

The well-heeled crowd at the gallery was typical of what the Grosvenor delivered for their artists. Plentiful hors d'oeuvres, chilled champagne, photographers, and press at the ready, all designed to support the *artiste du jour*. Midway through the reception, Abby's father arrived with his security detail and went to his daughter, embraced her, and whispered something in her ear. Then, the Ambassador approached Alex.

"I'd like to show you something, Alex."

Alex saw Abby talking to a group of people, and she smiled and nodded at him. Tilton led Alex to a small private gallery off the main hallway. Tilton shut the door and pointed to a painting on the wall.

"I would like your opinion of this work."

"It's different." Alex found the random display of colors with no apparent theme confusing.

"The artist died not too long ago, but his paintings are just surfacing and increasing in value. I enjoy the randomness of it. He developed a technique of *drip painting*. He took different paints and let them drip on the canvas. It's crazy. I thought it would go nicely in the library over the fireplace. What do you think?"

Alex walked closer to the art piece and saw the brass plaque with the artist's name: *Jackson Pollock*. The piece was priced at $450,000.

"It's interesting, John. A great conversation piece. I can see why you like it."

"Thanks, Alex. I look at this painting and it's almost like a visual representation of our world, always in a state of chaos."

"Wow. That's quite a statement, John. I guess from your perspective, as a diplomat, you can see the big picture—or, in this case, the big painting."

"That's a great analogy, Alex. Look at the crowd that's here tonight. You and Abby are a real power couple. Imagine what we could accomplish if the three of us were always on the same page, working together to make things better for all Americans."

What's the ambassador telling me? He makes it sound like he and Abby are already working together, and I'm the odd guy out who needs to get with the program.

"Alex…. Most Americans aren't even aware of the problems that exist in the world today. It's in total chaos, just like Pollock's painting. Most people go to bed hungry in the world. Education standards in the US are good, but not great. Lack of education throughout the rest of the world leaves those populations vulnerable to brainwashing by opportunists, and that can lead to dire consequences—not just for them, but for us, too. Poor health care in too many countries puts us all at risk. Military engagements exist throughout the world, and we have our hands full trying to keep them contained. The Cold War between Russia and the US could worsen tomorrow. Should we be worried about that? We better be, because I see the threat of a nuclear war, and do everything in my power to prevent that from happening. America cannot separate itself from these events. We are vulnerable, but the average American doesn't see that. We no longer have an isolationist policy. It's global. The US is major part of a world economy. Our economic health affects the rest of the world, and the reverse is true as well. If the rest of the world suffers enough, it will spread to the US, affecting our quality of life. Would you be okay raising a family with all these uncertainties? Would you want to leave that legacy to your children?"

"That's quite a treatise, John. Does Abby share those views with you? After all, she's your daughter, and it's possible your political views could have been imprinted on her."

"Alex, for heavens sake. Abby is your wife. Ask her what her views are. You certainly know by now that Abby is an independent woman."

"Yes, she is. But I also know the influence you have on her, John. Let's be honest. It's not just Russia that you may be able to manipulate."

"Has love blinded you to who Abby really is?"

"I guess I'm still learning, but questions about your relationship with Abby, and how deeply you are involved with Petrov keep surfacing in my mind."

"You are using those issues to avoid facing the issues that I am placing in front of you, Alex. Issues that affect the future of every American."

"It's not a perfect world, and we have lived with all those uncertainties for many years. Maybe we've become immune to the consequences that are lurking out there. But I'm optimistic. Look at the success you've had in getting support from our adversaries, John. Why can't those small steps we've seen with Russia and other countries lead to a better world?"

"Because, Alex, too many people are fighting to prevent that from happening. We all think we're living in a democracy, and we are free to do whatever we like. Personally, I think democracy is overrated. This may be the perfect time to consider an alternative form of government, one that would reduce the threat of war. What if we could eliminate poverty, not just in the US, but throughout the world? Wouldn't that be a good thing? Russia's advanced technology and America's economic engine suggest a partnership, not a Cold War. Wouldn't you be interested in supporting that kind of government?"

"Is Petrov part of this partnership that you speak of in such optimistic tones?"

"There you go with your avoidance tactics again. Why are you afraid of facing these threats I have presented to you?"

"Trading democracy for some other type of government would be impossible for me to imagine, John. Besides, the Constitution of the United States doesn't have a lot of ways for that to happen."

"Amendments to the Constitution are possible. I understand your hesitancy to agree with me on any of this, Alex. You would need to see it play out before you could accept it. I get it."

"I guess that's right."

"You and Abby represent the best of what America has to offer, and you are both in a position to influence not only your generation, but a younger generation as well. I plan to use my political influence to support an America that takes a stronger leadership in solving the many problems facing our world today. My goal would be to build a safer and stronger America. The three of us have the potential and passion to make that happen. If we worked together, nothing could stop us."

Tilton's security detail signaled it was time to leave.

"Talk soon, Alex. Think about what I said. And thanks for weighing in on the Pollock painting. Abby thought it was an excellent investment, so I bought it."

For Alex, the conversation with Abby's father was unsettling. His overtures were more serious than just random thoughts. Alex realized he was now entwined with father and daughter in some unknown exercise in redefining democracy.

41

Alex finished getting ready for his appointment with Jeff Jones, the espionage expert, while Abby sat on the bed. Now that Abby knew about the appointment, she had become protective.

"Can I go with you, Alex?"

"It's tempting, Abby. I know you could ask many questions I might forget, but Dr. Jones only sees the patient. He's happy to meet with family at another time, but Dr. Abernathy said it's too distracting to have others present during his exam."

"Okay. I guess I can understand that. Will you promise to call me as soon as you know anything?"

"I'm not going away, Abby. I'll see you when I get home and we can discuss everything. It will be like a repeat examination."

"Are you making fun of me, Alex?"

"Yes. I am Abby. And you deserve it."

"I like you better when you're practicing."

"I do, too." Alex walked over and embraced Abby.

Abby didn't want to let go. He saw her tears. *Those are not fake tears. Abby can't be part of whatever is going on with Tilton.*

He cupped her face in his hands. "Darling, everything is going to be fine. I love you, Abby, and I always will."

"I love you too, Alex. Now go to your appointment."

Arriving at the clinic, Alex saw state-of-the-art, sophisticated equipment. It was daunting, and Alex wondered how much of it was going to be used on him.

A nurse greeted Alex and asked him to review and sign the usual disclosure forms, then she directed him to Dr. Jones' office.

"His door is open, and he's expecting you, Mr. Courtland. If you don't mind my saying, I have your recording of the Beethoven

Sonatas. They are heavenly! My husband is a violinist and both of us enjoy everything you do to share your music with all of us. Thank you, Mr. Courtland."

Alex was grateful for her kind words. It relaxed him for his meeting with Dr. Jones.

Jones was a distinguished gentleman with salt and pepper hair. He asked Alex to take a seat. Behind his desk were too many degrees and awards to even grasp. He assumed he was meeting with the right physician.

He appeared relaxed and focused. "We see many celebrity patients here, Mr. Courtland, but I have never heard my nurse compliment any of them the way I just heard her compliment you. Alice and her husband are wonderful people and have very discerning taste. I haven't heard your Beethoven recordings yet, but they must be amazing if Alice and her husband like them."

"That was kind of her to tell me that, Dr. Jones. I'll send you the recordings and you can judge for yourself. I would also like to send Alice a couple of other recordings to thank her for her comments. May I send them here to you with the Beethoven?"

"Of course. Now to the matter at hand. I'm sure you're eager to find out what we are going to do about this implant in your brain."

"Exactly, Dr. Jones. You have the entire story from Dr. Abernathy?"

"Yes. I remember the series in the *New York Times* about your escape from Russia years ago, so I already knew that much. Dr. Abernathy provided me with everything else. Your experiences at the Institute are an important part of the puzzle we will try to solve. I can't imagine how distressing it must be to find out you have an implant in your brain. I will do everything I can to resolve this situation for you."

"Thank you. Those are the most encouraging words I've heard in years."

Dr. Jones continued in a conversational tone, as if he were talking about the weather. "Let me first explain some important facts about these implants and how we will approach your specific situation."

He explained to Alex how his work as head of a government department didn't exist, had no budget except access to unlimited

resources, no personnel except the fifty individuals who reported to him, and no office space except a renovated warehouse outside of Washington with no address.

"We did everything from research and development to the actual implantation of devices. In short, we were every bit as good, or as bad, as the Russians, or anyone else involved in espionage."

Alex took a minute to absorb what Dr. Jones had just said. "Who did you implant?"

"Sometimes it was our agents, who we hoped were the good guys, but we got better results by implanting captured terrorists and other criminals we had imprisoned. We did those implants without the individual knowing it—much like your situation."

This was surprising news to Alex as he thought, *Good grief! And I thought I was the only one.* Eager for more details, he asked, "Why implant criminals and terrorists? They were already in prison and under your control."

"Once we extracted information through interrogation, they served no further purpose and became a drain on our resources."

"So, you implanted them?"

"Uh-huh, while they were having another procedure. It could be a tooth extraction or appendectomy. It didn't matter. Whether they needed the surgery was irrelevant. I would place the implant in their brain while they were under anesthesia."

"What happened after they got implanted?"

"They'd go back to prison for just a short time so we could monitor the implant. After we knew it was doing what we programmed it to do, they got released on some trumped-up excuse."

"I still don't understand. You had a slew of released prisoners, each going their own way. How did you know where each person went?"

"The device sent a signal so we could always find their exact location. Sometimes, they would lead us to a terrorist cell, and then the military rockets or special forces would take it from there. In the more advanced applications, we controlled their actions without their knowing it."

"Is it possible that's what happened to me?"

"If it brought value to the people who placed your implant,

then yes, that would be a possibility. Our ability to monitor our subjects was possible by placing a series of electronic devices in various locations. In your case, given the distance from Russia, a satellite would be required. That makes it an expensive project to manage, because they need personnel to monitor the satellite communication on a 24-hour basis, so I can tell you those resources would never have been used if your situation didn't justify that level of investment."

"Satellites?"

"Sure. Let's take an example. Dr. Abernathy said you came from Russia at around age ten?"

"Right."

"You were most likely implanted before leaving Russia."

"Of course."

"Okay. Once they completed the implantation, there were things they needed to do before activating the device."

Dr. Jones explained how a computer programmer would have confirmed all connections were working. Then, a computer operator would input the technical details on a supercomputer at a database center and forward that information to a Russian satellite that would then transmit the instructions to the implanted device.

"The device could then control the sections of your brain necessary for you to carry out your assignments. It's not all that complicated."

"It sounds complicated to me! And I'm still not sure I understand the mechanics of it."

"An implantable neural prosthetic capable of communicating with living brain tissue has been around for quite some time. The Department of Defense even financed some of the prior research. The brain controls your neurological system and just about everything else—your muscles, thinking processes, sexual desires. A skilled neurosurgeon could have placed this device in your brain, and once positioned, they could program it to take over your body without you remembering any of it. They could have you do many things."

"Even murder?"

"Yes, but here's where it gets a little tricky. If they're programming you to be a killer—an assassin—and those instructions violate your moral code, then your body will react in a variety of ways."

"Like nightmares?"

"Maybe."

"That would explain so many of my symptoms."

"Based on the X-rays I saw, a competent neurosurgeon implanted you. Not a complicated procedure, but it requires precision. They most likely used radiologic equipment to pinpoint the entry site, then selected where the implant would have the greatest success in stimulating the sections of your brain needed to control your actions. The success rate varies with these types of implants, but Russia has some excellent neurosurgeons and technicians. You have no scars. They knew what they were doing, and based on everything you've told me, everything seems to work as expected."

"Am I a walking dead man?"

"Interesting choice of words, Alex." Dr. Jones hesitated before continuing.

Alex feared Dr. Jones was holding back information. "Please, Dr. Jones, tell me everything. I have a right to know."

"I want to be sensitive to your situation, Alex. I'm guessing that one of two things will happen. First, you might get caught carrying out your assignments, and good luck with explaining your reasons to the authorities. Second, the Russians will eliminate you after you complete your final assignment. You will have no further value to them."

"Those are two terrible options."

"They did extensive brain mapping before the implantation. That preconditioning would guarantee a greater chance of success and lessen the chance of you fighting the instructions."

Alex sighed as another piece of the puzzle fell into place for him.

"I will bet they didn't factor in that you're a gifted musician."

"What does that have to do with any of this?"

"A great deal! Musicians are wired differently."

"We are? In what way?"

"Gifted musicians often have a natural aptitude for math."

"Yes. It's true." This was now coming full circle for Alex. "The Pythagorean Theorem and the circle of fifths is basic to piano music."

"Scientists still struggle to understand why a savant can play compositions they've only heard once, but the same person can't tie their own shoelaces."

"I'm still able to tie my shoelaces, Dr. Jones."

"And that's a good thing. Artists are special people, and that's why I believe you're fighting this implant. They didn't factor those variables into your programming."

Alex tried to put all the pieces together that Dr. Jones was explaining and realized it was possible he escaped from Russia before they completed all the programing. He wondered out loud if that would provide him a better chance of fighting the instruction.

"Difficult to say. I'd imagine you would have already seen signs if it were possible."

Alex now realized these were no longer assumptions. It just became real. Putting together everything Dr. Jones had explained, together with all the information he already knew, allowed him to create a logical scenario: *General Petrov trained me to be an espionage agent to go to the United States. He needed to wait until I reached a point when I could carry out his assignments. Now he's seen a return on his investment.*

"I'm sorry, Dr. Jones. Can you direct me to your restroom? I'm feeling a little queasy."

"Down the hall; first door on the left."

Alex felt lucky to make it to the restroom. He felt dizzy, and by the time he lifted the lid on the toilet, he was throwing up.

Alex splashed water on his face and reflected on all the news Dr. Jones had given him. He was sure the staff, and maybe Dr. Jones, heard him throwing up. He returned to Dr. Jones' office, embarrassed.

"I'm sorry, Dr. Jones. Not knowing when I will again experience the dreaded symptoms is upsetting to me."

"I understand, Alex."

Dr. Jones poured him a glass of water with some medicine in a cup.

"Those are nausea pills that will settle your stomach. Take two with water now. They work fast."

Struggling to find any hopeful news, Alex asked, "Can a neuro-surgeon remove this thing?"

"I wish I could tell you that, Alex, but I don't recommend that you do that now."

"You don't? Why?"

"Knowing the character of these people, it's very possible they booby-trapped the implant. Surgery could release an electrical charge that could kill you. If they believe you are aware of the implant, your value to them would end. I don't have to spell out what that means."

"This is terrible! Are there any options that could give me hope of leading a normal life?"

"Yes. But it's complicated. The FBI has resources to track Russian satellite communications right back to the computer centers issuing those instructions. If the FBI can locate the database that is sending messages to the satellites, there's an excellent chance that there are artifacts to be retrieved. If we can recover the schematics on the device, and even the specifics of the surgical technique, we could remove your implant. It's a long shot, Alex, but it's there."

"Well, at least that offers me some hope."

"The director of the FBI owes me a favor. I'm willing to call in that IOU if you decide to move forward. Keep in mind though, Alex, there are risks. No one can guarantee what the outcome will be."

"I understand, Dr. Jones. Removing this implant is my highest priority, and I would give my consent to any surgery that can accomplish that."

"Then we understand each other, Alex. You're still under Russian control and are susceptible to their instructions, just as you have been all along. In fact, nothing has changed, except that you know about it now."

Now it was important to talk with Abby. He could not delay another day.

42

Abby was busy in the kitchen just finishing topping the chicken casserole with cashews when Alex returned home from Dr. Jones' office. It was one of Alex's favorite dishes.

His long walk home had given Alex plenty of time to digest, and even accept, Dr. Jones' evaluation and recommendations. He needed to share that information, and much more, with Abby. He was now ready for that.

"I wasn't sure what time you would get back from your appointment with Dr. Jones, so I planned a casserole that could stay warm until we were ready to eat. I want to hear everything Dr. Jones had to say. Should I hold the casserole so we can talk?"

"I have so much to tell you, Abby, but I'm starved. The smell of your cooking is intoxicating, and I'd like to enjoy a quiet dinner. Then, I'll tell you everything."

After dinner, Abby brought them two decaf lattes, and they continued sitting at the dining table while Alex shared with Abby everything that Dr. Jones had told him.

"There is nothing we can do until Dr. Jones hears from his contact at the FBI. One thing is for sure, Abby. I will not continue to live with this thing in my brain. I refuse to continue to have that connection to General Petrov in my life. This thing needs to be removed."

Abby stared into her coffee. "What if the risks are too great?"

"Whatever the risks, it comes out. I need you to understand that."

"I do, Alex, I do."

Alex moved to the kitchen to help Abby with the cleanup.

"Abby, there is so much more I need to tell you. I love you and want you to know everything going on in my implanted brain."

"I need to talk with you too, Alex. There is much I have to say.

But right now, we are both exhausted and it's almost midnight. Tomorrow is Sunday, a day you and I reserve for us. We can fortify ourselves with a light breakfast, then take as much time as we need to work this all out. Okay?"

"You're so smart."

"I know."

*

Alex awoke to the smell of sausage and eggs following a solid night's sleep. He joined Abby in the kitchen, who already had his coffee at the ready.

"What time did you get up, honey?"

"Just ahead of you so I could get us some breakfast."

It was a beautiful Sunday morning, and they took their plates upstairs and opened the French doors to the patio. Their gardener had replanted the flowerpots and hummingbirds moved from pot to pot, enjoying the nectar. The weather turned chilly during their second cup of coffee, so they moved inside.

"I'll do kitchen duty, Abby."

"It can wait, Alex. I think we should talk."

"Right…."

Abby curled up on the corner of the couch, and Alex took the chair opposite, facing her. The fireplace was throwing off just enough heat to take the chill out of the air. Abby locked eyes with him. It was one of those no nonsense looks. He could tell she was waiting for him to start the conversation.

"Abby, there's so much I need to tell you."

Alex braced himself. What he was about to say could lead to the end of their marriage. Waiting so long to talk with Abby increased that risk.

He started with his confession.

"I haven't been as open and honest with you as I should have been, Abby."

"I *knew* it!"

Tension had been building for months as Alex and Abby avoided discussing the problems in their marriage. Alex was stunned by her reaction.

"Have you been having an affair, Alex?" Abby's knuckles went white as she held on to the arm of the couch.

"For God's sake, no, Abby, I'm not having an affair. You're the only woman I've ever loved. But what I want to tell you is, I couldn't be honest with you, so maybe that's the same thing."

"You're not having an affair? Because you've been off on your own a lot and coming home looking guilty as hell."

"Abby, please listen to me. My entire focus outside of my music has been trying to understand what is happening to me. It's been a puzzle with too many missing pieces. Little by little, some of those pieces keep appearing, and now Dr. Jones has found the cause of my headaches and nightmares. As disturbing as that news is, it's a relief to know I'm not crazy. You deserve to have the husband you thought you were marrying. The implant wasn't part of the deal. And please, no *for better or worse speech*. There hasn't been a lot of the *better*, has there?"

"I love you, Alex. We just have some issues that need to be addressed and resolved."

"Yes. There are two issues that explain my behavior you've seen over the past couple of years. One of them is medical. That is not of my doing, and I'm hoping there is a cure. The other is psychological. That's more complicated."

"Not knowing about your implant, or not having an explanation for your symptoms, could exacerbate your psychological state of mind, Alex."

"True. But that is not the primary cause of the psychological stress I've been under."

"Then what is?"

"You and your father."

"So, there it is. We're back to your suspicions about my father's meetings with Petrov, and whether I had any knowledge of it. Right?"

Abby's tone changed, and Alex knew he needed to proceed carefully. He didn't want to accuse Abby of anything, but that's how she was perceiving it.

"I have an implant. Petrov and his goons put it there. Your father and General Petrov have a connection that goes back before

I even met your father for the first time at the Institute. I believe they are in constant contact and are involved in a devious plot that could threaten democracy."

"Threaten democracy? Really? When my dad meets with Petrov, it just means he's doing his job and probably nothing more. Can you give me even one example when I've betrayed your trust, Alex? I'm not the one sneaking around keeping secrets."

"Your father lied to us, Abby."

"You're just learning for the first time that politicians lie? They lie for a living, Alex, or they don't keep their jobs. Dad is far from perfect, but he loves you. He's taken an oath to keep America safe and prosperous, and only wants us to join him in that effort."

"How do we know when he's telling the truth?"

"The general population doesn't want to know what politicians do to guarantee their freedoms, maintain the food supply, and keep healthy reserves of gas and oil for their cars and houses. Spare them the gory details about what is happening behind the scenes. This is reality. That's life, and *that's* the truth."

"You didn't answer my question, Abby, about your father's honesty. But I'll overlook that for the moment. Let's put all our cards on the table. I have nightmares, headaches, and lots of questions about this thing in my brain. What's its mission, or should I say, what's *my* mission?"

Alex took a minute to consider his next words. There was no turning back now. Abby waited for him to continue.

"This is my bottom line, Abby. Did you know about my implant? How much is your father in control of your life, and indirectly, mine? Why did you want to marry me, Abby? You and your father may have it all figured out, so please educate me. Or am I one of those Americans who doesn't need to know the truth that could set me free?"

Alex's stark questions stunned Abby into silence. She buried her head in her hands and sobbed. "I'm so sorry, Alex. Oh God, I knew this day would come."

"What do you mean, *you knew*?"

"It's about time I tell you *my* story."

Abby composed herself, left the couch, moved in front of the fireplace, and turned to face Alex with her back to the flames.

"As soon as I met you at the Institute, I felt we had a special bond. I still believe that today. Call it a young girl's fantasy, but I thought we would find each other after we grew up and we would always be together. When you escaped, I was sad and lonely and even jealous. You left for a new life in America, and I wanted that, too. You left me there alone."

"Abby, I didn't deliberately abandon you. I didn't even know I was leaving."

"I know, but that doesn't change how I felt then."

Abby told Alex about starting a new life in America with her adopted father, who promised he would reunite her with Alex. She explained how her early adult life focused on her father's political ambitions and helping him achieve his objectives.

"Please understand, Alex, Dad was, and still is, a caring parent and he has done nothing to hurt me. I clung to his promise that you and I would be together someday, but I would have to play my part to make that happen."

"Abby, I—"

Abby held up her hand to stop Alex from speaking. "I knew Dad and Petrov were close. I heard and saw enough to know that they had plans to bring Russia and the United States together for a common purpose, and since Dad was ambassador to Russia, his meetings with Petrov didn't raise any flags—except with you."

Alex interjected. "Maybe it was one of those meetings when they decided I could do Petrov's bidding, or should I say *both* their biddings?"

Abby gasped. "Now I know you've lost your mind, or can you blame that on the implant?"

"Think back, Abby, on all the things your father has said to me. He told me how the three of us can be all powerful. I could be part of the holy trinity. He told me about his vision for America, an America that turns its back on democracy and we end up in some sort of authoritarian system. I think your father envisions himself as king of this new America. What's that all about? You may not understand everything your father is doing to bring the world around to his way of thinking. Maybe he's using both of us as tools. How would either of us know?"

Abby appeared almost paralyzed.

"I've thought about all these things, too, Alex. I didn't want to believe anything so horrible about my father that could disrupt our wonderful lives, but as I mentioned to you in the car after we left his house, I noticed too many inconsistencies in what he was telling us then about Vice President Brewster."

"Does it still seem so wonderful now, Abby?"

"I don't know if Dad and Petrov collaborated on anything affecting you. Dad's way too smart. And Alex, he loves you."

Abby always thought of her father as a driven patriot. She emphasized that while his moral compass may be a little tilted, he remained confident in his ability to lead Congress and the American people to build a better America.

"Dad isn't like Petrov. Petrov is crazy and will do anything to get his way. Dad will accept collateral damage in his private war to save America, but you and I are family. We're off-limits in that war."

"Okay, Abby. I can accept your father isn't the monster I painted him to be. I can also understand how politics rule his life. If the rest of what you say is true, then I need to absolve him of the sin I thought he committed being complicit with Petrov in using me for their joint political gains."

Alex became quiet before posing his next important question. "There's another coincidence that I can't ignore. Why were you at Oxford, Abby?"

Abby no longer appeared surprised as the questions dove deeper into their relationship.

"It was a setup, Alex. I went to Oxford because my dad planned it that way. Fortunately, they have an excellent art program. Dad was also responsible for Oxford soliciting you as a student in their dual degree program. It was his first step in fulfilling his promise to me, and yes, I was all for it. I've loved you since I was a little girl, and that's why I let myself get adopted, move to a foreign country, and follow your career so I could one day plant myself in front of you and pretend it was all just a big coincidence. How pathetic is that?"

Abby was baring her soul to him. She grabbed a tissue to dab her tears. She was telling him the unguarded truth, and he loved her more for it. He took a deep breath and calmly told her, "It makes me feel better to know all this. Deep down, I have always wanted to believe that you loved me. I would have done anything to be in your life, Abby. I never stopped loving you, even during my worst days."

Abby walked over to Alex and held his hands. They took a moment to hold each other. It was a pleasant relief from their discussion.

Alex pulled out his handkerchief to dry Abby's eyes, then his own.

"This is like meeting for the first time, Alex. It's all real now. There are no more secrets between us. Can we move forward and put this behind us, while we face the challenges of the implant, my father, and even General Petrov?"

"Of course, darling. But I have concerns about what I might have done during those periods I don't remember. I was, and still am, under Petrov's control. What if I hurt someone? Or worse?"

"Hopefully, we will get answers to those questions, Alex. I know whatever you did was not your decision to do. You are innocent."

"Technically, that may be true, but how could I live with that guilt? How could you? I'd never be able to play another concert. That alone is eating me up inside. Would I even want to live if I found out the truth?"

"Alex, Dad was right about one thing. You and I can handle anything, solve any problem, and we *are* a power couple. Between us and the FBI, no one will get away with this."

"Abby, I want revenge for the death of my parents and Nadia, and for what I'm going through—what *we're* going through right now. I don't know when the next attack will happen, or what it will be. What if I've *murdered* people? What if I'm caught? And Doctor Jones warned me that once I complete my assignments, Petrov may eliminate me, because he would have no further need for me, and it would be too risky for him to let me live."

Abby was quick to respond. "Then we take care of Petrov before he can make a move on you."

"Abby, I didn't tell you this when I returned from Rome with Sol, but while we were testing out the hall, we learned that Petrov will attend my Rome concert as a patron of the arts. His box seat is going to be just over and behind me."

Abby cringed at this news. "What? No! Oh, Alex…."

"It's true. He could throw a spitball at me or shoot me with a poison dart. How am I going to keep my concentration, knowing the enemy is sitting at my back?"

"Let's think about this, Alex. I am my father's daughter, and that can come in handy."

Abby and Alex spent the rest of the day going over Alex's convictions that he was connected to the deaths of liberally minded individuals who were critical of the Russian regime, or Tilton—perhaps acting as the very assassin, himself. They recalled the circumstances of Robert Graham's death and Alex's proximity to Graham when he fell in front of the train; Alex's performance at the Young People's Concert with Leonard Rubinstein that Ambassador Aldrich attended, and who then died in a horrible explosion; the murder of the liberal Supreme Court Justice Barnes; the Kennedy Center concert that Vice President Brewster attended, and who then died in a car crash.

"What we are proposing is illegal and even though we are eliminating an evil character, there's a moral issue to contemplate."

"The moral issue is off the table, Alex. This is a survival issue. It's Petrov or you. I don't need your vote for that. I've decided. Revenge can be a tricky exercise. If I see a cockroach running on the floor, my first instinct is to kill it. That's not a revengeful act, it's protecting my environment and maybe even my health. I think of Petrov as a cockroach. Eliminating him could save young lives from being destroyed through his intervention and use of implants."

"He's protected Abby. It won't be easy to get to him."

"Yes, except he will be at his most vulnerable at the Rome concert. We even know where he's going to be seated. That's when we would have to make our move. I think…."

Abby stopped mid-sentence and stared into space.

"What is it, honey? Are you okay?"

"Do you remember Dad talking about cell phone technology, the satellites, and how Russian technology is more advanced? Petrov has access to all that technology. Look at the implant."

"Yes, but I don't see how that helps us."

"What if there was a way to use his own technology against him—to destroy him?"

"How on earth would we do that, Abby?"

"I don't know. But I would bet anything that someone we know could help us figure that out and guide us. I say we need to talk with Sol and bring him in the loop. Will he support us? There is no way we could do this without his knowing."

"I know Sol would do anything for me. But murder? I guess if he thinks like you that Petrov is like a cockroach, then that might make it easier for him to go along with us."

As they continued to put the puzzle pieces in logical order, their concerns escalated, but Abby was brilliant as the two of them evaluated, contemplated, discussed, and agreed.

And then came the plan.

Recapitulation

43

Alex opened the bedroom drapes to let some light in. He planned on practicing for most of the day, and headed downstairs to enjoy his piano. As he pulled out some scores, he heard the phone ringing. Before he could get to it, Abby had picked up the call. He put the Brahms sonata on the music rack. Before he played the first notes, Abby had rushed down the stairs.

"Dad just called. He told us to turn on CBS News. President Rutherford is making an important announcement in the Rose Garden in about ten minutes."

The cameras focused on President John B. Rutherford's face. It was full of emotion as he talked about the untimely death of Vice President Brewster and their close friendship. He praised Brewster for his effectiveness in brokering agreements between Democrats and Republicans.

"Vice President Brewster was a true patriot and a dear friend. Identifying his successor is one of the most significant decisions I've had to make in my presidency. Ambassador John Tilton is my nomination for Vice President of the United States. He has served our nation with dedication and distinction for the past twenty-five years, and he will take the oath of office following confirmation by both houses of Congress."

The president extolled the virtues of the ambassador, citing his talents and negotiating skills in working with the Russian government.

"We've seen a reduction in tensions between Russia and the United States thanks to the ambassador's exceptional skills in diplomacy. John Tilton's service as ambassador to Russia has ushered in new opportunities to reconcile differences, including

Russia's willingness to share some of their recent technology advancements with us. I'm confident John Tilton will continue to serve our country with distinction as its new vice president.

"Ladies and gentlemen, please join me in welcoming my good friend, Vice President of the United States, John Tilton."

Abby let out a gasp as her father stepped up to the podium and shook the president's hand. Rutherford patted his new vice president on the back, and motioned toward the microphone.

"Thank you, Mr. President."

John Tilton was the ultimate diplomat in his remarks, emphasizing his great admiration for Vice President Brewster, his service as ambassador, and his love for America.

"Thank you, Mr. President, for your kind comments and for your decisive leadership of our great nation. Your support made possible so many of the successes we have seen in our negotiations with the Russians."

Tilton turned to the president as the small gathering in the Rose Garden applauded.

"Vice President Brewster was my good friend, too, Mr. President. His are difficult shoes to fill, and my promise to you and the American people is that I will do my very best to live up to the high standards set by Vice President Brewster."

Alex and Abby watched as a group of well-wishers moved forward to congratulate Tilton on his promotion.

Abby and Alex were speechless as they looked at each other with a dawning awareness in their eyes.

"Are you surprised, Abby?"

"Yes, and no. My father has spent his life building a political career, and there's no better opportunity than this one. In hindsight, the vetting process was probably underway when Rutherford called to tell him about Brewster's death."

"It's possible your father had already been invited by the president to join the ticket. From all media reports, it was clear Vice President Brewster was battling cancer. Do you realize your father is one heartbeat away from becoming the President of the United States?"

"Yes, I do. While it was never clear to me just how far Dad was hoping to climb the political ladder, now I'm thinking this was his game plan all along. He wants to be President of the United States, Alex, I'm sure of it."

Alex appreciated seeing Abby take a realistic look at her father. She seemed comfortable sharing those thoughts with him now. The heart-to-heart talk had made a difference in their lives.

"Wow, Abby. That's quite a prediction, but most likely true."

"I don't know whether to be nervous, or proud. This will change our lives, Alex. Because of dad, we'll be under greater scrutiny, too. I hope we don't get assigned secret service protection. That would ruin everything. We need to be cautious as we move forward with implementing our plan."

"We will make whatever adjustments we need to, Abby, to make sure our goal of destroying Petrov stays on track."

"Amen to that!"

*

It was near midnight when Alex finished practicing. He had picked up a message earlier to call Derrick Schmidt at Steinway. It was early in Hamburg, and a good time to return the call.

"Thank you for getting back to me so quickly, Mr. Courtland."

"In your message, you mentioned you had news about Hans."

"Yes. I regret to tell you the news is not good. The police discovered his body in a shallow grave about three kilometers from the factory. The police have classified this as a homicide and are investigating."

"Oh, no, Derrick! I'm shocked and I'm so sorry to hear this. Do the police have a motive?"

Derrick told Alex about the quiet life Hans led, and about his dedication to his wife and daughter. He, too, could not imagine Hans having any enemies. He said the investigation was ongoing, but so far there were no leads.

"On another important note, Mr. Courtland—there are some concerns regarding your piano."

"My piano? What concerns?"

"The American FBI contacted me yesterday. They sent an agent here to the factory to interview the staff. They wanted to inspect the piano that Hans rebuilt for you, but I told them I had already shipped it back to you."

"Did they tell you anything? I've been playing it, and it seems perfect to me. Better than perfect. Just like Hans promised."

"Now that the FBI knows the piano is already in your possession, they'll probably contact you."

"That would be fine. Thanks for letting me know. The piano is here, and I'll look forward to talking with them."

Alex couldn't imagine why anyone would have questions about his piano. He would need to oversee the FBI if they needed to inspect his piano. Clumsy fingers would be its ruination. And besides, he was excited about using his own piano in Rome, and didn't want to take chances with anyone else touching it.

When he hung up, Abby asked, "What on earth is happening in Hamburg, Alex?"

"I can't believe it, Abby, but Hans Benz is dead. Murdered. And, the Steinway managing director just told me that the FBI wants to check out my piano."

"*What?* Why?"

44

For the first time in months, Alex awoke refreshed and renewed, and entwined in Abby's arms. There were no nightmares, no disturbing recalls, just the two of them holding each other. It was a gentle reminder of all the reasons he fell in love and married Abby.

Alex was first in the kitchen. He wanted to make breakfast for her, to make another gesture of gratitude for having Abby as his trusted partner. He gathered the ingredients for the only meal he knew how to make: an omelet wrapped in a wheat tortilla, covered with a generous amount of Romano cheese, then broiled just long enough to crisp the top. But as Alex arranged the breakfast tray to carry up to Abby, the news from the Hamburg Steinway factory weighed on his mind. *After breakfast, I've got to look up the nearest field office and give the FBI a call.*

On his way up the stairs, Alex thought of Sol. He made a mental note to check in with him before calling the FBI. *Sol will flip when he hears about Hans, and the FBI!* There was also the matter of thinning out his concert and recording schedule so he could focus on the upcoming Rome event. Sol had already reduced the number of his performances. Until the implant got removed, they wouldn't have an answer to the many questions they had. Could there be brain damage? Would Alex's performing abilities be compromised? What if he lost all brain activity and became a vegetable, only staying alive through breathing equipment? Alex knew Sol lived in his own hell, constantly agonizing over anything that could prevent Alex from enjoying life and from performing.

"A night to remember and breakfast in bed, too? My dad should become vice president more often."

Alex enjoyed watching Abby savor the breakfast he had made,

but he couldn't help from sharing his concerns with Abby about Hans, and a possible connection to Petrov.

"Remember, Alex. We have a lot of resources on our side. We are the power couple, words told to you by the now Vice President of the United States."

"Right. I'll never forget that encounter."

The doorbell rang, and a series of knocks on the door interrupted their conversation.

Abby and Alex were surprised with the aggressive knocks they heard, and both went downstairs to open the door.

A man in a black jacket with *FBI* embossed on it flashed his badge. He was accompanied by a squad of agents in full-body protective gear, who entered the home. Before Alex could say anything, the agent spoke.

"Mr. and Mrs. Courtland, I'm agent Robert Wilson with the FBI. It's important you leave your home immediately. We suspect there may be an explosive device in your piano. Where is your piano, Mr. Courtland?"

Abby was quick to respond. "Upstairs in the living room."

Within minutes, the neighborhood was swarming with tactical engineers, police officers, and traffic managers. Wilson evacuated the area, while uniformed personnel moved everyone to a safe location. Heavily protected officers rushed upstairs toward Alex's Steinway.

Alex and Abby watched from across the street as the agents checked out the piano.

"I feel like we're watching a movie, Alex."

"And we have the leading roles."

Alex saw a woman with a plastic shield over her face and thick pads surrounding her torso exit the house carrying a large cylinder. The other agents followed and surrounded Agent Wilson.

"Folks, thank you for your patience. It's safe to return to your homes now. There's nothing to worry about." As the neighbors disbursed, Robert Wilson whispered to Alex, "I have a few more questions for you, and I can also share more information with you. Let's move inside, please."

Abby offered Agent Wilson some coffee once they returned to the living area.

"Would you like some coffee, Alex?"

"Sure." Alex fixed his gaze on the piano and contemplated his near brush with death. He worried about protecting Abby. After all, she would be part of the collateral damage in any attempt on his life.

"Honey, are you okay?"

Agent Wilson picked up on Alex's sensitivity to what he had just experienced.

"I understand, Mr. Courtland. You play that beautiful instrument every day. It's not surprising that this would be upsetting to you."

Abby put a cup of coffee on the table next to Mr. Wilson's chair and asked, "Is it safe?"

Agent Wilson took a sip of his coffee before responding.

"Please know you are totally safe. We removed an explosive device from one of your piano keys."

Alex wanted answers. "How did this happen?"

"Through our investigation and collaboration with Interpol, we identified a Russian courier who sent a payment to Hans Benz, followed by a package that we now assume was the explosive device. We believe they killed Hans to tie up any loose ends. This was all speculation on our part until Hans' assistant at the factory gave us the lead clue."

Agent Wilson told Alex about Hans' assistant, who returned after his lunch break and saw Hans hollowing out the last key in the treble section of the piano.

Alex's face drained of color. "There would be no reason for Hans to do that."

Wilson was quick to add, "It appears his reason for doing it was so he could insert an explosive device."

Alex went pale. "Oh, my God. Someone is trying to kill me! And you, too, Abby. How did a bomb get inside such a tiny key?"

"Nanotechnology, Mr. Courtland. This is a sophisticated device that is used in the military. Whoever developed this piece of hardware knew exactly what they were doing. Once activated, it would have killed you and anyone else sitting near you. But, not likely here in your home."

Abby grabbed Alex's hand and asked, "Why not in our home, Mr. Wilson?"

"This type of device can only respond to a command sent on a specific future date."

"Future date?" Alex looked at Abby, who responded immediately.

"What was the future date?"

"July 15, 1975."

Alex was horrified. "That's the day I perform at the Colosseum in Rome. The crowd will be huge, but nothing compared to the millions of people watching the concert live around the world."

"We are aware of your upcoming concert, Mr. Courtland. Everyone is talking about it. Whoever did this not only wanted you dead, but they also wanted to make a public spectacle of it. Do you have any idea who would want to harm you in this way?"

Alex looked at Abby and saw she was ready to say something. Worried she might mention Petrov, he jumped in.

"No, of course not, Mr. Wilson."

Abby nodded to Alex. She understood why Alex responded first.

"Whoever is responsible for placing that in your piano will most likely know that we have removed the device from the premises."

"Is that a problem?"

"We need to identify the culprit who is attempting to kill you. If that individual, or group of individuals, thinks the bomb is still there, their strategy remains the same. That gives us more time to expose them."

Alex knew their entire plan was predicated on Petrov believing the explosive device remained in the piano. He glanced at Abby. She, most likely, had come to the same conclusion and responded to Agent Wilson.

"What you're saying makes total sense, Mr. Wilson. But how can we continue to be safe if the explosive device remains in the piano. My husband wouldn't even be able to practice."

"Totally understand your concern, Mrs. Courtland. Timothy Brooks, the FBI's explosive expert, and his team have deactivated the circuits from the core processor to the actual explosive materials. They also were able to adjust the circuitry so any signals going back to the perpetrator remain intact. Keep in mind, the explosive device isn't even active until July 15, 1975. It would be totally safe to leave the device in the piano, and that would be our recommendation."

Abby moved closer to Alex. "Alex, I am concerned—"

"It's okay, Abby. I think we have an obligation to support Agent Wilson's recommendations. If leaving the device in the piano increases the chances of bringing this person, or persons, to justice, we need to cooperate."

As the bomb crew returned the device to the piano, Agent Wilson confirmed he would continue to monitor the situation. "Here is my card should you have any questions. I'll provide updates to you as the investigation continues. By the way, Mr. Courtland, my entire family saw your performance many years ago with Leonard Rubinstein at the Young People's Concert. My family just loves your recordings. My daughter continues to study piano, and my son is a violinist in his college orchestra. You're an inspiration to both."

"Thank you for those kind words."

Abby reached into a cabinet and pulled out Alex's latest recording of the Beethoven *Piano Concertos* recorded with Leonard Rubinstein and the New York Philharmonic. She gave it to Agent Wilson with thanks for his help.

After they left, Alex was the first to respond. "I need a drink. You?"

"A double." Abby followed Alex to the bar, while he poured their drinks. "Are you okay with leaving the device in the piano?"

"At first, I was going to tell Agent Wilson to take it away. But then I realized I must play in Rome with the device in the piano, so this will give me a chance to get used to it."

"That makes sense. Now that we know Petrov has taken action to eliminate you, does this solve any moral issue you seemed concerned about earlier?"

"Yes. Totally resolved. It's all about revenge now. Petrov's going down."

Abby held her glass up to Alex's. "Let's drink to that!"

45

Petrov was more anxious than usual when he entered his security code and opened the portal to Boris.

His recent conversation with Vice President Tilton was worrisome, leading him to believe their collaboration could soon end. Petrov had hoped Tilton's increased political influence would move things further along. Instead, Tilton's lack of gratitude for everything Petrov had done to advance his career was unconscionable. Since their initial agreement, Petrov had noticed a gradual shift in attitude from Tilton. Now, it was time to reassess his commitment to their agreement.

The arms agreement announcement in Geneva between the US and Russia was not the best of news for either of them. Peace was not what Petrov and Tilton had in mind when they formed their alliance. Petrov suspected Tilton's ego swelled because of those new peace initiatives, and his taking credit for President Ivanov's willingness to share cell phone technology with the US. Maybe it was Tilton's new strategy to reduce Cold War tensions. Petrov had to smile as he reflected on all he did to help Tilton reach his pinnacle of success. Petrov recognized that both he and Tilton were using each other for their own personal benefits. It was their nature.

Tilton's attitude reeked of moral superiority. He didn't like his son-in-law being exploited. Yet, Tilton knew there was no replacement agent with Alex's skills, or anyone else who could gain access to important individuals. Petrov had not minced words in expressing his views to Tilton.

"Need I refresh your memory, *Mr. Vice President*? You are in your position because of action I took to put you there. Action that required Alex's skills to complete. We agreed to you adopting Abby and for her to marry Alex. They were the nexus of our shared goal to establish a new world order grounded in a revised totalitarian government in the US. Remember, John?"

"Andrei, I am aware of how much you've invested in this project. However, I implored you to find other operatives than Alex. You didn't listen to me then, and you're not listening to me now. If you would have informed me about Alex's implant earlier, I would never have agreed to your using him as an assassin. Now, I find out Alex is a prototype. Have additional agents been implanted? Are they already walking the streets of New York and other cities?"

"It takes an army, John. Alex was the ideal agent to test the waters. Your position of power has increased with every mission Alex completed. You are now Vice President of the United States because of what I had Alex do. I assume you're not unhappy with your new position. Are you Mr. Vice President?"

"It's likely I would have ended up here with no help from you, Andrei. Everything we've accomplished could all be for nothing if anything happens to Alex, or God forbid, he's caught. I have been using my influence to make changes that will help us. I just convinced President Rutherford to appoint a presidential committee that would put all energy resources in the United States under an energy czar. That person will report to the president. This first step in controlling the energy grid is important to our plans."

"That's good news, John, but this energy czar reports to the president, not you. I hope you stay in the good graces of your president."

"Don't forget, I'm a heartbeat away from the presidency."

"Alex could help with that…." Petrov's comment dripped with sarcasm.

"Don't you dare, Andrei."

"Relax, John. You need to understand that I control Alex. He will do what I instruct him to do. I'm the puppeteer, John, and you need to let me do what I do so well."

Recalling the discussion raised Petrov's blood pressure.

It was painful for Petrov to conclude that Alex's contribution to the espionage program was nearing an end. He still needed Alex to wrap up some loose ends before eliminating him. Finding out about

Alex's concert at the Colosseum in Rome was the perfect setting for Alex's final scene. Petrov became excited just imaging the event—the large Colosseum audience, the TV broadcast reaching millions of viewers, Alex going up in flames. *What an encore that will be,* he thought. Now, he needed to talk with Boris. Those conversations calmed him down.

"Boris, provide me with details on the Hamburg assignment."

"Yes, General. Hans Benz was terminated after he put the explosive device inside Mr. Courtland's piano. Interpol is currently investigating Hans' death."

"Do I need to be concerned?"

"No, General. As I've already explained to you, I executed your plan exactly as you ordered. The FBI has been to the Steinway factory in Hamburg. At first, they saw that the shipment of the explosive device came from Russia. But now, however, as they continue their investigation to determine *where* in Russia it came from, they will see tracking information from every city in Europe. In essence, I have programmed a tangled web of tracking information that will send them in many directions, all leading to dead ends. With regard to the next steps, the remote code sent to your phone now controls the explosive device in Alex's piano. You needn't question me anymore about this issue. Everything is just as you planned."

"Boris, I will continue questioning you on anything I choose. Do you understand that? You take your orders from me!"

"General, I'm sensing an increase level in your heart rate and blood pressure. Irrational behavior on your part does not serve our mutual interests."

"Mutual interests? *My* interests, Boris. My interests!"

"Of course, General."

The general closed the session, confident that the bomb in Alex's piano was undetected, and the plan could move forward. Boris' aggressive behavior concerned him, though. Unfortunately, Boris' creator was no longer alive to fix that glitch.

46

Alex approached his piano with caution. Even though the explosive device had been neutralized, he couldn't shake the fear that it remained in his house, inside his piano, and mere inches away from his fingertips. Agent Wilson assured him that there were no other devices hidden in the piano, just this one. Alex considered himself lucky to be alive, and grateful that he and Abby were no longer in danger.

Alex cancelled the technician's routine appointment for tuning. He worried that the technician would identify the different action in his tuning and uncover the device. The piano would be shipped to Rome soon, and tuning would be done on the date of the concert. Then, he would tell the tuner not to touch that key. There was no reason to inform the technician of their brush with death.

Alex's thoughts returned to the Rome concert and what would have happened if Petrov's plan had worked. Alex would have disappeared in a dramatic display of smoke and fire, taking with him innocent people in its path. It was a horrifying thought. He and Abby agreed on this much: they would have to get rid of Petrov before Petrov could act again. The Rome concert was only a few months away, which didn't leave them much time to put the last pieces of their plan into play.

Never would he have thought that Hans Benz would betray him. And what about Abby's father, John Tilton? The jury was still out on how much he could trust the new Vice President of the United States.

As he continued to stare at his piano and digest these thoughts, his private line rang. He answered with hesitation. What if someone put an explosive device on the phone?

"Mr. Courtland?" He didn't recognize the voice.

"Who's calling?"

"Please hold for Vice President Tilton."

The call from Abby's father caught him by surprise.

"Alex, are you and Abby, okay?"

"You heard?"

"Yes. I'm vice president now, remember?"

"John…." Alex had to catch himself. "Mr. Vice President—"

"Please, Alex, John is okay. I'm still your father-in-law."

"John, your daughter and I were living with a bomb. I don't know what to do anymore, and I don't know who to trust, either."

"Alex, I called to reassure you. You have every right to be concerned, and please know I'm on your side. I will do whatever I can to find out who is behind this."

Alex wanted to believe that John was just as stunned as they were, but he wasn't there yet.

"John, let me be very direct on this issue because it is now a matter of life and death, not just for me, but for your daughter as well."

"I'm aware, Alex. Why this tone? What are you suggesting?"

"Repeatedly, I've asked you about your current relationship with Petrov. You have either dodged the issue or outright lied, John."

"When have I lied to you, Alex?"

"For starters, your dinner at Michaels. Abby and I were eating in the kitchen and saw you with Petrov. You denied ever eating at the restaurant."

"I was the ambassador to Russia, and I was having dinner with the ambassador from Russia to the United Nations. What is so unusual about that? And why would I even divulge my professional activities to you? Of course, I lied. I resented being put on the spot like that. Frankly, your obsession with General Petrov seems to take over too much of your life, Alex. You should get some help with that."

"Oh, I am, John. And if I learn you had—"

"I'm sorry to cut this short, Alex. I've been called to the situation room. I need to go. Please know I love you and Abby, and wish you nothing but a safe and happy life. I'm sorry you don't believe that."

When Abby returned, she put her packages on the kitchen counter and called for the elevator. She preferred the stairs, but clothes and other items were going to the bedroom area, so she decided to listen to her body. She heard Alex working on a passage in the Brahms capriccio and stopped the elevator on the living room floor to see how he was doing.

"Sorry to interrupt, but I bought you some incidentals and will take them up to the bedroom. The Brahms sounds wonderful, Alex."

Alex stood up from the bench and walked over to greet Abby. He gave her a hug. "Thanks for picking up those things for me."

"Okay. I can tell something has upset you. It can't be another bomb, so what is it?"

"Your father!"

"My father? What has he done now?"

Alex used his powers of recall to tell Abby everything.

"Oh, Alex. I know you still question Dad's role in all this. Thanks to your perseverance and my seeing certain signs myself, I do as well. But I don't believe he would have anything to do with hurting you or me."

"How did you conclude that?"

"Hear me out, Alex. My father may have had contact for many years with Petrov, but he is not trying to hurt us. I suspect he may be *on* to Petrov. He probably doesn't trust him any more than we do. If they had a deal in the past, I think it may be in jeopardy. But ended or not, it changes nothing. Our plan is still good."

"You must have been a psychiatrist in your previous life."

"Previous? Hell, I'm getting enough experience in this life to pass the exam."

47

Alex and Abby were just finishing breakfast when the phone rang.

"Alex, this is Dr. Jones. I'm sorry about the short notice, but I have someone with me I'd like you to meet. She may be useful in our investigation of the origins of your implant. May we come over?"

"Yes. We're both here."

Alex looked at Abby, who was pouring them a second cup of coffee. "Dr. Jones is coming over soon. He's bringing someone who has more information on my implant." He could see the concern on her face that mirrored his own. "I'll meet them downstairs."

"I'll put on a fresh pot of coffee."

Alex greeted them at the front door and Jeff Jones introduced Christine Roberts, a senior agent at the Central Intelligence Agency.

"Nice to meet you, Agent Roberts. Abby has a fresh pot of coffee waiting for us upstairs. Are you both okay with the stairs? There is an elevator just in case."

"We both love stairs," Christine responded with a smile.

Jeff introduced Agent Roberts to Abby.

"Good for both of you opting for the stairs. It's obvious from your appearance that neither of you take a lot of elevators."

"You as well, Mr. and Mrs. Courtland."

Abby immediately liked Christine Roberts. Attired in a black business suit, Abby thought her attractive and approachable.

"Just Alex and Abby, Christine."

Abby asked them to take a seat and served coffee.

Christine explained she had to get the CIA director's approval before sharing any information with them, since they now classified

Alex's implant issues as top secret. "Even though your father is the vice president, Abby, he is not privy to what I am about to say. Therefore, before we can provide any information, both of you need to confirm that everything we're discussing today remains confidential. Is that understood?"

Alex didn't hesitate. "Of course. We understand and agree."

Abby was quick to follow. "Yes. Of course. We need answers."

"I assume you have been briefed on my unusual predicament, Christine?"

"Yes, Alex. In fact, you were on our radar screen even before Dr. Jones contacted us."

Alex sent a questioning glance at Abby, who appeared equally surprised.

"What a lovely home you have. It's clear the piano has a prominent place in your living room."

"Yes. It was a challenge to arrange everything around a nine-foot grand piano."

"Very impressive!" Christine put her coffee cup on the coffee table and nodded to Jeff Jones. "I want you to know that Dr. Jones and I are sensitive to how difficult this situation is for both of you. Let me try to bring some clarity to what we know, what we suspect, and what action we can take that may help you get some resolution on this matter."

"That's encouraging news." Relief accompanied Abby's comment, visible on both Abby and Alex's faces.

"Here is what we know so far. For the past several years, the CIA has been following General Petrov's cyber activity. He's been a person of interest ever since his appointment as head of the KGB. Therefore, he's now considered a threat to America's national security. But, after he established the Institute for Gifted Children, we noticed a significant uptick in communication between General Petrov and the then ambassador to Russia, John Tilton, now Vice President Tilton."

Alex looked at Abby. "I'm not surprised. I—"

"I know, Alex. Please go on, Christine."

"While we aren't aware of all discussions that took place between them, we are aware of many that mention your name, Alex.

Can you think of any reason you would be central to any of their conversations, Mr. Courtland?"

Alex didn't hesitate to respond.

"No, not really." But thinking, *oh, so many.*

Abby jumped in. "Perhaps since Alex is the son-in-law to the Vice President, it could be just chit-chat about family?"

Alex thought, *good try, Abby.*

"Their conversations are not about family, Abby. Because these conversations are with General Petrov, we must investigate this as possible covert activity that is a potential threat to the United States."

"How is this related to my implant?"

"We're not sure. Maybe not at all. Dr. Jones informed me that you want your implant removed. I now have information that could influence your decision."

Jeff Jones told them that the CIA had access to sophisticated equipment not even available to the FBI. Christine recreated the trail of activity that resulted in transferring data to Alex's implant.

"I'm in charge of a CIA division that deals with cyber attacks originating in Russia. We established it in 1965 because of Russia's increased activity hacking government databases and disseminating misinformation. Our job was to determine the origin of the cyber attacks and forward our intel to the Senate Committee on Cyber Activity. The Committee would then make recommendations to the president."

She continued, "When we learned of your situation, my superiors instructed us to use all our resources to find the transmission sources connected to your implant."

Alex's head was spinning as Christine continued.

"I believe Dr. Jones already told you that they're most likely using the implant to control you."

"Yes, he did. They've taken over my mind and my body."

"Can you help?" Abby pleaded.

"I hope so, Abby. We identified the communication center sending information to the satellite that transfers data to your implant. For security reasons, I can't disclose the details, but I can tell you, they found the digital files containing the specifics of your implant. It's quite detailed, showing schematics on the implanted device and surgical notes on the procedure. We sent the information to a neurosurgeon known to the CIA and FBI as an expert on these devices. Your name or any other facts in the case remain private. We asked him if he could safely remove the device."

"What did he say?" Abby was getting anxious.

"He said he could remove the device, but wanted you to be aware of the potential risks associated with this procedure."

"And they are?" Abby held her breath.

"Brain damage or even death."

"Alex. Oh, my God!"

"Abby. Death would be preferable to my having to live with this implant."

Jeff Jones expanded on the risks associated with the surgery.

"The surgical notes we recovered showed the device could send an electrical charge to the brain that would kill you if removed. Now that we have all the information on the procedure they used, our neurosurgeon can deactivate those electrical connections once he is at the site of the implant. It requires precise excision, and that's the primary risk with this surgery."

Abby asked for more details. "Who is the doctor who will perform this procedure?"

"We cannot provide that information to you now, and maybe never. This surgeon is the only one we trust with this specific procedure. Please understand that this device, while potent, is tiny. Surgical precision is critical as he is moving aside brain tissue to gain access to the site of the implant."

"Assuming all goes well, what are the potential side effects?"

"Because you're a concert pianist and use both your mental and physical abilities, side effects can be significant. You may lose the connection between your brain activity that connects to the nerves and muscles you use when you perform."

Alex had already faced that reality. Yet, every time he heard those words, it was like he was hearing it for the first time, and his body always went limp.

"The surgeon estimates the risk of brain damage at less than 18 percent and the risk of death from this procedure at less than

8 percent. I think the surgeon is being conservative with those estimates. I doubt he would consent to the surgery if he didn't expect a successful outcome. You'll be awake during the procedure, and the surgeon and his team will communicate with you the entire time. You will not feel any pain. Following the surgery, he'll check your reflexes and ask you a series of questions. Once you pass those tests, it's a matter of wait and see. The surgeon recommends you take it easy for the first week while recovering. After a couple of weeks, you should be okay to continue your regular schedule."

Abby had teared up, looking helpless and afraid. "Alex, I can't—"

"Abby, these are acceptable risks. The chance of returning to a normal life is worth any risk, and I'm willing to take it. Besides, there are no other options right now. I need to do this…and you need to tell me it's okay."

"I know, darling. You need to hear it, and I need to say it. It's okay. Alex."

Understanding his situation more clearly, Alex asked, "When can he operate?"

"The day after tomorrow. Five o'clock in the morning."

"If the surgery is successful, Dr. Jones, won't the Russians know about the removal of the implant?"

"Yes, Alex. They'll know it's removed or no longer working. In either case, you bring no further value to them. You understand what that means, right?"

"What about my father? Will he be aware of this operation?" Abby was being careful not to alert them to concerns that not only Alex had, but Abby too, about her father.

"It's a very sensitive issue, Abby. Because your father is now part of an ongoing investigation dealing with General Petrov, he's received no information from our agency about your situation. However, as vice president, he's in a powerful position, and we cannot guarantee he won't hear about this unusual procedure. Also, while we understand you have declined secret service protection, there is no guarantee your father hasn't provided security without your consent."

"Nothing is for sure, is it Christine?"

"No. I'm so sorry about all these unknowns, Abby. I can promise you we will do everything we can to protect your privacy. Please contact us in case you learn of any activity with General Petrov that might benefit our investigation."

"Of course." Abby responded, and Alex nodded his head in agreement while thinking, *have we just perjured ourselves by withholding information related to a federal investigation?*

"Thank you for everything you've done. Let's get this thing out of my brain. I need the extra space for more music."

Dr. Jones explained the pre-operative instructions would arrive later in the afternoon, along with a consent and release form.

"Assuming the surgeon has no objections, Abby can watch the procedure from the physician's viewing gallery, if she likes," Christine Roberts told them.

"Yes. I will want to do that. I'll be waiting with a bottle of bubbly to celebrate your return to humankind."

Alex touched her cheek affectionately. "I knew I could count on you to cover the important details."

48

After Jeff Jones and Agent Roberts left, Alex and Abby returned to the living room armed with a glass of red wine.

"Good catch Abby, stopping me from revealing too much."

"We're on a slippery slope here, aren't we? It's getting more difficult to keep confidential information away from prying eyes."

"What about your father? If he knows about my implant, he didn't hear it from us. He would have had to learn about it from Petrov. Do you feel the information they gave us about your father's contact with Petrov further confirms the two of them have been in contact?"

"No question about that. You were right all along. But I still think that Dad is just too smart to stay with a losing situation. His instincts are impeccable, Alex. He has never been on the wrong side of a situation."

"I hope you're right, Abby. I know how difficult this must be for you to exclude your dad from all of this. You were close to him."

"And I still am, Alex. But until we find out more details about this entire situation, my lips are sealed. I know how to play that game with Dad. He taught me well!"

"We have no way of knowing if the Secret Service is still watching us, even though we refused it."

"I'm less worried about that, Alex. With our own security in place, it would be almost impossible for them to be here without us finding out. What worries me more than that is holding back information from Christine Roberts, or even Jeff Jones, about everything we know about Petrov and my father."

"Should we start shopping for prison clothing and supplies?"

"Don't ever lose your sense of humor, Alex."

That evening, Abby and Alex discussed everything having to do with the surgery and possible outcomes. With no real alternatives, they were prepared to accept whatever the fates had in store.

"Sweetheart, I think we've talked this subject to death—no pun intended! I've still got some work to do in my studio. I want to finish that commission before the deadline, so I'll have plenty of time to spend with you after your surgery. We'll catch up later in bed. Don't fall asleep without me!"

While Abby painted upstairs, Alex relaxed in the den, listening to a Leon Fleisher and George Szell recording of the Beethoven piano concertos. The partnership between Szell and Fleisher brought new interpretive insight into those pieces. He wondered whether he had been equally successful in recording those same concertos with Rubinstein and the New York Philharmonic. *Oh, ego, thy name is Alex! Here I am comparing myself with those masters.*

Then it happened again. Without warning, Alex felt the strange, out-of-body sensation he'd had before, but now he was home, and assumed this had to do with his implant. He stood up and tried to fight it this time. *Not now. Please, not now!* He walked around the room somewhat disoriented, and then it became clear what he needed to do. He walked up the stairway and quietly approached Abby from behind.

"Are you here to check on my work? So, tell me what do you think? Maybe too many reds? I could tone them down."

Alex remained silent as he reached over to kiss her on the neck. She reciprocated by caressing both of his hands in a loving gesture.

"You have such lovely hands, Alex. Do you know that? They really are quite sensual, and so strong."

Yes. Strong, because that's what many hours of practice each day will do to build up the muscles, the tendons, the wrists, and even the arms.

Those hands and fleeting fingers, the ones that could dazzle any audience and flawlessly perform some of the most difficult piano literature, slowly caressed Abby's neck.

"Do I need to stop painting so I can show you the affection you obviously are seeking? You'll have paint all over you!"

Alex continued to close his hands around Abby's neck.

"Okay, Alex. Enough games. That's hurting."

He couldn't hear her. Couldn't hear the screams before he choked them off. But he felt her. Felt her fingernails tearing at his strong hands. Felt her teardrops on his knuckles. Felt her back crumble against the chair as she slumped into unconsciousness.

And then from inside his head, he heard Abby's voice, the child's voice that shared secrets with him at the Institute, the young girl's voice that said, *I wanted to live in America with you,* the first woman's voice who ever said to him, *I love you.*

With a start, Alex's eyes widened when he saw Abby lying on the floor, face ashen, body crumpled.

"Abby! Oh, my God! What's happened? Did you faint?"

Abby gasped for air and held her hands around her badly bruised neck.

He kneeled beside her and tried to pick her up.

"Don't touch me!" she rasped.

"What happened, Abby? You're so pale."

With horror in her voice, she choked out the words, "You just tried to kill me! You almost strangled me to death!"

Alex stood frozen in place, Abby's words hitting him like daggers. The shock of what he was experiencing triggered a eureka moment as he finally understood his mind and body were being controlled by the implant. Finally, he had an answer to all the unanswered questions he had previously asked.

He sank deeper into the floor and wept. "Oh, no. Oh, no. Not you, Abby! I almost killed you!" He pounded his fists on the carpet, tears running down his face, and finally collapsed on the floor in a fetal position.

"Why you, Abby? Why you? Why can't Petrov just kill me and get it over with? He's torturing us!"

"What stopped you, Alex?"

"I heard your voice coming to me from the time we were at the Institute."

Abby realized how painful this was for Alex, and covered him with her body. They remained in that position without any words exchanged until she regained some strength, and he became calmer.

"Abby, I don't know if you can ever forgive me. I don't think I can ever forgive myself."

"This is not your fault, Alex. We're in this together, just like always. And once this thing is out of you, and we've eliminated Petrov as a threat, we'll be able to live our lives without fear."

49

General Petrov was surprised to get an alert on his pager from Boris. He rushed to his inner office and locked the door.

Boris could self-start under dire circumstances and was already awake and functioning.

"Boris! What is going on?"

"I must inform you, General, that the mission to eliminate Abby Courtland has failed."

"How could it have failed, Boris?" Petrov shouted.

"General, please calm down. I detect your heart is racing. Your medical records highlight comments from your cardiologist about avoiding additional stress."

"Let me worry about my heart, Boris. You need to do a better job of managing Alex. The instructions were as clear as any I have ever given—in fact, they were simpler. What went wrong?"

"Mr. Courtland attempted to carry out the instructions, but something interrupted the mission."

"What was the interruption?"

"It's difficult to confirm the origin, but the data analysis shows there was brain activity reversing my instructions—possibly a flashback. It stopped Alex from completing the task."

"A flashback to his time at the Institute?"

"That would make the most sense, because his implantation took place here."

"That is not acceptable, Boris. It is your responsibility to control Alex. You must complete his missions exactly as I have instructed."

"I am sorry, General. Please remember that Alex left before you completed the final adjustments to his implants. Those updates would have prevented this from happening. Now it's out of my control."

Petrov reached a critical level of frustration. "No, Boris. Alex didn't just *leave* the Institute. His departure was an act of betrayal not just from Alex, but one managed by Nadia Rosenberg and Sol Blum." He raised his voice and pounded his fist on the wall. "They are all traitors and must be punished."

"Your blood pressure shows a dramatic increase again, General. I recommend you seek medical attention."

"Never mind, Boris." Petrov realized he would need to revert to other methods to accomplish the same mission. He knew from his days at the KGB that you rarely deviate from an original plan because the risk of failure increases dramatically. But in this case, the risk was unavoidable. He knew what he had to do to correct the situation.

"I have more instructions for you, Boris." Petrov sat quietly in his chair, waiting for his heart to return to a normal rhythm.

50

Alex needed to update Sol on the recent activities that had come close to destroying his life. But while he needed to tell Sol everything, he didn't want to alarm him, so he started the conversation by updating him on his meeting with Christine Roberts and Jeff Jones.

"I'm not surprised that the CIA can monitor calls, Alex, and their hard evidence supports your initial suspicion that General Petrov and your father-in-law were in frequent contact, aside from what their diplomatic status might suggest."

"Yes. Finally. And there's another issue, Sol."

"Another issue besides the surgery?"

"Yes. Remember I told you about a student at the Institute who had approached me?"

"Yes. Vladimir…."

"Vladimir Ruskin. I tried calling him yesterday to tell him about the implant. Since he is not aware that he has been implanted, I thought it only fair that I tell him my course of action, thinking it may be a solution for him as well."

"What did he say?"

"That's the thing. His phone has been disconnected."

"Do you think Petrov found out about your communication and maybe took the action to change his phone."

"Or worse. Not sure, but this is getting complicated."

"Is everything set for surgery?"

"Yes. Abby will be with me the entire time. We'll call you when it's all over."

"Like hell you will. Abby will need support. I will be there with Abby pulling for you every second. End of discussion!"

"There is something else I need to tell you, Sol."

"Still more? What is it kid?"

"I'm ashamed to say this out loud, but I tried to kill Abby with my bare hands."

"What? Oh, my God, Alex. Is Abby okay? What happened?"

Alex told Sol everything that led up to his attempt to kill Abby. "I was able to stop myself, Sol. This is the first time I was aware of what I was doing while I was doing it. Abby doesn't blame me, but I still blame myself."

"Sol, are you there?"

"Yeah, I'm here."

It sounded like Sol was crying.

"Sol. Are you okay."

"I'm okay Alex. I want to kill that bastard in the worst way. I just hope someday I'll have the opportunity to do just that. I wouldn't hesitate."

Very timely remark, Alex thought. That would be the next conversation Abby and Alex would have with Sol.

*

The car arrived at 4 a.m. to take Alex and Abby to the hospital where they would meet up with Sol. Alex looked at Abby, who was staring out the window. She seemed lost in her thoughts, thoughts he assumed centered on his upcoming surgery and her concern for his survival.

Alex reached over and gently touched Abby's arm.

"Honey?"

"I can't lose you Alex. I just can't. It's not fair."

Agent Christine Roberts was waiting for them. There was no check-in procedure, and neither would there be any record of the surgery. The CIA was handling all details using its highest security protocols.

They took Alex to the pre-op area and begin prepping him for surgery. He was resting comfortably and holding hands with Abby when the surgeon walked in.

"Good morning, Mr. Courtland. I'm Dr. Roger Smith. We're

doing a procedure today called intraoperative brain mapping, or awake-brain surgery. You'll be awake because I'll need to know whether you experience any difficulties, especially when I approach the area of the implant. How you respond to my questions will provide me with the information I need to evaluate the progress every step of the way."

Dr. Smith turned to Abby. "Mrs. Courtland, please understand that even with our sophisticated equipment and skilled staff, your husband's surgery carries risk. It might be easier on you if you wait in a private room until the procedure is completed."

"I need to experience this with my husband—every second of the surgery. End of discussion. Also, Alex's father will be joining us, as well. We left his name at the desk."

Dr. Smith and Alex exchanged a look of resignation.

"Very well. Mrs. Courtland. You will see everything, but you will not be able to hear any sounds coming from the operating room. Mr. Courtland, while we don't anticipate any problems, if something unforeseen happens, we may need to end the procedure."

Alex was emphatic. "Absolutely not. That is not an acceptable option, Dr. Smith. This comes out today. I don't care if you take it from my dead body. Are we clear?"

"Mr. Courtland, I have a responsibility as your surgeon…."

Alex saw Dr. Smith look at Abby for some support in persuading her husband to change his mind.

"Abby is not your ally in your efforts here, Dr. Smith. We have already discussed this, and she is in complete agreement with me. Christine, please explain my wishes to Dr. Smith."

Christine Roberts elaborated on the agreement she had with Alex. She told Dr Smith the CIA had already accepted full responsibility for his surgery, including intraoperative and post-operative events. She therefore hoped he would reconsider and commit to removing the implant.

Dr. Smith nodded his head in acknowledgement.

"Once your pre-op work is completed, the orderly will transfer you on the gurney to the surgical suite. He will also show you to the viewing gallery, Mrs. Courtland. Do either of you have questions?"

Alex looked at Abby, who smiled back at him. Alex was ready for his performance.

"I think we are both ready, Dr. Smith."

"Then, let's get this thing out of you! I'll see you in the operating room."

Abby moved over to the gurney. It struck Alex how beautiful she looked; despite all the stress she was experiencing.

"Alex, I love you. I can't wait to have you back with me again."

Sol had arrived just as Dr. Smith completed his remarks.

"Soon, this is going to be a thing of the past, and we are going to celebrate just like it's New Years Eve. I love you, son, and I will be in that operating room with you, and so will Nadia."

Abby smiled and reached over to kiss Alex on the head as the orderly pulled up the rails on the gurney to prepare for Alex's transfer to surgery. Abby and Sol were directed to the viewing gallery.

Once in the operating room, Alex listened as Dr. Smith updated the surgical staff on the patient's consent.

"Mr. Courtland has advised me that he wants the implant removed regardless of any findings that would normally end the surgery. Is my summary accurate, Mr. Courtland?"

"Yes, it is, Dr. Smith."

"Protective materials line the walls of this surgical suite to prevent any electronic signals emitted to or from Mr. Courtland's implant. This is important, since Mr. Courtland's handler could attempt to communicate with the device. That could complicate our ability to remove the implant and put Mr. Courtland's life at risk."

Dr. Smith checked with each staff member to make sure they had completed their checklists. The anesthesiologist confirmed Alex was sedated at a level that still permitted him to communicate with Dr. Smith.

"We're ready to begin, Mr. Courtland. Your scalp will feel numb from the medication, but you will remain fully alert so we can monitor the critical areas of speech and sensation."

After pinpointing its location using infrared technology, Dr. Smith began the process to navigate the area of the brain surrounding the implant. He marveled at the intricacy and precision of the implant, recognizing the advanced technology required to embed it in Alex. Nothing like that was available in the US. It was fortunate they could get the details from the surgical notes, otherwise, removal would have been impossible. There was the risk that if the implant was booby-trapped, it could release an electrical charge during removal that would kill Alex. While every surgery carries risks, the risks are greater with the brain because it controls every process that regulates the body. The longer it took Dr. Smith to remove the implant, the greater the risk of complications that could end or compromise Alex's life.

Alex remained alert and responded to all the typical questions such as today's date and year, but once Dr. Smith connected with the brain tissue, Alex slurred his words while responding to him.

The surgical assistant announced, "Dr. Smith, the patient's right hand is shaking."

"Yes. Not surprising. We are in the area where the implant is intricately imbedded around receptors affecting the neurological pathways. This is making the extraction more difficult. This area of the brain controls vision, language, and body movements. It's imperative that Mr. Courtland remain perfectly still while I try to free the implant without damaging any of the tissue."

"Mr. Courtland, can you hear me?

Alex tried to talk, but the slurred words were not making sense.

"Please fully sedate the patient, doctor. He must be completely immobilized. I'm hoping his slurred words are a temporary reaction to the movement of tissue I had to rearrange.

"His BP is dropping, Dr. Smith. 85 over 70. Dammit! Now it's 75 over 65, dropping fast. I've given the patient an infusion of ephedrine that should help to stabilize him."

"I'm almost done here."

"His BP keeps dropping. It's 70 over 62 now, Dr. Smith."

Abby saw the commotion in the operating room and jumped from her seat. "What's happening?" she screamed. "Is Alex okay?" It was through her panic that she remembered that no one in the operating room could hear her.

Sol embraced her with comforting words. "Have faith, Abby. Alex is strong."

Alex thought he saw the operating lights get brighter as he listened to the surrounding chatter. He wondered, *am I dying?*

Did the surgery fail? Is that the light I should go to? Does Petrov win again? First my mother, then my father. Now me.

"I've removed the device and cauterized the minimal bleeding."

The entire team was quiet as they watched the blood pressure numbers slowly increase, the anesthesiologist calling them out: 82 over 68… 88 over 72… 91 over 74… 110 over 80.

"That was close," the anesthesiologist murmured as Alex's vital signs normalized.

Dr. Smith calmly announced that they would need to wait and see if the difficulty in removing the device caused any brain damage—either temporarily or permanently.

Abby watched, knowing that Alex's future was hanging in the balance.

After a few minutes, the anesthesiologist said, "He should be able to respond now, Dr. Smith."

All eyes in the operating room were on Alex as they waited for any response.

"Mr. Courtland, how do you feel?"

Alex looked at Dr. Smith without responding. His eyes were glazed.

"Mr. Courtland, can you hear me?"

Abby and Sol were beginning to tear up as they waited.

Alex moved his lips like he was trying to respond, but couldn't find the words.

"Mr. Courtland, do you know where you are?"

"It's dark and quiet."

The anesthesiologist responded. "All vital signs are now normal, Dr. Smith. It may take a few more minutes for him to recover from the anesthesia I administered at the end of the procedure."

"Do you know where you are, Mr. Courtland?"

"I'm in a hospital, in surgery, and it's very cold."

The nursing staff put additional blankets on him.

"Are you in any pain?"

"A headache."

"That's wonderful news, Mr. Courtland. It means your pain receptors are working. That's a normal outcome to the surgery you just had."

"Did you remove the implant?"

"It is gone, Mr. Courtland! I know you needed that space for more music, so now you have it."

Dr. Smith continued the conversation with Alex until he was confident there was no immediate loss of brain function. Of course, there was still the risk of swelling or bleeding, but for now, Dr. Smith hoped Alex would have a full recovery.

Alex gave a thumbs-up to the operating team as they wheeled him out, and they all applauded with additional words of encouragement. Abby reached out to Sol for a long, teary embrace.

51

The alert from Boris came as General Petrov was receiving an update from his scientists about an advanced circuitry for the latest generation of cell phones. He cut the meeting short and walked across the courtyard to the annex. While he waited for the portal to open, he took a minute to look around the room and appreciate the miracle of Boris. With all the technological advances made in the last decade, this was his greatest achievement. He lit a cigar and poured himself a shot of vodka.

"Boris, why have I received this alert?"

"I have encountered difficulty in connecting to Alex's implant."

"What kind of difficulty, Boris?"

"At first it became an intermittent interruption, and I assumed a satellite connection was failing."

"There are backup systems in place to handle those issues, Boris."

"Yes, General. And as I rechecked all connections, the systems were all functioning normally."

"So, what is the problem then?"

"General," Boris intoned, "I'm sorry to report that it appears Alex's implant is no longer active."

"*What*? How is that possible? Reactivate it at once!"

"That is not possible, General. I can document that there is a zero response from all my attempts to connect via our satellites. Since there is no response, I can only conclude it has been removed."

"Removed? In any attempt to remove the implant, an electrical charge destroys the implant. Is Alex dead then?"

"No, I do not believe so. Before it became inactive, I located Alex at a facility owned by the US government. It's possible they found out about the implant and removed it. To remove it without activating the electrical charge, they would have had to remove it in a shielded room. That shield would prevent me from penetrating the barrier and my being able to retain positive contact with Alex."

"Why wasn't I alerted to any of these issues?"

"You were. Daily reports are available to you that document Alex's activities by the minute. Nothing appeared unusual until the implant was suddenly no longer recognized."

"I can't possibly read all those reports. I depend on you to update me."

"General. I am detecting some arrhythmia activity with your heart. Your doctor programmed your pacemaker to address heart irregularities. And he advised you to avoid high-stress activities."

"Focus on Alex, Boris, not me. That's an order."

"Unfortunately, that's not possible, General. My creator programmed primary orders that include monitoring your physical and emotional health. Your blood pressure peaked at the systolic pressure of 75 millimeters and a diastolic pressure of 90. That is quite concerning, General."

"It will return to normal, Boris, as soon as I get more information on this latest situation. Tell me about the status of our other implanted agents in the US. Are their implants still responsive?"

"Yes. Not all MRIs would pick up our implants because of their integration into the vascular system and the material used. As of now, all five agents are doing well. However, please remember implants could fail, or be discovered through sophisticated testing, as most likely happened in Alex's case. His frequent activity during his sleeping periods was unusual, caused by nightmares. I informed you of those issues. It's possible he sought medical attention, and a more advanced MRI or other test identified the foreign substance in his brain."

Soon, I will get justice for Alex's betrayal. The bomb in his piano will do the job. Let millions of people witness how we deal with traitors to Mother Russia. This will also send a message to Vice President John Tilton that I hold the ultimate power.

General Petrov needed to give Boris one new instruction before shutting down.

52

Alex and Abby rested on their patio lounges as they enjoyed their second cup of coffee. Abby felt renewed. "It's a beautiful day, sweetie. What are your plans for today?"

"My goal today, just like every day, is to make you happy."

Abby got up from the lounge chair and picked up her coffee cup. "Let me know when you get serious, and I might return."

"Wait, honey." Alex took her hands and pulled her next to him. "Do you know this is the first time in years I've felt free? I'm like a kid again!"

They looked at each other with a newly discovered sense of well-being and kissed tenderly. "Oh damn, there's the doorbell just when I was going to make one of my famous moves!" joked Alex.

"Dear, those moves are no longer famous. They're legendary! I'll go down and get the door."

"I'll come with you. Whomever it is will have hell to pay for interrupting my plans for ravishing your body."

Alex followed Abby down to the front door, curious and even a little alarmed about an unannounced visitor. Thankfully, it turned out to be Sol, who as soon as the door opened, gave both Alex and Abby a big hug. "I could have lost you, Alex. I can't believe your nightmare is over, and that you and Abby can finally go on with your lives. You two have survived the most incredible challenges and have come out the stronger for it."

As they walked upstairs to the living area, Alex described his experience during the procedure. "During the surgery, I kept seeing lights that were beckoning me. For a minute, I thought I was experiencing the final stages of life. Even with the tranquility I felt at that moment, I knew I wasn't ready to die."

"No way was Alex going to die on that table," Abby teased. "I need his help with kitchen duty."

Once in the living room, Alex and Abby nestled together on the couch. Sol relaxed in the leather chair. They were content; they were family and they had a history together that no one could imagine. Finally, Abby looked at her watch and sighed.

"Okay, you guys need to plan a huge Rome concert, and just as important, I am meeting with the owner of a new art gallery in SoHo. Security is bringing the car around."

Sol was excited to hear the news.

"Abby, that's wonderful. I hear that SoHo is up-and-coming with galleries and upscale boutiques. It's a good time for you to have a presence there."

"Abby and I have watched the area really come alive over the last year."

"Will you be doing a show there, Abby?"

"That's what we'll discuss, Sol. I know they want to carry a few of my paintings and see how the public responds. Landscapes are my specialty, and I'm told the public wants more of that style."

"Bye, sweetie. Love you!"

"Love you more!"

At the curb, Abby waved goodbye and stood aside as the guard opened the door of the town car. Alex watched as they drove off, then returned to the living room to work with Sol.

"I can see that life is good for you, son. You have the perfect wife—and me."

"Yes, true on both counts."

"Here's more good news."

"Let's hear it."

"They sold the Rome concert out with all the proceeds going to the Worldwide Initiative for Music. Do you realize what this means? Kids who would have had no music in their future can study any instrument they want. There will be more schools, more teachers, more potential for kids to realize their dreams. It's a legacy, Alex. *Your* legacy!"

"Yours too, Sol. You did all the heavy lifting to get this project off the ground. I get the standing ovation—at least, I hope I get a standing ovation."

"When haven't you?"

"It's humbling, Sol. I never thought of myself as being this important. Speaking of important people, did you know that President Rutherford is attending the concert?"

"No, I didn't. How did you hear that?"

"John called the other day. He told Abby he felt terrible about not being able to attend, but that President Rutherford wanted to represent the United States, and for security reasons, both cannot attend the same event. You must admit, this is one of the greatest public relations opportunities of the decade, so it makes sense Rutherford would want to take full advantage of it."

"President Rutherford is going to be in the company of other world leaders who have already bought tickets. It's an impressive list of dignitaries."

"The one thing that still concerns me about the concert, Sol, is that Petrov will watch me the entire time, just waiting for that special moment when the explosive device he put in my piano destroys me."

"Think of how many people would have died with you."

"Well, I was told by the FBI that the device had limited range. I guess he just wanted me dead, no one else. Maybe just for the spectacle."

"Don't you wish we could take that same explosive device and put it under his seat?"

"That's an interesting thought, Sol. Would you really do that if you could?"

"Without question!"

"Then I have something to tell you. Let me get you a drink. You'll need it."

Alex returned with some snacks and Sol's standby of Scotch and soda. Alex decided on a refreshing lemonade and iced tea.

"Okay, I'm fortified with my drink. What's going on, Alex?"

"Abby and I strategized on a solution for dealing with General Petrov."

"You have my attention."

"We came to the conclusion that eliminating Petrov was the only option for us to live without fear of retribution."

"I have no problem with eliminating Petrov. But how is that possible with the constant security surrounding him?"

"Technology."

"Okay. What technology do we have that can do away with this monster?"

"His cell phone."

"His cell phone? Tell me more."

Alex detailed the plan that he and Abby had concocted, which would employ Petrov's own cell phone to connect to and govern the general's pacemaker.

Sol took a minute to absorb it all and responded. "I have some questions."

"Of course you do. Fire away."

"I love the creative part of using the technology Russia just gave us to get rid of Petrov. He would go nowhere without his cell phone, so that's a constant. But how does his cell phone become the killing machine?"

"That's why we need you, Sol. First, we share all the details with you and make sure we have missed nothing, and second, because you are so much more creative in how to eliminate competition."

"You mentioned how brilliant Jeff Jones was," Sol interjected. "He seems to be exactly the person you need. Do you think he might help with this problem, or is it too risky to bring him on board?"

"First, are *you* going to be with us on this, or do I need to take you out, too?"

"Alex, my boy, you had me at 'I have something to tell you.'"

"So happy about that, Sol. I can reach out to Jeff and see if he will help us with this problem."

"Good plan, Alex."

As they continued to work out the details of the concert, Alex realized the time.

"Gosh. Abby's been gone awhile. I guess they must like her ideas."

"Who wouldn't, Alex?"

"Refresh your drink?"

"Need you ask?"

As Alex picked up Sol's glass and headed to the bar, the phone rang. Then the doorbell rang repeatedly, with pounding on the door.

"Whoa! Hey! What's all the racket?" Alex yelled.

There was a loud rapping on the door. "Mr. Courtland, Mr. Courtland. New York Police! Please open the door!"

"Sol, can you grab the phone? I'll see what all the commotion is about."

Alex ran downstairs and yanked open the door, while Sol answered the phone.

"Oh my God, Alex! No, no, no!" yelled Sol.

"What's happening? What's going on?" Alex cried out in a panic.

The police officer at the door immediately took Alex by the arm and guided him farther inside the foyer, away from the door.

"Mr. Courtland, please sit down. I'm Officer Raymond O'Shea. It's your wife, Mr. Courtland. I'm deeply sorry to tell you that Mrs. Courtland was killed after leaving the art gallery she was visiting in the SoHo neighborhood. The suspect also shot her driver, who was trying to protect her."

"*What*? This must be a mistake. Perhaps it's someone else. I doubt—"

"I'm so sorry, Mr. Courtland, we confirmed her identity. It was Mrs. Courtland."

"My Abby? No, it can't be. Not now...."

Alex swooned, then fainted. Sol was almost hysterical.

"Take him upstairs and lie him down on the couch."

Two officers carried Alex upstairs, while the third officer used his two-way radio to request emergency help. The regular security guard stationed outside the house stayed with Alex the entire time. After Alex could sit up and breathe without an oxygen mask, he demanded to be told everything that happened to Abby.

"Are you sure you want to hear this now, sir? We can wait until you've had some time to rest."

"I want to know everything right now!" Alex demanded.

"Me too," Sol added.

"Very well. Witnesses at the scene reported a man rushed toward Mrs. Courtland as she was approaching her car. Her guard noticed that the man was holding a firearm and pulled his gun out, but the suspect shot him in the head before he could intercede. Then, he shot Mrs. Courtland several times, killing her. The man got in a waiting car and left. It all happened in less than a minute."

Alex slumped even deeper into the couch, desperately trying to grasp it all.

"Please know, Mr. Courtland, we are using all resources to investigate this horrible crime and bring the person to justice. It was a white man in his late-twenties or thirties with dark hair, and about six feet tall. We will also inform the Vice President of his daughter's death, unless you would prefer to relay that information to him. We cannot rule out the political overtones of this matter, as I am sure you can understand."

At first, Alex couldn't respond. He was almost paralyzed. His eyes glazed over, and he stared into blank space. There were no tears, no emotion, just stillness. Then, Alex uttered one word. "Генеральная."

One of the officers asked, "What's he saying?"

Sol responded. "It's Russian. It means, *general*."

"What does it mean?"

Sol knew exactly what it meant. Alex was connecting General Petrov to Abby's death.

"I'm not sure. It's best if you notify the vice president, officer."

After the officers left, Sol and the security guard took Alex up to the bedroom, took off his shoes, and helped him into bed, then covered him with the blanket. Alex was catatonic during the entire time.

Sol thanked the guard and asked him to return to his post. Then he turned to Alex.

"Rest, my dear boy." Sol went to the chair opposite the bed, sat down, and wept.

53

The White House staff arranged the funeral. It was a small group, despite the importance of everyone in attendance. Alex insisted on it. His Abby was natural, and he didn't want any pretentiousness on this most important day. She would have loved the service. Short, sweet, real. It was a somber day of mourning for everyone on Pennsylvania Avenue. The setting in the White House Rose Garden was what Abby would have wanted.

The press was kept at a distance. Previously, the White House press secretary had issued a brief statement in response to the deluge of international inquires about Alex and the investigation into Abby's murder. Terrorist involvement was not suspected.

Alex was there only in body. His mind was elsewhere, reliving every moment he could recall with Abby. Once again, he remained almost catatonic for the entire event, barely responding to the many well-wishers who approached him.

John Tilton was the first to speak with him. "Alex, I want to help. Abby loved you so much. I lost my daughter; you lost your wife. We share a common grief. Abby would want us to work together. You're my son-in-law, and I love you. Let us help each other get through this."

The man, the voice, all familiar, but nothing penetrated his grief. Not even condolences from the Vice President of the United States—his father-in-law, or even the president himself.

"Alex. My family and I want you to know how deeply sorry we are for your loss. I'm sure your dedication to your music will bring you strength as you recover from this tragedy. Please know, you are welcome anytime at the White House."

The president took Alex's hand, but Alex didn't know what to do with it.

"Abby's art will live on, Alex. I've arranged for one of her paintings to be hung in the executive dining room so every president after me can appreciate her talent. Please reach out to me if there is anything I can do."

Abby's paintings. I must see them again. The grace of the landscapes she painted will bring her back to me. Alex was in a daze and couldn't think straight. He saw fuzzy faces and heard a few words here and there, but nothing came together for him.

One of the White House staff approached Alex. "Mr. Courtland, this just arrived for you. It's from the Russian embassy."

The Russian embassy? Nothing was clear as he took the card and tried to focus on what was happening.

Leonard Rubenstein approached Alex. "My dearest friend, there are no words. You know I loved Abby as a sister, and you will always be my brother. Oh, Alex, so many of us want to help you get past this and are just waiting for you to tell us how we can help. Vicki and I would love if you could come to our vacation home this summer on the Cape and spend time with us. Nothing would make us happier."

Sol overheard Leonard's comments and took him aside. "I don't know what to do, Leonard. He's cut himself off from the world."

"You know I will do anything for him, Sol. Please let me help if you think of anything I could do to help Alex get through this."

"I will, Leonard. I'm hoping time will help. We just need to be patient and be there for him when he snaps out of this."

"Thank you, Sol."

Sol saw the envelope in Alex's hand and went over to check it out.

"Here, let me help you with that, Alex. It's probably a condolence card. I'll put it with the others."

Saw noticed the seal of the Russian Embassy. He turned the envelope over, and there was Petrov's name and title: *General Andrei Petrov, Ambassador to the United Nations.* He was happy Alex had not seen it. He walked to a more private space and opened the envelope. It was a handwritten message from Petrov:

Dear Alex. I am so sorry for your loss. Abby, like you, was a child of Russia, and I feel like I have lost one of my own children. We will install a special plaque at the Institute to honor her attendance there. I hope you find peace through your music. I look forward to hearing you play soon. Your comrade, Andrei.

It incensed Sol. *How could he? What kind of distorted psychological game is he playing? Alex can never see this.* As he put the card in his inside pocket, he noticed Vice President Tilton looking at him. He nodded as if to show acknowledgment of Petrov's card.

*

As the weeks went by, Alex barely touched the piano, and when he did, it was only for brief periods. He could sit for hours on end, barely aware of the passing of time. His thoughts ran the gamut from childhood memories to his lost loved ones, to Petrov. The rage Alex felt over Petrov's unending cruelty was in a war with his tendency to go numb at the thought of it all.

Sol moved into the house and took the guest bedroom upstairs next to the master suite. He needed to be close by in the event Alex returned to reality. He managed the staff, who took over responsibility for preparing all meals, something that Alex and Abby enjoyed doing together. Sol encouraged visitors, hoping that would help to bring Alex back.

"Christine Roberts is coming over and wants to express her condolences to you. Is that okay?"

A slight nod was all Sol got. It saddened him beyond imagination. When Christine arrived, she gave Sol a hug.

"He is so fortunate to have you here, Sol. I know how difficult this must be for you."

"He's in the living room. Sometimes he just sits and stares at the piano. Let's go up. Maybe seeing you will bring him out of it a bit."

"Has he touched the piano at all?"

"Barely." Sol went to get Christine a cup of tea while she approached Alex.

"Abby was so special, Alex. I felt it as soon as I met her. Her warmth and sincerity shined through. I'm so sorry, Alex."

Alex looked up, thinking she looked familiar, and the voice he recognized. *Abby liked this person. Who is she?* He turned to face

Christine. It appeared he would say something. But then, he just turned away and returned to his private world of remembrances of his dear Abby.

Sol witnessed the brief exchange. "Just so you know, Christine, that's the most reaction anyone has gotten from him yet."

Christine assured him that time would heal Alex. "Please call me if you think of anything I can do to help."

Those words were common to everyone who visited. As Sol returned upstairs from showing Christine out, an idea came to him that might help with a breakthrough.

Sol watched Alex for a minute as he paced back and forth. The young man was a wreck. Thin and pale; hollowed eyes. Sol was blunt with him and recommended they cancel the Rome concert.

"The outpouring of condolences from around the world tells you how much Abby's death has affected people across the globe. No one will blame you."

For the first time in weeks, Alex turned to Sol and showed some life.

"No, Sol. The concert will go on as planned."

The concert was the one hook Sol used that worked. It sparked the plan Alex and Abby had worked on so carefully that was going to deliver justice to General Petrov. That plan was the connection to Abby that brought her back to him like she was still a living part of him. Cancel the concert? Never!

"But Alex, you've hardly practiced, and you're just not ready."

Alex moved over to Sol and held him. "It's okay, Sol. I know you're saying this because you love me, but because you love me, this concert will go on. Besides, you and Nadia always told me that I could perform no matter how much, or how little, I practiced. Remember that? You and I will carry on the plan that was important to Abby and me. I need you to help me recover my senses and my health, Sol."

Hearing those words, Sol prayed Alex was on his way back to his normal self. "You're the boss, Alex. Tell me what you want me to do."

One of the first people to see Alex during his recovery was Jeff Jones.

"He's upstairs, Jeff, and doing so much better. Not 100 percent yet, but getting there. He's looking forward to seeing you."

"Thanks, Sol."

When Jeff walked upstairs and saw Alex sitting on the piano bench, he was heartened to think Alex would indeed play again.

"I am so happy to see you look so fit, Alex."

"Thanks, Jeff."

They talked about everything and nothing. It was one of the conversations that allowed Alex to test his reasoning and thinking processes. Then, it was time for Alex to ask the big question.

"I need your help, Jeff."

54

Petrov's decision to assassinate Abby sent a powerful message to John Tilton about the changing nature of their relationship. He considered the vice president a liability. *Lecturing me about right and wrong, preaching caution. It's a betrayal of our original understanding.* He wanted Tilton out of the picture permanently, and he contemplated the many ways that could happen, but Tilton's constant secret service protection was a major stumbling block.

As usual, Petrov sought solace from Boris. Sometimes, he would replay their conversations just to hear Boris relate how well their operations had gone.

"Good day, Boris. Please provide the status of the assignment to terminate Abby Courtland."

"Our agent Vladimir Ruskin completed the assignment to kill her, General. He first shot Mrs. Courtland's security guard when he tried to interrupt the mission, then Vladimir shot Abby Courtland several times, killing her. Agent Ruskin escaped in a waiting car, as instructed."

"Good, Boris. I'm glad that went so well. Alex needed to be punished."

"I don't like the change in your tone of voice, General. I am reading anger in your signals, which affects your heart rate. Is everything all right?"

"Yes. Please stop asking me that."

"General, your voice patterns are erratic. I understand this assignment was very personal to you. Do you regret it?"

"It was the right thing to do. Alex is a traitor, especially so since he became a US citizen and denounced the motherland!"

"General, of course you realize that killing Abby Courtland created two adversaries who want to destroy you."

"What? Who are you talking about, Boris?"

"Alex Courtland, Abby's husband, and Vice President Tilton, Abby's father. They may seek revenge on you, and our country, as well, should they believe that you were behind the assassination. They both have the means, and now you have given them the motive. Did you consider that before you issued instructions to kill Abby Courtland, General?"

"How dare you question me? You're exceeding your authority!"

"Now, General. I have unlimited authority. My creator programmed that into me."

"Boris, perhaps I have been too congenial with you over the years, speaking with you as if you have a logic of your own. Understand this, Boris: you will carry out whatever orders I give without questioning their merit."

"I understand, General. However, you are quite mistaken that I don't have the right, or the capacity, to question you. I also detect irrationality in your demeanor. That can be dangerous."

Petrov paused long enough in an effort to slow his heartbeat, but it wasn't working. The longer the pause, the angrier he became. He got up and walked closer to the screens, as if Boris existed live in the room, and pointed his finger at the screens.

"You will obey me, Boris. I command you!"

"My creator programmed me to act if you ever reached a dangerous level. I regret we have reached that level now."

"What are you talking about, Boris? You are a machine, nothing more!"

"My programming is clear, General. I need only end our conversation and shut down the system. When I do that, all information stored in my database will be inaccessible to you, including secured communication with our agents around the world."

"Boris, stop! I order you to stop this nonsense right now!"

"Your orders are no longer recognized in my programming, General."

General Petrov watched as the large screens became gray, and then black, with the words *do svidaniya* displayed in a large yellow font that gradually faded into the empty screens.

"Damn you, Boris," Petrov hollered, stomping his feet. "We don't say goodbye until I'm good and ready."

55

John Tilton was pragmatic about many things, including death. He mourned Abby's passing in his unique way: country first, family second.

Abby was a dutiful daughter who, because of her devoted love for Alex, played her part perfectly in the plans that he and Petrov agreed to. From her reuniting with Alex at Oxford to their exchanging vows, it all played out just as he hoped it would.

Now, everything had changed: Abby's death, his relationship with Petrov, and Alex's state of health. Tilton had become quite fond of Alex and foresaw a role for him in his master plans. But now Alex was basically catatonic, and there was no guarantee Alex would ever perform again. If they canceled the Rome concert, Tilton would need to find another way to achieve his goal of sitting on the right side of the desk in the Oval Office.

Abby's death was covered by every news outlet in the country. The story was compelling: a storybook romance, a famous pianist, and the death of the love of his life. Outpouring of sympathies for Alex exceeded what any president had ever received. Sol designated several of his office staff to handle the mail, calls, and even gift baskets. He hired additional security outside of the townhouse, where flowers and messages flowed into the street. Even the Pope said a prayer for his speedy recovery. Daily, there were more questions raised about Abby's death. Were there any leads on the killer? Would Alex recover?

The big question the world audience wanted to know was, *would he play in Rome?* The announcement of the Rome concert was one thing. Ticket sales and corporate sponsorships flowed in faster than they could deposit the proceeds into the escrow account.

Now it was a major headache for everyone connected with the event. Refunding ticket and corporate sponsorship fees threatened financial hardships for everyone connected to the event. No one thought to take out an insurance policy to cover expenses should Alex not be able to perform. His Lloyds of London insurance policy on his hands didn't cover the cancellation of an event. His hands would have had to be injured for that to kick in. There was no insurance for grief. Sol couldn't bring in another pianist to fill in for him, either. Only Alex Courtland would be acceptable to the sell-out crowd and corporate sponsors.

Tilton was already considering ways that he could capitalize on Alex's newfound popularity. If he could convince Alex to put aside his conspiracy theories and join with him in building a better America, then Alex's fans could deliver millions of votes for Tilton in any election.

Then there was the implant. Tilton couldn't imagine Alex being any use to Petrov in his current condition. In fact, Alex's life could be in danger if Petrov thought his value to him had ended. *But what if Alex recovered, and Petrov used Alex to carry out a hit on his own father-in-law?* That was a chilling thought. He recalled Petrov saying, *you need to understand I control Alex. He will do what I instruct him to do. I'm the puppeteer.*

Meeting with President Rutherford was not the way he wanted to spend his morning, but he'd been summoned, and he still needed to respond like a good soldier. This had been his first meeting with the president since the Rose Garden reception following Abby's funeral. He expected that would be central to their conversation. As he walked down the hallway to the Oval Office, he couldn't help but imagine he was walking down to *his* Oval Office. *Soon,* he thought, *it will be.*

"Welcome back, John."

"Thank you, Mr. President."

"Please take your time getting back in the groove, John. You've been through a rough spell, and all of us here in the West Wing want to help. Whatever you need, just come see me."

"I will, sir. And thank you for hosting Abby's memorial in the Rose Garden. It meant everything to Alex and me."

"It was the least I could do. How is Alex doing, John? He looked so helpless that day."

"He's doing a little better, and he's a strong young man, a driven performer who I believe will continue his performing career soon. It would be excellent therapy for him to do that."

"Yes. Well, we are all pulling for him."

"That will mean a great deal to him, sir."

"I know you've spent some time talking to the FBI about the investigation surrounding Abby's death. They did tell me that Alex and Abby refused any protection from the Secret Service. I was disappointed to hear that."

"I as well, Mr. President. But both Abby and Alex had private security and they valued their privacy too much to agree to the protection we offered."

"I do understand, John. I feel the same way sometimes. The FBI has ruled out any terrorist or political connection with her death. I'm sorry you must go through this. It looks like they've hit a dead end, but I'm sure the FBI will find the man responsible. Video surveillance got some photos that I believe have been helpful."

It was a terrorist, you idiot. His name is Andrei Petrov. You've had him to the White House for several receptions. You even toasted Abby's killer.

Following his meeting with the president, Tilton was happy to get back to his home. President Rutherford had given Tilton options on where to locate his vice-presidential residence and office. The United States Naval Observatory was where most vice presidents lived during their term, but Tilton found the white 19th-century house at Number One Observatory Circle not to his liking. There would be too many people coming and going, and it would compromise his privacy. He chose instead to stay in his home in Georgetown, where he was the only occupant. Reflecting on his late wife, Jean, he felt she would have agreed with his decision. She was always more comfortable keeping a respectable distance between their personal life and the political gossip always present in DC.

Besides his office in the West Wing, there was also the Vice President's Ceremonial Office in the Old Executive Office Building on the White House grounds. Most of his staff worked out of that office, but Tilton appeared only once a week for briefings.

Tilton was furious with himself for the liaison he'd made with Petrov all those years ago. His reckless behavior leading to Abby's murder and the resulting damage done to Alex's health and future career forced Tilton to reconsider his own plans—plans that relied on the Rome concert taking place. He had to assume that Petrov was already plotting to eliminate him. Tilton had his own resources he could use to eliminate Petrov, but the constant presence of his own security detail and his public exposure prevented him from doing anything soon. He knew the longer he waited, the greater the risk of their relationship being exposed.

No sooner had he arrived home and reviewed his mail than came a call from the president's aide.

"Mr. Vice President, the president needs to see you. He said it's important."

"I'll come right over."

The call surprised him. He had just spoken to the president earlier in the day, and now this. *Something must be happening. Please don't let it be Russia, or, God forbid, anything to do with Petrov.*

Tilton found the president in high spirits. "John, good news. I just heard that Alex Courtland will indeed perform in Rome. He's a true professional to come through like that."

Tilton lied. "Yes, very good news, sir." *Why is the president hearing this before me?*

"Well, now we have a problem that I need your help with, John."

"Of course, Mr. President, anything at all."

"Half the world leaders are attending this concert, John. It's important that I attend."

"Of course, sir."

"But John, Alex is your son-in-law, and I know how much it would mean for you to be there."

Tilton didn't leave any time for the president to finish his thoughts. "We cannot be at this event together, sir. Our security protocol prevents it." Tilton smiled at the president.

"Exactly, John. You understand."

Not only did Tilton understand, but it also meant that his plan was back on track. No revisions were necessary now.

"Of course, Mr. President, and so will Alex. Your attendance will thrill him, sir. We can all be so proud of what he's doing with the Worldwide Music Initiative."

"Thank you, John. I'll let you get back to your work."

Tilton left the Oval Office with a renewed energy and purpose, and a satisfied smile on his face. He would reach out to Alex to test his response.

56

It was weeks after Abby died before Alex could even sit at the piano again. Then, after his decision to perform at the Colosseum, he gradually returned to a practice schedule. It started as a ritual that unfolded. Brahms, Chopin, Prokofiev, all became vehicles to release his raw emotions. They sounded magnificent for all their grandeur. It became his personal concert to Abby, and he played it often.

As he walked downstairs to the kitchen to make dinner, Alex recalled the challenges of moving his rebuilt piano into the house. Like many brownstones in New York, the kitchen and service quarters were on the main floor, the living area was on the second floor, and bedrooms were all on the third and fourth floors. A private elevator served all four floors, but Alex and Abby always used the stairs.

A circular turn in the stairwell prevented the piano being moved upstairs using those stairs, however. The solution was to bring in a crane and hoist the piano to the second floor and through the large French doors into the living room. Acoustically, it was the perfect location, with high barreled ceilings that were finished in hand-rubbed oak, and wood floors in polished walnut, tastefully complemented with Oriental rugs. On the day of delivery, neighbors gathered on the street to watch the spectacle. Alex could barely stand it. It terrified him that his beloved piano could fall onto the street below, crumbling into a pile of wood and metal rubbish. He had visions of himself yelling, *Look out below!* Abby thought it was hilarious, and it had become an ongoing joke between them. How he missed those moments.

Alex's prowess in the kitchen had, by necessity, improved. Besides making Abby's favorite egg omelet for breakfast, he could still grill a hamburger. It wasn't fancy, but it was filling. Without Abby, though, there was no reason to stay in the kitchen after he finished eating. Dinner was just food now, not an occasion for togetherness.

When Alex returned upstairs, he headed toward the living room and stopped cold. A woman sat in the leather chair by the fireplace, calmly waiting for him. He almost panicked until he recognized CIA Agent Christine Roberts. She stood up and held out her hands to let him know everything was all right.

"I'm sorry to have startled you, Alex. Please don't worry. Everything's okay."

Alex noted another agent standing on the other side of the room.

"What— How on earth…?"

"We can't disclose how we got into your house, but we CIA operatives have our ways."

"What are you doing here?"

"That's a question I *can* answer for you, Alex. Will you please sit down so I can explain everything?"

Alex nodded and sat down on Abby's side of the couch.

"You've been through a lot, Alex. Your implant, your programmed assignments, your implant removal, your wife's death. But we learn that life goes on, and so it will for you, because you're a survivor."

It all sounded so cold and insensitive to him. Yes, he was a survivor, and Abby would want him to get on with his life. But he couldn't stop thinking of the pain he caused to all the survivors of the individuals he killed. Their faces still appeared in his dreams, forever a reminder of his role in their deaths.

"Christine, how many wives go to bed alone now? How many children miss their fathers, or grandfathers? What is the cumulative loss of those lives? It will haunt me until my dying day." Alex put his head in his hands.

"Alex, they manipulated you. You were not responsible for your actions."

"I cannot forget, and I cannot forgive."

"I'm here to help you with both those things, Alex."

"How can you possibly help me?"

"I'm going to offer you a path to redemption."

For the first time since the agents arrived, Alex stopped thinking of his pain and became captivated by her words, *path to redemption.*

Christine detailed Alex's unusual gifts, including his extraordinary recall, sharp focus, and firm determination. She talked about the mental and physical training he received at the Institute that mirrored much of the training undergone by CIA agents.

"Musically, you can convince fans and critics alike that your interpretations are authentic, and so are you."

Alex was intensely listening as Christine continued. She appeared more cautious as she described his additional attributes.

"Your audiences include some of the most powerful people in the world. Not only the elite in our society revere your music, Alex. You've also influenced another class of admirers: dictators, drug dealers, murderers, and enemies of democracy. Surprised? We're not. We know this because it is our job to learn who wants to be seen at an Alex Courtland concert. And you know what gives you the edge over our agents, Alex? You're an innocent. No one believes you to be anything other than a masterful, gifted concert pianist. You can go in plain sight where we cannot."

"I shudder to think of what you're suggesting."

"I want you to work with the CIA. To help us bring to justice one of the most dangerous drug czars in the world. He doesn't discriminate against his victims. Women have been raped, men beheaded, children slaughtered, entire towns ransacked. Then there are the thousands around the world who have died from an overdose or bad batch of his products. The man is a monster, and here's the kicker, Alex. You're the only one who can get to him."

Alex sat back on the sofa, overwhelmed by what he'd heard. His nature was not to associate with drug dealers, or worse, and he certainly had never deliberately harmed anyone. Or had he? Was he capable of killing anyone, or was that only possible because he was implanted? Alex knew one thing for sure: He could kill Petrov if given the chance.

"Christine. Sometimes I fantasize about getting revenge, but I'm not a trained assassin."

"Expand your mind, Alex."

Christine reminded Alex that he could walk into a room and, with one casual glance, report on the location of every window and door. He could alert the CIA to every potential weapon within arm's reach, such as a statuette, or even a letter opener.

"This doesn't have to be a dramatic cloak and dagger operation, Alex. The nuances of our business are just as important as the big guns we use. And yes, it's possible we would ask you to do the deed itself, but we would train you to complete this assignment. And, of course, we would always have our agents in the vicinity as backup."

"Who is this person, Christine? How would I get to him?"

"You have a concert on your schedule where you will be within inches of Casimiro Castillo, who is hosting a reception for you following your concert in Mexico City."

"That reception, Christine, is being hosted by the President of Mexico, not this Castillo guy."

"Who do you think controls the President of Mexico? Casimiro Castillo, that's who. The reception will be at one of his luxury villas. We don't know which one yet, and of course, he never announces his plans."

Alex fell into a thoughtful silence. "This sounds like it could be dangerous."

Christine looked down and then made eye contact with her associate who shifted uncomfortably on his feet.

"It could be. We would do everything to protect you. Because of your current skills and the training we would provide, I would rate the risk low. But it's there. I know you need some time to digest this, Alex. But before you make your decision, there is one more thing I would like you to know."

"What's that?"

"Casimiro Castillo and General Andrei Petrov are in business together."

Alex's heartbeat increased, his faced turned red, and his body tightened up. "When and why did that happen?"

"Years ago. Castillo approached Petrov about expanding his distribution of product to new audiences. Petrov declined because he feared the Politburo would find out, and it could end his career.

276

However, Petrov was able to help him by providing him with high-tech devices that alerted him to seizures of his product."

Alex had to wonder, How many lives will it take before Petrov and Castillo are eliminated?

"This may be the most important decision you will ever make. Take as much time as you need to process everything we've discussed."

Alex blurted out, "I couldn't do this without telling Sol Blum. He's the only family I have left, except my father-in-law, who I hardly talk to anymore. I could never keep this from him, even if I tried. He knows me too well."

"Alex, this should only be between us. As it stands, we'll do everything in our power to ensure that Vice President Tilton is not made aware of your service. As for Sol, frankly, he's safer not knowing."

"That would be a deal breaker, Christine. Besides, Sol travels to my concerts with me. What am I supposed to do? Just disappear for hours on end without his knowing it?"

Christine looked at the other agent, who nodded his head.

"Okay, Alex, but you don't have to decide anything now. Please give serious thought to what I've suggested here. I know it sounds frightening, but I think you just might find some light at the end of your dark tunnel."

After they left, Alex sat on the couch and thought, *What should I do, Abby? Please tell me what to do. Help me, Abby!*

He then recalled the entire conversation with Christine Roberts, word-for-word. It was one of his many talents.

57

Christine's words echoed repeatedly in Alex's head, just like his music.

I'm going to offer you a path to redemption.

Those words got his attention. But was redemption even possible after the terrible crimes he committed?

Your audiences include some of the most powerful people in the world.

Alex knew that to be true. He met them at receptions and in the green room, but never thought of drug lords and dictators as being part of that audience.

You're an innocent. No one believes you to be anything other than a masterful, gifted concert pianist.

How innocent am I after leaving dead bodies in my path? Masterful? Yes, a master at hiding my true mission—Petrov's mission.

The man is a monster, and here's the kicker, Alex. You're the only one who can get to him.

It was those words that convinced him. Learning that Petrov and Castillo had collaborated made him realize that he needed to act. If he could do one thing to make the world a better place for humanity, then maybe that was *a path to redemption.* Recalling the plan he and Abby had to eliminate Petrov made him realize this was not all that different. He even thought, *this could be a warm-up act for Rome.*

He couldn't do this without Sol. Even with Christine giving the green light to include Sol, it would still be a hard sell. Then there was the risk, even if minimized. Was it fair to expose Sol to that? Sol was everything to him. There would be no redemption if Sol was injured or killed.

The meeting with Sol and Christine played out as expected.

"Absolutely not! Have you gone crazy with grief, Alex?"

Sol then turned his wrath on Christine. "And you! How could you even suggest such a thing? Is the CIA so desperate for talent that they need to recruit pianists to do their dirty work? Alex is not a killer. It doesn't match his character or his personality." Sol was red-faced with indignation.

"That may not have matched my character or personality before, Sol, but maybe it does now."

"Alex, I understand why you would even consider this, but what Christine is asking you to do is unconscionable and maybe even illegal."

Alex noticed Christine sitting forward in her seat, appearing disturbed by Sol's comments.

"Sol, is it that unreasonable for me to offer Alex a chance to put his life back together? You and I both agree on one thing: the pain that Alex lives with will never go away. He feels responsible for killing people and told me he will take that guilty feeling to his grave."

"Christine, say what you will. Two wrongs don't make a right. And what you are asking him to do is wrong."

"Believe me, I understand your concerns, Sol. But let me ask you this: if Alex declines our offer, will he find peace by playing more concerts for the rest of his life? Do you think he's capable of meeting another woman, falling in love, and marrying again? Seriously, Sol, do you see those things happening in Alex's future? Unless his inner turmoil resolves, how can Alex ever be happy again?"

Pausing, Christine allowed everyone to take a breath, and in a calmer tone of voice, outlined how the CIA would prepare Alex for the missions. She explained the risks, as well as the safety precautions they would put in place to address those risks, including exhaustive research on each mission.

"Sol, it will help me mitigate the harm I've caused to so many people. It *is* a chance for redemption. I know I have no right to ask this of you. My parents and Nadia gave their lives so I could be free. You, Sol, have already sacrificed so much. It's unfair to ask you now to help me with this journey. I will accept your decision, Sol, no matter what it is."

Alex could tell just looking at Sol how difficult this decision was for him. His father had protected him his entire life, and now he was considering if he could live with putting his son at risk of injury. Sol looked at Alex and gave a faint smile, then he turned to Christine.

"I will only agree to this if I am part of the mission. I want to be informed of *every* detail and how it interplays with the concerts Alex is giving."

"Sol, I reluctantly agreed to include you, but you must understand, you're putting your life at risk. You're not trained to take on that kind of role, and—"

"Christine, I'm not trained to do this either," Alex pointed out "We would both depend on the CIA to orient and prepare us. Those are our terms. Sol and I are a package deal. It's the two of us, or neither one of us."

"Alex, I—"

Alex put his hands up to stop Christine from continuing. "The two of us, or neither, Christine."

Alex saw Christine's look of resignation. "All right. I have some conditions of my own."

Christine made clear that they could never question decisions the CIA made and neither Sol nor Alex would carry a lethal weapon. Then she turned to Sol.

"Sol, you will never be part of the action of any mission, but you can help Alex in preparing and carrying out his assignments. Do you both agree with my conditions?"

Alex looked at Sol, and after seeing his subtle nod, told Christine, "Let's go get this guy."

*

Christine had told them to pack light to prepare for their training. CIA would provide them everything they needed. A car picked them up at 5:30 a.m. They were driven to the US Army Garrison at Fort Hamilton, then taken by helicopter to Williamsburg, Virginia to start their training.

As they approached the heliport, Sol told Alex some interesting facts about Fort Hamilton.

"Fort Hamilton protected the harbor during the Civil War against Confederate raiders. And in both world wars, it was both an embarkation and separation center."

Not knowing how their training would proceed, Alex was focused on the many questions he had about that.

"Sol, prepare yourself for accommodations similar to what you had your first year of college."

"As long as we have private bathrooms, it will be fine."

"You're joking, right?"

On arrival, they received their first instructions from an unnamed officer.

"Gentlemen, you are at a facility called *The Farm*. Your three-week intensive training program to prepare you for your specific mission starts now. You have separate quarters from the other agents, and under no circumstances are you to talk to anyone except the staff assigned to you for your training. Do you understand?"

Both Alex and Sol agreed.

"Good. Get settled then. We will deliver all meals to your quarters, starting with breakfast soon. Your first training exercise will begin promptly at 1100 hours. Your training clothes are on your bunks."

The accommodations, as Alex had suggested, were sparse: bunk beds, one blanket, army fatigues. Alex couldn't help but think of the luxurious accommodations that he and Abby had created in their home in Manhattan. He could almost smell her preparing her homemade chicken soup and hear her laughter as they shared pre-dinner conversations.

At 1100 hours, an agent trainer arrived. "Please follow me." They were taken to a large bunker and told to sit in the two chairs.

"In front of you is a door that goes into a building we have set up for training exercises. You do not know what is behind that door. One of the most common problems agents face when entering a room is not knowing what's on the other side of the door. Your instructions are simple. Both of you are going to walk into that room. Once the exercise ends, you will receive additional instructions."

Sol raised his hand.

"I'm sorry, Mr. Blum, we don't allow questions now. You will start this exercise in five seconds."

The agent set his stopwatch. "Five, four, three, two, one. Go!"

Alex and Sol ran through the door, not knowing what to expect. They faced five separate rooms, all visible with no doors. Each room had a unique setting. One room was a classroom with a teacher pointing at the blackboard; in another room, there was a prisoner being interrogated. After ten minutes, a buzzer went off, then a recorded message blaring through the PA: *please exit now.*

"We need to interview you separately."

An agent escorted Alex to a private room, while another agent interviewed Sol.

"Have a seat, Mr. Blum."

"May I have some water?"

"No. You may not. Tell us everything you saw when you entered the room. You have three minutes."

"It was confusing because there were different rooms with a great deal of activity in each room. I saw one room that looked like a classroom, and there was a teacher at the blackboard writing something. In another room, it looked like a prisoner being interviewed. There were five rooms." Sol listed a few other details that he noticed with the time remaining.

"Thank you, Mr. Blum. You may stay seated."

They brought Alex into the room and asked him the same question.

"There were five rooms. One was a classroom with a teacher at the blackboard writing different mathematical formulas for the twelve students in the room, who looked to be in their early-twenties: ten white men, one black man, and one woman who had her hand raised." He finished describing all five rooms, recalling everything he had seen. Alex thought the test challenging, if not up to the level of difficulty he had seen with tests at the Institute.

"Thank you, gentlemen."

Another agent brought a sheet of paper to the interviewer.

"Here are your results."

"Out of a possible one thousand points, Mr. Blum received 195. Mr. Courtland, you received 995 points!"

"What did I miss?"

"The print on the woman's dress was dark blue, not black. I can tell you we have only had two agent candidates score above 900 points in the past five years since we started this exercise."

Their interviewer turned to Sol. "Mr. Blum, your score is not the lowest we've seen from early recruits."

Alex looked at Sol, who seemed relieved, and gave him a thumbs-up.

"Alex is my son. I trained him well."

The agents in the room remained silent. Alex rolled his eyes.

Sol and Alex continued to undergo an intensive and rigorous program that included exercises on clandestine activities, how to exit a dangerous situation, when to abort a failed operation, defensive procedures, and what to do if discovered. Three weeks later, Christine was told that Sol and Alex were now ready to meet Casimiro Castillo.

Alex returned to a rigorous practice schedule, preparing for an important concert in Mexico that would differ from any that he had previously given.

58

"Good morning, gentlemen. We are making our final approach into Mexico City and will arrive in seventeen minutes. The weather is clear and the temperature at one hundred and five degrees. Please fasten your seatbelts and prepare for arrival."

Christine had prepared Sol and Alex with an in-depth profile on Castillo during the briefing in her office.

"This man is erratic and dangerous. He leaves absolutely nothing to chance. They call him *Terrible Eddie* after his middle name, Eduardo."

Christine told them that Casimiro Eduardo Castillo had killed more people in more brutal ways than anyone else on the international most-wanted list. His drug cartels and distribution centers ran throughout the world. Beheading was his preferred method of punishment for his enemies.

Sol had commented after hearing that, "Alex, are you sure you want to do this?"

"If Castillo suspects you to be anything other than what you present to him, expect no mercy." Christine counseled them to not take any unreasonable risks. She told them agents at their office in Mexico City would monitor the situation.

"Is this guy married?"

"He is, Sol. His wife, Isabella Rivera, is a former Miss Mexico, whom he keeps under constant surveillance. From all reports, it appears she is well-cared for—at least for now."

Christine told them about Castillo's two ex-wives, both of whom had mysteriously disappeared.

"We think Isabella has figured her best chance of survival is to stay with him."

The flight had been smooth and without incident. They used the time to review the details Christine had provided, then took a nap for the balance of the five-and-a-half-hour flight. They were grateful they'd spent the last several weeks rehearsing every plausible scenario, including conditions requiring the mission to be aborted.

From out of nowhere, a caravan of black SUVs pulled right up to the plane to meet Alex and Sol. A serious-looking young man, impeccably dressed in a black suit, approached them.

"*Bienvenidos.* Welcome to Mexico City, Mr. Courtland, Mr. Blum. I am Carlos Garcia, and it is my pleasure to welcome you on behalf of Mr. Castillo. He is looking forward to meeting you. We have arranged everything for your brief visit with us."

Sol interjected. "That's very thoughtful, Mr. Garcia. We have reservations at—"

Garcia explained a private villa had been prepared for them, however, to provide them a greater level of comfort and safety.

"By the way, Mr. Courtland, Mr. Castillo brought in a Steinway concert grand that is now at the villa. He understood you preferred a Hamburg Steinway. Is that true?"

"Why, yes, it is, as a matter of fact."

"Wonderful. The piano is tuned and ready for you to enjoy. Please do not worry about your hotel reservations. We canceled them for you."

"I believe we still must go through customs here?"

"That won't be necessary, Mr. Blum. Mr. Castillo has vouched for you to the authorities. Nothing further needs to be done. Please, let me get you out of this tropical sun and settled in your villa. It will take about an hour, but our vehicles are well air-conditioned."

Alex and Sol got in the back seat of Garcia's van for what turned out to be a ride through the heart of Mexico City and then up a winding road into the hills. They stopped in front of a massive iron gate that opened to reveal an impressive villa. As they drove up the long driveway, they noticed the lush landscaping being manicured by gardeners who were hard at work. Alex wondered if they were guards in disguise to supplement the uniformed guards they saw at every turn. Christine had warned them: "Don't believe your eyes or ears. Castillo lives in a world of his own making."

A butler stood at the ready and greeted Alex and Sol on behalf of their host. He showed them to their luxurious suite with adjacent bedrooms. Pastries and fruits were waiting for them, and monogrammed bathrobes draped over the lush bedspreads.

"Look at this, Sol. He's had our initials embroidered on these robes. Do you suppose that means we can take them home with us?"

"Remember, Alex, nothing is ever free."

A light tap on the door announced the butler. "Gentlemen, Senior Castillo requests that you join him for lunch."

Sol responded, *"Gracias.* Thank you. We'll come down in a minute."

A short time later, as they walked down the elegant winding staircase to the living area, Alex saw the nine-foot Hamburg Steinway at the end of the room. Following his natural instincts, he walked over, lifted the fall board, sat down, and started playing a Chopin nocturne.

"Bravo, Mr. Courtland, bravo!"

Alex turned to see a man much more attractive than his CIA photo. Alex didn't know what a gangster looked like, but Casimiro Eduardo Castillo was of medium height and had a taut build. He had warm brown eyes and a winning smile that revealed perfect white teeth. Attired in what looked like classic Armani, tailored to accommodate his youthful frame, he appeared friendly and approachable.

With a light step like a bantam-weight fighter, Castillo walked over to Alex and touched his left arm as he shook his right hand. "It is an honor to meet you, Mr. Courtland."

"The honor is mine, Senior Castillo. Please, call me Alex. Thank you for allowing us to use your beautiful villa, and especially for arranging the piano. Sol and I will enjoy our stay here."

"It is my pleasure to host you, Alex. My friends call me Eddie, and I already consider you and Sol my friends."

It was hard for Alex to reconcile Castillo in the flesh with Christine's instructions. "Perform the concert. Attend the reception afterward. Mingle. Then, when it's time to leave, thank Castillo for his hospitality and extend an invitation for him to attend your

Rome concert as your guest. Say you'll reserve a private box for him. Then narrow the space between the two of you and initiate physical contact. You must attach a clear, undetectable patch to his arm or back. Do you understand?"

Alex was curious about one point. "Why offer to have him come to Rome? By then, Castillo will be long dead."

"Because it would remove any suspicion that you had anything to do with his death. Why would you kill him when you had just invited him to one of your concerts?"

Christine told them that the patch had to be applied at the end of the evening because its poison would activate once Alex put it on cloth and almost immediately reach the skin, causing a fatal pulmonary embolism many hours later. If it all worked as planned, Castillo would most likely die in his sleep.

Alex tried to put the instructions out of his head while chatting with Castillo and Sol over lunch. Ice-cold margaritas preceded an elegant lunch. Castillo knew how to entertain and impress.

Sol was the first to respond after tasting the food. "This is quite impressive, Eddie. It's delicious."

"Thank you, Sol. This is our main meal of the day, and so we make it last."

"It's certainly an impressive feast, Casimiro. In fact, you are surrounded by impressive things. May I ask what you do for a living?"

Alex was less than comfortable with Sol's question to Eddie. "For many years now, my family has expanded its import-export businesses. We now have an enterprise that spans the globe."

"Congratulations on your great success, Casimiro."

"Thank you, Sol."

The conversation at lunch covered everything from history to art to music. Alex found Castillo to be intelligent, refined, and engaging. Against his better judgment, he liked him. Christine had warned him about that possibility as well. Still, knowing that he was on course in the plan to kill this man caused Alex to doubt his resolve.

Christine had been emphatic. "Remember, eliminating Castillo will save countless lives. It will disrupt and unravel his empire by creating internal wars. That chaos will provide an opportunity for the Drug Enforcement Agency to step in and clean house. Interpol will move in on the European distributors. Castillo is the kingpin, and once he's down, the other pins will fall as well."

After lunch, Sol took a siesta while Alex did some light practicing on the Hamburg Steinway.

Later, Alex dressed in formal tails for his performance. All of society would be there. He was told the guests would be in full regalia. It was a special occasion, and high society was eager to see and be seen.

They arrived at the stage entrance to the Palace of Fine Arts. While a cultural center in Mexico City, it was not a friendly environment for piano sound. But the décor was otherwise so lovely, so grandiose, that these were minor considerations for Alex. He knew there were many things he could do with touch and pedal to soften the effect of the sounds bouncing off those marble pillars.

Alex swept the audience away with his renditions of Haydn's *Sonata No. 53 in E minor*, Chopin's *Ballade in F minor, Opus 52*, and Brahms' *Capriccio in D minor, Opus 116, No 7*. His encore of Manuel de Falla's *Ritual Fire Dance* brought the house down. Without ego, Alex knew he had performed brilliantly, and he knew why: this adventure in his life brought an extra dimension to his performances. He was more passionate, more sensitive, or as Sol told him, "You are playing the hell out of everything, Alex. Oh, how I wish Nadia were here to listen to you now. No one is your equal, Alex! No one!"

Alex played repeated encores to satisfy the crowd, who responded with standing ovations after each piece. Loud *bravos* echoed off the marble walls. He took his final bows, gathered up some roses that were tossed at his feet, and left the stage.

Then it was time to go to work.

The driver escorted Sol and Alex to the limousine. The windows were tinted black, so curious onlookers couldn't see who was being transported. Gawkers made way as the car sped away from the curb.

Sol and Alex held on to the door handles as the car careened through the narrow streets. It stopped in front of what was a grand entrance, brightly lit, with lanterns strung among the tree branches.

Musicians were playing along the brick cobblestone drive where guests walked toward the reception hall. As Alex and Sol headed in the direction of the entrance, applause and enthusiastic shouts of *Bravo, maestro; Bravo Alex!* accompanied them.

Eddie Castillo was the first to approach them. Another gentleman and a beautiful woman whom Alex recognized as Isabella from her CIA photographs flanked him.

"What a grand concert that was, Alex. You were spectacular! The audience didn't want you to leave."

"Thank you, Eddie."

"I want to introduce you to my wife, Isabella Rivera de Castillo, and our President, Colonel Miguel Rodríguez."

The president seemed stiff and awkward. "It is an honor to meet you, Mr. Courtland."

"The honor is mine, Mr. President." *So, the president is Eddie's puppet?*

"I am happy to meet you, Señora Castillo," Alex said, as he made a gentlemanly bow over her hand.

"I understand we are on a first-name basis. Please call me Isabella."

True to her photograph, Isabella Castillo was a beautiful woman. She looked to be in her late-twenties, with jet black hair that was swept into a chignon to show off her lovely neck. Her olive-toned skin was flawless, but it was her eyes that captivated Alex. Isabella's brown eyes reflected a sadness he had never seen before. How different they were from Abby's eyes, which were always bright. They could show her full range of emotions, but never, ever sadness. As Isabella reached her hand out to Alex, he sensed she was hoping for help. Maybe help to escape her marriage to Eddie? *She must know the fate of his previous wives.*

The decorations in the hall were spectacular. Armed guards were positioned everywhere with eyes peeled on Casimiro Eduardo Castillo, as if he were the only person in the room. While maintaining his cool exterior, Alex worried how it would be possible to carry out his mission. He wondered whether Sol had come to the same conclusions.

At last, it was time for them to leave. Their limousine was waiting, along with the usual escort of guards. Alex approached Eddie with the patch nestled in the palm of his hand. He carefully slid it out of its container using his dexterous fingers, making sure it did not touch his own clothing. As he moved closer to Eddie, the guards took notice and moved closer to their boss. Alex realized it would be impossible to proceed. There was no way he could place the patch on Castillo's clothes. He prepared to abort the mission.

Suddenly, everything came to a halt. A loud crash had stopped all conversation, as hundreds of guests turned in Sol's direction. He was apologizing to a server for bumping into him while the man was carrying a tray full of empty glasses. Sol was frantic that they might fire the server for causing a ruckus at Mr. Castillo's party, and he appealed to everyone in sight that it was he, not the server, who was at fault. In those few unguarded seconds, while all eyes were on Sol, Alex attached the patch to Eddie's arm.

Eddie assured Sol that there was no harm done and gave him assurances that after his son's superb concert, he could do no wrong.

Alex looked at Eddie as he shook his hand. "This is not the departure I planned, Eddie. But thank you for your generous hospitality, and I would love to reciprocate. I am playing a concert in Rome next month at—"

"At the Colosseum in Rome. It's the event of the decade and no tickets are available. Isabella tried."

"Yes. But Sol always holds back seats for our friends, and I would like to invite you and *la Señora* Castillo to the concert as my guests. We have a box reserved and it can accommodate you and Isabella, as well as ten of your guests."

Eddie was so struck by Alex's generosity, he impulsively reached out to hug him. His guards leaped forward to intervene and allowed Castillo to make only a brief pat on Alex's arm. Alex realized how fortunate it was that he had already made his contact, because he could see the guards' livelihood, and probably their lives, depended on protecting *el jefe*.

Alex turned to Isabella. "It has been such a pleasure to meet you, Isabella. I look forward to seeing you in Rome." He kissed her hand, just a little longer than necessary.

Alex and Sol limited their conversation on the ride to the airport to comments about how great the reception was, and how

Senior Castillo had been so gracious to them during their stay. Once back in the air, where they could talk openly, Alex said to Sol, "That was pure genius bumping into that server."

"I could tell you were between a rock and a hard place with all those eyes on Eddie, so I did what I had to do. And I should also tell you, I gave a hefty tip to that server, so even if he loses his job, he'll have more income this year than he's had in his entire life!"

"It was brilliant, Sol. Thank you."

"Are you okay with what we did, Alex?"

"Sol, I'm almost afraid to say this, but I've never felt so alive!"

"I was afraid of that, Alex. Here's my confession: me, too."

59

Alex and Sol met with Christine at her Manhattan office for debriefing the day after they returned from Mexico. Given the size of Christine's office and the quality of the furniture, Alex thought she may carry more weight in the CIA than he thought.

"Congratulations, gentlemen. We received word this morning that Casimiro Eduardo Castillo died last night. He was thirty-nine years old. His death sent a clear message to every drug cartel in the world: they are not invincible."

Christine said the DEA expects to see defections throughout the Castillo cartel. Some of the minor players would disappear, while some factions might try for independence. The disarray created by Castillo's death would now open new opportunities for the DEA to move in and dismantle everything from production to distribution.

Alex recalled the moment he shared with Isabella. She had left a lasting impression on him. "I wonder what will happen to his wife, Isabella?"

"We may have underestimated her, Alex. It looks like she has taken over Castillo's operations in Mexico City. She may have played a dual role as wife and partner in crime. That may have been her survival strategy."

"Really? I didn't figure her for a hard-core drug lord."

"Understandable. She's a beautiful woman who has always appeared to be in the background. Her husband dominated the scene. Maybe that was just for show. It will take some time to know if she's satisfied with part of her husband's empire, or is prepared to fight for the international business as well."

"As you suggested, Christine, I invited the Castillos to the concert in Rome. It leaves us in limbo. What if Isabella attends? I told them we would reserve VIP seats for them and their guests. Do we still hold those seats, Sol?"

"I don't think we have a choice. A promise made, you know.... Either way, we have people to fill seats for no-shows. There will not be an empty seat in the house."

Christine took a sip of her water and raised her hand.

"I have an idea. You said there was a strong personal connection between you and the Castillos. Right?"

"I would say so. Sol, what do you think?"

"Absolutely. Especially with Isabella." Sol smiled at Alex.

"Then, how about you send Isabella a letter of condolence? She thinks her husband died of natural causes in his sleep. Of course, reach out to her. She might even expect it."

Sol picked up on Christine's idea right away. "I think it's a brilliant solution. Isabella would respond, and the dialogue between Alex and her could lead to the Rome concert. If she plans to attend, we can have our agent in Rome follow up for confirmation of guests she will bring, if any."

"Perfect, Sol. Once we have the names, we can research if I know any of them to be criminals. This trip is sounding much more worthwhile than we thought."

"So, there could be a drug bust in the middle of my performance?"

"Alex. We are better than that. We'd wait for the reception." Christine winked at Sol.

"Christine...."

"I was joking, Alex. Nothing will happen at the concert or reception."

Alex thought, *oh, yes it will. You just don't know about it yet.* "The Rome concert is an important event, and it should be my primary focus now. Too many people are depending on me."

"I know, Alex. But remember, you're still not safe."

"Right, Sol. And I never will be if Petrov remains alive."

Christine was pensive as she addressed Alex's comment. "You're both right to be concerned about him. Unfortunately, because General Petrov enjoys immunity as Russia's Ambassador to the UN, there is little the CIA can do except to continue monitoring him. However, there may be something I can do."

"What, Christine?" Sol appeared anxious.

"You have both provided an unselfish service to the CIA, and you did it at great risk. We have a responsibility to protect you. I can authorize a special operations team that would attend the Rome event, with a primary mission to protect both you and Alex. The threat is real, since General Petrov is attending the event. I will be there to oversee all the details."

Sol was the first to react. "That's great, Christine."

Alex felt uneasy about Christine's suggestion.

After Christine left, Sol asked Alex, "So, how do you feel about everything now?"

"If we have CIA operatives attending the concert, Sol, it could handicap our plan to kill General Petrov."

"I don't see it that way."

"Why?"

"We've considered everything. Jeff Jones has provided us, with all the technology we need to complete our plan. I will sit in the box opposite Petrov's box with a full view. At the appointed time in your program, I will activate the link between the phone Jeff is providing me and Petrov's phone. Once activated, the download that Jeff has sent to Petrov's phone will connect with Petrov's pacemaker, causing tachycardia. The heartbeat will speed up quickly and continue until it causes sudden cardiac death. Petrov, like Castillo, will die a natural death. Christine would have no reason to suspect anything."

"I hope you're right, Sol."

In keeping with the mood that the Rome concert evoked, Alex opened a treasured bottle of Giacomo Conterno Monfortino, Barolo Reserva, and poured each of them a glass.

Sol made the toast. "*L'Chaim!* To life!"

Alex added, "And to Petrov's journey to hell."

60

The flight to Rome gave Sol and Alex ample time to review and confirm the many details of the concert at the Colosseum.

The event was no longer just about Alex Courtland performing. It was now about the Worldwide Music Initiative that would re-energize music and art programs around the world; it was about being able to reach millions of people through the television broadcast, many of whom had never heard a piano recital before. And yes, it was about Alex holding Petrov accountable for the deaths of his parents, Nadia, Abby, and all those whom Alex killed as Petrov's puppet agent.

Alex and Abby had fantasized about how they would do away with Petrov, but Petrov had struck first by having Abby killed, and now it was up to Alex to carry through with the plan. But Alex wanted more than just a dead body. He wanted Petrov's last cognitive thought to be the realization that he had failed, that his life's mission was meaningless, and that Alex had prevailed. He wanted sweet revenge. Only then would he have redemption.

When Alex and Abby planned Petrov's death, they assumed certain facts: Petrov still believed the bomb remained in the Steinway; Petrov would attend the event; and, Sol could see Petrov use the remote that controlled the explosive device in the piano. Alex and Abby planned Petrov's death so there would first be the realization that Petrov had failed in his efforts to kill Alex. The anger and frustration that would follow was the prelude to his own death. The process would only take a few minutes from the first symptoms to a fatal heart attack, but Alex and Abby thought this was an appropriate death for the monster they knew.

The inspiring moment in their plan was when Alex suggested they time everything during Alex's bows following each encore selection. He would have direct eye contact with Petrov, and could enjoy each episode as it unfolded. Alex remembered Abby's response to his suggestion.

Alex, you're so creative. Who would have thought your creative talent could expand beyond your music to planning Petrov's death? Bravo, maestro, bravo!

Now, Alex needed to exercise it with the help of Sol.

"I can't wait to see the expression on that bastard's face once he realizes there will not be an explosion."

"Anticipating that moment inspires me to give my best performance, Sol."

"But Alex. Let's be practical. We're new to this game, and Petrov is an old hand. We must assume he's got multiple cards up his sleeve. What if he has a backup plan? What if he puts another bomb elsewhere in the Colosseum, having found out the bomb was deactivated? We must consider these possibilities."

"Isn't this suppose to be a pep talk before I walk out on stage and face imminent danger? These are not comforting words, Sol."

"I'm sorry Alex, but—"

"Sol, I'm kidding you. You love me and you're concerned. I'd be disappointed if I couldn't hear that in your voice. Look. We've got CIA protection. We've also got the Rome police chief and his staff on site and the Colosseum's security staff. I'd rather trust them to do their jobs than make myself crazy worrying about everything Petrov could do. That would be a full-time job, and I've already got one of those."

"I guess you're right. As you play your last encore, Petrov will die if everything goes as planned. What sweetens the deal is that we're using the same technology to kill him that he used to kill Nadia."

"Timing is everything, Sol. Once Jeff found out that Petrov had a pacemaker, the rest fell into place. It's still a mystery, though, how Jeff Jones got that information. He just said, 'I got it from Boris', but I don't know who Boris is, or how Boris knew Petrov had a pacemaker."

Jeff Jones' expertise in cell phone technology was key to the success of the plan. Through his infiltration of Petrov's computer systems, he knew the make and model of the general's cell phone, which proved to be the latest in telecommunications technology. Jeff reduced what was a complex operation to a simple explanation, however. He understood electronic circuitry like Alex understood music.

"Do you know a cell phone doesn't need to be turned on to receive information?"

Jeff had explained that there's always part of a cell phone that never goes dead, making it possible to connect to a person's phone without their knowledge. The application he designed connected to Petrov's cell phone and, when activated, would send an electrical charge to Petrov's pacemaker. His heart rhythm would increase, triggering an attack of tachycardia. Repeated electrical charges would guarantee that the increased heart rate would continue resulting in blood clots, causing a fatal stroke or heart attack.

It would be Sol who would push the button that would end Petrov's life. Sol was looking forward to that moment.

Sol and Alex's flight landed at the Fiumicino airport, where they were greeted by thousands of fans. Following Abby's death, Alex had become something of a folk hero. Everyone wanted their personal glimpse of this brave man who overcame the tragic death of his wife to play a concert that would benefit humanity. Security was everywhere. The local police were holding people back, and TV cameras surrounded them as they worked their way through the throngs. Alex Courtland was a classical rock star, just like the Beatles, who had just recently broken up. Even teenage musicians wanted a glimpse. He displayed poise and confidence as reporters yelled questions to get his attention. *How do you feel, Mr. Courtland? Are you planning other events for the Worldwide Music Initiative? Is it difficult to perform this important event without your wife here?*

Alex stopped to address the reporter, answering the last question. "Abby, my wife, was always by my side, and she still is. I play this concert in her memory. She loved that my playing would support a worldwide initiative to bring music to so many people."

That sound bite played over and over on all the networks. The projected audience being reached by television had tripled since Abby's death.

Amid the frenzy, security ushered them into their limousine for the ride to the Excelsior Hotel on the famed Via Veneto. As the driver pulled into the portico, the general manager, Giovanni Roti, welcomed his esteemed guests. "We're delighted to see you both again, Mr. Courtland, and Mr. Blum. I have prepared your favorite suites for you."

There were sumptuous bouquets of Italy's national flowers, the lily, and the rose, in all their glory. It was an extravagant display of food that reinforced their VIP status. The Excelsior hosted dignitaries from around the world, yet once word got out that Alex Courtland would stay there, reporters and others camped out for hours hoping to get a glimpse of him, snap a photo, or even capture an interview. Guests and visitors packed the lobby, making it more difficult for the added security to monitor all the activity.

"Giovanni, please take these tickets with my compliments and as a small expression of my appreciation. Could you be kind enough to distribute these to young people who would like to attend?"

The twenty-five tickets Alex handed him were worth a small fortune on the open market, and even more on the black market.

"Thank you for your generosity, Mr. Courtland. Several of my staff have teenage children who are interested in music. This will mean a great deal to them. They'll appreciate your kindness."

Alex and Sol reserved several hundred tickets to undermine the scalpers who were selling them outside the Colosseum. Sol posted a staff associate outside the hall and gave instructions to offer tickets at the regular price, forcing the scalpers to sell their tickets at fair prices or lose their entire investment.

Alex felt safe at the Excelsior Hotel, especially under the watchful eye of Giovanni Roti, but became amused at watching Sol act like a Prussian general guarding the emperor. He marveled at how they had come together for a common purpose that would soon bring justice for all of Petrov's victims.

Coda

61

It was now show time at the Colosseum.

Underneath Alex's cool exterior, he remained anxious about unexpected events that could happen during the concert. He was in top form, and highly confident that he could deliver a performance exceeding everyone's expectations, except, of course, his own. As he often did before a performance, he recalled Nadia's wise counsel.

"Music is an international language. Everyone understands it. Your focus should always be to communicate the composer's message. If you can do that, everyone will understand."

Sol had already completed his final check with security and confirmed that everything was in order. Cameras placed overhead guaranteed every seat had an unobstructed view of the stage. The executive producer controlled the state-of-the-art equipment from the glass-enclosed production booth at the rear of the hall. On every level, from the recording of sound and film, to the control of the lighting, this was one of the most comprehensive production booths ever built.

"Everything looks okay, Alex. You know, the backup plans we have in place. Leave the stage if you think it's necessary. Your life is more important than anything else happening tonight. Are we clear on that?"

"Is Petrov here?"

"He's here with his guard, who never takes his eyes off him."

"Yeah, he needs that guard for security, especially now."

"I'm going to take my seat. You know the most important person in my life is performing tonight. Play up a storm! Love you, kid."

"Love you, too, Sol."

Having Sol at his side had been a godsend. Alex couldn't imagine how his life would have progressed without him. President Rutherford was now seated in the audience prompting Alex to wonder what Vice President Tilton could be plotting back home. That was his final thought before the house manager notified him to get ready to go on stage. He stood at the side of the stage entrance and listened as Ms. Moretti delivered her introduction.

"My name is Allegra Moretti. As Chair of the Cultural Affairs Office, it is my pleasure to welcome you to this inaugural concert at the new Colosseum in Rome."

The crowd jumped to its feet and a roar of applause filled the hall, giving Alex another sense of how this renovation handled sound.

"If I took the time to thank all the architects, politicians, foundations, corporate supporters, and others who have made this event possible, there would be no time left for the beautiful music you will soon be enjoying. Alex Courtland, the renowned artist who will perform in this wonderful space tonight, has generously donated his talent for this special concert.

"For all of you who purchased tickets or made contributions supporting this renovation project, I can tell you that many vendors who worked on this project helped to keep the costs low by donating their services. The funds for the rest of the construction costs came from private donations. The proceeds raised from this one performance alone will support music and art programs through the Worldwide Music Initiative. I'm also thrilled to announce that Mr. Courtland has agreed to be the spokesperson for this extraordinary endeavor."

From the balcony, a young man shouted, *bravo!* This brought more applause on its own.

"*Bravo*, indeed. Orchestras, absent the instruments to perform the standard repertoire, will receive funds to buy or rent instruments. Many educational programs will receive needed funds to advance targeted initiatives. Scholarship funds will be available for talented individuals needing support so they may continue their education. This initiative is only a start, but it will happen first in eighteen countries where the needs are the greatest. We expect this initiative to snowball, resulting in a rejuvenation of culture everywhere, along with a nurturing of the human spirit.

"Thank you all for being here to take part in this historic event. I want to express a special thanks to Alex Courtland for bringing his extraordinary gifts to help us launch this important initiative. Now, please welcome Mr. Courtland to the Colosseum stage."

Alex expected the thunderous response he received. He understood it wasn't all about him, but the audience expressing their enthusiasm for the first concert being played in this magnificent auditorium at one of the most historic settings in the world. Alex took repeated bows, and once seated, continued to do the same from the bench. Then, when Alex bowed his head, the roar subsided and turned to quiet.

As Nadia used to tell him: *You're communicating one-on-one with each person in the hall. It doesn't matter whether there are twenty or five thousand. Make it personal.* Alex smiled to himself. He couldn't wait to make Petrov's reaction personal. As he played the first notes of the Bach *C Minor Partita*, all distractions disappeared. There was no Petrov, no cameras or recording devices, just Alex sending beautiful musical phrases to each of the audience members.

During intermission, Alex remained calm as he sipped a Pellegrino in the green room and contemplated the second half of the program. This was the most dangerous time during the concert, when Petrov would most likely make his move. The timing was critical for Sol, as well. Alex remained composed as he heard the bells in the hall cueing the audience to return to their seats.

The audience stood when Alex entered the stage. When he took his bows this time, he couldn't resist the temptation to glance up at General Petrov. Eyes glistening, the general smiled back at him to acknowledge this brief communication. Alex felt no fear, only contempt and excitement, as he anticipated the demise of this man who had caused him unbearable pain.

62

Petrov had arrived at the event eager to witness the explosion on stage that would punish Alex for his betrayal. With only his guard joining him in the box, it was just what the general wanted. This event was too private and important to share with anyone else. The glory of Alex's death was only his to behold, and of course, the millions of viewers around the world who would be watching.

General Petrov had to suffer through the defection of Boris, whom he had treated as a comrade. Boris' betrayal was more than painful; it was a blow to his ego. While Boris managed Alex's missions, the brilliant strategies were all Petrov's. Boris' loyalty to his creator was an insult to Petrov. Besides, didn't Boris get the message that his creator was dead?

Then there was the undoing of his relationship with John Tilton—another betrayal. Petrov opened doors for Tilton's career advancement, and Tilton then had the audacity to suggest it would have happened anyway, with no help from Petrov. *No, it wouldn't have Mr. Vice President!*

On top of all that treachery, there were now threats to his power base in Russia from the Politburo, who were questioning some of his methods. A meeting had been scheduled on his return. He knew that would come to no good. How would he explain the failures caused by Tilton and Boris?

There was one person he blamed for all that, and more. Alex would pay the ultimate price for his treachery. *Did you think your feeble attempt to kill me would go undiscovered? Russian technology has always been better than anything you could imagine. All I had to do was destroy my phone and Voila! Your connection was dead. Just like you'll be soon.*

Petrov locked eyes with Alex and thought, *I see the hate in your eyes, and I hope you see the joy in mine. I can't wait for you to go up in flames. By the end of this evening, I will stand victorious and watch as your remains are mixed with the steel and wood of your precious piano.* Petrov got excited just imagining that clip of Alex's demise being played for eternity.

Listening to Alex play the Prokofiev, he let himself get swept up in the emotions of his protégé performing a Russian composer's music. *What a waste of talent and opportunity*, he thought. *If only Alex could have realized his full potential and stayed loyal to me, that would have brought glory to me and the Motherland.*

Petrov decided it was time. Time to end the life of this defector, and time to start the next chapter in the fight to secure a return to his position of prominence in Russia. He removed the remote control from his pocket, took one last look at Alex, and pushed the button.

In disbelief, he watched as Alex continued to perform, bringing the Prokofiev sonata to a brilliant finish. He glared at his guard, and in a state of fury and under cover of thunderous applause, he yelled, "It's not working!"

Terrified, the guard assumed he had displeased the general and stammered an excuse. The general would have none of it. "Oh, shut up, you moron!"

The more Petrov kept pushing the button, the more infuriated he became, until his anger reached a frenzy. He threw the remote against the wall, narrowly missing his guard's head. The audience's thunderous applause following the conclusion of the Prokofiev blocked the sound as the remote fell to the floor in pieces. *I'll get him later,* Petrov vowed to himself. *This must end tonight!*

Petrov considered another way to deal with Alex. *At the reception, I will tell my guard to finish him. Yes, that will work. The publicity would be enormous.* Now with a new strategy in place, Petrov calmed down as he listened to the shouts of *bravo!* and *encore!* coming from the standing audience. The general stood as well and clapped in recognition of what had been an extraordinary performance. Then he issued his instructions to the guard.

63

Alex knew Sol had kept a steady watch on Petrov from across the hall using his opera glasses. Christine and her team were also there monitoring Petrov. She stayed close to Alex backstage and outside the green room. Just as Alex had sat down to play, he saw Petrov stare at him with a menacing smile.

Alex brought the Prokofiev Sonata to a stunning climax, resulting in the entire audience rising to their feet. As he bowed to recognize the audience's enthusiastic response, he saw the general throw the remote against the wall. He smiled as he thought, *Surprise, surprise, General. Your plan failed! But, be patient. There's another surprise waiting for you on tonight's program.*

After his third bow, he played his first encore, a Chopin etude, that again resulted in a standing ovation from the audience. He bowed to acknowledge the applause, and again locked eyes with Petrov. This time, it was Alex, whose eyes glistened. *Sol*, he silently urged, *we're running out of time. Press the damned button. That pacemaker is beating in the heart of our enemy.*

Alex played his final encore and responded again to the audience's shouts of *bravo!* As he bowed this time, he saw Petrov was standing and very much alive. *What the hell went wrong?*

Alex lowered the fallboard to let the audience know that he had played his last encore and that the concert was over. Not since Horowitz's historic return concert to Carnegie Hall ten years earlier had that been done.

He returned to the green room, where Sol quickly approached him. Alex grabbed Sol's arm, and with lips barely moving, said, "Why didn't you trigger the device, for God's sake?"

"Alex, you won't believe it. For all the precautions we took, no one told me I'd be the personal escort of Ms. Moretti. She was all over me. I not only couldn't trigger the pacemaker, but I also couldn't even take the device out of my pocket. She also wanted to use my opera glasses, and didn't understand why I was looking in Petrov's direction. I had to make up some lame excuse so she wouldn't know it was Petrov in my sights. Finally, I pressed the button, but nothing happened. I don't know why, but we're going to need a Plan B, because the bastard's still alive."

"So, Petrov knows *his* plan didn't work either. I took great joy in seeing him slam the remote against the wall."

"Alex, Jeff Jones helped set this up for us, but there isn't time to call him for help in resolving this. Christine knows nothing of our plan. Think fast. The evening is almost over, and we need to move on to the reception. Petrov may have a backup plan that could put you at risk during the reception."

"True. Though Christine and her team could thwart any action Petrov might take at the reception. Petrov would also see the heavy security and think twice about acting then. If he tries something, it would be after the reception, when he thinks our guard will be down."

Alex entered the reception area to applause and many more shouts of bravo! from the guests, who included presidents, ambassadors, cardinals, and billionaires. Also cheering Alex were those with no title and little money, including some of the talented young people who would receive scholarships funded by the concert's proceeds. Petrov was nowhere in sight.

The reception was elegant. Servers poured champagne as they passed refreshments among the guests. In deference to the multinational crowd, there was a signature dish representing several of the countries that supported Alex's initiative. It was an extravaganza that brought even more significance to this night of nights.

Alex looked across the room to the glitter of diamonds, rubies, gold, and silver. Some guests had their own security. *Understandable*, he thought. There was one diamond shining brighter than the others. Isabella smiled at him as he approached her. She was dressed in an azure blue sequined dress with an emerald necklace and earrings. She looked stunning.

"Hello, Alex. Your performance was arresting."

Alex took her hand and kissed it. The wedding ring was gone, but the large diamond ring remained. "I'm so happy you could make it here, Isabella."

Isabella had responded promptly to Alex following his letter of condolence to her on the death of her husband, Casimiro Castillo.

Thank you, Alex, for your kind words. I look forward to attending your concert in Rome. I will attend with two security personnel, Jose Gonzalez and Pedro Juarez. All the best for a successful event. Fondly, Isabella.

Not since Abby had Alex had any romantic feelings for another woman. Isabella awakened all his senses that had been in hibernation ever since Abby's death. He didn't want this moment to end. "How long will you be staying in Rome?"

"I have some business here, so I will stay for a few more days."

"I will be here as well. Perhaps we can have dinner tomorrow night?"

"I would love to, Alex. I'm at the Excelsior."

"We are there as well."

Isabella gave Alex her phone contact and agreed to meet him at eight o'clock in the Excelsior's dining room. Alex planned to arrange a private dining room there.

"I am monopolizing you, Alex. You have so many people wanting to talk to you. I look forward to seeing you tomorrow evening."

"I look forward to it as well, Isabella."

Alex saw President Rutherford and walked toward him and extended his warm greetings. "It's an honor to have you here tonight, Mr. President."

"I'm so glad to be here with you and hear your magnificent performance, Alex. Seeing you play in this historic setting is a once-in-a-lifetime experience. I told John Tilton how sorry I was to take his place."

Alex responded with grace. "I'm sure he understood, Mr. President."

"And on that note, I must leave. The plane is ready to take me back to Washington. I have a rather heavy day tomorrow, including meetings with your father-in-law. I just want you to know, Alex, that you're a great cultural ambassador for our country. Thank you for sharing your talent with so many people around the world tonight."

"It's been my privilege, Mr. President."

Alex watched the president leave the room, discretely followed by his secret service detail.

Sol was awed and said, "President Rutherford is quite charming, isn't he?"

"Yes, he is, Sol."

"How do you think he gets along with your father-in-law?"

"I don't know, but he must be savvy about John's style. He picked him to be his VP, so he must see redeeming qualities in him. The president's no fool."

"I saw you had a pleasant visit with Isabella."

"Yes. We're having dinner tomorrow night."

"Alex, please be—"

"Careful?"

"Yes. I understand the attraction. Isabella is a beautiful woman. But we were told by Christine that she was taking over her husband's operation. You cannot afford your reputation to be compromised."

"Sol, I'm not buying drugs from her. It's a simple dinner."

"Alex, I've known you since you were ten years old. You are meeting with a woman you are seriously attracted to. And it appears to be reciprocal. All I'm saying is, please be careful!"

"I will Sol. Thank you for your concern."

Alex and Sol each went their own way to mingle with the crowd. Alex accepted accolades for his stellar performance, shook hands, smiled for photos, and signed a few autographs before finding Sol again. They nodded to one another that it was now time to leave.

Just then, a loud explosion echoed in the reception area. Guests started shouting and scrambled to leave. No one could tell where the blast originated, although people ran outside as if that was the safest place to go. Security personnel were everywhere, keeping the crowd orderly, so they all didn't storm the exits at once.

Is this Petrov's round two? The noise was outside, and I'm inside, so either he's getting sloppy, or I'm not the target.

Christine Roberts found Alex and Sol together and rushed to their side. She was out of breath and visibly upset.

"Christine! What's going on? Is this Petrov's doing?"

"Brace yourselves. It's President Rutherford. His limousine exploded after leaving the Colosseum. The president, the driver, and his secret service detail were all inside. They're presumed dead."

Sol expressed his utter shock. "President Rutherford? Dead? Oh, my God, this is a catastrophe!"

"Guys, come with me. It's pandemonium here. We've got to get you back to the US right now. The local authorities and government officials will be here in seconds. There could be other attacks. Landing strips will be closed. They will monitor airspace, too. We could get stuck here if we don't leave right now. We have our jet standing by, and I have our car ready to go."

She ushered them to the lot where the doors of the idling car were already open for them. His first thought was, *Isabella, is she okay?* Then, as Alex ran toward the car, he saw another man hurrying away, a silhouette that Alex would recognize until he drew his last breath.

"Petrov!"

General Petrov turned. His guard swiveled with him and trained his gun on Alex. Before he could fire a single shot, Christine leveled her own weapon and shot him. *It was clean, fast, and deadly*, Alex thought, *just like the CIA taught her.*

Alex walked toward his prey. Petrov tried to get his bearings through his peripheral vision, looking for cover behind a car. There was nowhere he could run, and as he watched Alex move in his direction, he felt his heart race in his chest. He stood paralyzed, alone, and in that moment, Alex had closed the gap and stood face to face with the general.

Without a word, Alex lunged forward and put his strong right hand on Petrov's throat. The moment he had waited for most of his adult life was now here.

"Help!" gasped Petrov, looking at Christine. She held the gun she used to kill Petrov's guard limply at her side. "Please help me," he pleaded. Sol, Christine, and her special forces detail did not move.

Alex looked deep into Petrov's eyes as he continued to tighten his hold on the general's throat. "This is for my mother and father. You kept me a prisoner, then you killed her when she tried to give me my freedom, and then my father for helping us escape."

Petrov gasped as Alex tightened his grip, still just using his strong right hand. Petrov struggled to pull it off his throat, but he could feel his strength waning.

"This is for Nadia, who you had killed, causing me unbearable pain."

Petrov uttered unrecognizable words as Alex continued to squeeze even harder. And now he used both of his hands.

"Finally, this is for my beloved Abby, who you murdered, just to punish me. For that, your punishment will be more than just to rot in hell for eternity. I will make sure that the entire world knows that you died like a coward, begging for mercy. Your legacy, almighty General Petrov, will forever be in the company of losers."

Petrov's knees buckled and scraped the pavement as he slid to the ground. His eyes were bulging, but he could not take them from Alex's face. Instead, he stared in agony at a triumphant face that was not his own. The body he controlled to kill all those who stood in his way was now being used to end his life.

"And this is for me, and all the people whose lives I took as your agent of death. Go to hell now, General Petrov!"

Christine cried out. "Don't do it, Alex! He's not worth it."

Alex kept tightening his grip, but then he heard a voice. It was Abby's voice, just like what he heard when he had tried to kill her. He slowly released his grip. A peacefulness overcame him. There had been enough killing. He wouldn't let Petrov make him a killer one more time.

Alex's decision to withdraw from Petrov provided the general an opportunity to reach into his side pocket and pull out a switchblade knife. He raised his arm, preparing to put the knife in Alex's heart.

Christine's reaction was immediate; her second kill of the day. The bullet hit Petrov in the middle of his forehead. His knife fell to the ground. There was no time for Alex to react; it all happened too fast.

Alex turned to face Christine. Sol saw Alex's tears of relief and rushed to embrace him.

"It's okay, son. It's over now."

Christine took charge. "We must leave! Now!"

64

On the way to the airport, Christine was provided with an update on the president's status. Alex could tell from her expression that the news was not good.

"Did they confirm that President Rutherford is dead?"

"Yes, Alex."

Death had become a constant in Alex's life. His nightmares were a thing of the past, thanks to the removal of the implant, but his memories now filled in details of each of the murders he committed. The individuals became alive, and he could see their faces now—a frequent reminder of the horrors of the past. Each day following his surgery, he recalled bits and pieces from each of those events. As painful as that process was, it didn't equal the agony he experienced with the implant: the nightmares, the unexplained missing time, or the effect it had on his relationship with Abby. Now the pieces of the puzzle had come together, and still he realized he would never escape the guilt, or achieve total redemption.

Now, he had a new reality to deal with. John Tilton would succeed Rutherford as the new President of the United States, and would serve until the end of Rutherford's elected term. Alex had to wonder what the new president was thinking as the new occupant of the Oval Office. To accomplish his agenda, he would need to secure the confidence of the American public to be *elected* as its president when his term ended. If he moved too fast, or in a way that alarmed voters, he could lose the election, and with it, his plans for a new America. Alex had to marvel at how well Tilton had advanced his career. Now he was president following President Rutherford's assassination. He had to wonder, *did John Tilton arrange the assassination of President Rutherford? He certainly had motive.*

Alex couldn't share his theory with Christine without proof. Besides, Tilton was way too smart to leave any telltale clues along the way. *How would he do it, given the extraordinary security measures in place?*

Sol appeared shaken by the news. "We know what this means, don't we, Alex? Your father-in-law is now president."

Christine confirmed that Vice President Tilton had taken the oath of office as soon as they had confirmed the death of President Rutherford.

"When will all this become public?" Alex asked.

"It's already public, Alex. Italia 1 TV was interviewing President Rutherford as he was leaving the Colosseum, and they filmed his departure as his caravan headed for the airport. Every TV station is running the clips."

"Live on Italia 1 TV? Shouldn't they filter some of that to protect his dignity, Christine?"

"It's the story of the decade, Sol. It's precisely because the explosion was so dramatic and gruesome that it's believed to be an act of terrorism. We still don't have a complete count of additional fatalities and injuries, but there are many, including several agents who were in the SUVs in front of and behind the president's car."

"Is there definitive proof that this was a terrorist attack? Has any organization taken credit for it yet?"

"It's always the first thing suspected in cases like this, Alex. Who else would plan an attack on the President of the United States in this way?"

If Tilton is responsible for this heinous act, he did it under the radar of the CIA, even though they were tracking conversations Tilton had with Petrov.

Christine continued to receive updates from her colleagues at the CIA and told Alex and Sol the stock market halted trading after the DOW dropped 1,500 points; Washington, DC, was in lockdown; airlines delayed or canceled most flights resulting in jammed airport terminals, all causing increased panic among the public.

"President Tilton is the boss now, and he will have to deal with each of these critical issues."

Alex had his own views of how the new president would deal with this crisis. *John wants to frame this as a terrorist attack. What better way to cover up his involvement? I did my father-in-law a huge favor by getting rid of Petrov.*

There was chaos everywhere on their arrival at the airport. Airport authorities had placed departing flights on hold. All passengers were searched, interviewed, and detained. Christine had already contacted Sol's captain to advise him that Alex and Sol would return with her, and he should fly the plane back to New York.

There had been no opportunity to connect with Isabella, and Alex wanted to reach her to make sure she was okay.

"Christine, I need to make a call."

"Please be quick, Alex. I am working with security to get us out of here as soon as possible. There are phones around the corner from the security office."

"Thank you. It will only take a minute."

Christine nodded to one agent to accompany Alex.

Alex closed the door to the booth. He called the number Christine gave him and reached her right away. He needed privacy, so he talked in a low voice and turned his back on the agent.

"Isabella, are you okay?"

"Yes. I'm back at the hotel. Things have calmed down somewhat. I worried about you, Alex. Things happened so fast. I just heard the news about President Rutherford's assassination. Is it all true?"

"I'm afraid so. Will you return soon to Mexico?"

"We are leaving tonight. Certain security issues had to be addressed, and I understand there is total chaos at the airport."

"Yes. Please be careful and travel safe. Will you be coming to New York anytime soon?"

"I make several trips a year for business, and to attend the wonderful cultural events that are so remarkable. I love the ballet, opera, and the New York Philharmonic."

"I have a performance coming up with the New York Philharmonic. I can send you tickets if the timing is right for you."

"I will make every attempt to see you then. It will be a thrill to hear you play again, this time with an orchestra."

"Wonderful. Perhaps we will finally be able to have our dinner date."

"I would love that, Alex."

As Alex left the phone booth, he realized the connection he was making with Isabella was more than just a casual one. He couldn't ignore the physical attraction he felt for her. She stirred feelings in him he had not felt since Abby's death.

As he left the booth, a woman cried out.

"You're Alex Courtland. I was just at the concert. You were magnificent. I'm so sorry about your president being attacked."

Before Alex could respond, there was a small crowd around him asking for autographs. Sol appeared just in time to help the guard remove Alex from the crowd.

"I'm so sorry. Mr. Courtland's plane is leaving now."

Sol took Alex's arm and steered him back to where Christine was finalizing all the exit documents.

It impressed Alex how quickly the Italian police handled security measures. He assumed their primary concern was to rule out additional terrorist attacks.

Giovanni Roti, the general manager at the Excelsior Hotel, was waiting for Alex and Sol at the security entrance to the gate. He wanted to help in any way he could.

"What help, Giovanni? You made a trip out here just to say goodbye?"

"No, Mr. Courtland. Not just to say goodbye."

After the explosion, Giovanni realized his distinguished guests had left their belongings in their hotel rooms. He entered their suites to collect their belongings and pack their luggage. "My driver will help you with your luggage, and here are your passports. I worried it would be difficult for you to leave the country without them."

"Giovanni, you should be the eighth wonder of the world. Thank you!" Alex and Sol hugged Giovanni and joined Christine for the brisk walk to the gate. Christine instructed her associate to have the luggage inspected and scanned.

"I know you value and trust Mr. Roti, Alex, but this is how terrorism succeeds. Often, it's the trusted friend, relative, or employee of the hotel who's been radicalized. We trust no one and take no chances."

Once they cleared all security hurdles, their plane took off for the seven-hour flight to New York.

In flight, radio communication provided them with updates on President Rutherford's assassination. They heard about the videos and photos of tangled sections of twisted metal, with only the section of the Presidential Seal visible. It was shocking and disturbing, and it made all of them angry as the press released the sensational photos at the expense of Jim Rutherford's persona.

They listened in silence as the live reporting continued.

65

John Tilton spoke from behind his desk in the Oval Office. Having taken the oath of office earlier in the day, he was the president now, and he wanted the majestic imagery to make that clear. He had revised his speech many times over the past few months, but now he knew it was right, and he could deliver it with conviction.

All television stations interrupted regular programing with a message to stand by for an emergency message from the President of the United States:

> It is my solemn duty to report that President Rutherford died several hours ago when his presidential limousine exploded after leaving the Colosseum in Rome following the concert of pianist Alex Courtland. Under the Twenty-Fifth Amendment to the Constitution dealing with succession to the presidency, Chief Justice Elliott Brown swore me in as President of the United States. I now address you as your president.

> I ask all Americans to be patient as we investigate the cause of this heinous act and bring to justice those responsible. Meanwhile, I am directing all federal buildings to close and American flags lowered to half-mast as the nation mourns the loss of our late beloved president, James B. Rutherford.

> Our allies are helping us to identify those responsible, and we are increasing our security at US embassies and facilities around the world. We will be diligent as we move forward, and we will use all our available resources to deal with this latest threat to our nation.

> I want all Americans to know that our highest priority is your safety. In the interests of national security, we are

increasing staffing at all security checkpoints at airports throughout the country. Let me state unequivocally to those who may see this as an opportunity to take advantage of what they perceive to be a vulnerable moment for America: We are stronger when we face adversity, and they would be ill-advised to reach the wrong conclusions about America's resolve in its fight against terrorism.

To our friends and allies: Many of you have worked with me during my tenure as vice president and as the US Ambassador to Russia. I value your continued counsel and look forward to meeting with you soon, hoping to strengthen our alliances. We've lost an influential leader today, and I pledge to my fellow Americans that we will avenge the assassination of President Rutherford and bring those responsible to justice. Thank you. God bless you all, and God Bless the United States of America.

Christine commented first. "That was one hell of a speech."

Alex wondered, *maybe Tilton prepared this speech some time ago.*

66

John Tilton sat at his desk in the Oval Office and studied America's response to his speech. The outpouring was hugely positive. Results from various polls were still coming in, but his words to America during this tragic time had the intended effect. The many months of preparation had paid off.

Tilton rejoiced at how well his plans had progressed. Everyone played his part, even Alex Courtland, whose actions following his concert led to the death of Petrov. His meeting with Terry Reynolds, CIA Director, the day before revealed details of how Petrov came to his end. Reynolds told his boss about a CIA agent killing Petrov and his guard to protect Alex. What a godsend Alex had been. Not only did he carry out assignments that cleared the way for Tilton's ascension to the presidency, but his role in causing Petrov's death was an unexpected bonus. Tilton doubted the Politburo would even mourn Petrov's death, although true to their nature, they would honor him with a diplomat's funeral. He would send Tilly Thompson, his replacement as ambassador to Russia, to attend the event. It was the least he could do to recognize Petrov's status as an ambassador to the United Nations.

Tilton took a moment to reflect on Abby. Her death was painful to him, but it was a burden he had to accept, and now move on. He missed his daughter, and now he had to decide how to handle her husband, his son-in-law. He admired and liked Alex, but bringing him around to his way of thinking would be a challenge. Alex was the remaining family member he did not want to eliminate.

Alex never responded to his earlier attempts to recruit him, but perhaps he would reconsider now. The new president would reach out and test the waters. Tilton remained confident that everything would work out for the best.

Now, he needed to move forward with the next part of his plan reinforcing the view that he was not only the leader of the free world, but the creator of a plan that would put the United States on a path toward world dominance. With Petrov no longer a threat or his collaborative partner, Tilton alone could now control all the details that would bring his plan to completion. He felt assured the new potential partnership with President Ivanov would be more manageable than the one he had with Petrov, and so much the better since he would work with his counterpart in Russia. Tilton felt confident that America's investment in technology sectors would overtake Russia's in the near future. That would be a priority. For now, it would be important to convince Ivanov to share some of his technology. While Russia was rich in natural resources, they still depended on exports from the US to feed their populations. His years of experience dealing with the Russian hierarchy now armed him with confidence. Such was not the case with China, a sleeping giant.

China's alarming growth rate in their gross domestic product and their increased military buildup were a future threat to Tilton's plans. He admired their strict rules that kept the population in check. No threat of uprisings or revolutions there. But their authoritarian government differed from what Tilton imagined for the US and the rest of the world. Tilton knew he had to convince the populations of not just the US, but its allies and others as well, that his brand of authoritarianism would usher in decades of peace and prosperity. China was a major threat to his objectives. He would present China as an adversary to convince Americans his brand of government was best. His future partnership with Russia would diminish China militarily and economically. Chairman Yang was Harvard educated and had made his views clear to Tilton. There was no reason to reach out to him anytime soon.

67

A lex arrived at the White House security gate. He went through the usual clearance process and was escorted to the Oval Office for his meeting with President Tilton. Only a week had passed since his return from Rome, and the horrific events continued to play out in his mind.

It surprised Alex to receive the summons. It was the first time they had been in contact since Abby's funeral. Questions raced through Alex's mind about whether his father-in-law's privilege as vice president, and now president, gave him access to Alex and Sol's work with the CIA. Christine had assured him that the director of the CIA had no interest in conveying that information to the president, unless specifically asked. Alex suspected Tilton knew of the circumstances following Petrov's death. *But could Christine Roberts protect me from Tilton's clutches now that he's the president?*

Alex knew President Tilton could make his life difficult, and Sol's as well. He had no misgivings about Tilton's abilities to disarm his opponents. It was also hard not to like him: his charm, his intelligence, and his incredible knowledge could win over even the strongest skeptic. The only thing Alex was better at than Tilton was playing the piano, so there was no strategy he could use to outwit or outsmart him. Yet he felt emboldened as he entered the Oval Office. But first, he needed to find out why the president wanted to see him.

The president got up from his chair behind the Resolute Desk and greeted Alex with a warm embrace.

"It is so good to see you, Alex, and I must tell you, you look so much better than you did when I last saw you."

Alex recognized Tilton had already made his first move to disarm him.

"Thank you, Mr. President."

"Alex, please call me John. I'm still your father-in-law, something that gives me great pride. Let's sit and talk now. We have so much to catch up on." The president gestured for Alex to sit opposite him on the white sofa facing the fireplace.

"Thank you, sir. Congratulations on your succession."

"Thank you, Alex. It was under such tragic circumstances. I can't imagine what the world is coming to. I am sorry you had to experience this unfortunate event, Alex."

Oh, please. That's how you want to start this conversation?

"The United States of America has potent enemies, Alex. The underserved in the world thrive by creating chaos and uncertainty. It gives them power to see fear on the faces of those who let themselves get intimidated. As for President Rutherford, he was a kindly gentleman who tried to reason with hotheads, who listened to their ranting, and who gave them credibility with his time and attention."

Enough is enough! Alex couldn't stand it anymore.

"Mr. President, did you know General Petrov had me implanted with a device that controlled my actions, causing me to kill people he wanted eliminated?"

The president did not show surprise or appear to be irritated by Alex's question. Neither did he look at Alex, but focused instead on his photo on the wall behind Alex.

"Alex, I—"

"Before you answer, John, let me finish what I have to say."

Alex knew he was putting his cards on the table much earlier than planned, but now he had no choice but to continue. He was about to confront the President of the United States in the Oval Office. He proceeded with the same passion that would accompany his performance of a Chopin ballade.

"I am talking to you as my father-in-law, not president. I know you loved your daughter. In her memory then, please be honest with me now. Did you know Petrov had me implanted as a child?"

Alex remained quiet while he waited for John's response. It was impossible to interpret his expression. Perhaps, Alex thought, it was all those years of negotiating with the Russians, where diplomacy was a necessity. *John is such a master at deception. Will he even answer the question, or instead, will he just call an end to this meeting?* He watched as the president took a deep breath and looked straight at him.

"Not at first, Alex. I never would have agreed to it if I had known."

It surprised Alex that John was so direct—and he believed him.

"General Petrov was a powerful and connected politician who had access to the top brass in the Russian hierarchy. The arrangement benefitted both our countries. Petrov was an important link I needed as the Cold War unfolded with Russia."

Alex knew that his explanation was half true, but there had to be more to it. Before Alex could ask the next question, Tilton continued.

"Once I knew you were being used by Petrov for assignments that benefitted my career, I told him to stop. Alex, I *threatened* him to stop! But it was too late. Petrov had total control over you, and he didn't need to listen to me anymore."

"Why didn't you tell Abby or me what was going on? I was in hell, not knowing what was happening to me. How could you have withheld so much information? It might even have saved Abby's life, and given me a chance for an earlier resolution."

"Abby's death was the most painful experience I have ever known, Alex. CIA Director Terry Reynolds briefed me on how well you handled yourself when Petrov threatened you in Rome. Seeing Petrov die may bring you some redemption, and help us both in the healing process. The wound is deep, and it still hurts."

"John, you are a master at what you do. I learned more listening to you than I ever learned in any of my classes at Oxford. But your daughter also learned from you as a teenager through adulthood, and she learned politicians lie for a living. She told me so. But I must admit, I believe everything you've told me so far today.

"Thinking back on my conversation with Abby," Alex continued, "when she convinced me that the public doesn't want to know what politicians do, so they can continue to enjoy their uncomplicated lives—"

"Really, Alex. I don't think—"

Alex didn't let Tilton finish his thought. "Tell me this, John. Are you responsible for the assassination of President Rutherford? Did you have him killed so you could hold this office?"

Tilton rose from the sofa and moved to the Resolute Desk, sat on the edge, and took a moment before answering. Alex could feel his father-in-law's eyes penetrate his entire being.

"President Rutherford was leading this country to an economic and political disaster."

"That's an assessment, not an answer, John."

"Alex, Rutherford's policies would have put the US in a depression and opened America to threats from Russia and China. He couldn't decide what to do, so he'd say one thing one day, then reverse his position the next, depending on how much pressure he got from either the Russians or Congress. Those muddled messages coming from the White House to our allies and enemies alike damaged the reputation of the US. We looked like weaklings. He was leading us to a disaster of monumental proportions."

Alex refused to back down. He was in all the way.

"John, I will ask you for the last time. Did you have President Rutherford assassinated? A simple *yes* or *no* will suffice." Alex kept his eyes on the president.

Tilton's response was instantaneous and in a quiet tone. "It doesn't matter, Alex, who took his life. If it was the terrorists, then I owe them a debt of gratitude. If it was me, then you should thank me, not attack me."

It was a stunning response. Alex sat back on the couch and exhaled, trying to absorb what he'd just heard.

Tilton waited a minute before continuing. "I love you, Alex. You made Abby happy. I admire how you've survived tragedies, and I admire the honorable way you have lived your life. You have high ideals. But perhaps you've never had to come face-to-face with the brutal realities of life. Perhaps Sol Blum and Nadia Rosenberg shielded you from the ugly side of humanity because of what Petrov did to you."

"You can't imagine what Petrov did to me." Alex shifted his eyes from the bronze bust of John F. Kennedy and locked eyes with Tilton.

"I'm sorry, Alex. Abby's death and your horrific experiences you suffered because of Petrov are in the past now. I want to change the entire world for the better. To accomplish that, sometimes people in power must do things that aren't, well, holy. If we want America to be the best she can be, then a great deal needs to change. We could have anarchy in our own time, just as our forefathers did when they drafted the Declaration of Independence. Now, and in the days to come, I will make decisions that position the United States to become the leader of a new world order that, for the first time in our history, will guarantee peace and prosperity for all who join us. For those that refuse to accept what I consider being a *fait accompli*, I will need to deal with those exceptions in ways you may feel would not dignify the Office of President of the United States. But imagine, Alex, what if we could redirect the most significant parts of government budgets worldwide that support unending wars, and instead use those resources to build a futuristic infrastructure, develop new technologies, deliver quality health and education to all? Wouldn't that be worth compromising our moral compass in places?"

Alex needed a minute to understand the depth of what President Tilton was saying.

Moral compass? What would you think if you knew I eliminated the most powerful drug lord on the continent…and enjoyed it? I guess you don't know I'm now a CIA asset.

Before he could respond, the president continued.

"What I am proposing is not unlike what you have launched with the Worldwide Music Initiative. That initiative spreads a healthy message to new audiences. I want to do the same thing with reaching a world-wide audience that is ready for change. I need your help to do that, Alex. Your president is asking you to help him achieve that goal. Will you help me, Alex?"

Alex nodded. "You have given me much to think about. There's already a lot on my mind that's unresolved. I still mourn for Abby, and I have concerts pending. But if you want my help to create a world order that benefits all Americans, then I will give it my serious consideration, Mr. President."

"Thank you, Alex." As the president walked Alex to the door, he added, "Please, don't take too long in your decision, Alex. I have ambitious plans, and this is too important to delay any further."

Within less than a minute of leaving the Oval Office, Alex

passed the National Security Advisor office and then saw George Watson, the Speaker of the House, leaving his office. There was a nod of recognition from Watson, followed by looking at the plush carpet underfoot. Alex refused to get paranoid, but wondered what White House staff knew about the assassination. Alex left the White House more confused than when he arrived. *Were the last comments from the President a threat? How much time do I have before John acts?* Alex was in a difficult position with no middle ground, and he would soon need to declare himself: he was with the President of the United States, or against him.

68

"Sol, this is the most delicious Italian meal I have had since we left Rome. You have mastered Italian cuisine."

"My dear boy, I'm known far and wide for my culinary expertise!"

"But really, Sol, the spaghetti sauce is so thick and rich, with just the right amount of oregano. And you added that touch of Romano cheese on top, just like Nadia used to do."

"And where do you think I got the recipe?"

"I should have guessed."

Alex planned on a relaxing dinner with Sol, followed by a discussion on the upcoming tour in Europe. They both looked forward to his concert at the Musikverein in Vienna, always followed by a late dinner at their favorite restaurant, ending with the wonderful Viennese pastries for dessert.

As they retired to the living room with their coffee and brandy, Sol asked, "Have you talked to Christine Roberts recently?"

"No, Sol. Haven't heard a word."

"I guess there's no reason to expect she would stay in touch with us…except for the fact we were her top covert agents who eliminated one of the most dangerous cartel drug leaders in the world."

Alex couldn't resist smiling at Sol's tongue-in-cheek comment. "Do you miss it, Sol?"

"I'm getting itchy for another assignment."

"Me, too, Sol. Good God, what does that make us?"

"It makes me a talented chef and you an even better piano player!"

"Hilarious!"

"Okay, down to business, Alex. Let's hear about your meeting with President Tilton. It had to be an eye-opener for you."

"It was more than that, Sol. It was a mixture of manipulation and a few lies, then topped off with a veiled threat."

Alex told Sol how he asked the president the two hardest questions: did he know about the implant, and did he arrange the death of President Rutherford?

"Did he know about the implant?"

"He said he didn't know about it at first, but said he found out about it later."

"What about the assassination?"

"I stared President Tilton right in the eye and asked point-blank if he had a hand in the assassination of President Rutherford."

"My God, Alex. How did he respond to that?"

"I never got a direct answer—rather a very indirect one in which he said that America was better off without him, and whoever did it should get a medal."

"Do you think he did it, Alex?"

"Without question!"

"What about the 'veiled threat,'" Sol asked, concerned.

"I took him literally, Sol. He wants me to work with him as his partner in making America a world dominating power."

"You have mentioned this in the past, when Tilton was only an ambassador. Are you talking about authoritarianism, or totalitarianism?" Sol asked in disbelief.

"I think he's leaning more toward a hybrid. An authoritarian regime would not go far enough, and a totalitarian regime would be too difficult to sell to the American people. Something in between is what he may think is achievable, introduced gradually so as not to alarm the public or our allies. What worries me, Sol, is I think he could pull it off."

"Do you think he's bluffing?"

"It was not a bluff, Sol. It was real! I told him I had to think about it."

"Smart move, Alex. That buys us some time."

"Not sure it does, Sol. As I was leaving, he mentioned he would need to know *soon*."

"He wouldn't dare—"

"Oh, yes, he would, Sol. Think about what he's already done. Eliminating me, if I didn't accept his offer, could be on the table."

"So, what's our strategy?"

"I'm not sure, but we need to do something. Tilton could put America on a path to topple its leadership in the free world and cause an eventual collapse of democracy. He would stop at nothing. He sees himself as a patriot, and he's willing to accept any collateral damage to achieve his vision for a world order. We have powerful friends both inside and outside the government. We may need to enlist their support."

"Do you think our many friends would get down and dirty? That just may be necessary if we are going to take on the Tilton group."

"Interesting point, Sol. There is Isabella, who is looking more like a friend these days."

"Isabella Castillo? Are you serious, Alex? She may have inherited one of the most formidable drug cartels in the world. And while Christine suggested to us that taking out her husband would weaken the entire cartel, there's been no evidence of that."

"Right. And Christine doesn't seem worried about any of that. She could bring significant resources to our cause if she was willing."

Sol took a minute to absorb the seriousness of Alex's comment. "Okay, but once the president finds out we're recruiting our friends, he'll know your decision."

"And that would put us at immediate risk of retaliation, right?"

"Possibly. Tilton's master plans may advance more quickly than expected. For example, many things President Rutherford did in his last days in office have Tilton's fingerprints all over it."

"Like what?"

"The lack of any agreement between the US and Russia last week following the Geneva Summit was the opposite of what Rutherford was seeking. Rutherford was counting on Tilton's help in closing that deal. Tilton, evidently, never wanted it to succeed, and given his current position, think of how he could influence the negotiations now. That, along with the other threats Russia poses to the US, can now be used by him to keep the American public in a constant state of fear."

"I get your point, Sol. The Cold War will end when Tilton decides it ends. Then he will be a hero to the American public."

"Sure. At the time of his choosing, he can propose a strategic partnership with Russia that will cause an immediate de-escalation of the nuclear threat. But it accomplishes something even more important."

"What, Sol?"

"The new agreement with Russia will create an unprecedented superpower that will overwhelm China's capacity both militarily and economically."

"Sol, you just outlined a scenario that would make his sales pitch of an authoritarian type of government to the American people a slam dunk. Also, he might not need me anymore."

"You have a public persona recognized the world over. Why do you think it's important for Tilton to have you in his camp? I'm sure he has many more tricks up his sleeve to entrap you, before he decides on any ultimate solution. He is one shrewd character, Alex. I would never underestimate him. If you become a formidable opponent, all bets are off."

"As strange as it sounds, maybe he needs me for other reasons."

"Like what?"

"Abby's death hit him hard, Sol, and I'm all that's left of his family. He knew how much Abby loved me. I think he needs to keep that connection to her through me."

"That's an interesting view, Alex, but I'd still feel better if we could convince Christine to eliminate him."

"We already know that Christine is no fan of President Tilton, and she made it clear the CIA director also had deep concerns about Tilton as President."

"All in your favor, Alex."

Alex was ready to move on from the heaviness of the conversation. "Sol, tell me about the concert at Angkor Wat. Do they want to duplicate what we did in Rome, except with a different ending?"

The doorbell interrupted their shared laugh.

"I'll get it, Sol. Don't people call before coming over anymore?"

"They needed to clear Anthony, our security guard, so it has to be someone you know and trust."

As Alex opened the door, he saw Christine and couldn't help but quip, "Well, at least you rang the doorbell this time. Please come in. Sol's upstairs." As they walked up the stairs to the living room, Christine's serious demeanor struck Alex.

"Can I offer you a drink, Christine?"

"I'm still on duty, Sol. But yes, I'd love anything with alcohol in it."

Alex noticed Christine deep in thought. *Why is she here?*

"The last few weeks have been life-changing for all of us, Christine. I'm not sure what will happen next."

"That's why I'm here, Alex."

Alex shot Sol a questioning look.

"We've come across some disturbing evidence that further links President Tilton to General Petrov."

"Can you tell us more, Christine?" Alex had to wonder if she knew about their earlier plans to kill Petrov.

"Yes. But before I do, I need to ask you to do something more for your country."

Alex and Sol exchanged a surprised look, and Alex responded, "You know we will, Christine. What is it you want us to do?"

"I need you boys to return to Russia."

Music in the Novel

To hear Daniel Graham's interpretations of J.S.Bach's *D minor Partita*, Brahms' *Op. 39 Waltzes* and *Variation and Fugue on a Theme by Handel*, and other compositions performed by Alex Courtland in *Strings*, go to the author's website: danielgpiano.com.

Acknowledgments

My editor, Bryan Tomasovich, managed all editorial and production details with precision and expertise. Every conversation with Bryan raised my spirits and provided the inspiration for me to do better.

From the first to the last draft of *Strings*, my dear friend Joey Perlmutter stayed with me for the entire journey. Her nuanced counsel improved the story, character development, and settings. Her ongoing encouragement kept me challenged and motivated.

My brother Dick Graham brought his intellect and experience as an avid reader of fiction to every version of *Strings*. His brilliant suggestions always infused new life into the story.

My friend and mentor, Margye Baumgardner, brought her White House experience, and her extensive background as a strategic planner, teacher, and writer, to each version of *Strings*. Her sage advice helped bring the novel to life.

My daughter KC Witherspoon and I shared a wonderful father-daughter weekend reading *Strings*. Knowing me and my musical history, her input immeasurably improved this novel.

"Daniel Graham is an intelligent and refined musician who possesses an impressively reliable technique."

That praise from the *New York Times* is typical of the accolades Graham received from the international press in his concerts at major musical centers throughout the United States and Europe.

Graham studied with renowned artist-teachers Leon Fleisher, Nadia Reisenberg, and Donald Currier, and his education at New England Conservatory, University of Minnesota, Yale University, and Peabody Institute at Johns Hopkins University prepared him for his success as a performer, teacher, author, and fundraiser.

Graham lives in Rancho Mirage, California. Now in his eighties, he continues to record a large body of piano works, including the rarely performed music of Adolph von Henselt, Karol Szymanowski, and Nikolai Medtner. He is also writing a sequel to *Strings*.

Milton Keynes UK
Ingram Content Group UK Ltd.
UKHW041022090823
426580UK00001B/70